T0359201

# WESTERN

*Rugged men looking for love...*

## Wrangling A Family
Kathy Douglass

## Second Chance Deputy
Alexis Morgan

# MILLS & BOON

WRANGLING A FAMILY
© 2023 by Kathleen Gregory
Philippine Copyright 2023
Australian Copyright 2023
New Zealand Copyright 2023

First Published 2023
First Australian Paperback Edition 2023
ISBN 978 1 867 29822 9

SECOND CHANCE DEPUTY
© 2023 by Patricia L. Pritchard
Philippine Copyright 2023
Australian Copyright 2023
New Zealand Copyright 2023

First Published 2023
First Australian Paperback Edition 2023
ISBN 978 1 867 29822 9

MIX
Paper | Supporting
responsible forestry
FSC® C001695
www.fsc.org

Published by
Harlequin Mills & Boon
An imprint of Harlequin Enterprises (Australia) Pty Limited
(ABN 47 001 180 918), a subsidiary of HarperCollins
Publishers Australia Pty Limited
(ABN 36 009 913 517)
Level 19, 201 Elizabeth Street
SYDNEY NSW 2000 AUSTRALIA

Cover art used by arrangement with Harlequin Books S.A.. All rights reserved.

Printed and bound in Australia by McPherson's Printing Group

# Wrangling A Family
## Kathy Douglass

MILLS & BOON

**Kathy Douglass** is a lawyer turned author of sweet small-town contemporary romances. She is married to her very own hero and mother to two sons, who cheer her on as she tries to get her stubborn hero and heroine to realise they are meant to be together. She loves hearing from readers that something in her books made them laugh or cry. You can learn more about Kathy or contact her at kathydouglassbooks.com.

Visit the Author Profile page
at millsandboon.com.au for more titles.

Dear Reader,

Welcome back to Aspen Creek, Colorado, where love is once more in the air. This time love is coming for Nathan Montgomery and Alexandra Jamison.

Nathan has seen his two brothers fall in love, but he is clear that a relationship doesn't fit in his five-year plan. Alexandra has been burned by love and has no interest in a man. She is content to raise her infant daughter and leave romance for others.

Then Nathan's brother enters him in the Aspen Creek Bachelor Auction. Alexandra—egged on by her friends—wins a date with him. Although Nathan and Alexandra hit it off, they agree that the date is a one-time thing. You've probably already guessed that it doesn't work out that way.

I love writing about couples who are determined not to fall in love. It makes it that much sweeter when they do. I hope you enjoy reading *Wrangling a Family* as much as I enjoyed writing it.

I love hearing from my readers. Visit my website, kathydouglassbooks.com, and drop me a line. While you're there, sign up for my newsletter.

Happy reading!

*Kathy*

# DEDICATION

This book is dedicated with much love
and appreciation to my husband and sons.
Your love and support mean the world to me.

# CHAPTER ONE

"LET ME STOP you right there," Alexandra Jamison said, holding up a hand and shaking her head. She needed to stop her friends before they got carried away by this ridiculous idea. "The answer is no."

"Don't say no so fast," Veronica said, her fork suspended halfway between her plate of shrimp scampi and linguini and her mouth. "At least not until you hear the entire plan."

"I've heard enough to know that I don't want any part of it." Alexandra replied.

"Perhaps you don't understand," Kristy said. "Because if you did, you'd realize it made perfect sense."

"I did understand," Alexandra said. Kristy was a sixth-grade math teacher and Alexandra suspected she was about to use her spoon to diagram the plan on her napkin. "We all bought tickets to the Aspen Creek dinner and bachelor auction. Now Veronica wants me to bid on a bachelor."

"It's for a good cause. The money raised will support several local programs for youth and new programs at the library." Veronica Kendrick, the children's librarian, was normally levelheaded, so this loony idea was out of character.

"I have no problem attending," Alexandra agreed. "It's the bidding on a bachelor that I don't want to do."

"Why not?" Marissa asked. Marissa and Alexandra were both nurses at the local hospital. Marissa worked in the ICU and Alexandra worked in pediatrics. They'd become fast friends when Alexandra moved to Aspen Creek five months ago. Marissa introduced her to Kristy and Veronica, and they'd become friends too. They got together regularly for dinner and conversation. Their bimonthly girls' night out had started so normally that Alexandra hadn't expected this at all.

"It'll be fun," Kristy promised.

"How is bidding on some guy I don't know so I can spend the night with him *fun*?"

"You don't have to spend the night with him. It's just a date," Veronica said.

"You know what I meant. Besides, it'll make me look desperate." She hadn't uprooted herself and her child only to have that reputation follow her here. It had been bad enough back home, where someone had started the rumor that she'd gotten pregnant in order to trap her rich, former boyfriend. It hadn't been true, but that hadn't stopped the gossip from spreading like wildfire around the hospital where she worked.

"No it won't. It will make you look like a caring member of the community who appreciates the importance of contributing to charity," Veronica insisted.

"You'll look like someone who wants to have fun," Marissa added.

"And you don't have to bid on a stranger," Kristy added. "You can always bid on someone you know."

Alexandra frowned. "That's even worse. Can you imagine bidding on one of the doctors I work with? That would be too weird."

"So no doctors," Kristy said, making a note on a piece of paper that seemingly materialized out of nowhere.

"Why am I the only one who has to bid on someone?"

"I would love to participate, but I can't," Veronica said.

"I'm the auctioneer. It would be hard to bid and conduct the auction at the same time."

"I suppose not," Alexandra conceded. She looked at Kristy and Marissa. "But what about you two? Neither of you has a steady boyfriend."

"So what? We have busy social lives and date quite a bit. You, on the other hand, only leave the house to work or meet up with us. This will give you the chance to go on at least one date."

"I'm not looking to get involved with anyone right now. I have my daughter to think about. Chloe needs all of my time and attention."

"Nobody is saying that you have to start a relationship. Just have dinner with a nice guy," Marissa said.

"And maybe go to a club," Kristy added, doing a little chair dance.

"That sounds okay in theory. But things have a way of getting complicated really fast. I'd rather not take that chance right now. I still think that you two should bid on someone. It sounds like fun. And it's for charity."

"Don't be so quick to say no. There won't be any complications. And we know plenty of men. Besides, we expect the bidding to go high," Marissa said. "We're going to have to pool our resources in order to win even one date."

"Really?"

"Yes. These aren't just any run-of-the-mill bachelors you'll be bidding on. These are some of the most eligible men in Aspen Creek. And from out of town too—a couple of the guys even live in Denver," Veronica said. As one of the coordinators, she would know.

"Didn't you even look at the list of participants I gave you at lunch yesterday?" Marissa asked.

Alexandra shook her head. "Why would I? The names

wouldn't mean a thing to me. Not to mention that I had no intention of bidding."

While Alexandra was speaking, Kristy rummaged through her purse. Now she pulled out the flyer advertising the Aspen Creek Bachelor Auction, pushed Alexandra's empty plate aside, and set the paper in front of her. "I had a feeling that might be the case, so I circled the names of men you might be interested in bidding on."

"That was such a good idea," Veronica said, rolling her eyes. "Let's see who *you* think Alexandra would like."

"Let's not," Alexandra said. She could have saved her breath. Her friends were too busy looking at the flyer to pay much attention to her.

When Veronica squealed, "Oh no, you didn't," Alexandra couldn't help but glance over to see who they were talking about.

"Who?"

"Dr. Hunt."

"What's wrong with him?" Kristy asked. "I think he's cute."

"We know," Marissa said. "So why are you trying to set Alexandra up with your secret crush?"

"I don't have a crush on him, secret or otherwise. I just appreciate how gentle he is when I bring Twinkie in for his exam."

"Is Dr. Hunt your vet?" Alexandra asked.

Kristy nodded. "Yes. And he's a good one. Twinkie adores him. And you know how cats can be."

Alexandra was a dog person, so she had no idea. But she nodded anyway. "You do talk about him a lot. Maybe you should bid on him for yourself. I'm willing to contribute to the cause if you think he'll go for a lot of money."

"Don't listen to them," Kristy said, waving her hands. "I don't have a crush on him."

"Right," Marissa said, stretching the word over several syllables.

"Who else is on the list?" Alexandra asked, getting into the spirit despite herself. Besides, looking didn't hurt anything. And hearing about the different bachelors would help her to learn more about her neighbors.

"Oh, you really are interested," Kristy teased.

Aspen Creek, Colorado, was a resort town and a very close-knit community. Despite the fact that the population of the town grew significantly during the winter months as vacationers came to ski and participate in other outdoor activities, and less so during the warmer months when people came to fish and hike, the town still managed to keep its sense of community. That was one of the things that had appealed to Alexandra.

"Not really. I'm an outsider. I need these bits of information to get a complete picture of the people in town," Alexandra said quickly. She'd moved to town to help her great-aunt who'd injured her hip. Alexandra's parents wanted to move Aunt Rose in with them in their suburban Chicago home, but she wouldn't hear of it. She loved Aspen Creek and refused to leave the home she'd lived in all of her adult life. As a compromise, Aunt Rose allowed Alexandra and her daughter to stay with her and provide the care she needed. Since Alexandra had just ended a disastrous relationship and wanted to start over fresh, it was the perfect solution for both of them. A man—even one that supposedly came with no strings—was not part of the plan.

"What can you tell me about him?" Alexandra asked, pointing at a random picture. He wasn't one of the ones that had been circled, and she wasn't any more interested in him than she was in the others, but she wasn't above gathering what information she could.

"That's Nathan Montgomery," Marissa said. "I still can't believe he agreed to enter."

"Why? Is he a selfish jerk?"

"Nothing like that. He's generous and supports all the fundraisers. It's just that Nathan's all work and no play. There is no room in his life for anything other than his family's ranch. I would expect him to write a check and be done with it."

"So he's the serious type." Someone who wasn't interested in a relationship was the type of man she'd want to bid on. Not that she was going to bid on anyone.

"That's putting it mildly," Marissa said. "And not at all the type of man I would choose for you. Now Party Marty would be a better fit."

"Party Marty," Kristy said with a smile. "I agree. He would be better."

Veronica nodded. "He'll definitely show you a good time."

A guy named *Party Marty* couldn't be further from what Alexandra wanted. "No. I don't think so."

"So who are you going to bid on?" Veronica asked.

"I told you, I'm not bidding on anyone. I'll be happy to watch the auction." Alexandra took a breath and said firmly, "I'm really not interested in going out with anyone."

"Even though there is no second date? No commitment?" Kristy asked, clearly disappointed.

"Even then. I have enough on my plate right now. So, it's a no for me." Alexandra handed the flyer back to Kristy. "I won't be bidding on anyone."

NATHAN MONTGOMERY GRABBED the crumpled flyer advertising the Aspen Creek Bachelor Auction from his back pocket and held it out to his brother Isaac, so that he could read it. Nathan barely reined in his anger. This nonsense had Isaac's fingerprints all over it.

"What's that?" Isaac asked without looking at it.

"It's a flyer advertising the bachelor auction."

"And why are you showing it to me? I certainly have no interest in it."

"I thought you might find one of the names particularly interesting."

Isaac dropped the saddle he'd been about to place on his horse, snatched the paper from Nathan, and began frantically searching it. "I'm not on here, am I? Savannah is laid-back, but I don't think she would appreciate me going out with another woman, even if it is to raise money for charity."

Savannah was Isaac's fiancée and one of the sweetest people Nathan had met. She'd suffered the loss of her first husband and child and had found happiness with Isaac. Nathan looked at his brother, his suspicion temporarily suspended. "Are you saying you didn't do this?"

"Do what?"

"Enter me in the bachelor auction."

"What? No. Why would I do something like that?"

"As a joke."

"Again, no. Although I have to admit the idea of you strutting your stuff down the catwalk is kind of funny."

"You think so? Well, I don't. I am not interested in anything to do with this shenanigan. But if you didn't do this, who did?"

"Maybe your name was added as a mistake."

"And my picture? No way. Somebody had to intentionally put me on the list."

"Good point. But instead of accusing innocent people, why don't you just call the person in charge and ask how you were added? There's a number right on the flyer."

"Good idea."

"I'm more than just a pretty face and great body." Isaac winked and then flexed, striking a pose. Despite his annoyance, Nathan laughed. Of the three Montgomery brothers, Isaac, the youngest, had gotten the majority of the charm, which had made him popular with the single women of Aspen Creek. Nathan didn't envy him though. He had goals that charm wouldn't help him accomplish. His serious nature and willingness to do the hard work was what had him in line to run the Montgomery Ranch when his father retired. Those qualities might not be what women were looking for, but they were going to help him make the business even more successful than it was now.

Right now, theirs was the biggest beef ranch in the state and enjoyed a superior reputation. But Nathan was eyeing more than Colorado or even the Midwest. Over the next five years, he wanted to expand the operation until they distributed their organic beef across the entire United States.

Being a rancher was in Nathan's blood. From the time he could walk, he'd followed his father around, mimicking everything he did. Nathan learned the business from the bottom up. He'd cleaned stalls, fed cows, participated in cattle drives, and arranged for the stock to be taken to market. The only time he hadn't lived on the ranch had been when he'd gone away to Howard University, earning first his bachelor's and then a master's degree in business. Although he'd enjoyed his time at college, he'd itched to return home to Colorado. Now, unless he was on a business trip or on a weekend getaway, he was on the ranch.

Nathan made a mental note to contact Veronica Kendrick when they were finished moving the cattle from their current grazing site to another. "I wonder what's keeping Miles."

"Probably Jillian or the kids. Besides, we aren't supposed to leave for another five minutes, so technically he's not late."

Nathan nodded. He knew that was true, but he liked to have everything in order ahead of time, just in case an issue arose at the last minute. He didn't like surprises.

"Hey," Miles called, jogging into the stable and heading for his horse. In a minute he'd saddled it and ridden up beside them. He looked at the flyer Nathan was still holding. "Oh, I see you have that. Good. With all of the busyness surrounding the wedding arrangements, I forgot to mention it to you."

"You're the one behind this?" Nathan's fist clenched, crushing the flyer.

"Yes. Is there a problem?"

"You have to ask? Of course there's a problem. Why in the world would you enter me in this ridiculous bachelor auction?"

"If you recall, you had me start attending those Chamber of Commerce meetings. They are such a waste of time. I agreed to go *once* because I was grateful that you babysat the kids so I could spend more time with Jillian. That one time morphed into me going every month."

"And I appreciate you taking that task off my plate."

"You say that as if I had a choice."

"So...what? This is your petty payback? Instead of coming to me with your issue like a man, you signed me up for this bachelor auction?"

"It wasn't like that," Miles objected.

"We all have to do our part to keep the ranch running. It is a *family* business. And the last time I checked you were part of the family."

"The ranch means as much to me as it does to you. And no, this isn't payback. When I have a problem with you, you'll know. But when I mentioned the fundraiser, you didn't let me go into detail. You just said that it was important that Montgomery Ranch be represented in a very visible way. To show that even though we are not geographically a part of Aspen Creek, that we are a part of the town in spirit. That whatever matters to the town matters to the Montgomery family."

Miles was quiet by nature, so this long speech was out of character. And unnecessary. Nathan wound his hand in a "get to the point" gesture. They had a schedule to keep.

"Well, Nathan, the fundraiser is this ridiculous bachelor auction. It was Deborah Lane's idea. But it quickly won the support of most of the women at the meeting. A few of the men even thought it was a good idea and signed up for it on the spot." He shook his head. "They decided to contact the single men in town to see if they were willing to participate. Apparently quite a few were."

"Nobody contacted me." He would have shut down that foolishness in a minute.

"That's because when they asked me if one of the Montgomery men was willing to participate, I said yes. Clearly I'm out. I'm getting married in three weeks. And Isaac is out because he's engaged. That left only you."

"You could have said no."

"Oh, how short your memory is, dear brother. The last time I said no about a fundraiser, you jumped all over me because I made the ranch look like a poor neighbor. I believe your exact words were *always say yes, Miles. Always.*"

"I remember that," Isaac said, not being the least bit helpful. But then, knowing Isaac, he hadn't intended to be. He delighted in being annoying. It was his superpower.

Nathan recalled the conversation too, although he wasn't

going to admit it now. "And somehow you took that to mean I wanted to be bid upon like a cow?"

"Don't turn this on me. I was just following your blanket order. If you want to back out, then that's on you."

"Oh, come on. Why would he want to back out?" Isaac asked. "This is the stuff dreams are made of."

"How do you figure?" Nathan asked. Even Miles looked interested in Isaac's reply.

"Dozens of women willing to spend their hard-earned money for a chance to go out with you. What man wouldn't love that?"

*Me*, thought Nathan. *I wouldn't*.

But he and Isaac were different. Before Isaac had met Savannah and fallen head over heels in love, his nickname had been Isaac "love 'em and leave 'em happy" Montgomery. He'd dated nearly every woman in town, somehow managing to remain on good terms with all of them.

Nathan had never been as popular with the women as Isaac. But then, nobody was. Being a ladies' man wasn't among Nathan's goals. Not that he was opposed to relationships. They had their place. And time. And now wasn't the time for him to become involved with anyone. The ranch kept him busy and he wouldn't be able to give a woman the attention she deserved.

Not that he hadn't tried on more than one occasion. His last relationship had been a colossal failure. Janet had been a single mother of a six-year-old. He and Billy had been wrecked when the relationship ended, and Billy and his mother had moved to Iowa. But Nathan had learned his lesson—no dating single mothers.

There was an order to things. First he would establish the ranch as the premiere beef ranch in the nation. Then—and only then—would he look for a woman to share his life.

He didn't see what the big rush was to find a woman and get married anyway. After all, he was only thirty years old. There was plenty of time for a relationship in the future.

He'd explained himself to his brothers and parents several times, but they didn't understand. He wasn't going to waste his breath saying it again. "I don't want to lead anyone on."

"Lead them on how? They're bidding on one night. Dinner and maybe some dancing. Or a movie or concert. Nobody is expecting a marriage proposal. Or even a second date," Isaac said.

"Really? If that's all they want, why would they spend all that money for one date?"

"You got me," Miles said. "The whole idea is silly to me. There are plenty of other ways to support a charity. Like writing a check."

"Because it's fun," Isaac said. "You two really are sticks-in-the-mud. I can't believe we're related. Let me break it down for you. Not every date has to lead to a relationship. Sometimes people do things just for the sheer pleasure of it. Like bid on a date at a bachelor auction. Don't read more into it than is there."

"When did you get all logical?" Nathan asked. "You're actually making sense."

"I don't want to be out here all day. Savannah and I have plans for the evening, so I don't have time for you to have an existential crisis over something that doesn't matter. Take the winner to dinner and take her home. Thank her for her time and her charitable donation, and leave. Easy."

"Right?" Miles agreed. "What's the big deal? And it will generate goodwill for the ranch. That's something that's important. If you back out, we'll lose that goodwill and maybe even stir up some bad blood."

"And you definitely don't want to do that," Isaac said.

"No." That was the last thing he would ever want. The ranch was everything.

"Good. Now that it's settled, let's get this show on the road," Isaac said, leading the way from the stable, Nathan and Miles behind him.

As he rode out to the pastures beside his brothers, Nathan tried to convince himself that it was going to be as easy as Isaac claimed.

But he had a sneaking suspicion that the auction was going to be much more complicated than that.

# CHAPTER TWO

ALEXANDRA STEPPED INTO the ballroom and then looked around. The decorating committee had outdone themselves with red, pink, and white roses in marble vases. Enormous crystal chandeliers hung from the twenty-foot ceiling, illuminating the spacious room. There was a buzz of energy in the air, and despite telling herself that she really didn't want to bid on anyone, excitement built up inside her.

She spotted her friends at their table. She'd left work a few minutes later than scheduled and had needed to rush home in order to get dressed. Although she hadn't planned to make a big deal of this, she'd bought a new dress and shoes for the night. It had been a while since she'd been shopping, and she'd gone a bit over budget. But looking at the other women dressed in their designer finery and showy jewelry, she was glad that she'd done it. She knew that she looked good in her sleek black dress and heels.

Her friends had a table in a prime location near the end of the catwalk—probably because of Veronica's position as the auctioneer—and she made her way over to them.

"We thought you had backed out," Marissa said, rising to give Alexandra a hug.

"No. I got caught up at work."

"That's what your aunt said when I called, but we figured she was covering for you."

"Aunt Rose? No way. She tried to convince me to bid on

a guy." Aunt Rose might be in her late sixties, but she had a very young attitude and was up for anything. Including parachuting out of a plane with her partner in crime, Bella Stewart, which is how she'd injured her hip.

Alexandra sat in a chair and looked around. "So where are the eligible bachelors?"

"They're here. They're eating dinner, same as us."

"Don't tell me that they have dates."

"I have no idea," Marissa said. "Why would that matter to you? You aren't bidding on anyone."

"Unless you changed your mind," Kristy said hopefully.

"No. I'm still not bidding," Alexandra said firmly. "But I'm willing to contribute to the cause. I just wanted to get a peek at the men before the bidding started."

"You won't have to wait long," Veronica said. She glanced at her watch, then stood. "I'm about to get the auction started."

"Good luck," Alexandra said.

Veronica smiled and then winked. "I was made for this."

Veronica took her place behind the podium and a hush immediately came over the room. "Welcome to the first and hopefully not last Aspen Creek Bachelor Auction."

There was a roar and applause, and Veronica smiled as she waited for silence before continuing, "I am Veronica Kendrick, your host for the event. Before we start, I want to remind you that tonight's auction is raising funds for charity. Specifically, funds for children in underserved communities as well as children's programming at the library. So, ladies, raise those paddles, open up your wallets and get ready to bid. I guarantee you'll get your money's worth. Our sixteen bachelors will each walk the catwalk, so you'll get a chance to meet them all before the bidding begins. Now, without further ado, let the auction begin."

NATHAN STOOD BACKSTAGE and looked at the other bachelors. They were all laughing and talking among themselves, as if being paraded in front of the entire town was a good thing. Nathan knew a lot of them, counted a few among his friends, but he didn't feel at ease enough to engage in conversation. Although he'd had time to get used to the idea of participating in the auction, he still couldn't shake the feeling that he was making a big mistake.

He knew all of the benefits that would result from the auction and had reminded himself of them repeatedly since he'd discovered he was a participant. Money would be raised for charity. Although the town was well off, there were always needs to be met. People to help. He was all for that.

And there was the goodwill that the ranch would accrue. Not only in Aspen Creek, but in the state as well. Nathan wanted to take the business nationwide, which required him to make contacts. He wasn't convinced that this was the best way to bring attention to the ranch, but backing out would definitely do harm to their reputation, something he would never tolerate.

"You don't look like you're expecting to have fun," a man said, approaching Nathan.

"Is this supposed to be fun?" Nathan replied.

He grinned. "That's how I was sold on it."

"Sounds like you talked to my brother, former most eligible bachelor of Aspen Creek."

"Former?"

"He's engaged now."

"Don't say it like it's a life sentence."

"I'm not opposed to commitment. Just not now." He held out his hand. "I'm Nathan Montgomery, by the way."

"I know. I grew up here. I guess you don't remember me."

Nathan gave the other man a long stare. He'd prided himself on his memory, but it was failing him now. Still… there was something familiar about the guy, but Nathan couldn't place him. "Sorry. I feel as if I should know you, but I can't recall your name."

"That's okay. I look a little bit different these days. I'm Malcolm Wilson."

"No kidding? You look a *lot* different. The Malcolm I remember was a short, scrawny guy."

Malcolm grinned. "I'm what my mother refers to as a late bloomer. I grew over a foot my freshman year in college and put on fifty pounds of muscle."

"What brings you back to town after all these years?"

He was a little hesitant. "It was time for me to come home."

Nathan nodded. "Well, this is certainly a way to make your presence known."

"So you haven't heard any talk about me?"

"Should I?"

"I don't know. If there's one thing I remember about Aspen Creek, it's that people like to speculate and gossip. My family owned a small ranch. I figured people are wondering what I plan to do with it."

"It's possible that they are. I don't live in town, so much of the news doesn't reach me. Besides, I don't gossip, so nobody would approach me with that kind of talk. But hey, welcome home."

"Thanks."

The backstage coordinator, Evelyn Parks, entered the room and clapped her hands. She was a member of the Aspen Creek Chamber of Commerce and the main reason there was always so much conflict at meetings. "It's time. You'll each be given a number. When it is called, you'll walk on stage. Walk down the catwalk and then return to the stage and line up. Across, so that everyone will have a good look at you. Then you all will exit and return backstage, waiting until your number is called to be bid on."

"Showtime," Malcolm said, patting Nathan on the shoulder before going to get a number.

Nathan put on the cowboy hat he had been holding. He'd wanted to dress in black jeans, a white shirt, and his cowboy boots, but Isaac had nixed the idea. His brother had reminded him that the auction was for charity, and that he had to look his best to get the most money. So now Nathan was wearing a black suit, black shirt, and dress shoes.

"You don't intend to wear that hat, do you?" Mrs. Parks said, her tone of voice making it clear what she thought of the idea. Her snooty attitude only hardened his position.

"I absolutely do," Nathan said. He might have left his cowboy boots under his bed, but the hat was nonnegotiable. No hat, no Nathan. "I'm a rancher."

"But you look so nice without it. And my Melanie is here and plans on bidding on you. You don't want your hat to turn her off, do you?"

Nathan managed to suppress a shudder. He and Melanie had been classmates. They'd never gotten along but over the years they had managed to keep their distance. Then one day, for a reason known only to herself, Melanie decided that the two of them would make a good couple. He'd done his best to disabuse her of that notion, but clearly he hadn't been successful. Ever since he'd realized that he couldn't back out of the auction, he had tried to put the upcoming date out of his mind. He hadn't considered the possibility that the winner might be someone he found completely unlikable. He could only hope that Melanie didn't win.

"I'm wearing my hat. Not only in the auction, but on

the date as well." That last bit was a bluff, but she didn't need to know that.

Mrs. Parks compressed her lips and stalked away, her wide back stiff. Another volunteer handed Nathan an eight-by-ten cardboard with a number on it and then wrote Nathan's name on a clipboard. Wouldn't you know it? Nathan was number sixteen. He would be the last bachelor. He didn't know if that was good or bad. Maybe the women would have run out of money by then and he would go home by himself. A reject. Embarrassed before the entire town.

Nathan shook his head. He didn't want to date anyone, so why did the thought bother him? Besides, going last could be good. They would be building up to him. If he had the charm and magnetism of Isaac, he might believe that to be the case instead of what it actually was. He'd been talking to Mrs. Parks and had been the last person given a number.

He noticed that Malcolm was standing three people ahead of him. As the men walked onto the stage, there was a burst of applause and some cheers.

The things he did for the ranch.

He just hoped the whole mess would be over soon.

ALEXANDRA WATCHED AS the men walked onto the catwalk as their numbers were called, in what was intended to be the teaser before the auction started. Even subtracting the handful of outsiders, it was hard to believe that this many good-looking men lived in this pleasant resort town. And yet, each man who crossed the stage was even more handsome than the one before.

"Dr. Trevor Hunt," Veronica announced, breaking into Alexandra's thoughts. A handsome man in his early thirties stepped onto the stage and Alexandra sneaked a look at Kristy. She was staring at him like Alexandra stared at chocolate. Her friend might try to deny it, but it was clear that she was attracted to the veterinarian.

"You should totally bid on him," Alexandra said to Kristy.

"No way. He's my cat's vet. That would make things awkward between us."

"On the other hand, he might appreciate being bid on by a friend instead of a stranger."

"Do you think all of the women here are strangers? Granted, a lot of them have come in from out of town, but most of them live in Aspen Creek. Believe me, plenty of them will be bidding on him, so it's unlikely he'll end up with someone he doesn't know."

"If it's all right with you, it's all right with me."

"It is."

Alexandra turned her attention back to the stage, watching as the men continued to cross the stage. Finally they got to the last man, who Veronica introduced as Nathan Montgomery. Alexandra had only seen him on the flyer the other day. The picture had been small, and it had been difficult to make out his features beneath his cowboy hat. Truthfully, she hadn't tried all that hard to see what he looked like. Now curiosity was getting the better of her.

And then he strode onto the stage as if he owned the place.

Alexandra took one look at him and barely managed to catch the gasp before it escaped her lips. The man was absolutely gorgeous. Dressed in all black, he had the best body Alexandra had ever seen. Even beneath his suit jacket, his broad, powerful shoulders were unmistakable. His well-formed chest tapered down to a trim waist. There was no disguising the muscular thighs of his long legs. He walked down the catwalk with confident strides. When he reached the end, he tipped his cowboy hat at the audience, eliciting cheers before turning and walking away.

Alexandra let out a sigh, glad that she hadn't swooned in front of her friends.

"What do you think?" Marissa asked, elbowing Alexandra out of her trance.

Alexandra smirked. "He's all right, I guess. If you go for that kind. He's a solid six."

"Right," Marissa replied, clearly not fooled. "Too bad you aren't going to bid on anyone."

The bachelors made their way backstage as the crowd applauded.

Bachelor number one remained on the stage. The bidding started at one hundred dollars. In two minutes of fast and furious bidding, that sum had risen to six hundred dollars. And women were still raising their paddles, going even higher.

Finally the bidding stopped at seventeen hundred and seventy-five dollars. *Wow.* Somebody really wanted to win a date with him. Alexandra turned to Kristy. "Is he someone important?"

"What do you mean?"

"I mean is he a big shot? A politician? A millionaire?" When her friend only stared at her, she continued. "He went for a lot of money."

"Oh, that's Marty Adams. He owns a restaurant in town. He also has a brand of barbecue sauce that's sold in stores across the country."

In that moment, it clicked. "That's Party Marty?"

"Yes. The woman who won a date with him is going to have a fantastic time."

"So all of the bachelors aren't going to go for that much?"

Kristy laughed. "I doubt it. Why? Have you changed your mind about bidding? There are lots of good men available."

"And we'll contribute if that's what is holding you back," Marissa added. "After all, it's for a good cause."

"I know. The library."

Marissa leaned in. "And getting you to go on a date."

Alexandra only shook her head. She wasn't sure getting her on a date was worth that much money.

The bidding didn't slow as the night progressed. In fact, the excitement built with each man and Alexandra was swept up in it. The energy had practically reached a frenzy by the time the last bachelor sauntered down the catwalk. Nathan Montgomery. His cowboy hat was fixed in a way that partially obscured his face. But what she could see of his handsome profile was enough to make her blood race. His brown skin was so perfect, she wondered if he got regular facials. That ridiculous thought didn't last a minute before she shooed it away.

From his confident and slightly irritated stance, and the way he commanded the room, it was clear that Nathan Montgomery was a man's man. The type who would never have a facial because he was too busy with more important things. Business? She wasn't sure, but he definitely didn't seem the type to be in this auction, no matter how good the cause.

She clenched the paddle that had sat unused on the table throughout the auction.

Marissa raised a questioning eyebrow.

"I'm just testing it out," Alexandra said weakly.

Kristy and Marissa laughed.

"There's no shame in bidding," Kristy said. "After all, the money will go to help kids."

Alexandra held her paddle in her lap as the bidding began. It started slowly and she wondered if the other women in town knew something about Nathan Montgomery that she didn't. Suddenly she felt sorry for him. He had pride just as much as she did. She knew what it was like to be embarrassed.

When the bidding stalled at five hundred dollars, a respectable number although lower than the other bids, Veronica spoke from the podium. "Do I hear five-fifty?"

"Seven hundred dollars," someone called in a smug voice, as if she'd knocked out all of the other competitors and knew it.

"Will anyone go higher? Do I hear seven-fifty?"

Nathan Montgomery turned slowly on the runway and looked in her direction. Although she couldn't see his eyes under the brim of his Stetson, she practically felt his gaze burning into her own. Her skin began to tingle and she jumped to her feet.

"Seven-fifty," Alexandra called, as she raised her paddle.

"I guess you want him after all," Kristy said with a smirk, as Alexandra sat again.

"One thousand dollars," that annoying voice called.

"Eleven hundred," Alexandra said firmly before turning to her friends. "Who is that bidding against me?"

"That's Melanie Parks. She was Nathan's nemesis for years. You can't let her win," Kristy said. "Nathan deserves better than her."

"That's right. This is war," Marissa said, then jumped to her feet. "Twelve hundred dollars!"

"You just bid against me," Alexandra said, poking her friend in the side.

Marissa clapped her hands against her mouth and sank into her chair. "Sorry! I got carried away."

There was silence.

"Anyone else have a bid?" Veronica asked.

Alexandra shot Marissa a look and then bid. "Twelve hundred and fifty dollars."

After a short silence, Veronica spoke again. "Going once. Twice. And the winner is paddle 58. Alexandra Jamison."

There was a pause and then explosive applause. Once more Alexandra felt her gaze being pulled over to where Nathan Montgomery stood. He tipped his cowboy hat at her and then strode down the catwalk. Alexandra couldn't tear her eyes away, not blinking until he had disappeared behind the curtain.

Somewhere in the recesses of her mind, she heard Veronica announcing that the event had been an unqualified success. She then told the winners where they could pay their donation and meet their dates. Now that it was over, the rush from winning faded and Alexandra no longer floated on air. She'd landed back to earth with a thud as reality struck her.

She'd just bid a ridiculous amount of money to go on a date with a man she'd never laid eyes on before tonight. What had she been thinking? Why had she spent so much money?

And on a *date*? That was the last thing she should be doing right now.

"Wow. You did it. You bid on a bachelor," Kristy said, grinning broadly.

"I wasn't sure you would," Marissa said. "Especially since you were so set against it."

Alexandra wasn't sure if she was in shock, but she couldn't bring herself to move. Or breathe. Or anything else. "I was a bit surprised myself. But I guess I finally got sucked into the action. And look at me now," she said weakly. "The winner!"

"Well, don't just sit there. Go pay and meet your date," Kristy said.

Alexandra nodded as she stood up, grabbing her purse. "I'll be right back."

"I feel as if I should contribute something," Marissa said, opening her purse. "After all, I did kick the price up by a couple of hundred dollars."

"You pay for my dinner next time we go out and we'll call it even," Alexandra said. When she and Owen had broken up, she'd sold most of the expensive jewelry that he'd given her. She hadn't wanted a reminder of how easily he'd turned her head. And of how wrong she'd been about him. But there was no way she was giving even one earring back to him. This wasn't exactly how she'd planned to spend the money, but a petty part of her that she rarely indulged reveled in the knowledge that Owen was funding her first date with another man since their breakup.

By the time Alexandra reached the cashier, there was no one in line. Alexandra set her paddle on the table and gave her name to the volunteer. A woman standing near the table shot Alexandra a dirty look before stomping away.

"Pay no attention to her," the cashier said. "Melanie is just upset that you outbid her."

"Oh." So *that* was Melanie. Alexandra slid her credit card into the reader and then approved the amount.

"Your cowboy is waiting," the cashier said, gesturing to where Nathan Montgomery stood. There were a couple of other bachelors nearby, but they were talking to other women. Veronica was standing close to one of the bachelors, engaged in what looked like a heated discussion. "Go introduce yourself to Nathan. Thank you for your donation. And have a great date."

"Thank you." Suddenly Alexandra felt shy, which was ridiculous. There wasn't a shy bone in her body. But experience was trying to teach her to think before she acted. Something she clearly had yet to learn. She'd just impulsively outbid a woman for a date with a man she wasn't sure she wanted to go out with simply because he'd looked divine in a cowboy hat. Well, there were no givebacks, so she needed to move ahead.

Inhaling deeply, Alexandra walked over to Nathan Montgomery.

"Hi," she said.

"Hi." He removed his hat and held it in his hands in front of him. She had the feeling that he didn't remove his hat often. "It appears that you have won a date with me."

"Yes." He'd spoken a bit stiffly and Alexandra was consumed with doubt. Had he hoped some other woman would win? "I hope that's all right with you. I ran into Melanie Parks at the table and she seemed a bit upset with me. If there's something between you two that I'm not aware of, I can always bow out."

"Absolutely not," Nathan said, immediately. "We are definitely not dating. We don't even run in the same circle of friends. Believe me, I am happy that you won the bidding war."

Alexandra smiled. She was relieved although she wasn't sure why. "Okay."

They stood there staring at each other. Clearly neither one knew what the next step should be. Since she was the one who'd won, perhaps the onus was on her to take the lead. She sighed. "I've never done anything like this before, so I'm at a loss as to what to do next."

"Why don't we sit down at one of the tables and figure it out?"

She nodded. Now that the auction was over, people were beginning to leave, so there were several empty tables to choose from.

Nathan held out his arm, allowing her to precede him. As she passed by him, she inhaled and got a whiff of his

cologne. It was subtle and outdoorsy. She'd never smelled
it before, but it was on the way to becoming her new favorite scent. She bypassed two tables and found one near
the corner of the room, where they would have a bit of
privacy. Nathan held out a chair for her and she sat. Once
she was comfortable, he took a seat across from her. There
were a couple of empty glasses on the table and he pushed
them aside.

"You know my name, but over all of the applause, I
couldn't make out yours."

"It's Alexandra Jamison. I'm new to Aspen Creek. I'm
a pediatric nurse."

"Nice to meet you, Alexandra. I guess you already
know a bit about me."

"Not really."

"You didn't read my biography on the flyer?" He lifted
one side of his mouth in a wry smile that she found oddly
appealing and that had her stomach do a little flip-flop.

"Well, to be honest, no. I had no intention of bidding
at all. My friends kind of egged me on and here we are."

"So… It was spur of the moment?"

"Yes."

He smiled and a dimple flashed in his cheek.

Their eyes met and she felt the same tingling sensation she'd experienced when he'd glanced at her from the
runway.

"Are you sure there's no woman waiting in the wings."

"Positive. I don't date much, to tell you the truth. Now
my brother Isaac on the other hand? All he has to do is
breathe and women fall at his feet."

"You must have some fans. After all, you went for a
lot of money."

He smiled. "Only because your friend jumped in."

Alexandra laughed. "She told me that she got caught up in the moment."

He threw back his head and laughed. The sound was robust and merry. "Perhaps you should have a talk with her about her emotions. If that keeps up, she could cost you a lot of money in the future."

"Well, since I don't plan on bidding on another man, I'm safe." She looked at him. "If you plan on doing this again, you're going to be at the mercy of some other woman. Like Melanie."

"Trust me, this was a onetime thing."

"You sound so definite."

"That's because I am. My brother is the one who signed me up. I only found out about it after the flyers had gone out. It would have looked bad for me to back out."

"Oh. Then maybe you need to have a talk with your brother," she said. "Otherwise you might become a regular attraction."

He smiled and butterflies fluttered in her stomach. Where had they come from?

"You're okay, Alexandra. This date just might turn out to be fun after all."

"I was just thinking the same thing. So, where would you like to go?"

"You just spent a lot of money, so you should decide."

"I don't know many places. If you don't mind, how about you make a few suggestions and we decide after that?"

"I can do that."

He reached into his inside jacket pocket and pulled out his cell phone. "If you want to give me your number, I'll call you. Then we'll both have each other's numbers."

She nodded and then reeled off her telephone number, which he dialed. In a second, her cell phone rang. Alexandra added Nathan's number to her contacts and then put her phone into her purse. "I'll call you tomorrow, if that's okay?"

"That's fine." He stood, placed his hat on his head, nodded, then strode away.

Heart racing, Alexandra watched him make his exit. She had the strange sensation that the date with Nathan Montgomery wasn't going to be as forgettable as she'd thought.

And neither was he.

## CHAPTER THREE

ALEXANDRA STEPPED INTO her aunt's house, slipped off her shoes, and placed them on the mat beside the door. After exchanging numbers with Nathan, she'd hugged Kristy and Marissa goodbye. Veronica had still been talking to the man Alexandra had seen her with earlier, and she hadn't wanted to disturb them.

"How was the auction?" Aunt Rose asked, glancing up from her rapidly moving crochet hook. Before Alexandra could answer, Aunt Rose turned to Crystal, Alexandra's teenage babysitter, who was crocheting too, although without the same speed or skill. "You're doing a good job."

Crystal smiled. "Do you think I'll be finished by my dad's birthday? It's in four weeks."

"Yes. And he's going to love that scarf." Turning back to her niece, she repeated, "Well, how was the auction?" without missing a stitch, as if she hadn't been the one to interrupt the conversation.

"It was fun," Alexandra said.

"Did you bid on anyone?"

"Yes."

"Good girl. And did you win?"

"Yes."

"Is this the bachelor auction for the library funds?" Crystal said, putting down her crocheting. "I told my dad to enter, but he just laughed and shook his head. He's never going to find a girlfriend if he doesn't try."

Alexandra didn't know what to make of that comment, so she ignored it and answered Crystal's question. "It was the bachelor auction. And speaking of your father, I should get you home. Just let me check on Chloe."

"She was very good," Crystal said, suddenly all business. She set down her crocheting and picked up a piece of paper from the coffee table. Although Alexandra had told her it wasn't necessary, Crystal insisted on writing detailed notes of everything Chloe did. "She finished her dinner right after you left. We played for a while. She had a bottle at eight thirty and was asleep by nine."

"Thank you. I know that she was in very good hands." Alexandra went to Chloe's bedroom and looked at her sleeping daughter. Her little girl was growing up so fast. Chloe had kicked off the blanket and Alexandra straightened it. Her heart overflowed with love as she caressed her daughter's face. Chloe stirred and Alexandra reluctantly pulled her hand away.

Being a single mother wasn't easy, and it certainly hadn't been her plan, but Chloe was worth it. Owen was missing out on everything. Not that he cared. He was perfectly happy living his life as a bachelor, seemingly interested in making the world a better place, all the while ignoring his flesh and blood.

Alexandra had met Owen at a fundraiser for childhood cancer research. He'd been so charming. So concerned about the sick children and their worried parents. So sensitive. What a joke. He'd burned rubber in his haste to get away when Alexandra had told him she was pregnant. His family was wealthy and connected—his mother was on the board at the hospital where Alexandra worked. His family wanted her to go away quietly and tried to use their influence to get her fired.

But Alexandra hadn't been without resources of her

own. Her mother, Clarice, was the chief of thoracic surgery at that same hospital, and the administration hadn't wanted to risk losing her. Not only that, Alexandra's father was a renowned attorney who'd won hundreds of millions of dollars for his clients. No one in their right mind wanted to go up against Lemuel Jamison in court. If Alexandra had wanted to fight with Owen, she would have won. But she hadn't wanted to battle with him. She'd just wanted to be done with him forever.

In exchange for Owen relinquishing his parental rights, Alexandra had agreed not to seek child support. Of course, Alexandra's father had insisted that Owen create a substantial trust for Chloe. Money couldn't replace a father, but it would guard against financial hardships in the future.

Alexandra closed Chloe's bedroom door, shutting down all thoughts of Owen as well, and then returned to the living room. Crystal had packed up her crocheting and was fastening her jacket. Alexandra grabbed her purse and then took out the agreed upon pay and handed the money to Crystal.

Crystal smiled and shoved the money into her pocket. "Thanks."

"You're welcome."

"I called my dad to let him know you were home. He said that you didn't need to drop me off. He was just leaving the store, so he said he'd pick me up."

Crystal's dad had been a ranch hand, but he'd recently purchased the feedstore in town. "That's nice of him."

The doorbell rang and Alexandra opened the door, letting in Crystal's father.

"How was the auction?" Clay asked.

"Fun. Although I hear you turned down an invitation to enter," Alexandra joked.

Clay grimaced. "That's an invitation I was happy to decline."

"You would have had fun, Dad," Crystal said as she came to stand beside them.

"Your idea of fun is a lot different than mine," Clay said, draping an affectionate arm over Crystal's shoulder and leading her out the door.

"Well, I guess I'll turn in," Alexandra said.

"You don't think you're getting off that easily," Aunt Rose said, patting the pillow next to her. "I want to know everything that happened at the auction. So come sit down and give me all of the details."

"Give me ten minutes to change and I'll tell you everything. Can I get you some tea?"

"No thanks."

Alexandra changed out of her new dress into her pajamas, washed off her makeup, then went back to the front room.

"So, who did you bet on? More importantly, who did you win?"

"Nathan Montgomery."

"Really?" Aunt Rose's eyebrows rose and she laughed. "Of all the men in town, that's the last man I expected you to want to date."

"What makes you say that?"

"Now don't get all huffy. It wasn't a criticism of you or him."

Alexandra blew out a breath. She didn't know why she'd been so touchy. "I know."

"He is a good-looking man, that's for sure. I should have bought a ticket. That way I could have bid on a bachelor or two."

"Really?"

"Sadly there weren't many men in my age group."

"None, to be honest."

"And I don't think those younger men could keep up with me. Of course, I could always teach a young one a thing or two."

Alexandra laughed. "You just might be right."

"Of course I am. So, where are you and Nathan going on your date?"

"We're going to figure it out later."

"That's good. I'm glad that you're starting to get out. You need more than work and Chloe in your life. You need to have fun. A hot fling is just what the doctor ordered."

"It's just one date," Alexandra reminded her aunt, a little appalled—and maybe amused, if she admitted it to herself—at Rose's racy suggestion.

"Well, of course it is, dear. That's how all flings start. On that note, I'm going to hit the hay." Aunt Rose put her crochet hook into her ball of yarn and stood. She gave Alexandra's cheek a gentle pat. "I'll see you in the morning. Good night. Have sweet dreams."

Alexandra was pleased to see that her aunt no longer needed her daily help—if she ever had. When Alexandra first arrived, she'd been surprised to see that her aunt hadn't been as badly hurt as Alexandra had been led to believe. Rose had been getting around—if slowly. Now Alexandra was beginning to suspect that either her aunt had exaggerated the state of her health, or she had conspired with Alexandra's parents to get her out of town after the collapse of her relationship. Either way, coming to Aspen Creek had been a balm to her soul.

Although she loved living with her aunt, Alexandra didn't want to overstay her welcome. After all, Aunt Rose was a senior citizen who'd enjoyed the peace and quiet of her big, rambling house. She probably longed for the days when she had the house to herself. Now she had two people living with her. And one was a baby. Alexandra tried to keep the mess and noise to a minimum, but that was nearly impossible.

Alexandra had brought up the topic of leaving a couple of weeks ago, but Aunt Rose had shut down that conversation. She'd said that Alexandra and Chloe were welcome to stay for as long as they wanted. Since Alexandra was still trying to figure out her next move, and she and Chloe were comfortable here, she had been glad to hear it.

Once Alexandra was alone, she leaned back in her chair and closed her eyes. Though she tried not to, she couldn't stop thinking about Nathan and how handsome he was. Of course, every man in the auction had been good-looking, but none of the others had sent shivers racing down her spine from just looking at him. But that didn't mean she had to act on her attraction. She had no intention of getting involved with anyone for the foreseeable future. She didn't trust any man with her heart—or Chloe's—right now. Not only that, she didn't trust her judgment. So no matter how appealing she found Nathan Montgomery, he was off-limits.

She would go on their date. And then he would be out of her life.

NATHAN SWIPED HIS forearm against his forehead and leaned against the top rail of the fence. He and his brothers had just driven the cattle from one grazing area of the ranch to the other. Most days he enjoyed spending hours on horseback, but today was not one of those days. No matter how he tried, he hadn't been able to get comfortable in the saddle, and he'd been relieved when they'd finally arrived.

He raised his face to the sky. The sun was directly overhead, and he knew that it was only a little bit past noon. Even so, he felt antsy. And he knew why. Alexandra was going to call him today. Knowing that had made it impossible to keep his mind on the task at hand. Twice Miles had spoken to him, and he'd barely heard it. Isaac had finally called him out on his behavior.

It was dangerous to be distracted around animals of this size. The cattle generally stayed with the herd, and there were several trained dogs to keep them in line if they should decide to make a break for it. Even so, Nathan knew he needed to get his head back on straight. Now.

"What's up?" Isaac asked as he and Miles walked over to him.

"Just thinking."

"About that woman who won a date with you at the auction?" Miles asked.

"I can't believe you have the nerve to mention the auction to me," Nathan said, rather than answer.

"You came in third, right behind Marty and the mayor. You raised a lot of money for charity and gained a lot of goodwill for the ranch."

"That's the only reason I'm talking to you today."

Miles laughed and shook his head.

"So are you thinking about her?" Isaac asked.

"Why are you asking me that?" Nathan didn't know why he didn't just answer the question directly. It wasn't a crime to think about her. Alexandra was attractive. Intriguing.

"I'm curious," Isaac said.

Nathan waited for his brother to make a wisecrack and was pleasantly surprised when he didn't. Somehow he forgot that Isaac was actually an adult, capable of having a serious conversation. But the change in his brother's attitude hadn't come with age. Several months ago, Isaac had been named the guardian of a baby girl. To Nathan's surprise, his brother had changed his ways overnight and become a devoted father. Then he'd become involved with Savannah, putting his "love 'em and leave 'em" reputation behind him for good.

"I guess I am thinking about her. She was interesting."

"And sexy."

Nathan raised his eyebrow and gave his brother a hard look.

Isaac laughed and raised his hands in front of him in surrender. "There's no need for you to give me the death stare. I'm just saying she's attractive. That's all. I'm happy with Savannah and not the least bit interested in any other woman. Much less one who has caught your attention. It's about time you found a good woman and settled down."

Nathan laughed. "I know you didn't just say that to me. Not after you've been out with every woman from here to Denver and back."

"That was before. And now that I've seen the light, I want you to enjoy the same happiness that Miles and I have found."

Miles nodded. Miles and his fiancée, Jillian Adams, had been childhood friends. They'd dated through high school and college before breaking up and marrying other people. As divorced single parents, they had found their way back to each other over the past year, and their connection was stronger than ever.

"I think I'll pass. I have goals that I want to achieve before I even think about getting involved in a serious relationship."

"We know. Your five-year plan," Isaac said, frowning.

Miles rolled his eyes. Nathan already knew his brothers didn't approve of his plan. Luckily, Nathan didn't need their approval.

"Exactly."

"Then why are you standing here daydreaming about Alexandra?"

Before Nathan could think of a suitable reply, his brothers had walked away and mounted their horses.

Isaac looked over at him and called, "Come on. We need to get finished. I want to get back to Savannah and Mia. And you know Jillian will be waiting for Miles. They have wedding plans to finalize."

Nathan shook himself. He was acting like a lovesick teenager instead of a man of thirty. If he was going to run this ranch when his father retired, he needed to keep his head in the game. He couldn't tolerate distractions, no matter how gorgeous the package they came in.

Alexandra was proving to be a distraction he couldn't afford. They'd barely met, and she was already affecting his work. After their date, he was going to have to put her out of his life so he could stay on course. He felt a sharp pain in his chest at that thought. What in the world was that? Why had he felt that pang? It had to be the stress of the day. Or something physical. There was no way his heart would ache at the thought of not seeing a woman he hadn't even known twenty-four hours ago.

He mounted his horse and then got back to work, blocking all thoughts of Alexandra from his mind. It took more effort than it should have, but he managed to stay focused for the remainder of the day.

When he got home, he showered and then looked through the refrigerator for something to heat up for dinner. Two years ago he'd had a five-bedroom house built on the property. He might be single now, but one day he planned to marry and have a family, and they would need a place to live. Building a house now had solved the problem before it had arisen.

Each of his brothers had homes of their own on the ranch too. His parents still lived in the house where Nathan and his brothers had grown up. His mother always cooked plenty of food in case they dropped in for dinner. Nathan ate with his parents on occasion but didn't want to take advantage. Besides, after a hard day at work, he appreciated his solitude.

Antsy and unsettled, he prowled around the kitchen. He knew his nerves were attacking him because he was waiting to hear from Alexandra. He could take control and call her, but he wouldn't. Not because he was afraid it would make him look desperate, although that was a distinct possibility. It was because she had told him she would call. He would trust her to do that at her convenience.

He grabbed a steak out of the refrigerator and seasoned it. Then he stepped onto the patio overlooking his in-ground pool, threw some charcoal on the grill, and lit it. While he waited for the fire to burn down, he lit his firepit, then went back inside, where he threw together a salad and boiled some water for corn. Every once in a while, he picked up his phone to be sure that he hadn't somehow missed Alexandra's call.

They hadn't set up a time for her to reach out. For all he knew, she could be at work. She'd told him that she was a nurse, but he had no idea what her schedule was.

Once the charcoal was perfect, he put the steak on the grill and then sat on a lawn chair in front of the firepit and looked over at the ranch. This was his favorite view of all. There was something about the hills and valleys with the occasional stand of trees that soothed his soul. And no matter which direction he looked, there was nothing to intercept his view. No parking lots. No strip malls. Nothing but nature at its finest.

When the food was ready, he grabbed a cold beer and

then set his dinner on the table. The days were getting shorter and the evenings cooler. Still, there was enough light to see by and the firepit provided sufficient warmth for Nathan to be comfortable while he ate.

As he enjoyed his meal, he let his mind wander. He wasn't the least bit surprised when he found himself thinking about Alexandra. Their conversation last night had been short, but he'd found her to be both intelligent and entertaining. Friendly with a good sense of humor.

She was unmistakably beautiful, but she didn't come across as overly concerned with her looks. She'd been absolutely stunning in her black dress that had clung to her curvaceous body. When she'd walked, he had been mesmerized by the gentle sway of her hips. She was about five-seven, with long, shapely legs that seemed to go on forever.

The phone rang, bringing him back to the present. He immediately looked at the screen. *Alexandra*. He smiled as he answered.

"I hope it's not too late to call," Alexandra said instead of hello. "My daughter didn't feel like going to sleep at bedtime. I had to rock her for a long time tonight."

*Daughter?*

"I didn't know you had a child." He wanted to call back the words a second after they'd burst from his lips. They hadn't come out at all as he'd intended. They'd sounded... bad.

"Yes." She was silent for a moment. "Is that going to be a problem for you?"

He heard the strain in her voice. The barely disguised hurt and disappointment.

"Not at all," he hastened to assure her, uncertain if he was being entirely honest. Odd that she hadn't mentioned her daughter before. But when? And why should she reveal personal details of her life to him? It's not as if they were going to see each other after their date. This wasn't the start of a relationship, so he didn't have to worry about getting attached to her daughter. He didn't have enough time for one person, so he certainly didn't have enough time for two.

"Okay," she said quietly.

He didn't know her well enough to tell if she'd accepted his answer, so he decided to act as if she had and replied to her earlier comment, "It's not too late. Unlike your baby, I don't have to go to bed this early."

"That's good to know."

"How old is your daughter?"

"She's almost one. She's growing so fast every day and I'm just so impressed by how smart she is. How talented. She really is the best little girl in the world." She gave a strangled chuckle. "Sorry. I didn't mean to go on about her. Parental pride run amok, I suppose."

"I didn't mind. I wouldn't have asked about her if I hadn't been truly interested." He loved kids and hoped to have a few of his own one day. But he wasn't anywhere near ready for that role yet. He was just fine playing uncle for the time being to his nieces and nephew.

"Thank you. I was so worried about calling you this late," Alexandra said, then laughed. It was a happy sound that made him smile. "I know you're a rancher. I thought that you guys have to get up early. At least they do in the movies."

"Ah, so I take it that your knowledge of ranching is limited to what you've seen on television."

"And what I read about in books." There was a pause. "But I want to learn more."

"Really? If you want to know more about ranching, ask away. I would be happy to answer any questions you have."

"What kind of ranch do you have?"

"Cattle ranch. It's one of the largest in the state. We breed the best organic beef you'll ever taste in your life."

Although he couldn't see her expression, he felt her smile. The minute that fanciful thought entered his mind, he shoved it aside. That was the kind of idiotic thinking that romantic fools indulged in. No one had ever accused Nathan of being romantic or a fool. In fact, the women he'd dated in the past had accused him of being cold and distant. Uninterested in getting to know them or caring about their hearts. Truth was, he couldn't deny that accusation. Messy emotions could only disrupt his plan. Not that he hadn't tried to be more responsive.

When Janet broke up with him, she'd told him that she'd grown tired of coming in second behind the ranch. He'd been late for dates one too many times or been distracted when they'd been together. Seeing himself through her eyes had been informative and had led to the realization that he wasn't in a position to have a relationship. It would be unfair to a woman for him to pretend otherwise.

"Is that right? Is your beef served in the restaurants in town? If so, I might have eaten it."

"We're in a lot of restaurants in the state, including Aspen Creek." He'd brokered several of those deals and had many more lined up. "If you want, we can go to one of those places for our date. Then you will definitely know that you've enjoyed a Montgomery steak."

"That sounds good. What is a good day for you?"

"How about this Saturday? That is date night."

"So it is." She sounded pleased. He hoped he hadn't given her the wrong idea. He wasn't interested in a relationship. He was simply fulfilling his obligation. Perhaps he should have gone with a Tuesday night. That would have been safer. Well, it was too late to change now. "That sounds like a plan."

The conversation had come to a conclusion, but Nathan was reluctant to end the call. Sadly, he was out of practice with the whole "get to know you" small talk, and the silence between them stretched as he searched for a suitable topic to discuss with her.

Before he could think of something, she spoke. "I suppose I should let you go. I imagine you have to get up early tomorrow."

"I'll call you this week so we can firm up plans for Saturday. Okay?"

"Sounds like a plan."

They said good-night, but Nathan held the phone for a few long seconds after the conversation ended. Though he told himself to play it cool, one thought echoed through his mind.

He was going to see Alexandra again. And he couldn't wait.

## CHAPTER FOUR

"WHAT'S UP?" ISAAC ASKED, the minute Nathan opened his front door the following Saturday. Ordinarily Nathan was happy to see his brothers, but he didn't have time to shoot the breeze. He was trying to get ready for his date with Alexandra. He'd been looking forward to tonight all week.

"What are you doing here?" Nathan hadn't meant to sound so abrupt, but the words were out there and he couldn't call them back now.

"Just visiting my big brother," Isaac said, pushing away from the doorjamb, stepping around Nathan and into the foyer.

There was a smirk on his brother's face, so Nathan knew he was up to something. Making himself at home, Isaac headed for the kitchen and Nathan followed. Isaac grabbed a beer from the fridge and then leaned against the counter. "Don't you smell nice? Got a date?"

Nathan took the unopened bottle from Isaac's hand and returned it to the refrigerator. "As a matter of fact, I do. What are you doing here? It's Saturday night. Shouldn't you be spending time with your fiancée? Or spoiling my niece?"

"Mom is having a grandmother's night with all of the grandkids. Savannah and the other bridesmaids are taking Jillian out tonight. So I'm on my own."

"And what? You decided to come over here and annoy me?"

"I figured you would be settling in to watch the game. I thought we'd order a pizza and watch it together."

"Well, now you know that I have plans, so you can show yourself out." Nathan walked up the stairs to his bedroom, trying to ignore his brother, who was right on his heels. When he reached his bedroom, he tried to close the door, but Isaac simply stepped inside.

"Come on in," Nathan said sarcastically.

"Don't mind if I do," Isaac said with a laugh. He sat on a chair and crossed his feet at the ankles.

Nathan grabbed his suit from the closet. It was the same one he'd worn to the bachelor auction, with a different shirt to switch it up.

"You aren't wearing that, are you?"

Despite telling himself that his brother was just messing with him, Nathan felt a seed of doubt form in his stomach. "What's wrong with it?"

"Nothing, if you're going to a funeral."

"Are you kidding? A black suit, white shirt, and red tie is classic."

"You'll look like a church deacon. She'll take one look and think you're about to collect the offering."

Despite himself, Nathan laughed.

Uninvited, Isaac stepped into his brother's closet and began to shift hangers aside, shaking his head and mumbling to himself as he discarded one jacket and shirt after the other. "Is this all you have? Work clothes and a bunch of boring suits that look like someone Dad's age would wear?"

"There's nothing wrong with my wardrobe."

"Where are you taking her?"

"We're going to dinner and then, depending on how that goes, maybe dancing at Grady's."

"Then the suit is definitely out. What time are you leaving?"

"Half an hour or so. Why?"

"You're lucky we're the same size. I'm going home and getting you something decent to wear."

"That's not necessary."

Isaac sighed dramatically. "You're going out with Alexandra, aren't you?"

"How did you know?"

"You don't leave this house unless someone—usually me—drags you. Besides, she won a date with you at the bachelor auction. One plus one and all that." Nathan frowned at his brother, who continued, "That is one gorgeous and stylish woman. You want to impress her, don't you?"

"That's a stupid question." Though this was going to be their only date, he wanted to put his best foot forward and show Alexandra a good time. After all, she had dropped a bucketload of money.

"Then you don't want to show up in the same suit you wore to the auction. You need to wear something else. I'll be back in ten minutes."

"Nothing flashy," Nathan said.

Isaac rolled his eyes. "I wouldn't dream of it."

Nathan shoved the suit back into the closet and shook his head. He couldn't believe he was letting Isaac get inside his mind like this. But aggravating as it was to admit, Isaac had been right about wearing a suit to the auction. That's what the other bachelors had worn. And Nathan had raised the third highest sum. He had known the suit was too formal for Grady's without being told. That's why he'd intended to leave the jacket and tie in the car if they went to the club.

He heard his front door open and a minute later his brother was stepping into the room, several hangers draped over his shoulder. Isaac had brought three shirts, four jackets, and two pairs of pants for Nathan to choose from. As he inspected the coordinating clothes, Nathan had to admit that his brother had chosen well. The clothes were dressy enough to be acceptable at the restaurant and casual enough to wear to the club.

Nathan grabbed a black collarless pullover, a flint gray blazer, and fitted black trousers. After putting them on, he checked his reflection in the full-length mirror. *Not bad.* He glanced over at Isaac, who was lounging on a chair, texting on his phone. "What do you think?"

Isaac looked up and grinned. "Looking good. Much better. You look almost as good as I do in them."

Nathan shook his head. "I would have been fine in my suit too."

"It's pitiful that you actually think that. If you want to change back, you can."

Nathan fastened his watch. "No time."

They walked down the stairs and out of the house. Isaac clapped Nathan's shoulder. "Have a good time tonight."

"I plan on it."

"And if things work out, be sure to give Miles the credit."

"There's nothing to work out. One date. That's it."

"Famous last words," Isaac said with a laugh.

They climbed into their cars and drove away. As Nathan neared Aspen Creek, his excitement grew. He couldn't wait to see Alexandra again. There was something so enticing about the way her thick black hair had skimmed her shoulders every time she shook her head when she'd spoken or laughed. He'd thought about that—and her—more times than he should have this week.

But it was more than her physical attributes that had him pressing the accelerator harder as he sped down the highway. Although they'd only had a couple of conversations, he'd liked what he'd seen of her so far.

Nathan wasn't given to making snap decisions. He knew that people often pretended to be something they weren't. Only after a long time, when they couldn't keep up the act, did the real personality shine through. Even if they didn't have bad intentions, they always tried to put their best foot forward in an effort to make a good first impression. Which was why he'd hadn't allowed himself to get carried away by his reaction to her. She seemed too good. Too perfect. Nobody could be that wonderful.

He looked at his clothes and then laughed out loud. Ironically, he was doing his best to impress Alexandra. He wanted her to enjoy herself tonight. Given what she'd paid, it was the least he could do. But he wasn't going to try to be something that he wasn't. He could try to be as charming as Isaac, but he knew he would never be able to keep it up for long. He was going to be himself and hope for the best. Minus the clothes, which he liked, and which were admittedly better than his. Alexandra was going to see the real Nathan Montgomery. Either she would like him for himself, or she wouldn't.

And really...why did he care that much? He wanted them both to enjoy themselves, but this wasn't the beginning of a relationship. It was their first—and last—date.

He exited the highway, then headed for Alexandra's neighborhood. It was a nice one, but then that could be said of the entire town. There was no poor side of Aspen Creek. There were the affluent and there were the dirty rich. Nathan didn't spend much time in town, but as far as he knew, everyone got on well together.

When he reached Alexandra's aunt's house, he turned off the car and then blew out a deep breath, ridding himself of sudden unexpected tension. He didn't know why he was nervous. It wasn't as if this was his first date in his life. He'd gone out before. Besides, this wasn't a big deal. They weren't going out to discover if there could be something between them. He already knew the answer to that. *No.* There was no room in his life for a woman. This date was simply the fulfillment of an obligation. Once the night was over, he and Alexandra would go their separate ways.

That reminder firmly in his mind, he got out of the car, climbed the stairs of the grand house, and pressed the doorbell. Before the ringing stopped, the door opened. And then Alexandra was standing before him. She was positively stunning. His mouth dropped open. When he realized that he was staring, he closed his mouth and snapped to attention.

"Hello. I hope I'm not too early," he said, even though he knew he was right on time.

"Nope. You've got perfect timing. I just got Chloe to fall asleep. Come on in. I need to get my coat and speak to my babysitter. Then I'll be ready to go."

"Of course." He winced internally at the mention of the babysitter, a reminder that Alexandra was a single mother. After his last relationship, he had developed a hard and fast rule against dating women with children. Even casually. Kids were easy to love. Easy to get attached to. So it was best to avoid them altogether.

Alexandra proceeded him into the front room, and his eyes followed each step she took. Her red dress fit like a glove, showcasing her sexy body. The fabric stopped in the middle of her well-toned thighs, revealing smooth brown skin that his hands ached to caress. Her matching high heels accentuated her world-class legs. She was dressed perfectly for dinner as well as a few hours at Grady's.

"Hi, Mr. Nathan."

He lifted her eyes from Alexandra's round bottom and

smiled at Crystal, the daughter of one of his former ranch hands and current owner of the feedstore. "Hi. How are you?"

"I'm good. I'm babysitting Chloe for Ms. Alexandra. And Mrs. Rose is teaching me how to crochet."

"That's good. We miss seeing you around the ranch. Miles and Isaac said you were the best babysitter they ever had."

"I miss everybody. But now that we live in town, I can't always get out to the ranch to babysit anymore. Will you tell them hi for me?"

"Of course."

Alexandra introduced Nathan to her aunt, who smiled. "It's nice to meet you. You guys have fun. And don't worry about a thing. Crystal has everything under control."

"I know." Alexandra hugged her aunt. "Have a good evening. And either of you can call me if you need to."

"We'll be fine," Crystal said confidently. "I've been babysitting for years."

Nathan and Alexandra exchanged smiles at the teen's comment. Alexandra picked up her jacket and Nathan immediately took it from her, helping her to put it on. He inhaled and got a whiff of her sweet perfume. It was intoxicating. Once her jacket was on, he stepped away, resisting the temptation to bury his nose in her neck and breathe in her scent.

When they were settled inside his sedan, he turned on the radio to an easy listening station. The sound of the saxophone came over the speaker, and he looked over at Alexandra. "I guess I should have asked before I turned on the radio. What kind of music do you like?"

ALEXANDRA SMILED AT Nathan's question. She'd been a bundle of nerves all day and his query put her at ease. Though she'd been looking forward to the date all week, dread and worry had been mixed with her excitement. It had been months since she'd been this eager to spend time with a man. Things with Owen definitely had left her wary.

But she didn't feel wary around Nathan. She wasn't worried that he wasn't a good person. Her friends had made it clear that he was. More than that, she was starting to trust her instincts again. They might have led her astray with Owen, but she believed they were right with Nathan. He was honest and trustworthy. He was a good man. The kind of man she could fall for.

That's what had her worried. She didn't want to like him as much as she did; didn't want to be excited about seeing him. She definitely didn't want to open her heart to him. That leap was just too much right now. But his simple question had reminded her that she'd gotten ahead of herself. This was a simple date. A fulfillment of an obligation. She'd been worrying over nothing. "I listen to just about anything."

"No favorites?"

"Not really."

"Come on, everyone likes one type of music more than others."

"My favorites change. It really depends on my mood. Some days are instrumental days. Others are hip-hop. Or classic rock. Or Motown. Of course, in a couple of years my preferences won't matter. I'll be playing the *Bluey* theme song on repeat."

He laughed. "My brothers have kids and I can tell you that will absolutely happen. I confess that I have a couple of kid playlists that the littles—that's what I call my nieces and nephew—make me play whenever they're around."

"*Make* you play?"

"Little kids are monsters."

The idea of a big strong man like Nathan being at the mercy of preschoolers made her laugh. "How old are they?"

"Benji is four. Lilliana is three and Mia is one-and-a-half."

"I have heard about the terrible twos, but I don't believe it can be as bad as all that. It seems like a good nap would get that behavior all sorted."

"If only it was that easy. Of course, your little girl is probably still at that sweet and charming age."

"Yes. She's truly a happy baby. She loves being held and playing with her toys. She's my greatest joy."

"Can she walk?"

"A little. She takes a few steps here and there. But when she's in a hurry to get somewhere, she drops down on all fours. She crawls much faster than she can walk. She had just gone down for the night when you arrived. Otherwise I would have introduced you." She glanced at his strong profile. "Do you have any kids?"

"Me?" He shook his head. "No."

"Do you want any?"

"Maybe one day. I'm definitely not opposed to the idea of being a parent. But I'm not in any hurry either. I'm content to be the favorite uncle for the time being."

That answer was disappointing, but she didn't know why it hurt her heart. It was his truth. And much better than creating a child and shoving it out of his life as Owen had done to Chloe. Besides, she and Nathan were not on their way to starting a relationship. They were simply going on the date that she'd won. Then they were going back to their regularly scheduled lives. She needed to remember that.

"It's a lot easier to be an uncle than a father," Nathan continued. "When they spend time with me, it's only for a few hours at a time. And I always know that I have backup in case I need it. I'm responsible for them for that short period, but when they go home, my responsibility ends. I imagine being a parent is endless worrying."

She huffed out a breath. "I try not to stress too much about every little thing, but I catch myself fretting more than I like to admit. You'd think that being a nurse, I would be more relaxed, but that's not always the case. I still panic about things that are completely out of my control."

"There will be no worrying tonight. We're going to have a good time. A relaxing time."

"That sounds like a plan. Where are we going for dinner?"

"We have reservations at Bliss on Your Lips."

"Really? I'm new to town and even I know reservations there can take up to a month to get and almost twice that long on a Saturday night. How did you get them on such short notice? Did you break a date with someone else?"

He laughed. "You're funny. No. I didn't break a date. I told you, I don't have a girlfriend. And I can't recall the last time I went on a date. My brother is engaged to Jillian Adams. Her brother, Marty, owns the restaurant. Since we're practically family, he found a table for us."

"Party Marty?"

Nathan gave her an odd look. "You know him?"

"No. We've never met. He was in the auction with you, and one of my friends pointed him out."

"He's popular. Hence the name."

"If you go for that type."

"And you don't?" Nathan sounded surprised.

She frowned. "Not even a little bit."

Nathan nodded as if pondering her response. After a moment, he pulled in front of the restaurant and stopped the car. A uniformed valet ran over. Nathan handed over the keys, pocketed a claim ticket, then helped Alexandra from the car. Nathan held her arm as he led her to the restaurant's entrance, where a uniformed young man greeted them, then opened the door, holding it while they stepped inside.

Alexandra looked around and sucked in a breath. Amazing. She'd known this was a first-class establishment, but even so, she was impressed with the decor. It was exquisite. The luxurious design was as timeless as it was elegant. A two-story chandelier divided the space into an enchanting bar area and an opulent dining room. The tables, draped in pristine white cloths, and lavish blue chairs created the perfect ambience for fine dining.

"This way to your table," the hostess said, pulling Alexandra's attention back to her.

As they walked past the diners, Alexandra inhaled, and her lungs were filled with delicious aromas.

The hostess stopped at a table near large windows that provided an unobstructed view of the mountain peaks.

Nathan held Alexandra's chair and then sat across from her.

"Your server will be here to take your order shortly," the hostess said, handing them each a menu before departing.

Alexandra set her menu on the table and then looked at Nathan. "This place is so chic. It's breathtaking. I absolutely love it." She was gushing, but she couldn't help it.

"I'm glad that you think so. Just so that we're clear, I'm paying for dinner."

"No way. I don't think that's the way it's supposed to go. I won this date with you, so I think I'm supposed to pay." At least that's what she thought. The details had been vague at best.

"That's where you're wrong. You paid for the date. For my company." He winced as he said the words. Clearly he was as uncomfortable with the notion as she'd been at the time. "We're here together. That means that the check is mine."

"That makes sense in a twisted way."

"I'm glad you agree." Nathan picked up his menu. Clearly, in his mind, the case was closed.

"What's good here?" Alexandra asked, glancing at Nathan over the top of hers. He was almost too handsome to look at straight on and foolish butterflies danced in her stomach. She forced herself not to stare. Not that she would be alone in doing that. She'd noticed the way women's heads swiveled as he walked through the restaurant. But no matter how good-looking he was, she wasn't going to let her attraction get out of hand.

Alexandra had no doubt that he had earned his reputation as a hardworking rancher and serious businessman, yet it was easy for her to see that there was more to Nathan Montgomery than that. Beneath that commanding exterior beat the heart of an interesting man. Though she knew it was a bad idea, she really wanted to get to know him on a deeper level.

Lucky for her, Nathan had given no indication that he was interested in more than fulfilling his obligation to go on this date with her. One and done. And since that fit in with her plans, she should be glad. Despite all of his good qualities, he had one glaring flaw. He wasn't interested in becoming a father. He was enjoying his bachelorhood, which was his right. She appreciated his honesty. But she had a child. She and Chloe were a package deal. There was no way she would ever consider becoming involved with a man who wouldn't love her child as his own.

But she needed to get her life back on track before she added another person to the mix. That's what made Nathan perfect for her. They were both clear about what they didn't want. A romance. Or anything that went past to-night. So she was free to let down her hair, so to speak, and just enjoy his company.

"Everything is good," he said, pulling her thoughts back to the present where they belonged. "I generally like the steak. It's Montgomery steak so I can vouch for the quality. They cook it perfectly. It's tender and juicy with just the right amount of smoky flavor. But if you prefer chicken or fish, that will be good too."

"You had me at steak. And since this is Montgomery steak, how can I say no?"

"Good decision. Especially since you're in beef country."

"And having dinner with a Montgomery cattle rancher," she said with a smile.

"That too."

He returned her smile and her heart did a foolish pitter-patter that she tried to ignore.

"Before I moved to Aspen Creek, I didn't think of Colorado as ranch country."

"Most people don't. They think of skiing and other winter sports. And rightly so, since there are some great resorts in the state—including here in Aspen Creek."

"That's exactly what I thought. Probably because I only visited my aunt in the winter. And naturally we went skiing and ice-skating."

"Too bad you never came in the summer. You missed fishing and biking season. And of course hiking."

"I don't get the popularity of hiking. It's just a fancy name for walking outside."

He shook his head and chuckled. She could get used to that sound. "It's more than just walking outside. You're challenging yourself physically, all the while enjoying the beauty of nature."

"Like mountain climbing?"

"Not exactly. But that's also fun. You should try it while you're in town."

"I'll think about it."

"And from the sound of your voice, you've given it all the thought you intend to."

She laughed. "Wise man."

"How long are you going to be in town?"

"That's still up in the air. I'm in the middle of figuring out my next move."

"How is that going? If that's not too personal a question."

"Not at all. I'd like an objective opinion."

"I don't know how objective I can be. I happen to think Aspen Creek is the best place in the world to live. I don't understand why people would choose to live anywhere else."

"Part of the charm of Aspen Creek is the small-town feel. That would be lost if too many people lived here."

"True." The waitress came and took their dinner orders, returning within minutes with their drinks and appetizers. By unspoken agreement, they didn't pick up the strands of that conversation until they had tasted everything. It was just as delicious as it looked and smelled.

"So, what factors are you considering," Nathan asked, spearing a seared scallop with his fork.

"Well, first I have to consider my daughter. Chloe is my first priority. She needs to be happy."

"What about her father?"

"Owen isn't in our lives. When I told him that I was pregnant, he let me know in no uncertain terms that he wasn't interested in being a father." Even after all this time, saying the words hurt her. And made her furious. She took a deep breath and then blew it out slowly. "And since I wanted my child to grow up loved, I didn't try to change his mind. We agreed that he would give up his parental rights and I wouldn't sue him for child support."

"He didn't want his child?" Nathan's voice rang with disgust.

"No. And I was not going to try to force him to be in her life. Chloe deserves better than that."

"So do you."

The sincerity in his voice warmed her heart and she smiled. "Thank you."

"Did you come to Aspen Creek looking for a fresh start?"

"Yes and no. I had been trying to figure out my next move when Aunt Rose hurt her hip. When she was released from the hospital, my parents wanted her to move in with them. Aunt Rose wouldn't think of it. She loves her independence. We were all worried about her, and I was thinking of getting a new job, so I asked if I could come and stay with her for a while. She agreed. Since I'm a nurse, I could help care for her."

"That makes sense."

"Yes. But I wasn't here long before I realized that Aunt Rose didn't need all that much help. I sometimes wonder if she didn't exaggerate her injury in order to give me an excuse to move here. A new purpose in life so to speak."

"Would that be so bad?"

"Not really. Because I can tell you that I was devastated by the way things went with Owen," Alexandra said, and then paused. She didn't ordinarily share so much of herself, and never with someone she just met. Yet here she was, opening up to Nathan. It felt right, somehow, so she continued, "Never in a million years would I have thought he'd treat me and Chloe that way. He seemed like such a good guy. Concerned about all the same things that concerned me. Making the world a better place might really be important to him, but he definitely wasn't husband or father material. Too bad I didn't see that in the beginning. I would have saved myself so much needless pain."

"Maybe you didn't see it because he didn't show it to you. The guy probably guessed that if you knew all about him, you wouldn't want him. And he wanted to be with you enough to lie and hope that it would be enough for you."

"Wow. That's very kind of you to say. But Owen doesn't deserve it. I don't think he gave my feelings a second thought. He did what was best for him."

"Then you're definitely better off without him. And so is Chloe."

"Agreed." She took a sip of her wine. It was delicious and deserved to be savored over pleasant conversation, not soured by bitter topics like her failed romance. "Enough about me and my failed relationship. I'll be happy to never mention Owen again."

The waitress appeared with their meals then, and Alexandra inhaled the wonderful aroma of her steak. Nathan must have read her mind because he smiled. "Wait until you taste it."

She picked up her knife and cut a slice. It was tender and juicy. She popped it into her mouth and a moan of pleasure immediately followed. "Oh my goodness. This is good."

"I'm glad you think so. That makes all the days of hard work at the exclusion of everything else—including a social life—worth it. Being single-minded has paid off."

"I don't believe that for a moment. There's more to you than just being a cattle rancher. You've already shown that much."

His eyebrows lifted as if he were trying to figure out when and how he'd given himself away. "Have I?"

"Yes. Consider the way we met. That was a charity auction. You didn't have to participate, but you did. To be honest, I don't think I would have had the nerve."

"Let me tell you a little secret," he said, a mischievous smile on his face. "If I could have thought of a way to get out of it without damaging the ranch's reputation and simply made a cash donation instead, I would have done it in a heartbeat. But nothing came to mind."

She laughed. "You should have tried harder. I could have come up with an excuse on a moment's notice. My car ran out of gas. The dry cleaner ruined my dress. The moon is too full. Anything."

He laughed. "*The moon is too full?* Where were you when I needed you? You weren't around, so I was stuck standing up on the stage while my mom's walking buddy bid on me." He shuddered.

"Which just shows what a good sport you are."

"Maybe." He leaned back in his chair. The look that he gave her made her heart flutter. "But I like the way things worked out."

# CHAPTER FIVE

NATHAN COULDN'T BELIEVE he'd just blurted out that comment. Especially since he was determined not to lead Alexandra to believe he wanted more than this one date. This was why he focused on business and left the wining and dining to Isaac. He supposed he could play the game, but that wasn't his style. Being honest had served him well in business. It would do no less in his personal life. He'd always been clear with women that he wasn't interested in anything serious right now. Business came first. And it would for the foreseeable future.

"I'm pretty pleased with everything myself," Alexandra said. Her smile was warm and he felt his body heat rising. Still, he reminded himself yet again that there was no room in his life for a woman. Even one as appealing as Alexandra. But then, since she wasn't looking for anything either, there was no danger that she would expect a commitment from him.

He swallowed more wine, taking the opportunity to sneak a peek at her. When she glanced up and caught him staring, her cheeks took on an attractive pink tinge.

"Well, the night is young. There's plenty of time for us to spend together and get to know each other better. That is the best way, you know."

Wait, why did he just say *that*? That almost sounded like he wanted her to be in his life for more than tonight.

Something he'd already decided was definitely *not* going to happen.

"True. You really are wise to be so young."

"It comes from being the oldest child."

"As the youngest child, I'll have to take your word for it." She batted her long lashes at him. "Of course, we can talk while we eat. I can get to know more about you over dessert."

He nodded. When she looked at him like that, he would tell her anything she wanted to know. "Absolutely. You've probably already guessed that I love living in Colorado. There is something good to do every season, and I try to do it. Although I like being a rancher, I like the business side more. There's something about looking for new opportunities and then finding them that I find so fulfilling. Finding new markets for our beef. Negotiating contracts. I enjoy it all. Of course, I'm not a big fan of schmoozing clients, but it goes with the territory."

"Really? I'd take a dinner I didn't have to cook any day of the week. Especially if it's this good. Where do I sign up for schmoozing?"

She flashed him a smile that made his heart skip a beat.

Ordering himself to calm down, he focused on their conversation. "I take it there's not much wining and dining in nursing."

"Not even a little bit. But there are other advantages. I like interacting with the patients, doing what I can to help them to feel better. Sometimes an encouraging word mixed with the right amount of medicine is all it takes to brighten a patient's day."

"What made you decide on nursing?" Despite telling himself to stick to generic, impersonal topics, he wanted to know what made her tick. He'd already decided that she was off-limits, so what was the harm in learning more about her?

"Medicine was one of the two career options in my family."

"I hope you're kidding."

She shrugged. "In a way. My mother is a doctor. She's a thoracic surgeon. Chief of her department. My father is a lawyer. Those are the careers that I saw at home. I know people joke about joining the family business, but it often happens. Children follow in their parents' footsteps." She gestured at him and he nodded.

"I see your point."

"My brother, Joshua, is a doctor, and my sister, Victoria is a lawyer. I liked medicine, but I didn't want to be a doctor. Not that there is anything wrong with that. I just felt like nursing was more for me."

"And are all of you happy with your career choices?"

"We are." She took a bite of her steak and then pointed her fork at him. "And we've done it again. We're talking about me. Tell me about your childhood. Something unexpected. Something that is completely out of character for you."

"Hmm." He thought for a minute She'd told him bits about herself, so it was only fair to share. But he didn't want to talk about being rejected by former lovers. He needed to keep the mood light. "My brothers and I had a singing group."

Her eyes widened and then she laughed. The sweet sound made his heart race and he ordered himself not to react that way again. "Really. What kind of music did you guys sing?"

"Oh. A little of this and a little of that. Ballads. Dance music. Boy band. Whatever was popular."

"How old were you?"

"Young. Junior high school age."

"Did you guys play instruments?"

"No. Our friends played for us. We were sure we were going to be big stars. You know, sold-out concerts in stadiums full of screaming fans. Grammy awards. The whole nine yards."

"I get the picture." She tilted her head. "Who was the lead singer?"

"I was. But in all honesty, Miles should have been. He's the best singer in the family by far."

"So why were you the lead singer?"

Nathan shrugged. "I was the oldest."

"And age has its privilege?" One corner of her mouth lifted in a half smile that made the blood race through his veins.

"That's the way I saw it at the time. It wasn't easy, knowing that my younger brother had more talent than I did. I figured that since I was older, I should have been better. I could rope and ride better than Miles and Isaac, so to me, it logically followed that I should be able to do everything better. Including sing. Of course, I couldn't."

"That had to be a hard lesson to learn."

"Trust me, it was a shock to my system. I liked being better at everything than they were. I didn't understand that learned skills were different from innate talent. I didn't learn it back then. Truth be told, I'm still learning it."

She grinned. "Growing up stinks, doesn't it?"

"Yes. Nobody likes being a reasonable adult."

"So where did you guys perform?"

He leaned back in his chair, as he thought back to those days. "School talent contests. We actually did well in a couple of them. We came in second in one and third in the other. Once we performed at a birthday party."

"Oh. The big time."

The mischief in her voice made him realize just how much fun he could have with her and alarm bells began ringing inside his brain. He ignored them.

"You'd better know it. For about a week I walked around like a big shot. I just knew we were on our way." He laughed.

"Your one brush with fame." She giggled. "Then what happened?"

"Nothing. The gigs dried up. And practicing wasn't nearly as much fun as performing. One big fight and it was all over. Still, it was fun while it lasted."

She gave him an admiring smile. "You sang in a band. That is something I would have never guessed about you."

"Your turn," he said.

"To?"

"Reveal something unexpected about yourself."

Her brow wrinkled as she appeared deep in thought and that expression was sexier than it should have been. "Well, I can safely say that I have never been in a singing group. You and your brothers might be good singers, but I can honestly say I have no musical talent at all. Okay, that's not completely accurate. I can't sing but I took piano lessons as a girl."

"Did you like it?"

"Not as much as Joshua did. He's excellent. He could play professionally if he wanted to. I was nowhere near as good. After five years of private lessons, I finally convinced my parents to let me quit. In a pinch, I might be able to play 'Für Elise' and a little bit of 'Moonlight Sonata.'"

"That's it?"

"Yes. I did a lot better in my dancing lessons."

"What kind of dance?"

"Oh, you know, the usual. Ballet and tap when I was in grammar school. In high school I added jazz and modern, which I preferred. Lucky for me, those lessons stuck. I'm a great dancer."

"She said modestly," Nathan said with a grin.

"If I'm going to be brutally honest about my flaws, I'm going to be just as honest about my skills."

"I like the way you think."

She winked. "It works for me."

"If you're up to it, I'd like to take you dancing. That way you can let me see your moves."

"I am totally up for dancing. Just say the word and I'm ready." She lifted the fork with the last bit of her steak to her mouth and shimmied in her chair. The innocent move was enticing. He couldn't wait to see her body move in time to the music on the dance floor. Not only that, but at some point the DJ was likely to play a slow song and Nathan might get the chance to hold Alexandra in his arms.

"Would you like anything else? Dessert?"

"No. Everything was delicious, but I don't have room for another bite."

"Then let's get going."

He paid the check, including a tip, then escorted Alexandra from the restaurant. Once they were in the car, he turned to her. She was staring at him, a smile on her face. Her sweet expression did things to his insides that he had difficulty ignoring.

"I can't remember the last time I went dancing," he confessed.

"It's been a while for me too."

"I'm taking you to Grady's. It's the most popular club in Aspen Creek. It's the best kept secret in town."

"I've never been there. I was supposed to go with my friends one night, but Chloe got sick, so I had to cancel."

"They have a great house band—Downhill From Here—and one of the best DJs around. Occasionally they have a guest band, but I don't know if one will be there tonight."

"And the crowd?"

"Everyone is friendly. It's a mature crowd—everyone is there to have a good time."

"Sounds like fun."

"It is. We'll be there in a few minutes. I hope you have on your dancing shoes."

She held up a foot and he took another opportunity to check out her calf. It was shapely and sexy as hell. Her shoes had four-inch heels, but he'd seen women dancing in higher. He didn't know if their feet hurt, but he'd never heard one of them complain.

He parked, helped her from the car, and they went inside Grady's. Up-tempo music played. It was loud, but not too loud for conversation. The room was enormous, and the border of the room was lined with black and silver booths.

Nathan led her through the room and they found a booth near the dance floor with a view of the stage. A DJ was spinning records and several people were already on the floor. Alexandra and Nathan dropped their jackets onto their seats.

Nathan smiled at her. "Do you want to dance, or would you rather watch for a while?"

Instead of speaking, she shook her shoulders and wiggled her hips in a move that sent his mind down a road it had no business traveling. And yet, he couldn't stop imagining Alexandra in his arms. In his bed. He forced the image away. No matter how enticing she was, they weren't going to be spending any time in his bed. Or hers.

"You don't even need to ask."

He took her hand and led her to the dance floor. Her skin was warm and soft, and her hand fit perfectly in his. Electricity shot from his fingers and throughout his body.

He knew he should release her hand, but what was the fun in that? He didn't feel like being responsible right now. Besides, no harm could come from just holding hands.

She spun around and his eyes instantly shot to her sexy bottom. Hypnotized, he was frozen in place.

She turned around and stared at him. She stopped moving and frowned. "Please don't tell me you can't dance."

"Oh, I can dance," he said, beginning to move. He did a few fancy steps and then looked at her.

She smiled and nodded, then began to dance again. "Oh yeah. You have the moves. I think you'll be able to keep up with me."

They danced together as if they'd been partners for years. As one song merged into the next, it became clear that Alexandra had been blessed with natural grace. Her moves were easy and flowed in time to the music. She also possessed an innate sexiness that was making him sweat. He wasn't looking for romance or even a one-night stand. Those things always ended in disaster, hurt feelings, and disappointment. Yet that knowledge couldn't make his body behave in the way that he wanted.

"Why are you frowning?" Alexandra asked as she shimmied up to him and brushed her hand against his chest, a teasing smile on her face. "Don't tell me that you're counting the steps in your head."

Laughing, he reached out and grabbed her waist, holding her in place. The motion from her hips as she moved to the music was nearly his undoing, and he had to force himself to concentrate on what he'd been about to say. "Cute. I don't need to count."

The up-tempo music faded into a slow song, and she draped her arms across his shoulders, looping them around his neck. He slid his arms around her waist as if holding her pressed against him was the most natural thing in the world, and they swayed together to the ballad. He closed his eyes and savored the moment as the saxophone slid into a sultry solo. Although he'd danced with many women in his life, he'd never felt anything quite this satisfying.

As they danced, Nathan was struck by just how well they fit together. Not just physically, although their bodies fit together like two puzzle pieces. It was the *way* they moved. It was as if she sensed where and how he was going to move before he did. And he was just as able to anticipate her next move. They were completely in sync. She moved closer and her sweet scent wrapped around him, inflaming his desire even more.

"This is nice," she said and sighed. "I could get used to this."

ALEXANDRA WANTED TO call back the words the instant they'd fallen from her mouth. She couldn't believe that she'd thought them, much less said them out loud. But from the way Nathan jerked, she knew that he'd heard her.

She stepped back, creating the physical distance she needed. Luckily the song ended right then, so her movement looked natural. The DJ announced that the house band would be playing soon and everyone began to vacate the dance floor.

Although the light was dim, Alexandra could still see the expression on Nathan's face. He looked as stunned as she felt. She needed to get a hold of her emotions and her mouth before things got out of hand. She and Nathan were perfect for each other because neither of them was looking for a relationship. This date was a onetime thing never to be repeated. Yet somehow, dancing close to him and being held in his strong arms, she'd lost track of that important fact.

Nathan was turning out to be totally different than she'd

expected him to be. He was charming. Funny. He'd gone out of his way to put her at ease. His personality and great body made him the total package.

But she hadn't anticipated just how good she would feel in his arms. How heavenly moving together to the music would be. Being held in his embrace, even just while dancing, had revealed that his muscles were just as hard as they looked. His years of physical labor had definitely paid benefits.

And he smelled so good. When she'd been in his arms, she'd gotten a whiff of his masculine scent. It was more than his cologne that appealed to her. It was his own natural scent that had teased her all night. Tempting her to forget her vow to keep him at a distance.

Even though she was in danger of crossing the line, she didn't want the night to end yet. "I guess we should sit down so we can watch the band."

Nathan nodded and she breathed a sigh of relief. She hadn't ruined everything. The date would go on.

"Would you like something to drink?" Nathan asked.

"I would love a soft drink," she replied. Hopefully it would cool her off.

"I'll be right back," he said and then headed for the bar. He was back shortly with their drinks.

Alexandra and Nathan didn't talk much as the band played. They were just as good as Nathan promised, and when their set was over, Alexandra and Nathan rose to their feet and applauded with the rest of the crowd.

"That was great," Alexandra said.

"They always put on a good show."

The conversation lagged. Clearly her words from earlier in the evening still lingered in the air, casting a pall over the evening. She decided to take the reins of the conversation since she was the one who'd caused the unease between them. "About what I said earlier…"

"Forget about it."

"I will. But first I want to repeat that I'm not looking for a relationship. I don't have room in my life for a man. Nor am I interested in one."

"Same here."

"Actually, I don't think I'll ever be ready to put my heart on the line in a relationship."

Something that looked like disappointment mingled with sorrow flitted across his face before vanishing. "Don't say that. You never know what will happen in the future. You might meet someone. You should keep your options open."

"I don't see you running to get involved with anyone."

"Not right now. But I'm not against the idea. I want to get married in a few years, after I have accomplished my goals with the ranch. Right now, I'm not in the position to have a relationship. I don't have time to give a woman the attention she deserves. I tried a few times before and it always ended in disappointment. And pain. I'm not willing to take that risk when I know I'm not in a place to be a full partner. I'm not selfish enough to do that."

"That's exactly why I'm not interested in a man. Not because I have a ranch to run, but because I know that I don't have anything to offer a man. My heart wouldn't be in it. Nobody deserves to be disappointed and hurt. Especially when it can be avoided."

"Then we're in agreement."

"Totally," Alexandra said, although being around Nathan made her wish things could be different. But they couldn't so she forced down her longing and disappointment. "And on that note, I suppose we should get going. It's getting late, and I have to drive my babysitter home."

"Crystal is a nice girl. Her father used to work on our ranch, and she used to babysit for Miles and Isaac."

"Chloe loves her. So does Aunt Rose. I told Crystal that if we get home late, she could go to sleep if she wants, since Aunt Rose is there."

Nathan laughed. "How did that go over?"

"Poorly. She told me that she was a professional and would be staying up."

They put on their jackets and then moved through the crowd. When they were outside, Alexandra glanced up at the sky. The moon and stars were shining in the deep blue expanse. It was just so beautiful that it took her breath away. She'd lived in Aspen Creek for months, but she was still struck by its beauty.

The night had grown chillier while they were inside, and she shivered.

"Cold?" Nathan asked.

"A little." She tightened her jacket around her, shoved her hands into her pockets, and moved closer to him.

"Then let's get moving," Nathan said, wrapping his arm around her shoulder. The heat from his body encircled her, warming her. Despite telling herself that the attraction should be ignored, his nearness made the fire inside her grow hotter and she leaned closer.

Once they were inside the car, Nathan turned on the heat. Alexandra leaned back and allowed herself to reflect on the night. It had been wonderful, and she hated to see it end.

When they reached her house, Nathan parked. "I'll get your door for you."

"Thank you."

As Nathan rounded the front of the car, Alexandra couldn't help but smile. It was so nice to have someone spoil her. Nathan Montgomery was proof that chivalry wasn't dead.

When her door opened, she took his hand and allowed him to help her from the car. As they climbed the stairs to the house, her heart began to pound with anticipation. This hadn't been a traditional date—she'd paid for his time—but even so, she wondered how it was going to end.

Would they simply say good-night before he walked down the stairs, and she went into the house? That seemed a bit bland. Cold even. Not a fitting end to the great date they'd had. Or would they shake hands? That seemed too businesslike even for a serious businessman like Nathan.

Or, would they kiss? On the cheek? Or on the lips? Her heart skipped a beat at the thought. She ordered herself to stop this ridiculous line of thinking. She'd never put this much thought into the end of a date before. But then, she'd never been in this position before either. Never been as attracted to a man before. Never wanted to kiss a man this badly.

Never been so sure that kissing Nathan was the wrong thing to do.

Alexandra had forgotten to turn on the porch light, so the moon and stars provided the only illumination. As a result, she and Nathan were standing in the shadows. It felt intimate. Cozy.

She turned to look at him, only to find him staring at her. They gazed into each other's eyes for a brief moment. Neither of them spoke, but in that moment they didn't need words to communicate. His eyes grew dark with intensity. Then he reached out and brushed a strand of hair behind her ear, then caressed her cheek.

She placed her hand on Nathan's chest. His heart was pounding, beating in time with hers.

One corner of his lips lifted in a sexy half smile. "Alexandra, I really want to kiss you now."

Her breath caught. "So, what's stopping you?"

Slowly, as if giving her a chance to reconsider, Nathan lowered his head. Anticipation built inside her, and by the time his lips brushed against hers, she was burning with desire. Her knees weakened and she grabbed on to his shirt. Electricity spread throughout her body, leaving a tingling sensation in its wake.

Nathan wrapped his arms around her waist, and she moved closer, molding her body against his. She opened her mouth to him, and his tongue swept inside, deepening the kiss. Their tongues danced and tangled, and she savored the taste of him. She moaned and tried to get even closer to him.

Gradually she became aware that Nathan was slowly easing back, ending the kiss. Resisting the urge to cling to him, she struggled to regain control of her ragged breathing. Even though the kiss was over, aftershocks reverberated throughout her, prolonging the pleasure. Alexandra tried to talk, but she couldn't manage to gather enough words to form a coherent thought.

"Wow," Nathan said. "That was totally unexpected."

"Yeah." Alexandra shook her head in a futile attempt to clear it.

"And it shouldn't have happened," Nathan said. That statement was as good as cold water in the face. Her mind was clear now.

"I know." She had regained enough strength to stand without his assistance, so she stepped away from him. "Let's just consider that a temporary loss of control."

"A momentary lapse in judgment," he said. His voice was low. Gritty.

"And one that won't be repeated."

"It can't be repeated."

She nodded. "Agreed."

He edged away from her. "I need to get going."

"And I need to take Crystal home."

He started down the stairs, hesitated, then turned back to her. "It's been great getting to know you, Alexandra. Maybe I'll see you around."

"Yeah. Same."

Alexandra watched until he had driven away before she stepped inside the house and closed the door. Though she'd only just met Nathan, a feeling of loneliness swept over her and she longed to call him back. But she couldn't. Their date was over.

And he was out of her life.

## CHAPTER SIX

"HOW WAS YOUR date last night?" Michelle Montgomery asked Nathan the following day. Even though they all lived on the same ranch and saw each other during the week, Nathan's mother cooked a big dinner every other Sunday, so the family could spend quality time together.

Even though Miles and Isaac were engaged, and building their lives with their respective fiancées, they still took the time to join the family for dinners. Just not as early, as they had children to wrangle—which was why, on this Sunday, Nate found himself alone with his parents.

"How did you hear about that?" Nathan asked. He and his mother were setting the dining room table. He had placed the embroidered cloth that they'd used for every Sunday dinner for as long as he could remember onto the big dining room table, and his mother was smoothing out wrinkles.

"Was it supposed to be a secret?" Pausing, she glanced up.

"No. I guess it wasn't."

"Then did you have a good time?"

He nodded, and despite wanting to play it cool, he couldn't suppress his smile as he recalled the night. "Alexandra is very nice. We had dinner and then went to Grady's."

"I don't think I know her."

"She hasn't lived in town long. Alexandra is a pediatric nurse. She and her daughter are staying with her great-aunt, Rose Kenzie, for a while."

Michelle set a fork on a napkin and then looked at him. "You seem to know quite a bit about her."

"We had to talk about something."

"That's true. After all, she did spend a pretty penny on you." Michelle's eyes sparkled with mirth.

"Exactly."

"I still can't believe you participated in the auction. Isaac, yes. That's right up his alley. You? Not so much. I'm glad you stepped out of your comfort zone."

"You know I'll do anything for the ranch. Goodwill goes a long way."

Michelle frowned, something she rarely did and pointed a fork in his direction. "There's more to life than this ranch, you know."

"I know. But the ranch is important."

"Like finding a nice girl," Michelle said as if he hadn't replied. This was her favorite topic of discussion. Before his brothers had become involved, her focus had been split among the three of them. As the last man standing, Nathan got her undivided attention.

"There's time for that," he said as always. Not that it mattered. Michelle would not be deterred.

"Now that your brothers are settling down, you should take a page from their books."

Nathan inhaled and slowly blew out the breath. "You and Dad always told us to follow our own paths. That's what I'm doing."

"Did someone mention me?" his father said, coming into the dining room, a stack of plates in his hands. Edward was in his late fifties, but his posture was as erect as ever. He was just as strong as he'd always been. There was no man Nathan admired more than his father.

"I was just reminding Mom that the two of you raised us not to follow the crowd."

"That's right. A man has to blaze his own path."

"There's nothing that says he has to walk that path alone," Michelle countered, laying the last fork on a napkin with extra emphasis.

Edward laughed. "I take it that you've decided to make a match for Nathan now."

"Now that Isaac and Miles are part of a couple, she's turned her sights on me," Nathan said mournfully.

"You have to admit that your brothers are with wonderful women."

"They are."

"You had better get out there before all of the good women are gone," Michelle said.

"Michelle," Edward said softly. "Leave the boy alone. He'll find someone when it's time."

"Thank you," Nathan said.

"Besides, you know how stubborn he is. The more you push him, the harder he'll pull in the opposite direction."

"Hey!" Nathan objected.

"Eventually he'll realize that you're right," Edward said.

Nathan frowned. "Just whose side are you on?"

"Nobody's. I don't take sides, you know that."

"Who's pushing?" Michelle said innocently. "All I did was ask him about his date last night."

"Oh yes. The date with that woman from the auction," Edward said. "I imagine it must have been pretty awful."

"What makes you say that?" Nathan asked.

"She had to pay a man to go out with her. Only a desperate woman would do that. So, what was wrong with her? Was she rude? Boring?"

"Alexandra was none of those things," Nathan said.

"She is kind, smart, and very interesting. She bid on me as a way to support charities."

"So, there was nothing wrong with her?" Edward set a plate beside the silverware and glanced at Nathan, a skeptical expression on his face.

"No. She was perfect."

His father flashed a *gotcha* smile. "Is that right?"

Nathan narrowed his eyes. "This was a setup. The two of you are working together to get me to settle down."

"Proof of how well two people can work together," Edward said. He put an arm around Michelle's shoulder, pulled her close, then kissed her cheek.

"So, how was the date?" Michelle asked.

"It was fine. But it's not going to be the start of a relationship if that's what you're asking."

"Why are you so certain?" Michelle asked.

"Especially if you think she's perfect," his father said with a grin.

"Because we talked about it. Neither of us is interested in a relationship. She's might not even stay in Aspen Creek." Just saying the words caused an ache in Nathan's chest, but he ignored it.

"Hmm," Michelle said. "I didn't know that."

"Now you do. So can you please drop it?"

"If that's what you want," Michelle said. "I was just making conversation."

"It is." Nathan grabbed the glasses from the cabinet and then placed them beside the plates.

"Did I mention that Carol's daughter is moving back to Aspen Creek? She could use a friend."

"Mom," Nathan said. "I'm fine on my own."

"Really? Then why are you so grumpy?" Michelle asked.

"Hey, we're here," Miles called from the entry, the door slamming closed behind him.

"Thank goodness," Nathan muttered to his parents' obvious amusement.

A minute later, Benji raced into the room, his sister, Lilliana, hot on his heels. Jillian followed more slowly, a cake carrier in her hands.

"Hi, Uncle Nathan," Benji said, wrapping his arms around Nathan's leg.

"Hi, Uncle Nathan," Lilliana echoed, grabbing his other knee and holding on.

"Hey, it's the littles," Nathan said. He leaned down and scooped them up, holding them in his arms. "Have you been good?"

They nodded, managing to look as innocent as angels. Nathan wasn't fooled for a moment. He babysat them from time to time. He'd been caught off guard the first time, but now he knew the havoc they could wreak when they were together. After spending a few hours alone with them, he was always as exhausted as he'd be after putting in a full day of work.

He set them on their feet. "Go say hi to Grandma and Grandpa."

Nathan walked over to Miles and Jillian, who were smiling at each other. Their wedding, two weeks away, was a long time coming. Although they'd broken up with each other years ago and subsequently had disastrous marriages, it had always been clear that they belonged together. Nathan was happy that they'd found each other again and wished them a lifetime of happiness.

But married life was for them. Not him. An image of Alexandra's face flashed before him, but he set it aside.

A relationship was not in the cards for him right now. Especially not with a single mom.

"What's going on?" Miles asked.

"Nothing really," Nathan replied to his brother before kissing Jillian on her cheek. "Excited about the wedding?"

"Only two weeks to go," Jillian said gleefully. "Then we'll be a family officially."

"As far as I'm concerned, you've always been a part of this family. But I'm glad you guys are making it official."

"Best decision I made in my life," Miles said.

"Darn right," Jillian said. "And don't you forget it."

"Never." Miles's voice was serious. A vow. The look he and Jillian shared was so intimate Nathan felt as if he was intruding on a private moment.

He was about to excuse himself when Jillian spoke. "I'm going to help get food on the table."

Once they were alone, Nathan turned to his brother. "Nervous?"

"Not even a little bit. I'm marrying the love of my life."

"I know the four of you will be so happy together."

Miles was nodding when the front door opened. Isaac and Savannah stepped inside, each holding one of Mia's hands.

Edward stepped into the room. "Well, look who finally got here. It's Grandpa's baby girl."

"Pa-pa," Mia exclaimed. She pulled her hands free and ran across the room as fast as her little legs could take her. When she reached Edward, he bent over and scooped her into his arms and planted a kiss on her cheek. Laughing, she kissed him back. Edward tossed her into the air, and she laughed again.

"I'm about to put dinner onto the table, so go wash your hands," Michelle said, coming into the room. She reached out her arms for Mia, who shook her head and then leaned against Edward's chest. "All right, little one. I know how you love your Pa-pa. I'm partial to him too, so I can't blame you for having good taste."

"Do you need help?" Savannah asked.

"I could always use another pair of hands," Michelle said, looping arms with Savannah and returning to the kitchen.

"You know your mother is thrilled to finally have daughters," Edward said, before carrying Mia out of the room to find the other kids.

"Yeah, and she's looking for me to add a third," Nathan said.

"So, are you going to step up, big brother?" Isaac asked. "Or are you going to break Mom's heart?"

"Don't start," Nathan said, shoving his brother's shoulder. "I already had the conversation with her and cleared the air. She understands that I'm not going to be bringing a woman into the family."

"You don't actually believe that's the end of it," Miles said.

"Of course I do." As much as he could. He knew that his mother would try to stay out of his love life, but that eventually she would revert back to her old ways. She couldn't help herself. She was a romantic at heart. She was happily married and believed everyone would be happier if they were part of a matched set. Like socks.

His brothers exchanged glances and then looked back at him. Isaac smirked. "No, you don't."

"You're right. I'm just hoping for a reprieve. With the wedding coming up, she should be distracted for a while."

"The wedding is practically here. Once that's over, she'll be turning her attention back to you," Miles said.

"Not if Isaac and Savannah start planning their wedding," Nathan said, turning to his youngest brother.

Isaac laughed and shook his head. "Sorry, we won't be able to save you. We will be getting married, but we aren't ready to set a date. We want to take things slowly. Given Savannah's past, that's understandable."

Savannah had been married before she'd met Isaac. Her husband and four-year-old son had been killed by a drunk driver. She'd moved to a cabin bordering the Montgomery ranch in an effort to escape the pain. She and Isaac had met and quickly fallen in love.

"How slowly?"

"We're thinking about late next summer. Or maybe early next fall."

"Really? That's great," Nathan said. "You guys deserve all the happiness in the world."

"Thanks."

"Dinner is on the table," Michelle called from the dining room. "Are you going to stand around talking, or are you coming to eat?"

"Eat," they chorused.

Michelle was a big believer that the children should be included at the table with the adults, and Benji and Lilliana were sitting on booster seats and Mia's high chair was scooted up to the table. After saying the blessing, Michelle began to serve the roasted chicken, baked macaroni and cheese, green beans, and rolls.

Dinner was a lively affair with plenty of conversation and laughter. After dessert had been eaten, Nathan and his brothers cleared the table, put away the leftovers, and cleaned the kitchen. Everyone hung around for a while longer, relaxing and talking while the kids played. When Nathan headed home, his stomach was full, yet he felt oddly empty.

Being around his brothers and their fiancées made him long for more in his life than work. Not a romance. His mind remained unchanged about that. But after his date with Alexandra, he appreciated the value a woman's presence could bring to his life. Spending time with her had been more pleasurable than the solitude he usually enjoyed. And she was certainly a lot more fun than his brothers. A little female companionship every now and then wouldn't hurt. A woman who could be his friend. Just a friend.

Too bad she wasn't interested.

ALEXANDRA LAUGHED AS she wiped smeared spaghetti sauce from Chloe's face.

Echoing her, Chloe laughed and then clapped her hands, clearly pleased with something.

"All done. Time for your bath." Alexandra unstrapped Chloe from her high chair and carried her into the bathroom. Once Chloe was in the warm water, she began to play with her toys. Alexandra sat on the side of the tub, watching as her daughter poured water from one cup to another.

This had been a good day. Aunt Rose had met up with some of her friends for a matinee followed by an early dinner and then a Spades tournament, leaving Alexandra and Chloe on their own. Mother and daughter had spent the day playing with dolls and blocks.

Although Alexandra had enjoyed playing with her daughter, her mind kept drifting to Nathan and their date. No matter how hard she tried, she couldn't stop replaying the highlights of the night. The memories had been complete with the emotions she'd felt, including the ones she'd done her best to suppress.

Everything about dinner had been perfect. The food had been delicious, living up to the restaurant's reputation. Nathan had been so easy to talk to and their conversation had flowed easily. The night would have been a success if the date had ended there.

But it hadn't. They'd gone to Grady's. Dancing with

Nathan had been the ultimate pleasure. He definitely had the moves and she'd enjoyed watching him in action. But it was being held in his strong arms as they danced to slow, sexy songs that had taken the night to even higher heights. Even three days later, she still got goose bumps at the recollection.

She'd hoped to hear from Nathan, but as one night became two, she realized that he wasn't going to contact her. Of course, she had no reason to expect him to reach out. He'd been clear that he wasn't looking for a relationship. The night, as wonderful as it had been, was a one-off. It was the fulfillment of the bargain they'd made at the auction—not the start of a romance. Since she'd only agreed to bid on a bachelor on the condition that it was a one-time thing with no expectation of keeping in touch, she shouldn't feel disappointed.

Though he'd tried to deny it, she knew he had some reservations about her being a single mother. She'd heard the surprise in his voice when she'd mentioned Chloe. Of course, surprise didn't equate to reluctance. She might be reading too much into the tone of his voice.

Not that it mattered. Truth be told, she wasn't in a position to start a relationship. Her little girl needed all of her love and attention. Just caring for Chloe took all of her energy. There was only one of her, and she was pretty tapped out at the moment. And her heart was still too bruised to risk with another man, no matter how good it felt to be around him.

At least that was what she told herself. Now she wondered, if she met the right man, would she be willing to make space for him in her life? Willing to take a chance on loving him. If things had worked out with Owen, she would be in the exact same position—loving her child and loving a man. Of course, in that fantasy world, Owen would have loved his daughter, and her care wouldn't have fallen exclusively on Alexandra.

"And why am I thinking about that now?" Alexandra asked herself.

Chloe splashed the water, getting some of it on Alexandra. Deciding that her daughter had played long enough, Alexandra grabbed soap and a washcloth. Alexandra washed Chloe and then wrapped her squirming child in a towel and carried her into her bedroom and got her dressed for bed. They played until Chloe began to yawn and rub her eyes.

"Story time," Alexandra said, grabbing two books and Chloe's blankie. She sat in the rocker and snuggled her daughter on her lap and began to read. It wasn't long before her Chloe dozed off. Alexandra kissed the top of Chloe's head before she laid her in her crib and tiptoed from the room.

She was trying to figure out which television program to watch when her cell phone rang. Grabbing it, she answered without looking at the display. "Hello."

"Hi. Is this a good time?"

Nathan's deep voice sent shivers down Alexandra's spine. She'd long since given up on hearing from him, so this was a pleasant surprise. Telling herself to be cool, she answered in a voice she hoped didn't betray her excitement. "It's perfect."

"Good. I was just thinking of you and decided to see how you've been doing."

"Funny, I was just thinking about you and how much fun I had Saturday." The honest words popped out of her mouth before she had time to stop them. So much for playing it cool.

"It was a good time. I can't recall the last time I had that much fun."

"Same. You asked how I've been. I've been fine. Things are good at work. Aunt Rose has resumed her life and is as active as ever. Chloe is the sweetest baby in the world. She's even more so now that she is asleep."

Nathan laughed, a rich sound that reverberated through Alexandra. She'd almost forgotten how much she liked his voice and how deeply it affected her.

"So you're enjoying some 'you' time."

"It's like being on vacation." Alexandra laughed.

"I understand that. But you have told me about everyone but you. How are you?"

She blew out a breath. "I'm managing. Getting my feet beneath me."

"Have you decided whether to make the move to Aspen Creek a permanent one?"

"Not yet." She paused. Talking about that wouldn't help her make that decision. She believed the answer would come to her eventually. "How are things on the ranch?"

"Good. I spent most of today working to close a deal in a new market. We've done a lot of preliminary work these past months. Now we're setting a date for an in-person meeting to seal the deal."

"That sounds great. Good luck with that."

"Thanks."

Alexandra tucked her feet beneath her and got comfortable. She and Nathan hadn't known each other very long, but it felt natural to be talking to him at the end of the day.

"You mentioned that you have never been to a ranch."

"Not yet."

"Would you like to visit mine? Seeing it will give you more information about Aspen Creek. You don't want to make a decision without all of the facts."

"I'd love to." Did he think he needed to convince her to visit? She wanted to see the ranch. More than that, she wanted to spend more time with him. No number of reasons why she should keep him at a distance could change that.

"When is a good time for you?"

"I work three twelves—Mondays, Thursdays and Fridays. Any other day works for me."

"How about Saturday afternoon?"

"That's perfect."

"And it goes without saying that your daughter is included in the invitation."

Alexandra's heart warmed at his words. Although she tried to deny it, Owen's rejection of his own child had made her wary of men. A part of her expected each of them to want nothing to do with her daughter, so Nathan's welcoming attitude was a pleasant surprise. Maybe she had read too much into the tone of his voice before.

"Thanks for thinking of her, but Chloe won't be able to attend. One of Aunt Rose's friends is bringing over her granddaughter for a playdate." Alexandra chuckled. "My little girl has quite the social life. Besides, I'm not sure the ranch is the right place for a child."

"You're kidding, right? I grew up on a ranch. It's perfectly safe."

"I suppose. Maybe it's the city girl in me, but I need to check it out first. Just to be on the safe side."

"Since you're a city girl, I'll allow your skepticism."

"Thank you," Alexandra replied, smiling.

"I'll see you then. Good night."

"Good night." Alexandra ended the call and smiled.

She was going to see Nathan again.

It was early, so she immediately sent out a group text to her friends.

I just talked to Nathan.—Alexandra

Really?—Kristy

So much for one and done.—Marissa

He must have said something good for you to message us. So spill.—Veronica

He invited me to his ranch.—Alexandra

Wait. I need details. We need to talk.—Kristy

In a minute, they were all on the line, talking over each other.

"One date and he's inviting you to meet the parents? That was fast," Kristy said, laughing. Marissa and Veronica joined in.

"Okay, now you're scaring me," Alexandra said. "I mentioned wanting to see the ranch. I didn't say a word about meeting his parents."

"We'll stop teasing you. Seriously, that sounds like a good time," Marissa said.

"What are you going to wear?" Kristy, the most fashionable of the friend group, asked.

"Jeans and gym shoes I suppose." She hadn't had much time to think about it.

"Not gym shoes," Veronica said. "Get some cowboy boots."

"And a nice cowboy hat to finish the look," Kristy added. "There's a Western-wear shop in town. They have lots of cute clothes. They have a lot of overpriced touristy stuff in front, but locals get their stuff from the room in the back."

"Get them soon so you can break them in. You don't

want to walk around in boots that hurt your feet," Marissa said. "You won't have any fun that way."

"And you won't be nearly as cute either," Kristy added.

"True on both points," Alexandra said. Not that she should be worried about looking cute for Nathan. "How long will it take to break them in?"

"A couple of days should do it," Kristy said.

"I'll go tomorrow."

"What time?" Veronica asked. "I'll take my lunch and we can go together."

"Sounds good. How about noon?"

"Perfect."

"Be sure to send pictures to Marissa and me," Kristy said.

"I will," Alexandra promised.

They said good-night and then ended the call. Alexandra told herself that spending time with Nathan wasn't a big deal.

Her pounding heart let her know she hadn't fooled herself.

LATE THE NEXT MORNING, Alexandra got Chloe dressed to go shopping. Despite telling herself not to make a big deal of it, she was excited about the prospect of seeing Nathan again.

Aunt Rose was sitting on the sofa, doing some needlepoint, when Alexandra carried Chloe into the room and put on her jacket. Aunt Rose looked up and smiled. "Where are the two of you going?"

"I'm going to buy some cowboy boots and a cowboy hat."

"What brought this on?"

"Nathan invited me to visit the ranch, and the girls convinced me that I should get boots and a hat."

"That's a good idea. I haven't been to a ranch in ages, but boots are definitely better than regular shoes. After all, you never know what you'll step in."

Alexandra wrinkled her nose. "I hadn't thought of that."

"You aren't going to turn into a wimpy city girl, are you? Surely you're sturdier than that."

Alexandra laughed. "Are you forgetting that I brought two suitcases of designer clothes with me? Not to mention all the shoes and purses. I am a city girl."

"I haven't forgotten that at all. And since I appreciate good quality clothes, I think that was a good idea. It's easier to take what you want out of your closet than it is to purchase something new in a pinch. But sturdiness has nothing to do with the clothes you wear and everything to do with the kind of person you are inside. You never struck me as the type of woman who would break out in a sweat if she stepped in a little bit of cow poop. Am I wrong?"

"No. I'm a pediatric nurse, remember? I've been thrown up on, bled on, peed on. I don't think there is a bodily fluid that hasn't landed on me at some point."

"Good."

"I'm sure you meant that in a way other than how it sounded."

Aunt Rose laughed. "Don't be so sure. I just might have a mean streak."

Alexandra shook her head. "That's not possible."

Aunt Rose simply smiled mischievously.

After draping Chloe's diaper bag across her shoulder, Alexandra picked up her daughter. "We won't be long."

"You know you can always leave Chloe here with me."

"I know. But I don't want to take advantage. Besides, it's nice outside and she could use a little fresh air."

"You could never take advantage. But I agree about the fresh air. Have a good time."

Alexandra buckled Chloe into her car seat and then headed for downtown Aspen Creek. Aunt Rose's house was in one of the more established residential neighborhoods in town. Each house was large and set on a one-acre lot. Most of Aunt Rose's neighbors were senior citizens, although a couple in their thirties moved in across the street a week ago. The neighbors were friendly and doted on Chloe, but if Alexandra chose to make her move to Aspen Creek permanent, she would have to seriously consider a different area. It would be unfair to raise her daughter in a neighborhood that didn't have kids her age for her to run and play with.

When they reached downtown, Alexandra parked and then got the stroller from the trunk. She strapped Chloe into the stroller and looked up. Veronica was walking down the street.

"Perfect timing," Veronica said as she came to stand beside Alexandra.

"I could have picked you up at the library."

"No need. The library is only two blocks away." Veronica leaned over and tapped Chloe on her nose. "And how is my favorite little baby today?"

Chloe cooed and kicked her legs in response.

"She's having the best day ever," Alexandra answered.

"Does she know how to have any other type?" Veronica asked and then straightened.

"If only you knew," Alexandra joked. Chloe was a good baby, but she still had the occasional bad day.

They reached the Western-wear store and stepped inside. As expected, several tourists were wandering about, trying to find the perfect souvenir. A woman with an elaborately decorated cowboy hat perched on her head was standing in the middle of the room, holding two different fancy boots in her hands, as if trying to decide which pair to buy.

Scooting around the woman, Alexandra and Veronica walked down a narrow hallway to the back of the building. They stepped into a room that was just as well lit as the one in the front. Clearly the owner valued the residents' business as much as he did the vacationers' money. Veronica made a beeline for the earrings on a counter while Alexandra looked at the hats.

A middle-aged salesman approached Alexandra and gave her a friendly smile. "How can I help you?"

"I'm looking for boots and a hat," she replied with a smile of her own.

"Sure. We'll get your feet measured and then you can take a look around. How does that sound?"

"That makes perfect sense to me."

He led her to a row of chairs and then pushed one aside so she could place the stroller beside her.

Alexandra took off her shoes and the salesman quickly measured her feet.

Veronica returned and glanced at the salesman. "Hello, Mr. Carter. How are you doing?"

"I'm just fine, Veronica. How about you?"

"No complaints. This is my friend, Alexandra. She's Rose Kenzie's niece."

"Nice to meet you. And how is Rose doing these days?"

"She's fine. Up to her old tricks."

"Give her my best."

"I will."

Alexandra took Chloe out of the stroller and then headed over to the boots. She looked at a few and then picked up one that she liked.

Veronica picked up a boot and held it up. "What do you think of this one?"

"It's nice." Alexandra held up the boot she held. It was the same style as the one in Veronica's hand. While Veronica had picked up a black boot, Alexandra held a brown one.

"Great minds and all that," Veronica said.

"Clearly."

When Mr. Carter returned, he looked at the boots they held. "I'll be right back with both colors."

Choosing boots proved easier than choosing a hat. There were so many to choose from, each as gorgeous as the next. Although Alexandra didn't expect to wear the boots or hats more than a couple of times, she still wanted to look good. After she'd narrowed it down to two that complemented her face the best, she sought Veronica's opinion.

"The first one," Veronica said.

"Really? I was leaning toward the second."

Veronica took a picture of Alexandra wearing each hat and then texted them to Kristy and Marissa. They immediately texted back. Predictably, the vote was split.

"You could get both," Veronica said.

Alexandra shook her head. "And have two hats that I won't wear more than once? Nope."

"Let Chloe decide. After all, we haven't consulted her."

Veronica was currently holding Chloe, so Alexandra held a hat in each hand and then turned to face her daughter. "Which one do you like best?"

Chloe actually looked at the hats as if she was seriously contemplating the decision. Then she smiled and reached out for the hat in Alexandra's right hand, choosing the hat that Alexandra liked a little bit better.

"That settles it," Veronica said. "Although I still think you'll look great in either one of them."

"The real question is, will Nathan think I look good in it."

"Really? Interesting. Do go on."

Alexandra clapped a hand against her mouth. Had she really just said that? She couldn't believe that she'd actually thought it, much less said it out loud. Nathan's preferences shouldn't be a consideration. "Forget that you heard that."

"You're kidding, right?"

"More like hopeful."

Veronica mimed locking her lips. "Your secret is safe with me."

"Thank you."

Her friend smiled. "I just wonder how long it will be safe with you."

## CHAPTER SEVEN

NATHAN WATCHED AS Alexandra drove through the double gates and onto the paved driveway. She pulled over and stopped to let him get in. He'd offered to drive into Aspen Creek and pick her up, but she'd turned him down, insisting that she could drive herself. He climbed into the passenger seat and fastened his seat belt. The ranch was over fifteen thousand acres, and his house was off the beaten path. It was easier to show her where it was than to give her directions.

"How was your drive?" he asked, taking a moment to look at her. She'd pulled her thick hair into a ponytail at the nape of her neck, giving him a perfect view of her face. Her skin was clear and glowing. Her rich brown eyes were sparkling with excitement. But it was her full lips, parted in a smile, that attracted the majority of his attention. He knew how soft those lips were. How heavenly it was to kiss them, feeling them move beneath his. How sweet she tasted. How easy it would be to be distracted by her presence and do something foolish—like fall for her.

Even knowing the danger she posed to his five-year plan, he hadn't been able to resist calling her. He'd needed to see her again.

"Good. Peaceful," she said.

He forced himself to focus on the conversation, and not the slender legs in tight jeans. "Glad to hear it."

"It really is a straight shot from town. And it's quite

scenic. I haven't been out of town since I moved here. I'm beginning to see what I missed."

"We'll make up with some of that today. There are some really scenic spots here. Drive down the driveway until you reach a split in the road, then head to the right."

"Okay."

"My parents' house is straight ahead. I would introduce you to them, but they're spending the day in Denver."

The sound she made was a cross between choking and laughter. He was trying to figure out its meaning, when she spoke. "That sounds like a nice way to spend a Saturday."

"It's nice to see my parents taking it easier now. When my brothers and I were younger, they worked really hard. My brothers and I don't work every day, but back then, my father did. More often than not, my mother was by his side. Dad might not have worked a full day on Sundays, but he still worked a few hours. When we were older, my brothers and I tried to keep up with him."

He glanced over at her. She was watching the road, but he could tell that she was listening.

"Make a right and then follow the path around the lake," he instructed. The road wasn't paved, but tracks had been worn in the dirt.

"You're right. I never would have found your house."

He nodded.

"What was it like growing up on the ranch?"

He smiled as memories rushed back. "I had a great childhood. My parents never forced us to follow in their footsteps. If one or all of us had chosen other careers, Mom and Dad would have supported us. Despite the fact that my brothers and I have vastly different personalities, we all wanted to be ranchers."

"Does that cause conflict?"

"Occasionally, but not often. Despite our differences,

we have a similar outlook on life. And we're close friends. I know Miles and Isaac have my back. And I have theirs."

"Sounds a lot like my family. My brother, sister, and I all look out for each other. Of course we have a tendency to butt into each other's business a little too much."

"As siblings do."

"When we were kids, my brother, Joshua, did all the talking, and my sister, Victoria, and I did all the listening. At some point, she joined him. Now that we're older, it goes in all directions. It's nice to know that they respect my opinion."

She drove around the lake and stopped in front of an impressive house. "Wow."

"You like it?"

"It's breathtaking. And not at all what I was expecting."

"What were you expecting?"

She shrugged. "A log cabin maybe. Or a white clapboard house like in *The Wizard of Oz*. Something more ranch-y. Definitely not something from the pages of *Architectural Digest*."

"A few years back, I built a smaller house. I was gone a lot then, so I let my brother and his ex-wife live there. When I decided to build what I wanted, I decided on this design. I actually like the modern look. Some people might find the glass a bit too much, but I think it fits well with nature. And I get views from every room in the house, which I love."

"I'm not an art critic or architect, but I think it's perfect."

"Wait until you see inside."

Once they were standing beside the car, she leaned against her door and stared at the house with undisguised awe. His parents and brothers had been shocked when he'd shown them the plans for the house. They'd been sure he'd build something more traditional. Something safer. After all, he was by far the most conservative of the brothers. Or, as Isaac liked to say, he was more of a stick-in-the-mud than the others. Nathan didn't deny it. But when it came to his house, he'd wanted something bold. Something that reflected another part of him. The part of him that wanted to step outside the box and be a bit more frivolous. More daring and unpredictable. So he and the architect worked together to design this five-bedroom house of glass, steel, and stone that overlooked the lake.

He led her up the wide stone exterior stairs and through the oversize double glass doors.

"This is something else," she said, as she stood in the two-story foyer, her head back as she looked at the exquisite crystal chandelier. "I don't think I would ever leave for work. It's all so beautiful. I would just stand here and just stare."

"Believe me, I did a lot of that when I first moved in. I couldn't believe that it was my house. Although I was involved in every step of the process, I couldn't imagine how it would feel to stand inside on that first day. Every day I find something new to marvel over."

"I love the finishes you chose. I heard that marble feels cold, but nothing about your house feels cold."

"What would you rather see first, upstairs or the main floor?" Once more he was doing something he never did. He didn't usually invite women to the ranch—they tended to read more into that than he'd intended—and he certainly didn't give them tours of his home. It didn't make sense, yet he couldn't seem to stop himself.

"This is your home, so you should decide what you want to show me and what is off-limits."

"Let's start upstairs." Apparently nothing was off-limits. He led her up the curved stairway to a wide landing.

Alexandra looked over the rail, taking in the view from the second floor. "Wow. Again."

Though it shouldn't affect him, her obvious delight with his house stroked his ego. Nathan led her to the far end of the second floor, to his home office. It was quiet and decorated in a minimalist style.

"This is so spartan," Alexandra said.

"I have everything I need. Desk, chair, fridge, and microwave. Get the work done and get out is my motto."

"Does it work?"

"You'd be surprised by how well."

He showed her the four guest suites, each of which had a walk-in closet and a luxurious attached bathroom. The rooms were sunny and spacious with gorgeous views of the ranch from each window.

Alexandra gave him a sweet smile. "Nice. I imagine that you have a hard time getting your guests to leave."

He could have told her that he didn't have guests, so that wouldn't be a problem, but instead he simply nodded. He didn't want to give her the impression that he was cold and unfeeling. Friendless.

Alexandra was stepping into the hallway, so he led her to the last door. His master bedroom. Although she had been nothing but complimentary, Nathan was suddenly worried about what she would think about his bedroom. While he'd paid a designer to decorate the other rooms, he'd done the master bedroom himself. He'd wanted it to be a reflection of himself.

"Is this your sanctuary?" she asked. As usual, Alexandra's eyes sparkled with pleasure, which put him at ease. Not that he should have been uncomfortable in the first place. This was his home after all. He was the only one who had to like it. Even so, he inhaled deeply before swinging open the double doors.

As she had in the other rooms, Alexandra went to the middle of the room and turned in a slow circle, as if trying to absorb the feel of the room into her soul before moving. In the guest rooms, she'd run her hands across the comforters or picked up a random art object to study it. Now she didn't move, letting her eyes do the inspecting. Nathan appreciated that she showed respect for his personal items, but suddenly he didn't want her to keep her distance. He wanted her to feel free to sit on his bed and touch his belongings. Touch him. He wanted her to feel at home.

He shook his head at that thought and tried to push it away. That was going a little too far.

"I like it," she said, pulling his attention back to the here and now.

He blew out a breath, relieved that she had no idea what he'd been thinking. "Thanks."

"I like the colors you chose. They seem to bring in the outside. And of course, the view is outstanding." She crossed to the floor-to-ceiling wall of windows with their view of the lake and the mountains in the distance. "Just waking up to this must put you in the best mood."

"It does." There were nights when he'd lain in his bed and just stared out at the starry sky or across the vast acres of land to the outline of the mountains in the distance. Nothing compared to watching as lightning flashed in the dark sky on stormy nights.

"I'm jealous," she said, a smile belying her words.

"Why?"

"My aunt lives in a great neighborhood, but the views don't compare to this."

"There's no reason to be jealous. Consider this your invitation to visit the ranch anytime you feel like it."

She gave him a look he couldn't interpret and then crossed the room until she was standing near enough for him to touch. His hands ached to reach out and caress the smooth brown skin of her cheek, so he shoved it into his pocket. "You might want to reconsider that statement. For all you know, I might show up one day with my daughter in one arm and my bags in the other. Then where would you be?"

"Good point," he said, but the picture she'd painted held some appeal. Although he was the oldest son, he was the only one without a family of his own. Miles had Jillian, Benji, and Lilliana. They would officially become a family in a week.

Isaac had his sweet baby girl and was engaged to the love of his life. Although he and Savannah hadn't set a date, they were a family in every way that mattered.

Suddenly Nathan felt as if he had fallen behind, which was ridiculous. He was the one who'd set the schedule for his life. He followed his own timeline. He'd created his five-year plan. If he wanted to adjust it, he could at any moment.

That straight in his mind, he showed Alexandra his closet, which was twice the size of the ones in the guest room and then let her explore his bathroom. After she admired the steam shower and soaking tub, they went back down the stairs and returned to the foyer. Once there, he led her through the living room, dining room, den, family room, and finally the kitchen. With each of her exclamations of pleasure, his pride grew.

By the time they stepped onto his back patio, he was nearly bursting. She smiled. "This has to be the best home I've ever been in. And it's not just the architecture, although that is spectacular. I really like how warm and welcoming it feels."

"That's what I was going for. I want it to feel homey."

"You succeeded."

"Now would you like to see the ranch?"

"I would."

He flashed her a grin. "I don't suppose you know how to ride a horse?"

"You are correct. But I'm willing to try if it's necessary."

"Not today. We can make do with a Jeep."

"Okay."

They made small talk as they walked to his garage. Once they were in the Jeep, he drove down the paved road until it ended, turning into gravel and dirt. He slowed so that the uneven road wouldn't jostle her too much.

Alexandra planted a hand on her cowboy hat as she looked around. Watching her reaction, Nathan realized that he had begun to take the beauty of the ranch for granted. Now he allowed himself to see it anew through her eyes. Without a doubt, the ranch was on the most beautiful land in the country, and he realized just how blessed he'd been to call it home. He could walk for hours, days even, and not leave Montgomery property. He was in the middle of making a deal that would add even more acreage to their ranch.

The Duncan brothers, who owned the adjoining ranch, had finally agreed to sell. It had taken months of extensive, and at times painful, negotiations, but they had finally settled upon terms that made everyone happy. All that was left was to sign the contract.

"Where are your cows?" Alexandra asked.

"Grazing in one of the north pastures. We have to move them often so that they don't overgraze an area. We add supplemental food of course."

"They don't live in barns?"

"Not ordinarily. But we've built breaks to keep them from getting too cold on the range."

"Do you have pigs and chickens? Do you grow corn and beans?"

He shot her a look. "You mean like Old MacDonald?"

She shook her head. Although they were traveling at a slow pace, there was still enough wind to play with her thick, black hair. A few locks blew into her face, and she used her free hand to brush them back behind her ears. "Sort of."

"Yes and no."

"Oh, that's not confusing at all."

He laughed. "Yes, we have chickens. No pigs though. We don't raise them to sell. My mother just likes having fresh eggs. They taste so much better than store-bought. Mom also has a big garden where she grows all kinds of vegetables. Again, for personal consumption. Nothing compares to a salad made with fresh vegetables. We can sneak into her garden and grab enough for a salad for two."

"Oh no. You aren't going to include me in your larceny."

He laughed. "My mother won't mind. She's always giving vegetables to us. She grows more than she and my father could ever eat. And believe me, when it's time to harvest them, she has plenty of eager help."

"Harvest? Just how big is this garden?"

He shrugged. "I don't know. An acre, give or take."

"And she calls it a garden?"

"That's what it is."

"They definitely do some things bigger in ranch country."

"Everything is bigger in ranch country."

She raised an eyebrow, and he realized how suggestive his comment must have sounded. He could have tried to take the words back but didn't. That would only attract more attention to them. Besides, he didn't mind if she thought he was flirting with her. Because he was. "I'll keep that in mind."

"You do that."

He drove over a hill, parked, and they climbed out of the vehicle. The ground was covered in gold wildflowers that whipped in the wind. A stand of tall trees in the middle of the field provided a bit of shade. Birds flew across the sky, chirping and filling the air with their songs. Squirrels and rabbits darted across the grass, as if disturbed by Nathan's and Alexandra's presence. In the distance a few deer drank from a babbling brook.

"I love it here. It looks like something out of a fairy tale," Alexandra whispered, as if speaking too loudly would ruin the enchantment.

"It's one of my favorite places on the ranch. I thought about building my house here, but somehow it seemed wrong. Intrusive. As if I would be defiling something beautiful. I like to come here and soak up the atmosphere. Then I leave it, as perfect as I found it."

"You generally don't drive here, do you?"

He shook his head. "No. I usually come here on horseback. But I made an exception because I wanted to show it to you." He didn't want to give too much thought to why it had been so important to share this place with her. The answer might not align with his five-year plan.

And he wasn't ready to adjust that just yet.

ALEXANDRA TRIED TO keep her delight at his words under control. After all, she wasn't looking for a relationship. Neither was he. So why was she having such difficulty remembering that? And why was it so easy to imagine herself—and Chloe—spending more time here with Nathan? Whatever the reason, it ended now. She wasn't going to let her feelings lead her into possible heartbreak. She was going to stick to more general topics.

"I had a few preconceived notions about the ranch. None of them have proven to be accurate."

"Like what?"

He sounded genuinely interested so she answered honestly. "Well, for one, I thought that animals would be a lot closer to your house. Like I would walk out the back door and encounter bulls and cows."

"That could be true on some ranches. Especially smaller ones. Well, maybe not that close, but certainly closer than here. And given the time of year, our cattle might actually be grazing closer to the houses."

"And I thought that it would...smell. You know, like the zoo, only a million times worse."

He threw back his head and laughed. She liked the sound it made as it echoed across the vast acres. It was bold and robust, as confident as the man she was coming to know. "You know, there is a certain smell to nature that you get used to over time. If you would like a more up close and personal view of the ranch more in line with what you pictured, including the smells, we can do that."

"Would you think that I was weird if I said yes?"

"No. I want today to be everything you imagined it would be."

They traipsed back down the hill and climbed back into the Jeep. This was such a new experience for her and she was enjoying it more than she'd expected. She'd seen some of the most famous tourist attractions in the world and amazingly the ranch ranked up there with them. Perhaps it was the handsome tour guide showing her around that made the day so special.

He certainly was holding her attention. He'd looked incredibly dapper in his suit the night of the auction but dressed in jeans that fit his muscular thighs perfectly, and a plaid shirt that hugged his sculpted torso, he looked even more appealing. Just looking at him made her mouth water and stirred up longings she didn't want to feel. She used to believe that it was okay to look as long as she didn't touch. That didn't apply in Nathan's case. Looking at him was dangerous. Especially when she wasn't sure she could stop at just looking. Nor was she certain that she wanted to.

As they rode across the grassy hills and valleys, Nathan entertained her with amusing stories about growing up on a cattle ranch. He and his brothers had learned early on that the cattle weren't pets, nor was it safe for them to forget that the huge animals could crush and kill them in mere minutes.

"Did you ever ignore the rules and do something dangerous?"

"Like what?"

"I don't know…walk along the fence rail where the cattle were?"

He shook his head and gave her a quick look. They were driving across the grass and there was no danger of them running into another vehicle. "No. You forget, I'm the oldest brother. When my parents weren't around, I was responsible for keeping Miles and Isaac safe. I couldn't very well do something dangerous when I knew that one or both of them would mimic my behavior at a later date."

"Did you ever want to do something crazy or risky?"

"No. Maybe it's a result of being the oldest, but I never could forget that I had to be a role model." One side of his lips lifted in a quirk and her stomach gave a silly little lurch in response. Nathan was objectively handsome, so naturally she would enjoy looking at his gorgeous face and muscular body. There was nothing worrisome about that.

But when her body started to react like a schoolgirl with a crush? Then it was time to dial it back. Fast.

She'd already made one mistake with Owen. True, she'd been more than physically attracted to him. They'd spent a lot of time together and she'd liked the person that he'd appeared to be. He had talked for hours about helping the less fortunate in their communities as well as around the world. All appearances indicated that he'd been sincere. He donated to worthy causes and even helped establish a nonprofit to help homeless youth find homes, get GEDs and jobs.

But that generous spirit had only been a facade. A way of sanitizing his otherwise dirty interior. He hadn't really cared about people. Not really. He'd only been concerned as long as he was able to keep them at a distance. Or in a situation where he could maintain an air of superiority. His heart hadn't extended to love for his own child.

And why was she thinking about Owen now when she was in the company of this charming man? Oh yeah, *because* he was charming. She needed to remind herself not to make the same mistake with Nathan. She couldn't allow herself to get swept away by his charm and good looks. Even if he was truly as wonderful as he appeared, a relationship was the last thing she needed right now. Not that Nathan had given any indication that he was looking to start a romance with her. He hadn't once hinted about today being anything more than it was—an opportunity for her to see his ranch up close.

True, he'd flirted with her earlier, but it had seemed spontaneous, not something that was part of a playbook. And that made him even more appealing to her. But she needed to slow down. In fact, she needed to *stop*. She wasn't looking for a relationship. That was one of the reasons she'd been eager to move to this small town. To her way of thinking, the odds that she would meet someone she found attractive had been a million to one. Now it looked like her math had been off a bit.

Alexandra heard the sound of the lowing before she saw the cattle. She inhaled, and her nostrils were filled with their odor. She coughed. With each passing second, the odor and the noise grew even stronger.

Nathan stopped the Jeep and turned to her. "We can get out here and walk the rest of the way if you want."

She felt a bit of trepidation. "They aren't going to charge us, are they?"

"What? Not up for that kind of adventure?"

"No. I'm wearing boots, not gym shoes. I'm sure they'll slow me down." She held up her leg so he could see her boots.

"Those are nice. They look new."

"They are. I got them especially for this visit."

"Did you now?"

"Yes. I'm hoping that I can get more use out of them. I won't be able to wear them at work, and to be honest, I haven't been to many places where women were wearing boots."

"Where have you been?" he asked as they walked toward the cattle.

"Not too many places. You already know about my dinner at Bliss on Your Lips. My friends and I have treated ourselves to dinner at a few other fancy restaurants. That's it."

"I see. Well, you're getting some use out of them now. I don't know a lot about women's fashion, but I imagine you can wear them to the grocery store. Or running errands."

"I suppose."

They'd reached the fences surrounding the cattle. The cows were eating the grass and milling around. There was lots of room for the animals to move which she was pleased to see. Although she didn't consider herself to be an animal activist, she did care about the living conditions of the animals that would become the food she ate. She wanted them to have a good quality of life. Apparently Nathan and his family felt the same way.

Nathan held out his hand and she took it as if it was the most natural thing in the world to do. They swung their hands as they approached the cattle. He stopped at a safe distance and then they just watched for a while without talking. It was nice. This was different from the way she'd spent most of her Saturday afternoons when she'd lived in Chicago. It was even different from the way she'd been spending her free time since she moved to Aspen Creek.

And she enjoyed it. The weather was warm and the sky was clear. There was something soothing about standing quietly and watching the cows.

She wondered how Chloe would react to seeing the animals. Would she delight in listening to them moo? A part of her wondered if she should have taken Nathan up on his invitation to include her in the day. But that might prove risky. She didn't want Chloe to get attached to someone who wasn't going to be a permanent part of their lives. Since neither she nor Nathan was looking for a relationship, things between them were temporary. It would be best for her to keep Nathan at a distance until she had a better handle on things. He hadn't even met Chloe yet. Perhaps that was for the best.

After she'd had her fill of looking at the cattle—and being downwind of them—she suggested that they stroll around for a bit. It was all so scenic and so peaceful. So isolated. It was as if they were the only two people in the world.

That thought stopped her in her tracks. She'd learned

the hard way that fantasy and reality rarely intersected. *Once upon a time* was not the way relationships began in real life. Now that she was a mother, she needed to keep both of her feet firmly on the ground. She couldn't set her child up for the heartbreak of disappointment.

"I suppose I need to get going," Alexandra said after a while. The day had been wonderful, but she didn't want to overstay her welcome. Besides, Chloe was at home. She needed to spend some time with her.

Nathan looked surprised and for a long moment he didn't speak. A part of her wanted him to protest, to insist that she stay longer, but the rational part of her hoped he wouldn't. She didn't know if she was strong enough to resist his appeal for much longer. She needed to create some distance from him so she could remind herself why she didn't want a man in her life right now.

"Okay. Let's get you back to your car."

"I had the best time. Thank you so much for inviting me."

"You're more than welcome."

They got back into the Jeep and drove over the field. Nathan took a different way back to his house, showcasing even more beautiful spots. She saw a few men in the distance, but other than waving, Nathan paid no attention to them. The drive went quickly, and Alexandra was actually sad when his house came into view. He parked and then they turned and faced each other.

She sighed. "I suppose I need to get out of your Jeep."

"We both do. I left my motorcycle at the front gate, so I'll ride back with you."

"You have a motorcycle?"

He nodded. "Surprised?"

"Totally." She grinned at him. "You're more fun than you let on."

He winked. "Let's keep that between the two of us. I have a reputation as a stick-in-the-mud to uphold."

Alexandra burst out laughing. "Your secret is safe with me."

They got out of the Jeep and into her car to ride back to the front gate. When they arrived, he didn't get out of the car. Instead, he looked at her as if debating with himself. Since she had internal battles quite often, she waited patiently until he appeared to reach a decision.

"My brother is getting married next week."

That was not at all what she was expecting him to say. She nodded. "I remember. You told me. That's a good thing. Right?"

"Yes. I'm happy for them. It's just my mother. She's caught up in the whole romance thing. It's only my two brothers and me. Now my mother has wedding fever. She thinks we all need to settle down. Miles is getting married. Isaac is engaged. And then there's me."

"Don't tell me she's matchmaking."

He gave her a look that spoke volumes.

"Yikes."

"That about sums it up. She's on a mission. Before she was too busy helping Miles with Benji and worrying about Isaac's revolving door of women, to do more than throw a random woman in my direction. But that's all changed. I'm the sole focus of her attention. I'm afraid to answer my door for fear that she'll be standing there with a single woman by her side."

"Now you're exaggerating."

"Maybe a little. But she's on a mission. Last Sunday, she asked about our date."

"How did she know we went out?"

"My mother knows everything. I made the mistake of telling her how good a time we had. I could see the wheels turning in her head. She was just thrilled at the idea of adding another daughter-in-law to the family. When I told her nothing was going to happen between us, she wasn't happy. Especially when I told her that it was mutual. The next thing I knew, she was mentioning some friend's daughter. I tell you, she's not going to rest until she has me in a relationship."

"So what are you going to do?"

"The only thing I can do." He paused. "I'm running away from home."

Laughter burst out of Alexandra's lips. "You are hilarious."

"Desperate is more like it. You would be too if you knew my mother."

"I would help you if I could. I suppose I could write her a letter and ask her to give you a reprieve."

"I wish that would work. No, the only thing that will get her off my case is if she sees me with a woman." He paused, and now she could hear the wheels in *his* head turning. He spoke slowly. "Are you busy next Saturday?"

"No." The word sounded normal, not betraying the caution she felt. "Why?"

"Do you want to go to my brother's wedding with me? I need someone to keep my mother off my back for a few hours."

She laughed. "That's some kind of invitation. No wonder your mother is worried about you ever having a girlfriend."

He gave her a sheepish grin. "I guess that didn't come across as smooth."

"Not even slightly."

"Well, let me see if I can do it better the second time." He cleared his throat and then spoke in a sexy voice that a radio DJ would envy. "Alexandra. If you are free this

Saturday, I would be honored if you accompanied me to my brother's wedding."

Despite knowing that he was only putting on, the timbre of his voice set butterflies free in her stomach. She wouldn't stand a chance if he ever decided to woo her for real. She couldn't let him have all the fun, so she injected her voice with a double dose of sex appeal. "Nathan. I would love to be your date for your brother's wedding. What time should I expect you?"

There was a brief pause before he responded. "The ceremony starts at two. I'll pick you up at noon if that works for you."

"That's fine. I'm looking forward to meeting your family." She realized how that came out and hastened to clarify her statement. "In a general way. Not that I'm hoping to become a part of it."

"I didn't think you did."

"I love weddings," she added, just to be on the safe side.

"That's good." He inhaled and then blew the breath out slowly. His Adam's apple bobbed up and down twice. "But more than being my date. I need you to pretend to be my girlfriend."

"Oh." She was too shocked to cover the wariness in her voice. "What would that involve?"

He shrugged one of his massive shoulders and looked slightly embarrassed. "I guess just act like you like me."

That wouldn't be hard because she did like him. Perhaps too much. But since neither of them were looking for romance, this could work to her advantage too. She might not want a boyfriend, but she wasn't opposed to having a male friend to spend time with occasionally. Having a make-believe boyfriend might be fun.

It had been a long time since she'd had fun. Aunt Rose

was right. She needed more in her life than work and Chloe. Alexandra couldn't suppress a grin. She loved a good caper. "I can hardly wait."

# CHAPTER EIGHT

ALEXANDRA CHECKED HER appearance in the mirror before going downstairs to wait for Nathan. This was the first wedding she'd attended in a long time. Although her relationship with Owen had ended disastrously, and she was not interested in trying again, she loved weddings and all the trappings. She liked seeing the bridesmaids' dresses and their bouquets. She was always excited to see the bride's wedding dress. Her heart always beat a little faster as she listened to the emotionally spoken wedding vows. There was something so hopeful about witnessing a happy couple promise to love each other forever. If only she didn't know what could go wrong if they didn't keep those promises.

But what she was really looking forward to was seeing Nathan again. No matter how hard she tried to convince herself that this was subterfuge and not a real date, her heart still sped up with the realization that she was going to be spending the next few hours with him.

That feeling was in direct opposition to her plan to avoid romantic entanglements at all costs. But there was something about Nathan that made sticking to her plan next to impossible. Lucky for her, he had no problem sticking to his five-year plan. He was so determined not to be roped into a relationship that he was willing to bring a pretend date to his brother's wedding.

No, that wasn't accurate. She wasn't his pretend date.

She was his real date—just not his real girlfriend. His plus one for the reception. She wouldn't lie—especially not to his mother—but if her presence gave people the impression that Alexandra and Nathan were a couple, well she couldn't be responsible for that. She was helping Nathan out of a tight spot. Helping him convince his mom that he didn't need a matchmaker after all.

She just needed to make sure that *she* didn't start to believe there was something romantic between them.

She turned from side to side, then made a minor adjustment to the bottom of her pomegranate-red dress. It was fitted from shoulders to just above her hips, hugging her breasts and waist before flaring out over her knees. It was perfect for an afternoon wedding and reception.

Alexandra had taken extra time with her hair and makeup, and she looked good, if she did say so herself. She went downstairs, where Chloe was on all fours and Crystal was chasing her around the room.

"I'm going to catch you," Crystal said, making Chloe laugh.

Aunt Rose was sitting on the sofa. She smiled and shook her head.

Crystal looked up when Alexandra entered the room. "Wow. You look really pretty."

"Thank you." Alexandra smiled then scooped up Chloe, planting a big kiss on her cheek.

"I bet all of the men will want to dance with you," Crystal continued.

"I don't know about that."

"My dad might. He's going to the wedding. He doesn't have a date, so if he asks you to dance, you should say yes."

Alexandra wondered if Crystal's dad had any idea how much matchmaking Crystal did on his behalf. "I most certainly will. Don't forget, I have Chloe's food and bottles all set up."

"You told me already. And I know when to give her a snack and which ones she likes best."

Alexandra smiled. "You really are a great babysitter."

Crystal beamed. "Thank you."

Chloe pushed against Alexandra's chest, straining to get down so she could resume her game of chase. Sighing, Alexandra set her on the floor and then watched as Chloe began crawling around the room while Crystal followed behind her. The doorbell rang and Alexandra hurried to open it. Nathan was standing there, dressed in a black tuxedo, and her heart stuttered. She couldn't tear her eyes away.

"Whoa. You are absolutely gorgeous," Nathan said. His eyes swept over her body, male appreciation in his eyes. Although he hadn't touched her, his gaze had been so hot and intense that her body began to burn.

She told herself that he was just playing a part—after all, she was his pretend girlfriend—but her heart and brain didn't seem to be communicating. Her foolish heart wished he'd been sincere.

"Thank you. And might I add that you look pretty dapper yourself?"

Before she could stop herself, she reached out and straightened his bow tie. When she realized just how intimate that act was, she pulled her hands away and folded them in front of her. There was no reason to pretend when their intended audience wasn't around to see.

He struck a pose, something completely out of character, and winked. "I'm one of the groomsmen, so I had to wear this tux. But we need to get to the resort now."

"Okay."

Chloe crawled over and grabbed a fistful of the cuff of

Nathan's pants. Immediately Alexandra leaned over and picked her up. "Sorry about that."

"Don't be." Nathan gave Chloe a long look. He appeared slightly stunned and his voice sounded different. Strained. "This must be your little girl."

"Yes. This is Chloe."

Nathan grinned. "She's a little cutie."

Chloe reached a hand to Nathan, and Alexandra took a step back before her daughter could touch him. "Her hands are a bit grubby. The last thing I want is for her to mess up your tux."

Crystal came over and took Chloe into her arms.

"Thank you. I'll see you later." Alexandra grabbed her wrap and purse from the bench in the hallway and then waved to Aunt Rose and Crystal, blew a kiss to Chloe, and she and Nathan left. She didn't know what to make of Nathan's reaction to Chloe. He had said all of the right things, but something had been off. But then, no doubt he had a lot on his mind with the wedding and was a bit stressed. And first meetings were always a bit strained, so she decided not to make too much of it.

When they were inside his sedan, she turned to him. "Which resort are we going to?"

"I forgot, you're still getting to know Aspen Creek. Jillian—the bride's—family owns one of the most successful resorts in Colorado. They host weddings throughout the year. Miles and Jillian's wedding will be there, of course."

"That sounds wonderful. I imagine it will be quite beautiful."

"As are all the weddings held there. Of course, I know they pulled out all the stops for this one."

"Forget being a rancher, you should have been a tour guide. What else can you tell me about Aspen Creek?"

Nate laughed. "What do you want to know?"

"Anything. Everything. You grew up here, right?"

"Technically, yes, although I really grew up on the ranch. The town is a lot different than it was back then. It wasn't the tourist destination that it is now. The locals all knew about the skiing and outdoor activities, but it was a much smaller place in those days. Very tight-knit. Even those of us who grew up on ranches felt like we belonged."

"That sounds nice."

"It was. Even though the town has grown over the years, it still feels the same. I'm not sure how it happened, but about ten years ago, Aspen Creek went from being Colorado's best-kept secret to an overnight vacation destination of the rich and famous. Now tourists from all over the world vacation here. Aspen Creek is home to many former winter Olympians. They teach skiing, skating, and other things."

"Really? Maybe I'll take a lesson. It would be nice to learn something from the best. What lessons have you taken?"

He shrugged. "Over the years? Skiing. Ice-skating. Snowboarding. Everything they offer."

"Nice. What did you and your friends do for fun?"

"When you live on a ranch, there is a lot of horseback riding. We also skied, went ice-skating, and snowmobiling in the winter. In the summer we met up at the local swimming hole. Or fished and hiked. Everything you can think of, we did."

"You actually had a swimming hole?"

"Yeah."

"Why? I mean, I saw your swimming pool. Didn't your parents have one?"

"Yes. But there was something special about the swimming hole. Maybe the absence of parents was the draw. All of our friends would meet there. We'd hang out for hours. On cool evenings we'd build a bonfire, play music, and dance. Or sit around and talk. Now that I'm older I appreciate having a heated pool in my backyard."

"You can definitely get more use out of it."

"You would think. But I put in so many hours at work that I don't get to swim as much as I used to. I do spend a lot of time in the hot tub though." He glanced at her. "Feel free to come over and use it at any time."

"That's pretty far to go just to sit in your hot tub."

"You'd also get to enjoy the pleasure of my company."

"There is that. But I work full-time. I have a little girl and I need to spend time with her."

"I have nothing against kids. You are more than welcome to bring her with you."

"Really?" Alexandra's heart warmed at Nathan's words. He'd said something similar before, but she'd tried to convince herself that he was being polite. Maybe he hadn't been. Still, she had her reservations about letting Chloe spend a lot of time with Nathan. This charade wasn't going to last forever. Eventually Nathan's mother would cease her matchmaking and he wouldn't need her around. Alexandra would understand his absence, but Chloe wouldn't. Even so, his attitude was a wonderful surprise. Owen hadn't been interested in Chloe, so Alexandra hadn't expected Nathan to be interested either. "Of course, she probably wouldn't want to spend time in the hot tub."

"No. I suppose not. But my invitation to bring her to the ranch still stands."

"I'll keep that in mind."

They arrived at the resort a few minutes later. Nathan parked, then helped Alexandra from the car. Alexandra took one look around and gasped. The view was absolutely breathtaking. She'd never seen anything as scenic. The mountains soared over the resort, appearing to reach the clear blue sky. The trees surrounding the enormous stone building were filled with twinkling white lights. Large urns filled with roses were spaced along the winding path and up the stairs leading to the wide double doors. It was quite romantic, and she couldn't wait to see how the interior had been decorated. No doubt, it was even more romantic.

"Where is the wedding going to be held?"

"In the rooftop chapel. Miles and Jillian had wanted a small, intimate ceremony. Then the parents—or rather the mothers—got involved, and the guest list grew. Now there will be close to a hundred people attending."

Alexandra laughed. "That could still be considered intimate, since it's a wedding."

"That's what the mothers keep saying."

"I hope your brother and his fiancée are okay with the way things ended up. This is their day after all."

"Miles couldn't care less what they do. He's said on more than one occasion that all he wants is to be married to Jillian. Whatever makes her happy makes him happy. And Jillian is no shrinking violet. She'd speak up if she didn't like something. At the end of the day, this will be her dream wedding."

They reached the chapel, and a tuxedoed usher handed them a folded program before they stepped inside. Alexandra looked around and smiled. It was even more beautiful than she'd expected. Every surface was covered with vases filled with pink and white roses. There had to be thousands of them, filling the air with wonderful perfume. Gleaming crystal chandeliers hung from the high ceiling. Rows of chairs covered with white linen and pink bows were divided by a wide aisle. Vases of flowers lined the aisle. An enormous rose-covered arch stood at the front of the room. Alexandra couldn't hold back her sigh. The entire room was a vision.

But as gorgeous as the chapel was, it was the view from behind the floral arch that took her breath away. The floor-to-ceiling windows provided an unobstructed view of the snowcapped mountains. This was the perfect backdrop for a wedding.

"Are you taking notes for your own wedding?" Nathan joked.

Alexandra shook her head, ensuring that the ludicrous notion couldn't take root. "No. Marriage isn't in my plan. You know that. But I'm not above admiring perfection when I see it."

Nathan glanced around. "It is rather nice."

"*Nice* doesn't come close to describing this room."

He shrugged. "What can I say? I'm not the romantic in the family. Remember, I'm the one who's all business all the time."

Alexandra smiled. He might want other people to believe that—he might even believe it himself—but she thought he was selling himself short. There was more to Nathan than business. He was kind and generous. Funny and playful. Thoughtful and considerate. Nathan possessed so many admirable traits that she couldn't begin to name them all. "I'll keep that in mind."

"Do you want to find a seat or would you rather hang out in the lobby? I need to meet up with Miles and the other groomsmen. I hope that's okay with you."

"It's fine. I'll just hang out in the lobby for a bit. I'll go inside a little closer to the start of the ceremony."

Nathan stared at her for a moment, his dark gaze unreadable. A spark of something she couldn't name arced between them and her knees weakened. Then he shook his head, gave her shoulder a gentle squeeze, and left. Alexandra stared at his retreating back, not breathing until he'd disappeared around a corner.

After a while, wedding guests began to arrive, so Alexandra went inside and found a seat near the center of the room.

Minutes later, a middle-aged couple approached Alexandra and the woman spoke. "Would you mind if we joined you?"

"That would be wonderful." Alexandra stood aside so the couple could enter.

"Are you saving a seat for anyone?"

"No. Feel free to sit next to me."

"Thank you." They sat down and then pulled out their phones. The woman stood up and took a few pictures of the chapel. When she was satisfied that she had a shot of everything, she put her phone back into her purse and then turned to Alexandra. "We're Richard and Jerilyn Brown. We know the bride and the groom. Their mothers are two of my dearest friends. I can't tell you how happy we are to see Miles and Jillian get married. Aren't we, Richard?"

Richard had been sneaking looks at what appeared to be some sporting event on his phone, but he managed a nod. "Yes, we are."

Jerilyn rolled her eyes. Clearly she wasn't fooled for a moment. Then she looked at Alexandra, an expectant expression on her face. Not sure what she was supposed to say, Alexandra smiled. Jerilyn sighed. "How do you know the bride and groom?"

"I don't really. I moved to Aspen Creek several months ago. But I know Nathan, the groom's brother. He invited me as his date."

"Really? How long have you and Nathan been dating?"

Alexandra was glad that she and Nathan had anticipated this line of questioning and had prepared an answer. Even so, she was still caught a bit off guard. She hadn't expected to be confronted by the first wedding guest she encountered. Alexandra decided to use this conversation as a trial run. It was a good opportunity to fill in any gaps in the cover story.

Alexandra turned in her seat to better face Jerilyn. She noted that while Richard was still looking at his phone, he was also listening to the conversation. Apparently gossiping was a gender-neutral sport. "Nathan and I haven't been dating long at all. We met at the Bachelor Auction. I actually won a date with him."

"Don't tell me that he decided to use this as the date." Jerilyn shook her head in disgust and then harrumphed. "That man had better get his head out of the ranch business. Now, his brother, Isaac, has always been a favorite with the ladies. He has enough charm for two people. Nathan could learn a thing or two from him."

"I don't know about Isaac or his charm. But this isn't our date," Alexandra said, quick to correct the older woman and defend Nathan's honor. "Nathan took me to dinner at Bliss On Your Lips and then to Grady's for music and dancing."

"Really." Jerilyn smiled, clearly impressed. Alexandra didn't know why it was important to her that the other woman have a good opinion of Nathan, but it mattered. Jerilyn's friendly smile turned sly. "You must be pretty special for him to take you to such an expensive restaurant on a first date. That's certainly not his style."

"Perhaps Nathan was just waiting for the right woman to come along," Richard chimed in. He patted his wife's hand. "Like I did."

Jerilyn's light brown cheeks pinkened, and she giggled like a schoolgirl. "Oh you."

Richard kissed her cheek and then turned his attention back to his phone.

Alexandra smiled, grateful that Richard had interrupted

the conversation. She knew that the other woman meant no harm, and Nathan probably wouldn't care a whit about the other woman's opinion of him. But *she* cared. She decided to change the subject. "How long have you been married?"

"Thirty-two years."

"That's nice." It always filled Alexandra's heart with joy to see happily married couples. Especially ones that had stood the test of time. They worked to balance the disappointment she felt whenever she thought of her failed relationship. Knowing that love could actually last a lifetime tempered the pain she'd experienced.

"Does attending this wedding give you ideas about your future with Nathan?"

Where did that come from? Apparently she hadn't changed the subject as completely as she'd hoped. "It's kind of early for that kind of decision. After all, Nathan and I are still getting to know each other."

"It doesn't always take a long time to know when you've found the right one. It didn't take me long to know that Richard was the one for me. I took one look at him across the diner and that was all it took. I was a goner. I knew I would love him forever. Of course, it took him a bit longer."

"Really? How much longer?" Alexandra loved a good how-I-met-my-spouse story and could listen to them for hours. Especially if it took the heat off her and Nathan.

"Two hours."

"Oh, you have to tell me everything."

Jerilyn looked at her watch and then back at Alexandra. "We have a few minutes before the ceremony is scheduled to start, so why not? I was at the diner with two of my friends. It was the summer before my senior year of college. He had graduated from college the year before and had moved to Aspen Creek to manage his uncle's music venue.

"The instant that I saw him, I was intrigued. Neither of my friends knew who he was, so I decided to find out. I walked up to the bar, where he was studying the dessert menu and told him that the chocolate brownie with whipped cream was my favorite. He nodded but didn't say anything. When my food came, I returned to my table and my friends. I was a bit disappointed that he hadn't asked for my number."

"I bet."

"My friends and I were just finishing our dinners when the waiter brought over three desserts. Chocolate brownies with whipped cream. He said it was courtesy of my friend at the bar. I looked up, but he was gone. The waiter slipped me a note from Richard. I still have that letter to this day. It read: *Thank you for the dessert recommendation. If you don't have a boyfriend and would like to get to know me, please call.* He'd written his telephone number. I called him as soon as I got home."

Alexandra sighed. "Wow. That is so perfect."

"It really was. I practically swallowed my brownie whole. Then I raced home and called him. We got married three months later."

"That's a beautiful story." One Alexandra couldn't relate to. Although she and Owen had seemed to hit it off right away, it hadn't lasted. How wonderful must it feel to have a relationship last for years. To survive the ups and downs that life threw at you. How sweet it must feel to recognize the person meant for you on sight.

Could love at first sight be real? Alexandra hadn't given it much thought, but she supposed that it could exist in one form or another. She might be a romantic at heart, but she was also a realist. Maybe even a bit of a skeptic when it came to things like that. Even so, she wondered if there was a man she could fall in love with. If not at first sight, maybe after a few sightings.

*How about Nathan?*

That thought came from out of nowhere, startling her. Before she could try it on for size, the pianist began playing, indicating the start of the ceremony. While Alexandra and Jerilyn had been speaking, more guests had begun to arrive and talk quietly. Now a hush came over the room.

Alexandra turned to face the front just as the robed minister and the groom, who looked quite handsome in his tuxedo, stepped into the room and stood before the floral arch. Alexandra's attention was then drawn to Nathan, who was standing beside his brother. Although Miles was the groom, it was Nathan who attracted and held her attention.

She'd seen him in the tuxedo earlier, but that hadn't made her immune to the impact his appearance had on her. The jacket was tailored to fit his broad shoulders and then tapered to his trim waist. The pants fit his muscular thighs before coming to rest on his shiny black dress shoes. His posture was erect, befitting a man of his presence. It was impossible to tear her eyes away.

There was no sense denying the obvious. Alexandra stared down at her clasped hands. Then she looked up at Nathan, who turned at that moment to glance at her. Their eyes met and held. He smiled and her heart skipped a beat. Incredibly, the other people in the room seemed to disappear and the music faded to nothingness. It was as if Alexandra and Nathan were the only two people in the world.

That feeling shook her to her core and her palms began to sweat. There was no way she was going to start fantasizing about Nathan. Especially after he'd been perfectly clear that there was no romance in their future. He was focused on accomplishing his five-year plan for the ranch.

She was fine with that. Especially since she wasn't the least bit interested in giving her heart to anyone.

The romantic atmosphere must be getting to her and playing havoc with her emotions. Weddings, with their love songs and floral arrangements, were romantic by design. Love was being celebrated, so naturally her thoughts would travel down that path. Once she was in her normal environment, the foolish thoughts would vanish into thin air.

She felt a poke in the side and turned to see Jerilyn smiling at her. "You can fool some of the people in here, but you can't fool me. I can see what's going on between you and Nathan. You can't keep your eyes off each other."

Alexandra's mouth fell open as she tried to think of a suitable response. Nothing came to mind. Perhaps she not only fooled Jerilyn into thinking she and Nathan were dating. She had fooled herself.

"Don't worry. Your secret is safe with me." Jerilyn smiled and then winked. "For now."

The procession began and Alexandra turned her attention to the middle aisle. As she watched the wedding party enter, she tried to get a grip on her suddenly turbulent emotions. She couldn't fall for Nathan. That was a heartbreak waiting to happen.

She smiled as the flower girl and ring bearer walked down the aisle. The little girl looked positively angelic in her frilly dress and the little boy looked charming in his tuxedo.

When the wedding march played, Alexandra joined the others and stood as she watched the bride enter on her father's arm. Even from a distance, Alexandra could feel the happiness radiating from the other woman. Jillian's smile was luminous, and there was a look of unmistakable joy on her face. Alexandra had never seen a more beautiful bride.

Despite warning herself of the dangers of getting

swept up in the moment, the entire ceremony was just too beautiful and emotional for her to remain a dispassionate observer. Alexandra's heart overflowed as the bride and groom recited the vows they had written themselves. When Miles and Jillian jumped over the broom and then kissed, Alexandra rose to her feet, applauding with the rest of the guests. Overcome by emotion, she felt her eyes fill with tears, but swiped them away before they could stain her cheeks.

As the bridal party recessed down the aisle, Alexandra tried not to stare at Nathan, but she couldn't pull her gaze away. He still had the proud and happy expression on his face he'd worn as he'd watched his brother get married. He was obviously close to his family. Their relationship reminded her of the one she shared with her siblings.

"That was truly beautiful," Jerilyn said, stirring Alexandra from her musings.

"It truly was," Alexandra agreed easily. "They are so obviously in love. It's so easy to picture them living happily-ever-after."

"Yes. But they took the long and winding road to get here."

"What do you mean?" The bridal party had returned and were now standing at the front of the room. The ushers were at the back of the room, directing the guests row by row to go to greet the couple. The usher had not reached them, so Jerilyn and Alexandra had time to talk.

"Jillian and Miles dated for years. Everyone expected them to get married right out of college. But they didn't. At least not to each other." She waved her hand as if the detail was too insignificant to be of any concern.

Alexandra nodded, indicating that she was following the story.

"Well, neither Miles's nor Jillian's marriages lasted. But—did you notice the ring bearer and the flower girl?"

"Yes. They are so adorable."

"Aren't they? Well, Benji is Miles's son, and Lilliana is Jillian's daughter. So when they got back together, they got a little something extra. Now they're one happy family."

"That's so romantic," Alexandra said honestly. And it gave her hope. Not that she was carrying a torch for Owen. She wouldn't take him back even if he came with a lifetime supply of chocolate. But it was nice to see that people who belonged together eventually ended up together. It was nice to see that there was a way back and that one mistake—even one as big as marrying the wrong person— hadn't been able to stop true love.

The usher came up and directed them to join the line greeting the happy couple. When Alexandra reached the bridal party, she smiled and said hello. Nathan smiled when he reached him and brushed her hand gently. The slight touch was enough to send shivers dancing down her spine. This wedding was definitely playing havoc with her emotions. It was a good thing that she and Nathan had been clear about their intentions. They were only pretending to date in order to keep his mother off his case.

For the first time, she admitted that she could very easily fall in love with him. The thought was shocking, and she felt her knees weaken.

She somehow managed to get hold of herself enough to murmur "congratulations" to the bride and groom before returning to her seat. After the receiving line ended, Nathan joined Alexandra. She smiled up at him, trying to slow her rapidly beating heart.

"The bridal party took a lot of pictures yesterday and some before the ceremony, but the photographer still wants to take more before we move on to the reception. Do you mind waiting?"

"Not at all. I'll just sit here."

"Thanks." He flashed her a grin before returning to stand before the arch. The two photographers took numerous pictures of the wedding party before dismissing all but the bride and groom.

Nathan approached her once again, a smile on his face. As he drew nearer, Alexandra couldn't help but admire his handsome face and muscular body. It was indisputable that he was one of the most attractive men she had ever known. There was something about his aura that wouldn't allow her to resist him for any length of time.

When he was standing beside her, he reached out a hand. She took it and rose. His fingers were warm and strong as they wrapped around hers. There was unmistakable power in his grip.

"Where is the reception going to be held?"

"The resort has a beautiful ballroom."

"It can't possibly be more beautiful than this."

"Maybe. Maybe not. I'll let you be the judge. If you're ready, we can go there now."

Alexandra nodded. Though it was dangerous to her heart, she knew that she would follow Nathan anywhere.

## CHAPTER NINE

"MAY I HAVE this dance," Nathan said. The reception was in full swing, and the dance floor was rapidly filling. He had fulfilled his obligation as co-best man. He'd posed for even more pictures once Jillian and Miles entered the ballroom and had danced with the bridesmaid. Isaac had wanted to make the toast and Nathan had agreed. Isaac knew just what to say to amuse the audience all the while making the bride and groom happy. Nathan had never liked having the spotlight shine on him, so he was relieved when his official duties had been completed. Now it was time to party.

"I suppose so," Alexandra said, a smile on her face. He noticed that she smiled easily and often. It was a sincere smile that reflected her inner happiness. And it was quite disarming.

She placed her soft hand into his. He felt a spark of electricity at the contact. He was becoming increasingly attracted to her, so his reaction wasn't unexpected. Nor was it unwanted. Filled with anticipation of holding her in his arms again, he led her to the dance floor. The ballroom was enormous and even with the elaborately decorated tables spaced around the edge and the stage where the band was now playing, there was still plenty of room to dance. The band was playing a ballad and Nathan pulled Alexandra close, then wrapped his arms around her tiny waist.

He'd been looking forward to holding her next to him

from the moment she'd opened the door this afternoon and he'd seen her standing there. Dressed in a reddish dress that accentuated every inch of her body, she was quite easily the most beautiful woman he'd ever seen. Even in the sea of jewels and designer dresses, she stood out.

Alexandra's wraparound satin dress was demure, but there was no disguising her sexy body. Over the past few days, he'd tried to convince himself that the rightness he'd felt the last time they danced had been a figment of his imagination. Now, with her soft breasts pressed against his chest, he acknowledged that he hadn't exaggerated things. In fact, he might have undersold his reaction.

They moved together as if they had been dance partners for years as opposed to only one night before. This wasn't something that he did frequently, but he was willing to make an exception tonight. Truthfully, he had made several exceptions since Alexandra had become a part of his life.

That thought shocked him and he stopped dancing. Alexandra stepped back and gave him a questioning look. He got himself together and pulled her against him once more, and they began to sway to the music. Though his body moved in time to the beat, his mind was miles away. One question kept echoing though his brain. Why had he thought that Alexandra had become a part of his life? Sure, the notion held certain appeal—too much appeal for his comfort—but he had his plans, and she didn't fit into them.

He knew rationally that he could make a place for a woman in his life if he wanted to. But women needed time and attention. Two things that he was unable and unwilling to sacrifice. Any time he spent with a woman was time that he couldn't spend working on improving the ranch. Time that would delay implementation of his five-year plan.

Sacrificing his time was fine every once in a while. He did like the occasional break. And he wasn't opposed to a no-strings-attached fling here and there. After all, he wasn't a monk. But anything serious or long-term? That was a nonstarter. So why was he considering making an exception with Alexandra?

Maybe it was the environment. He'd been surrounded by wedding planning for months. All of that talk of love and happily-ever-after had taken its toll on him. Today— with the promises to love and cherish forever and songs about devotion—had been even more of the same. Even a single-minded businessman wasn't immune to the effects of being bombarded by romance nonstop.

But it was more than the perfume scented air, the abundant flowers, and the flowing champagne that was affecting his thinking. It was Alexandra.

Nathan inhaled deeply in an effort to clear his head. Instead he got a whiff of her intoxicating scent and found himself being swept up by his emotions again. Although it was the opposite of clearing his mind, Nathan breathed in again, allowing the scent to completely envelop him.

Nathan could try to resist her appeal, but he knew it was senseless to try to control his reaction. Apparently he was powerless when it came to Alexandra.

"Do you have a nickname?" he asked, blurting the first thing that came to his mind. Anything to stop his mind from traveling down the road it was going. "You know, like a shortened version of Alexandra?"

"Not now. When I was younger, my friends and family called my Lexi."

"*Lexi.* I like that. Why'd you stop using it?"

She shrugged, and he felt her smiling against his shoulder. "I grew up. When I started college, I wanted a more mature-sounding name. Lexi didn't seem professional enough to be a nurse's name. So I became Alexandra."

"I understand."

"What about you? Does anybody call you Nate?"

"Not if they expect me to answer."

She laughed, and he not only heard the sound, he felt it.

The song merged into the next. This one was a line dance, and Nathan reluctantly released Alexandra. He enjoyed the dance, but he much preferred slow dancing, where he would be able to hold her.

When the dance ended, Alexandra grabbed his hand. "I need a break."

"How about we get a drink?"

He turned and nearly ran into Isaac. Naturally his brother would appear at the worst time.

"Hi. I'm Nathan's brother Isaac." He held out his hand to Alexandra, who took it, and then he gestured to the woman standing beside him. "And this is Savannah, my fiancée."

"Nice to meet you both."

"Alexandra and I were just going to get a drink," Nathan said.

"That's a good idea," Isaac said. "But before you do that, you might want to introduce Alexandra to Mom and Dad."

"Right." He should have done that earlier. After all, he'd brought Alexandra with him in order to convince his mother he didn't need her interfering in his love life.

Isaac nodded, then he and Savannah walked away.

When they were alone, Nathan turned to Alexandra. He hoped she wasn't too uncomfortable with the idea.

She grinned and grabbed his arm. "I suppose it's time to put on the show."

"You're okay with this?"

"Of course. This is why you brought me, right?"

"Yes." But he was beginning to believe that wasn't the only reason. And that could be a problem.

Nathan led her over to where his parents sat, smiles on their faces. Nathan quickly made the introductions.

"It's so nice to meet you both," Alexandra said, her look encompassing his parents. "I've heard so many nice things about you."

"It's nice meeting you too," Michelle said. "Won't you sit down so we can talk?"

Nathan smothered a groan.

"They don't want to talk," Edward said. "These young people want to dance. And I would like a few more dances with my best girl too."

"Oh you." Michelle giggled and took the hand Edward held out to her. She glanced at Alexandra and Nathan. "Enjoy the rest of the night."

Nathan kissed his mother's cheek before leading Alexandra away.

"That wasn't too bad," Nathan said.

He introduced her to Miles and Jillian. They got their drinks and then returned to the dance floor. After a few dances, the leader of the band announced that the bride was about to throw the bouquet.

"Yeah, I definitely need to get off the floor," Alexandra said, picking up her pace.

"Oh no. All the single ladies are supposed to try to catch the bouquet. It's tradition."

"I'm not interested in getting married."

"Don't tell me that you believe that catching the bouquet has any type of special powers? Are you the superstitious type? Oooh." He waved his hands as if conjuring up a ghost.

"Not at all."

He leaned closer, teasing her. "Then what's the harm? What if none of the other single ladies get in line? Think about how sad Jillian will feel."

Alexandra shook her head. "You are incorrigible."

"So I've been told."

"I'm going to stand in the back and I'm not going to try to catch it."

"Famous last words."

Alexandra shooed Nathan away and then joined the women assembling in the middle of the dance floor. Although catching the bouquet was supposed to be good fun, it was clear from the way some of the others were boxing out that they were taking it quite seriously. Perhaps they really did believe that catching the bouquet was the first step toward catching the man.

Jillian held up the bouquet and then turned her back to the women who were clustered close together. Alexandra expected Jillian to pretend to throw the floral arrangement in order to amp up the tension, so she was surprised when the flowers went sailing through the air. And landed right in her hands.

THERE WAS A smattering of applause and some good-natured groaning as the other women walked away. Jillian and Alexandra posed for a few pictures before Alexandra returned to Nathan's side. He nodded his head toward the bouquet, a wide smile on his face.

"Don't say a word."

"Oh, but I have to. It looks like your plan went awry."

Alexandra shook her head. "I don't know how it happened. One minute I was standing there, way behind everyone, minding my own business."

"And the next?"

She held up the small bouquet, letting the flowers do the talking for her.

Nathan laughed and draped his arm over her shoulder, pulling her next to his side. They fit together so perfectly that for a moment she wished their relationship was real. They got their drinks and found a quiet corner to talk. After two songs, Alexandra set her empty glass on a table and shimmied her shoulders in a clear signal that she wanted to dance.

Alexandra and Nathan danced to just about every song, stopping only to sip some champagne when they got thirsty. By the time the party began to wind down, Alexandra was certain that she had never had a better time in her life. She was actually sorry for the night to come to an end.

She and Nathan recounted the events of the day as he drove her back home. They laughed and talked easily and she was surprised to realize that Nathan was parking in front of Aunt Rose's house.

"Wow. I can't believe we got here so soon," she said, managing to mask her disappointment.

"Time flies when you're having fun," Nathan quipped.

"True. I guess this means our time together has come to an end."

Nathan got out of the car, and Alexandra waited patiently while he circled it and then opened her door for her. She took his hand and let him help her from the car. When he didn't release her hand, she smiled to herself and held on to his.

Her heart began to pound as they climbed the stairs and approached the front door. Memories of the last time they'd said good-night played in her mind. Despite reminding herself that they'd agreed the kiss couldn't ever be repeated, her heart sped up in anticipation of the possibility. Their decision had made sense at the time, since they had no plans of seeing each other again. Now Alexandra wondered why she had ever thought the no-kiss rule was a good idea. Now that she was so close to Nathan that the heat from his body caressed hers, she couldn't imagine not wanting to kiss him. Just the thought of his lips capturing hers made her feel tingly all over.

Surely one little kiss wouldn't hurt anything. They could go back to their previous relationship afterward. The moment the thought crossed her mind, she knew she was lying. It wouldn't be one little kiss. If she had her way, it would be several extremely hot kisses. Heck, she was longing for a live and in color make-out session. If only they hadn't gotten out of the car, they could be necking like teenagers in his back seat. That thought made her laugh out loud.

"What's so funny?" Nathan asked, turning to face each other.

"You won't get it."

"Really? I have a great sense of humor."

"Now that's funny," she said, laughing again.

"You've hurt my feelings."

"I'm sorry." She didn't think he was being serious, but she could be wrong. They were standing in the shadows, so she couldn't see his face. The last thing she wanted to do was offend him. Not simply because she didn't want such a perfect day to end on a sour note, but because she liked him as a person and wouldn't want to hurt him.

"Prove it. Tell me what you found so funny."

"All right," she said. It didn't make sense to hide her feelings from him. And if she was lucky, he'd been thinking the same thing. A girl could hope. She took a deep breath and then blurted out, "I was thinking that we should have stayed in the car so we could make out."

He huffed out a laugh that did little to mask his surprise. "Wow. You just put it out there."

She shrugged. "You asked."

"That I did." He paused for several long seconds and

suddenly she felt anxious. Maybe honesty wasn't always the best policy.

"You can always forget I said anything."

"Why would I want to do that?" He reached out slowly, and she held her breath as she waited for his hand to caress her cheek. His touch was gentle. Sweet. Of their own volition, her eyes floated shut, and she leaned into his palm. He brushed his callused thumb over her lips and desire pooled in her stomach.

She forced her eyes open and looked at him. His eyes were dark with longing that made hers even stronger. "So what are we going to do?"

He moved even closer. So close that she could feel his heart beating. "What's the worst that could happen if we kiss? You know, one more for the road?"

"I can't think of even one negative thing," she whispered.

"Then let's go for it," he murmured, a second before his lips captured hers in a searing kiss that took her breath away. They'd kissed before, and the memory of that kiss had been etched in her mind. But compared to this one, that one had been a peck. She opened her mouth to him and his tongue swept inside. Moaning her pleasure, her tongue tangled and danced with his. Hungry for more, she pressed closer, molding her body against his.

She had no idea how much time passed, but when he began to pull away, gradually ending the kiss, she was gasping for breath. Slowly she became aware of her surroundings. They were standing on her aunt's porch. She straightened her dress and then leaned against his chest. His breath was labored, and she felt his chest rise and fall beneath her forehead.

After she'd regained her composure, she leaned back and glanced into his face. His eyes were just as intense as before. Maybe more so. Needing to lighten the mood and diminish the sexual attraction crackling between them, she smiled. "I knew we should have stayed in the car."

A startled expression crossed his face a moment before he barked out a laugh. "Making out in the car would definitely be a new one for me."

"Really?" She allowed her voice to reflect the skepticism she felt. He might be the serious "all work and no play" type now, but she didn't for a moment believe he'd always been that way. After all, he'd been a teenage boy with raging hormones once. She couldn't believe the girls in town hadn't been all over him back then. "I find that hard to believe."

"Perhaps I should have said since I reached adulthood."

"That sounds more believable if a little bit…"

"A little bit what? Boring?"

"Sad. Even at our age we should experience the joy— and terror of being discovered—of necking in the back seat of a car."

He laughed. "I'll keep that in mind."

She eased back, slowly increasing the distance between them. When no part of her body enjoyed the pleasure of touching his, she sighed. "I suppose we need to say goodnight now."

"Yes. I really enjoyed spending time with you. Maybe we can do it again sometime."

"I'm willing whenever you are." Alexandra realized that saying that made her sound desperate, but it was too late to call the words back. Besides, she'd only spoken the truth. She would enjoy spending more time with Nathan. They were both clear about where they stood, so neither of them would have to worry about getting a broken heart.

What more could they ask for?

# CHAPTER TEN

"So, YOU AND ALEXANDRA?"

Nathan turned to look at his brother. Isaac was leaning against the fence, an exceedingly annoying expression on his face. Since Miles was honeymooning in Fiji, Nathan would be stuck dealing with Isaac on his own for the next ten days. Although he had matured a lot since Mia and Savannah had come into his life, his core personality hadn't changed. He still possessed that pesky little brother attitude that Nathan expected him to have at ninety.

"I brought her to the wedding Saturday. You saw her."

"And I noticed the way that you wouldn't let anyone else near her all night. I barely had the chance to say two words to her."

"That's not true. She was free to interact with whomever she chose."

"But when the real party started—you know dancing and talking—you were glued to her side. She might not have noticed, but I saw the way you mean mugged every man who even looked like he might come over to talk to her or ask her to dance."

Nathan couldn't deny that. But he wasn't going to admit it either. His time with Alexandra had been limited, and he hadn't wanted to share her with anyone. "She was my date, so I was responsible for her. She's new to town. She doesn't know which guys are serious and which ones would try to take advantage of her."

"So you were doing your civic duty?" Isaac laughed. "How big of you. We both know that every guy there was a stand-up type. Or they wouldn't have been invited."

Of course he knew that. But he'd felt strangely protective of her. More than that, he'd felt possessive, which was ridiculous. She didn't belong to him. They weren't involved romantically. Besides, he didn't believe that a person could own another. People stayed in relationships because they wanted to. That is the only way it could work.

"Did you want something?"

Isaac's grin spread slowly. "Just to tell you that I like Alexandra and to invite the two of you to have dinner with me and Savannah."

Nathan hooked the heel of his boot through the fence and thought for a second. He liked Savannah. She was the perfect woman for his brother. He enjoyed her company and thought Alexandra would too.

Going to dinner could be fun. It would also be a good way to keep his mother off his back. They hadn't had Sunday dinner this past week, and Nathan had been looking forward to having a reprieve. It hadn't come. His mother had called him before noon Sunday. She'd grilled him about Alexandra for so long he was surprised he didn't have sear lines on his body.

After seeing them together at the wedding, his mother had decided that they belonged together. Now Michelle would stop trying to set him up with a friend's cousin's next-door neighbor. Mission accomplished. But he might have succeeded too well, because now his mother had zeroed in on Alexandra. He could tell that she was already planning their future. She'd dropped hints about him bringing Alexandra around so she could get to know her better.

Although Alexandra had agreed to go to the wedding with him as part of the charade, he wasn't sure she would be amenable to carrying it on endlessly. After all, she'd been clear that she wasn't interested in a relationship. That's why he'd invited her to the wedding. She was a safe date who wouldn't be interested in trying to become a part of his life. If he asked her to continue the pretense for a while longer, she might think he was trying to intrude on hers.

He thought he'd been clever. Now it looked like he had outsmarted himself. If he told his mother that he and Alexandra weren't dating, she would start setting him up again. He didn't want to live through that. Just the thought was enough to make him break out in hives.

There was only one thing to do. He needed to convince Alexandra to extend their pretend relationship. She'd been so leery when he'd mentioned the charade and he'd been afraid she wouldn't go along with his plan. But since it was only make-believe, she'd gone along with it.

But the pretend relationship was starting to feel like a real one. That was a problem. Neither of them wanted anything that was remotely like a commitment. If he made too many demands on her time, she might back out. This was going to take a masterful negotiation.

"Let me get in touch with Alexandra and get back to you."

"Whoa. That is totally unexpected. I thought we had moved past that part of the conversation."

"We can. If your invitation wasn't sincere, that's fine."

Isaac laughed and raised his hands. "Oh no you don't, Nathan. You aren't going to weasel out that easily. Talk to Alexandra and get back to me."

"I'll let you know." He pushed away from the fence and headed for his horse. "Let's get back to work. Time's a wasting."

As they worked, Nathan's mind kept wandering to Alexandra and the last time he'd seen her. She'd been so radiant and full of life. Just being around her had made his heart beat faster. Thinking that she wouldn't be a part of his life had left him feeling empty. Bereft even, something he hadn't expected.

He hadn't wanted their time to come to an end, but he'd known that they couldn't pursue a relationship. So there was no reason for them to keep seeing each other.

Now he could spend time with her without having the expectations that accompanied a relationship. That is, if he could get her to agree. Alexandra's reluctance to date had just as much to do with time constraints as it did with an unwillingness to risk heartbreak. Although he could promise that her heart would be safe—he didn't want her love and wasn't giving his—a fake relationship could take just as much time as a real one.

Somehow, he would have to persuade her that he wouldn't take up too much of her time. Now that he had a reason to talk to Alexandra again, he couldn't wait for the workday to end so he could phone her. Just the thought of hearing her sultry voice sent blood pulsing through his veins. So naturally, they kept finding holes in the fence, and repairing them made the day drag on. He was relieved by the time they'd finished, and he stepped into his house.

After a quick shower followed by an equally quick dinner, Nathan grabbed his phone and dialed Alexandra's number. His heart sped up as the phone rang and he took a deep breath. He didn't want to sound like a teenager whose voice was changing, squeaking whenever he talked to a girl that he had a crush on.

The call went to voice mail. Disappointed, he left a message. The depth of his disappointment gave him pause. Perhaps it was a good thing that she didn't answer. He didn't want to get too attached to her. Maybe he needed to take a step back and rethink this plan.

"WHAT ARE YOU doing here?" Lynn, one of the night shift nurses, asked Alexandra on Tuesday night as she came into the locker room. "Isn't this your day off?"

"It was," Alexandra said, turning to look at her friend and coworker. "Carla had an emergency and needed to switch schedules, so I came in for her."

"Is she still having trouble with her ex?"

"Sadly, yes," Alexandra said. Although she was disappointed that Chloe wouldn't have a father in her life, she was relieved not to have this kind of drama. Alexandra reached into her locker and took out a bag. "I didn't have plans. But now my shift is over. I have one thing to do, and then I'm going home."

"What's in the bag?" Lynn asked, draping her stethoscope over her neck.

"It's something for Emma. I'm still trying to lift her spirits."

"That's nice. I hope it works. I'm fresh out of ideas."

Emma was a seven-year-old who'd been injured in a car accident. The little girl hadn't been responding to treatment. Worse, she showed little interest in trying and refused to cooperate. "I'll let you know how it works."

Alexandra closed her locker, slapped a red hat on her head, picked up the bag and then headed to Emma's room. The girl's mother, Robin, glanced up when Alexandra stepped inside. The worried expression on her face morphed into one of confusion.

"Ho, ho, ho," Alexandra said loudly. "Merry Christmas."

Emma had been staring listlessly out the window. Now she turned to look at Alexandra. "It's not Christmastime."

"It's not?" Alexandra said, doing her best to sound perplexed. "Are you sure?"

Emma giggled. "Yes. Christmas is in December. That is not now."

"Oh no. How embarrassing. And I have on this hat." Alexandra pointed to the red elf hat on her head. "I suppose I should take it off."

Emma nodded. "Yes."

Alexandra removed the hat and set it on the empty table. "What am I going to do with this?"

"With what?" Emma pushed herself into a sitting position.

Alexandra pulled a gaily wrapped box from the bag and held it up. "It has your name on it. Do you suppose Santa got confused too?"

"Can that happen?" Emma asked, looking at her mother.

"Maybe," Robin said.

"I should probably give it to you," Alexandra said. "I don't want Santa to get angry with us."

Emma's arm and hand had been injured and she hadn't been participating in her therapy. Now she reached out for the box. Alexandra stepped up to the bed and handed over the package.

Emma placed it on her lap. "I wonder what it is."

"Open it and see," Alexandra urged.

Emma's mother reached out to help her, and Alexandra shook her head *no*.

Alexandra had worked with Emma's physical therapist, who'd wrapped the box. Now Alexandra watched as the little girl struggled. It took some effort, but eventually she managed to remove the paper and tape.

"A doll! It's a doll." Emma turned the box so her mother could look. "It's a new doll."

"Wow. That's wonderful."

"I want to play with her."

"That sounds like a good plan," Alexandra said. "What are you going to name her?"

"Jenna. That's my sister's name."

"And it's a good one."

Alexandra hung out for a few more minutes, watching as Emma played with the doll. She was livelier than she'd been since she'd come to the hospital and was actually using her hands as much as she could.

Satisfied that the little girl was on the mend, Alexandra picked up the hat. "Well, I need to get going. Have fun with your doll."

Emma nodded. "Bye."

"Thank you so much," Robin said.

"You're welcome. Good night."

Alexandra was tired but happy as she headed home. She checked in on Chloe, grateful that her little girl was safe and healthy. Then she took a quick shower and pulled on a pair of her comfiest pajamas. While she ate dinner, she checked her messages. When she heard Nathan's voice, her heart skipped a beat.

She debated about whether it was too late to call and then decided to take a chance. "Is it a good time?" she asked instead of saying hello.

"It is the best time."

His answer made her smile. "Sorry I missed your call. I switched days with a friend."

"Are you tired?"

"No. I took a shower and now I've got my second wind."

"Great." She heard him inhale and then blow it out. "I was wondering if you are free to talk."

"Of course. We're talking now."

"Actually, I was hoping we could talk in person."

"That sounds ominous." She managed to keep her sudden stress from her voice.

"It's not. Everything is fine."

"Okay. Then come on over."

"Great. I'm on my way. I'll be there in a little while."

Alexandra ended the call and changed into a pair of faded jeans, a purple top and purple socks. She pulled a comb through her hair and then added a purple floral headband to hold it away from her face.

Her mind raced wildly as she waited impatiently for Nathan to arrive. Was he going to tell her that their friendship was over? If so, why would he do that in person? And why was that such a big deal?

Fortunately, the doorbell rang before her mind could travel too far down that road, and she walked to the door.

"Come on in," she said, softly. She held out her arm, gesturing for him to precede her into the living room. "Would you like something to eat or drink?"

Nathan shook his head and sat on the sofa where she'd indicated and looked around the room. With high ceilings, crown molding, and comfortable old furniture, the room was charming and cozy. He took a deep breath and forced himself to relax. "Maybe in a little while. But you go ahead if you want something."

"I have my cocoa." She picked up a mug and then took a swallow. "I love hot cocoa. I can't get enough of the stuff."

He couldn't get enough of watching the way her tongue darted out and dabbed at the tiniest bit of chocolate at the corner of her mouth. It was so erotic that he began to sweat. Perhaps he should have taken her up on her offer. He could use a cold drink right about now.

She leaned back against the chair and then crossed her ankles. She looked relaxed and he found himself relaxing too. It was amazing how at ease he felt with her. It felt completely natural to unwind with her at the end of the day.

"So, what did you want to talk about?"

He was glad to get right to the point. "I have a proposal for you."

She pressed her hands against her chest, smiled, and batted her eyes. "This is so sudden. I thought we were just friends." His breath stalled. Before he could say anything, she burst out laughing. "Sorry. I couldn't resist. Breathe before you pass out."

He inhaled. "You really are funny."

She grinned, clearly still amused. "You just looked so shocked. Then you looked like you might keel over at any minute. You know I was just teasing, right? We agreed that neither of us wants a relationship."

"I know we said that. But maybe I could change your mind."

Her eyes widened. "About having a relationship? Are you serious?"

Now it was his turn to laugh. "No. I was thinking about the wedding. We convinced a lot of people that we were a couple."

She nodded slowly, clearly wary.

"We could keep a lot of people off my back if we pretended for a while longer."

"By people, you mean your mother?"

He nodded. "As long as my mother thinks that we're involved, I won't have to worry about a strange woman showing up at Sunday dinner."

She looked a bit skeptical. "And you believe you can avoid this if I pretend to be your girlfriend."

He heard the confusion in her voice and was instantly reminded that he'd thought the idea was ludicrous. But it was out there now. "Yes. That's the plan."

"I don't know, Nathan. It sounds complicated."

"It isn't."

"Sure it is. It's not as if your mother is the only person in town. Other people will see us as well. Eventually our friends and my coworkers will hear about our supposed relationship. That's a complication if I ever heard of one. And that's just the beginning."

"Are you worried about a potential boyfriend hearing that you're involved?" He didn't know why the thought of Alexandra being with another man irritated him, but it did.

"Not even a little bit. I have no plans of seeing another man. A relationship is the last thing that I want."

The relief he felt was outsized. And disturbing. This pretend relationship shouldn't matter that much to him. If Alexandra decided she wanted to have a real relationship in the future, that was her right. It had nothing to do with him.

"Then why do you think this will be complicated?"

"Because. You can't just tell your mother that we're dating and have that be the end of it. You live on the same ranch. If you go about your regular routine, she'll know. In order for this to work, she has to see us together. That means we have to spend time together."

"I know. Is that going to be a problem?"

ALEXANDRA INHALED DEEPLY before answering. It didn't take a genius to know that this was not going to be as simple as Nathan believed. Things like this never were. Pretending to date would be playing with fire. No matter how hard they tried to ignore the simmering attraction between them, it was real. The kisses they'd shared were the hottest of her life. Pretending to be involved romantically could lead to complications. Even knowing that she could get burned, she was hard-pressed to think of kissing Nathan as a negative.

Alexandra realized that Nathan was still waiting for her

response. Before she could give him an answer, she needed more details. "How long would this last?"

"I don't know. I guess until we convince my mother that we're serious. She needs to believe that I'm willing to have more to my life than the ranch. Once she's convinced, we can stage a breakup."

"I don't know. I don't need that kind of drama. Are you sure there isn't some other reason you want to do this?"

He smirked. "You know, I am quite the catch."

She laughed. "I don't doubt it."

"I suppose having a girlfriend could help with business. Occasionally I have business dinners and a date would help."

She nodded. "I can do social events. At least on some weekends with enough notice."

"This goes both ways. I'm willing to be your pretend boyfriend whenever you need one."

"I'm not expecting to need one, but thanks for the offer."

He rose, paced to the window and back. Then he sat on the edge of the couch. She'd never seen him so nervous. Obviously this meant a lot to him. "So...will you do it?"

Alexandra knew she should say no, but she couldn't do him like that. He was kind and generous and he needed this favor. And to be honest, she liked spending time with Nathan and wouldn't mind seeing him more often. She was just afraid of getting hurt.

But this plan could be the best of both worlds. She could spend time with Nathan—enjoying his quick wit—and hopefully his hot kisses—without risking her heart.

"Well," Nathan prompted when she didn't respond.

She sucked in a breath. If she agreed, there would be no turning back. But then, she wouldn't want to. "I'm in. I'll be your pretend girlfriend for as long as you need."

His brilliant smile set butterflies free in her stomach,

and she felt tingly all over. "Now we need to put our plan into action."

"How about now?" She flashed him a saucy grin. "Do we need to synchronize our watches like they did in old movies?"

He chuckled. "I think we can skip that. When are you available to date?"

"My social life is limited to girls' night out every couple of weeks, so other than work, I'm free most of the time. Of course, I have a child who needs a lot of my attention."

"I don't want to take away your time with your daughter. In fact, if you're okay with me being around your daughter, I don't see a reason why she can't be a part of our dates."

"Really?"

"Yes. If we were dating for real, I would want to have a relationship with her. As much as you would allow."

Tears suddenly pricked her eyes and Alexandra blinked them away. She hoped Nathan hadn't noticed. She knew that Nathan was kind, but she was still caught unaware by how considerate he was. Owen hadn't been interested in Chloe, so Nathan's willingness to welcome her daughter into his life was especially touching.

"I think that would be nice."

"Great." He paused and inhaled. When he spoke again, his voice was husky. "I don't have kids, and my experience is limited to my nieces and nephew. But you can trust me. Chloe will always be safe with me."

"I appreciate you saying that. But you don't have to worry about being alone with Chloe. Since we're only pretend dating, we'll always be together."

Chloe was one of the reasons that Alexandra didn't want to get involved with a man. She didn't want her little girl to become attached to someone who might not stay in her life. Alexandra would rather be alone than break her daughter's heart. She knew letting her daughter get close to Nathan was risky. But in this instance, she believed the benefit of having another person around to love her was worth the risk. After all, she didn't want her daughter to become afraid to love.

Besides, Alexandra didn't expect their fake relationship to last long enough for Chloe to become attached to Nathan. A few dates here and there should be enough to convince Nathan's mother that he had more in his life than work.

"I also know that you're worried about letting Chloe get too close to me. You don't have to be. No matter what, I'll always take care of your little girl. Her heart will be safe with me."

Alexandra's vision blurred and she blinked. This pretend relationship was becoming more emotional than she'd anticipated. It was time to get back to the purely pragmatic issues.

"We should do something together soon," Alexandra said. Just saying the words made her heart pound and for a brief moment she second-guessed her decision to agree to this plan. One thing was certain, she and Nathan couldn't kiss again. Alexandra might have a lot of willpower, but it took more than willpower to control her heart. It would be too easy to fall for Nathan.

"What do you have in mind?"

"I had a great time visiting the ranch. I think Chloe would enjoy seeing the horses. That is, if you think that it's safe." And Chloe's presence would keep them from possibly becoming too affectionate.

"Remember, I grew up on the ranch. I was sitting on a horse in front of my father when I was younger than she is. My nieces and nephew have already been on horses with my brothers."

"Are you saying that you want to put Chloe on a horse?" Alexandra couldn't disguise her shock.

"Yes. Unless you're opposed to the idea."

"I've never been on a horse, so I certainly don't think that I can comfortably hold her."

He laughed, and the robust sound sent shivers down her spine.

Oh, she was walking a line here. It would be so easy to fall for him.

"I wasn't going to suggest that. If you're okay with it, I'll hold her on the horse with me."

"I think she might like it."

"And what about you? Would you like it?"

"Riding on a horse with you?" The image his words created in her mind was quite enticing. She could imagine how good it would feel to sit in front of him and lean back against his strong chest. How wonderful it would feel to be close enough to inhale his masculine scent while the heat from his body kept hers warm.

"That's not what I meant, but now that you mention it…" His voice lowered seductively, and his eyes appeared even darker.

Alexandra swallowed before answering. Even then, her voice was barely louder than a whisper. "I think that I can ride on my own. And I would love seeing Chloe on a horse in front of you."

"Then how about Saturday?"

"That works for me."

"Then it's a date."

## *CHAPTER ELEVEN*

ALEXANDRA SET CHLOE onto the floor before she ran to open the door. They were going to visit the Montgomery ranch today. Although Alexandra was perfectly capable of driving and had offered to do so, Nathan had insisted on picking them up. This is what he'd do if they were dating for real. According to him, they would never fool his mother if he acted out of character.

Dressed in a blue plaid shirt that emphasized his muscular torso and faded jeans, Nathan looked like he'd stepped out of a men's magazine. He smiled, and her heart nearly burst from her chest. It was so sweet and tender that she could almost believe that he was truly interested in her.

Shaking her head at such a foolish thought, she smiled back. "Welcome. Thank you so much for coming to pick us up."

"It is a date," he said, as if that explained everything. And to him it did.

"I suppose it is."

"And if this was a real date, I would do this too." Before she could guess his intent, he leaned over and brushed a kiss against her cheek. His gentle touch was devastating. Electricity shot through her body and her temperature rose at least five degrees. He pulled back and then looked at her, a twinkle in his eyes. "I hope that was okay to do."

"If we are going to make this look real, we need to stay in character at all times."

He smiled and nodded. Alexandra had no idea what it would be like to date Nathan, but if this was an example of how he treated a woman, it must be wonderful.

Alexandra led him into the front room. Chloe was standing, using the coffee table to keep her balance. She looked up and flashed a snaggletoothed grin. Alexandra scooped her up and then turned so that her little girl could get a look at Nathan.

She believed that you could tell a lot about a person by how they treated children. Nathan leaned over and smiled at Chloe. "Hello, Chloe. My name is Nathan."

Chloe grinned and then leaned her face into Alexandra's breast. After a moment, she turned her head and peeked at Nathan. Alexandra had a busy life and frequently took Chloe with her when she ran errands, so her daughter had been around many people. It was rare for her to be shy, so Alexandra wasn't sure what to make of her daughter's behavior. After a few seconds, Chloe lifted her head, looked at Nathan, and babbled a few syllables at him.

"Is that right?" Nathan asked.

Chloe nodded and chattered some more.

Alexandra watched with pleasure as Nathan and Chloe interacted. After a moment, Nathan stood to his full height, then took a good look at Alexandra and Chloe. He grinned. "You two look so cute."

*Cute* wasn't what Alexandra had been going for, at least for herself, but she tried not to feel disappointed by his comment. After all, he wasn't her real boyfriend. She'd been feeling a little bit frivolous today, so she'd dressed herself and Chloe in the same color. They were each wearing orange tops and blue jeans. Alexandra had found a cute pair of cowboy boots and a cowboy hat for Chloe.

"Thanks. I thought this would work in case we took pictures."

"Oh, we're definitely taking a few pictures to memorialize the day. Especially since this is Chloe's first time on a horse."

"Well then, let's get this day started."

Alexandra nodded and the trio left on their adventure.

Nathan removed the car seat from Alexandra's car and then secured it in the back seat of his car. Once Chloe was settled in her seat, Alexandra and Nathan got inside. Nathan started the car and then paired his phone to the car's sound system. Children's music began to play through the speaker.

Alexandra glanced at Nathan. "This is a surprise."

"I told you, I have a kids' playlist. My nieces and nephew like listening to it, so I figured Chloe would too."

Apparently Nathan's thoughtfulness was limitless. "She is starting to appreciate music. This is one of her favorite songs."

Chloe was too young to sing, but she made happy sounds and clapped.

Nathan flashed her a wicked grin before turning his attention back to the road. "Quiet as it's kept, a few of these songs are starting to grow on me. I've caught myself singing one every once in a while."

"A couple of them are quite catchy."

"It was a bit unsettling to find myself singing about being a pizza and a family of sharks at first but now I just go with it."

Alexandra laughed. "It takes a big man to admit that he likes kids' songs."

"Hold on a minute. I didn't say I liked listening to them.

I just said that they pop into my mind and out of my mouth at the strangest time."

"Well, I'm glad we got that straight," Alexandra teased. "I would hate to ruin your reputation as a serious rancher and hard businessman."

"Is that my reputation?"

"You don't know?"

He shrugged. "It's hard to know what others think about you. It's generally not something they discuss with you."

"True. Does having that reputation bother you?"

"I don't see why it should. I am focused on running the ranch."

"Is that enough for you?"

"It is for now."

She nodded. She knew that was true. He wouldn't need her to pretend to be his girlfriend otherwise. He would have a real one. One day, after he'd accomplished his business goals, he would find a woman to love for real and stop pretending.

That was one more reason why Alexandra couldn't allow herself to forget that this relationship was only make-believe.

NATHAN TURNED ONTO the road leading to the ranch and then drove straight to his house. After he parked, Alexandra got out of the car and then helped Chloe from the car seat. As he watched the mother and daughter duo, he felt a strange stirring near his heart. There was something about being around the two of them that filled him with a sense of peace. Not that peace was lacking in his life. It wasn't.

He didn't want to waste time pondering his feelings and trying to figure them out. He had a full day of fun planned. Before they headed for the stables, he wanted to drop the baby gear in the house. He grabbed up the assorted paraphernalia that babies needed and then led the way up the stairs.

They stepped inside and he dropped Chloe's play mat and bag of toys beside the front door. Though Alexandra had only been to his house once, it felt as if she belonged here.

"Would you like something to eat? Drink?"

Alexandra shook her head. "No."

"In that case, we should take Chloe out to see the horses."

Alexandra smiled brightly and his stomach did a ridiculous flip-flop. "I'm looking forward to seeing them too. And the cows. I had such a good time before. I couldn't stop thinking about it."

"Why didn't you say something? I told you that you could come back anytime. I meant it."

The look on her face nearly broke his heart as he realized that she hadn't believed he'd meant it when he said she was always welcome. He wondered how many times she had been disappointed by someone who'd broken a promise to her. Chloe's father would have to be at the top of the list.

What kind of man deceived a woman as sweet as Alexandra then abandoned his own child? How could a man live with himself when he had no idea if his child—his own flesh and blood—was safe and warm? How could he function without knowing if that child had enough to eat?

"Is something wrong?" Alexandra asked. Her soft voice was troubled, and her normally smooth brow was wrinkled.

No doubt his unpleasant thoughts were written all over his face. He forced his disgust for the other man away and smiled. He didn't want to waste time with Alexandra thinking about someone who wasn't worth it. "Not at all.

Everything is perfect. Whenever you're ready, we can go to the stable."

"I'm ready now." Alexandra picked up her daughter and looked at her. "Do you want to see a horsey?"

Chloe babbled and grabbed a fistful of Alexandra's hair and gave it a tug. Alexandra winced and tried to work her hair free.

"Do you need some help?" Nathan asked, even though he was unsure what good he could do.

At the sound of his voice, Chloe turned in his direction, pulling Alexandra's hair even harder.

"Yes," Alexandra said.

In a flash, Nathan was at her side. He leaned over and tried to free Alexandra's hair. He didn't want to hurt Chloe by being too rough, but he didn't like seeing Alexandra in pain. How could he help one without hurting the other? "What should I do?"

He realized that asking the question probably made him look foolish. Truth be told, he did suddenly feel incompetent. Not at all like the man with the plan.

"If you could hold Chloe, I can work my hair free from her fingers."

"That I can do." He reached out and took the little girl into his arms. He held her gingerly, careful not to squeeze her too tight. "Come here for a minute, Chloe."

The baby gave him a long look and then settled into his chest. She didn't loosen her grip on Alexandra's hair, so Alexandra had no choice but to come along. Nathan inhaled and got a whiff of her perfume. It was light and sexy. Tantalizing. His mind was immediately filled with erotic images, and it took immense effort to force them away. He was supposed to be helping Alexandra, not fantasizing about kissing her senseless and then making love to her until they were both weak.

Once he had Chloe firmly in his arms, Alexandra reached up and began to free her hair from her daughter's hand. She opened the little fingers one by one and then pulled her thick hair away. Chloe laughed and then clapped her chubby hands in pleasure, oblivious to the pain that she'd caused her mother.

Alexandra stood to her full height, which was several inches shorter than his. Her body might be small, but the impact it had on his was enormous. The heat from her body reached out and wrapped around him, pulling him nearer to her. Like a moth drawn to a flame, he was powerless to resist. Their eyes met and he froze, unable to do anything other than stare into hers. Her eyes were a rich brown, and suddenly they were filled with unmistakable longing. The urge to kiss her was strong. Before he could move closer to her, he felt a hard slap on his face.

He jerked.

"No, Chloe. No hitting," Alexandra said. "I'm so sorry."

Nathan just laughed. Perhaps Chloe had been able to read his mind and hadn't approved of the thoughts he was having about her mother. "Don't worry about it."

Alexandra stepped away, then gathered her gorgeous hair into a messy ponytail on top of her head. A pang hit him as he realized just how much he'd liked seeing her hair float free around her face and shoulders, shifting as she moved. But then, it appealed to Chloe too. No doubt she would grab a fistful the first opportunity that she got.

Nathan nodded toward Alexandra's hair. "Does she pull it often?"

"Yes. She's a regular Ms. Grabby Hands. That's why I no longer wear earrings or necklaces around her. I took a chance and left my hair down today. I was trying to be cute. Clearly that was a mistake I won't make again soon."

"You're just as beautiful either way," he blurted out

before he could think the better of it. It seemed like the right thing to say. Something a real boyfriend would say. But would a fake boyfriend compliment her appearance when there was no one else around to hear him? No one else over the age of one, that is.

"Thank you." Her voice was barely above a whisper. Her surprised yet gentle smile swept away all of his concerns. Nathan didn't know how many people commented on her appearance these days. In his mind, she was worthy of compliments every day. She was the most beautiful woman he'd ever laid eyes on. Though she was physically stunning, she was equally as beautiful on the inside.

They stood beside each other, silently assessing the other for a moment. When he realized that he was becoming hypnotized by her, he blinked and stepped back, creating a safe distance between them. Her nearness was wreaking havoc with his mind, affecting him in ways he hadn't anticipated. "Come on. Let's go see the horses."

She nodded and reached out for her daughter. "I can take Chloe if you want."

"That's not necessary. She doesn't weigh a thing. Besides, I think that she likes me. Don't you, sweetie?"

Chloe smiled and then leaned her head against his chest. This little one was quickly stealing his heart.

When they stepped outside, he set Chloe on his shoulders, something his nieces and nephew loved. There was something about being high enough to see everything that appealed to the little ones whose view was generally more limited. As expected, Chloe chortled gleefully and kicked her heels against his chest.

He was wearing a cowboy hat, so she wasn't able to grab his hair. Not that it was as long as Alexandra's.

"Is she okay?" Alexandra asked.

He heard the concern in her voice and smiled at her.

"I won't let her fall. I have her by the heels with one hand and my other is behind her back. She's perfectly safe."

"I know. I guess it's the mother in me."

"I can set her down if that would make you more comfortable."

She glanced at her daughter, who was babbling and having the time of her life. "No. I trust you."

Those three little words pierced his chest and touched a place in his heart that he hadn't known existed. He didn't know why Alexandra's trust meant so much to him, but it did. Perhaps it was knowing that someone had broken her trust along with her heart. He didn't know.

He was determined to prove himself worthy of that trust.

# CHAPTER TWELVE

ALEXANDRA ORDERED HERSELF to calm down as she walked beside Nathan in the stable. Her heart had started to race the moment that he helped her free her hair from Chloe's strong little fingers, and it hadn't slowed yet. He'd been standing so close that if she had moved even one centimeter in his direction, they would have been touching. For one blissful moment, she'd thought he might kiss her. Thought she would let him. Thankfully Chloe had broken the moment before Alexandra did something stupid that she would regret.

Nathan wasn't her real boyfriend. She didn't know why she was having such a hard time remembering that and behaving accordingly. It was easy to remember when he was far away from her. It was only a problem when he was near—like when their eyes had met and she'd been captured by his gaze. There was no way around it. Nathan Montgomery was the stuff that fantasies were made of.

Life wasn't a fantasy. There were no fairy godmothers waving magic wands and turning pumpkins into carriages.

Alexandra looked over at Nathan. He was laughing up at Chloe who was clearly thrilled to be sitting on his broad shoulders. The sight made Alexandra's heart ache for all that her little girl was missing by not having her father in her life. Alexandra knew that lots of children were being raised in single-parent homes and that they were happy.

There was no reason Chloe wouldn't thrive as long as she had Alexandra's support.

The expression on Nathan's face as he looked at Chloe touched Alexandra's heart. Clearly it was important to him that Chloe enjoyed herself.

A horse neighed. Chloe let out an excited squeal and craned her neck, trying to find the animal. She twisted on Nathan's shoulders and Alexandra's breath caught in her throat. Before she could gasp, Nathan had swung Chloe around and was now holding her against his chest. Her back was against his body so she could look at the animals without having to turn around. Chloe stretched out her arms, trying to touch the massive animal.

"It looks like she's a fan of horses."

"Looks like," Alexandra agreed.

"If you hold her for a minute, I'll saddle a couple for us. I figure a short ride around the corral will be just right for this little one."

Nathan turned and closed the distance between them. Alexandra admired his wide shoulders and muscular chest. When she realized she was staring, her cheeks got hot, and she glanced away. Once again she reminded herself that their relationship was only pretend. Not only were they not dating now, they wouldn't be dating in the future. Even so, she couldn't stop her heart from pounding as he came near. Nor could she prevent the tingles that skipped up and down her spine when their hands brushed.

He took care to place Chloe in Alexandra's arms and made sure that Alexandra had a secure hold on the baby before stepping away.

Alexandra watched as he walked away, noting that he looked just as good from behind as he did from the front. They might only be pretending to be involved, but her body was feeling the attraction for real.

Nathan moved quickly and efficiently as he put a blanket on the back of each horse, followed quickly by a saddle. Once he'd tightened everything, he grabbed the reins and led the animals through a wide door and into the corral. He looked over his shoulder and smiled at Alexandra. Her heart leaped in reply.

"Come on out here."

Chloe babbled a reply as if speaking for herself as well as Alexandra.

"Coming," Alexandra replied, walking into the corral. The dirt was packed and felt secure under her feet. Even so, she was glad she'd worn her cowboy boots.

When Alexandra reached Nathan, she smiled at him. "How are we going to do this?"

"Let me show you how to mount the horse. You can practice getting on and off. Once you're sure that you can get on by yourself, you can hold Chloe while I get on Excalibur's back. Then I'll hold her while you get on Snowflake. How does that sound?"

"It sounds like a plan." If she could pull it off.

Alexandra held Chloe while Nathan demonstrated how to get on the horse's back. He moved smoothly. Skillfully. The confidence that he demonstrated was proof that he'd done this thousands of times over the year. And it was a complete turn-on.

He swung off the horse's back and stood beside Alexandra. He took Chloe and then smiled. "Now you try. Put your left foot into the stirrup and then swing your right leg over Snowflake's back. I'll be right here in case you need assistance."

Alexandra inhaled a deep breath and then put her foot into the stirrup as Nathan had instructed. She grabbed the reins and then swung her right leg over the horse. When she was sitting in the saddle, she looked around and *whoa*. She was up high. The horse moved beneath her, and she gasped. Then Snowflake stilled. Alexandra smiled. It wasn't that bad. Actually it wasn't bad at all. She kind of liked it. Chloe must have felt the same way when she'd been on Nathan's shoulders.

She slid off the way that she'd watched Nathan dismount.

"Well?" he asked.

"Piece of cake."

"I thought you'd feel that way. You're a natural." With that, he handed over Chloe and then swung up on Excalibur's back. His horse was positively enormous, but Nathan was totally at ease on it. He held the reins in one hand and then leaned over for Chloe. Alexandra lifted up her child and watched with a bit of trepidation as he took her daughter into his arms and settled her on the saddle in front of him. Chloe giggled and wiggled her whole body in excitement.

"Well, we don't have to wonder if she likes horses. She's definitely a ranch child at heart," Nathan said.

"Apparently." Alexandra started to get on Snowflake's back. At the last minute, she pulled out her phone and snapped a few pictures of Chloe and Nathan on Excalibur's back for posterity's sake. Then she slid her phone back into her pocket so she could mount the horse. Alexandra mentally reviewed Nathan's directions, then swung up into Snowflake's saddle. The horse took a step or two and then stilled.

"You did that like a pro," Nathan said. "Nobody could tell me you haven't been riding for years."

Alexandra winked. "I had a great teacher."

"How about we walk around the corral?" Nathan suggested.

"Sounds good. Besides, I don't think Chloe will be

happy with just being on the horse's back. She knows that she is supposed to go somewhere."

Nathan gave Excalibur the signal to move, and the horse began to walk slowly around the corral. Alexandra gave Snowflake a gentle kick, and she began to follow Excalibur. Although Chloe hadn't yet mastered the art of talking, she was perfectly capable of expressing her feelings.

Alexandra urged her horse to go faster so that she and Nathan were riding side by side. As expected, Chloe was smiling brightly as she enjoyed this new experience. But it was Nathan's expression that held her attention. She'd never seen him as relaxed as he was now in his natural element.

Then he glanced down at Chloe, and Alexandra's breath caught in her throat. It was a look she'd seen many times on her own father's face whenever he looked at one of his children. It was a look of pure pride.

That thought brought Alexandra up short. She couldn't start deluding herself. Nathan was her friend. Period. It was foolish—indeed dangerous—to slot him into a role that he hadn't signed up for. Their relationship was a figment of their imagination. That was the way they both wanted it. The only way it could be.

"I think our Chloe is a natural. She'll be riding on her own before long."

*Our Chloe.* Alexandra knew he didn't mean anything by the careless comment, but even still it warmed her heart. It should have been a siren, providing a warning of an upcoming danger. Yet somehow it wasn't.

She wasn't looking for a daddy for Chloe. She and her daughter were a complete family. They were doing fine on their own. There might be a time in the future when Alexandra met a man she would risk her heart for. But that time wasn't now. And Nathan wasn't that man.

Just because there was no romantic future for them didn't mean she couldn't appreciate the kind of man he was. He was thoughtful and considerate. Gentle. With a physique that was second to none. He had the muscular body that came from hours spent doing hard, physical labor. Strength radiated from every pore of his body. He also possessed enough sex appeal to make her mouth water whenever he was around. Being near him made her entertain thoughts that had no business crossing her mind. He was her fake boyfriend. Given her desire to protect her heart, she shouldn't be thinking those thoughts about anyone.

Yet, she couldn't stop from fantasizing about how good it would feel to be held in his strong arms as she leaned her head against his solid chest and breathed in his masculine scent. And his thighs. They were so muscular. She felt her eyes straying to them, sneaking peeks when he wasn't looking. Nathan was everything a man should be. He was the man dreams were made of. Not the G-rated variety. She began to sweat as her imaginings grew even more erotic. A groan slipped out of her mouth and she bit her bottom lip.

Nathan glanced over and caught her staring. She felt her skin grow warm under his gaze and hoped like heck that her runaway thoughts weren't written on her face. She didn't want him to know she was lusting after him. One short step away from pouncing on him and having her wicked way.

It probably wasn't a new experience for him. Lots of women had bid on the opportunity to have a date with him. But none of those women were staring at him hard enough to drill a hole in his magnificent body. She smiled.

"This is so much fun," she said, in an effort to cover up the fact that she had been staring at him.

"Even though we are moving at a snail's pace?"

"I suppose this is the best pace for Chloe."

"Not really. She's very secure. We can go a little bit faster. That is, if you're comfortable with the idea."

She nodded. "At first I was a little nervous about even putting her on a horse."

"That's completely understandable. She is your baby."

"Yes. But now, I'm not scared. I trust you not to let any harm come to my daughter."

He looked at her, as several expressions crossed his face in rapid succession. She saw shock and surprise quickly followed by pleasure and pride. When those emotions fled, they left an undecipherable expression behind.

Nathan gave her a tender smile. "Your little girl will always be safe with me."

A lump formed in her throat. She swallowed twice before she could speak. Even then, her voice was a raspy whisper. "I know. So we can go a little faster if you want."

He nodded. "Just a little."

He jiggled the reins and Excalibur went slightly faster. They weren't galloping or even trotting by any means, but they were going fast enough that Alexandra could actually tell that they were moving. Chloe cheered with happiness and then began gurgling as they slowly circled the corral.

After they'd made the circuit twice, Nathan turned and looked at Alexandra. "I think that is probably enough for now."

Alexandra sighed. She'd been enjoying this moment of freedom and relaxation. "Already?"

He nodded in Chloe's direction. "We don't want to overdo it."

He led Excalibur through the stable doors, and she followed on Snowflake. When they were inside, Alexandra slid from the back of the horse. She was about to take

Chloe from Nathan when he dismounted, clearly unbothered by the little girl in his arms.

When he was on the ground, Chloe strained toward the horse. After it became clear that the ride was over, she began to fuss.

"Sorry," Alexandra said.

"Don't be," Nathan said, unfazed. He lifted Chloe over his head, releasing and then catching her several times. "I'm not pleased when I don't get my way. Believe me, if I could get away with crying, I would."

A startled laugh burst from Alexandra's lips. "That would be a sight to see."

Nathan grinned and lowered Chloe and held her against his chest. "I know you're upset little one, but we have a whole day planned. Okay?"

Chloe stopped fussing and frowned as if trying to understand what Nathan was saying. Then she threw her head back and laughed. After a moment, Nathan laughed with her.

"What's so funny?" Alexandra asked.

Nathan looked at Alexandra. "Sorry. That's a secret between us friends. Right, Chloe?"

Chloe nodded and babbled a reply.

"All right," Alexandra said. Foolishly, she felt left out.

Nathan brushed a kiss on Chloe's head, in much the way a father would, and then smiled at Alexandra. "You take the baby and I'll take care of the horses."

Alexandra held out her arms to Chloe. Generally her daughter would come to her eagerly, practically jumping into her arms. Instead, Chloe pursed her lips and then buried her head on Nathan's chest. Clearly her little girl was enchanted. Alexandra couldn't blame her. She would love to sink into Nathan's strong arms. Unlike Chloe, she couldn't be so bold. Alexandra doubted that Nathan would simply chuckle and rub her back.

"Come on, Chloe." Chloe didn't budge. Alexandra looked up at Nathan. "I don't know why she is acting this way."

"I guess she likes me."

"Of course she does. My daughter has good taste."

The slow, sexy smile that Nathan flashed her curled Alexandra's toes in her cowboy boots. They were only pretending to be in a relationship, but if she wasn't careful, she would fall in love with him. Then where would she be?

NATHAN GAVE CHLOE'S back a final rub and then handed the little girl over to her mother. Chloe clung to him for a moment longer, before giving him a bright smile and releasing his shirt. Then she practically jumped into Alexandra's outstretched arms. That move nearly stopped his heart. The last thing he wanted was to drop the baby. Alexandra didn't bat an eye. Apparently Chloe's daredevil ways were nothing new to her.

He loved his nieces and nephew, but he'd never felt the same tenderness holding them that he felt for Chloe. When he'd learned that his date at the bachelor auction was a single mother, he'd been a little bit leery. Even though the date was supposed to be a onetime thing, he hadn't wanted to deal with someone who was looking for a daddy for her child. When he'd realized Alexandra wasn't looking for anything permanent, much less a father for her child, he'd been relieved.

Now though, it wasn't relief that he felt. After spending just a few minutes with Chloe, he felt a surprising protectiveness and attachment. Not that he was thinking of altering the plans for his life. He was not considering anything remotely like that. Being an uncle was enough for now.

And yet...

"I have her now," Alexandra said, pulling Nathan away from his musings.

Nathan nodded. As Alexandra's hands brushed his, he felt a spark of electricity. He inhaled and the sensation traveled throughout his body, not sparing a single spot until his entire body was sending one message to his mind. He wanted more than a brush of hands from Alexandra. He wanted full body contact. Of course, that wouldn't be happening. Theirs was a relationship in name only.

He wasn't opposed to a purely physical relationship. He'd had a few in the past and they'd been mutually beneficial. But what he and Alexandra had was entirely different. They were becoming friends. That relationship would last much longer than one intense weekend. Therefore, he couldn't cross the line, no matter how tempting the notion was.

He reluctantly stepped away, removed the horses' saddles, then led them to their stalls. Nathan tried not to notice that Alexandra was following behind him, talking to Chloe as they kept up with him. She pointed out other horses and mentioned little details about them.

"This one is black," she said, coming up to Midnight. "Isn't he pretty?"

Chloe babbled in response.

"And this one has gray and white spots," Alexandra said.

Nathan told himself to focus on the task at hand, but it was hard to concentrate with Alexandra's sexy voice distracting him. It was low and appealing and sent his imagination into overdrive.

"This is just pretend," he said to himself softly. "So control yourself before you make a big mistake."

"Did you say something?" Alexandra asked, coming to

stand in front of Excalibur's stall. As with the other horses, the door leading to the corral was open, so the horse could go in and out at will.

He gave the horse a final brush before exiting the stall and stepping into the aisle. "No. I was just talking to myself."

"I didn't mean to eavesdrop." She flashed him a sweet smile that sent the blood racing through his veins. That reaction was totally inappropriate for someone who was supposed to think of Alexandra as a friend. Especially since his five-year plan didn't include her.

"Not to worry. I wasn't saying anything that needs to be kept confidential."

She laughed and his heart lurched. Her laughter was carefree, and it reached a place inside him that previously hadn't existed. That part liked the idea of being with Alexandra on a more permanent basis. He quickly silenced that thought before it could take root in his head. Or heart.

"Come on. Let's go in the house. I think we could use a snack." And he could use a cold drink.

"Sounds good," Alexandra replied, oblivious to the way her nearness was tantalizing him.

As they walked to the house, Nathan caught himself sneaking looks at Alexandra. He loved the elegant way she moved. She didn't walk as much as she floated. The way her slender hips swayed was extremely sexy. And enticing. She stepped close to him, and her sweet scent wafted around him.

He told himself to calm down and think of something else, but he couldn't stop his mind from fantasizing about spending intimate time with her. Why was it so hard to remember their relationship was purely a work of fiction?

When they stepped inside his house, Nathan grabbed Chloe's belongings and then led them into the kitchen.

Alexandra took Chloe into the adjoining family room, set her on a plastic mat, and gave her a quick diaper change. Once that was done, she put Chloe on her play mat and gave her a couple of toys. Chloe ignored those and then crawled over to the mini piano Nathan kept for the nieces and nephew to play with when they visited. She plopped onto her diapered bottom and began pounding on the keys. After a moment, she began to sing.

"She's quite musical."

Alexandra laughed. "I don't know that she has much natural talent. Of course it might be too early to tell."

"Oh, I think she has pretty good pitch. And she's very comfortable in front of an audience."

"You can tell all of that?"

"I have some experience performing. Remember?"

"I'll never forget that story. Do you have any videos?"

"My mother does. She keeps them as blackmail material."

Alexandra shook her head. "She probably keeps them because she was proud of you and your brothers."

"That's what she claims, but I'm not fooled."

"Do you miss performing? Ever think of getting the band back together again?"

"God, no. It was fun when we were kids. But we're grown now."

"So you don't miss singing?"

"I still sing from time to time. Not in public, but around the house while I listen to the radio."

"If I turn on a song that you know, will you sing for me?" Her eyes widened as if she suddenly realized how intimate that question sounded.

"You mean, would I serenade you?" He didn't know why the idea suddenly held such appeal, but it did.

"I guess it probably sounds a little bit ridiculous."

"No. Actually, it doesn't." He told himself that he would sing for any of his friends if they asked, although it wasn't true. He never sang for anyone. "You pick a song and I'll gladly sing it for you."

She smiled. "Now I feel like the pressure is really on me."

"Why would the pressure be on you?"

"Because. Now I have to come up with the perfect song. Are you partial to any type of music? Would you prefer a ballad? Or would you prefer an up-tempo song?"

"It really doesn't matter. Just name a song that you like and I'll sing it. If I don't know it, I'll learn it."

Her face lit up with pleasure. She was positively radiant. "Are you serious? You're willing to do all of that? For me?"

"Yes." Nathan would sing for her. He'd do anything to make her happy.

And that truth was more than a little unsettling.

# CHAPTER THIRTEEN

ALEXANDRA TRIED TO slow her racing heart. Nathan wasn't making a big deal about singing to her, so why was she? For all she knew, he sang for women all the time. That thought bothered her more than it should have. After all, she and Nathan were only pretending, so it shouldn't matter to her if he sang to every woman in Colorado. They weren't in love.

Chloe stopped "playing" and "singing" and then got on all fours and crawled over to Alexandra. When Chloe reached her, Alexandra took her hands and then helped her to stand. "That's a big girl. Look who's standing up."

Chloe chortled and then began bouncing up and down, laughing happily as she did so.

"Hey," Nathan said. Chloe tried to drop on all fours, but Alexandra kept holding her hands. "Let's walk."

"Can she walk on her own?"

"Yes. But she prefers to crawl."

"I suppose she wants to stick with the familiar."

"Crawling is faster. My little girl is impatient to get where she wants. She's all about speed."

He laughed and the sound raised goose bumps on her arms. She didn't understand why she was having such a hard time ignoring her attraction to him. Generally, once she made up her mind, it was done. She didn't waste time waffling. There was no second-guessing. She'd already decided that there was no room in her life for a man. That should be the end of it. So why wasn't it?

Now she found herself fighting feelings that she hadn't expected to have. And they were growing stronger with every moment that she spent with him.

The rational part of her wondered if she should end the farce before it got out of hand. Falling for him wasn't part of the plan. So she was going to knock it off. He was just a friend. And that was how she was going to think of him from now on.

"Do you need help in the kitchen?"

"No. I actually enjoy cooking. I find it quite relaxing. I try to cook as often as I can."

"What's your favorite thing to make?"

"I don't really have a favorite. It's more that I go through phases."

"What do you mean?"

"There was a time that I was all about French foods. I'm talking everything from coq au vin to Crepe Suzette. Then I was all about Greek food. Then seafood."

"Really? That's interesting. What are we having for lunch?"

"Given the fact that we have a little one with us, I thought we would have grilled cheese. It's a favorite of the little people in our family." His brow wrinkled. "She can eat grilled cheese, can't she?"

"Yes. She's almost one so she can eat a lot of finger foods, as long as they're cut into very small pieces."

"I have American cheese, but I also have mozzarella."

"Oh. I think she would like that."

"I'm going to make chicken and vegetable stir-fry for us."

"Oh. I like the sound of that."

"Then sit down and keep me company. I did all of the prep work earlier, so this will be a piece of cake."

Alexandra sat in one of the chairs at the island and held Chloe in her lap. She handed Chloe a stuffed toy and then watched as her daughter played with it. The moment felt so quiet. So normal. They could have been a family. Of course they weren't, and she reminded herself not to get caught up in a fantasy world.

Nathan and Alexandra talked as he prepared lunch. When it was done, he put the food on the table. He grabbed a high chair from the pantry and set it beside Alexandra's chair. She gave him a puzzled look.

He shrugged. "Remember, I have little ones over for dinner from time to time. It was easier and much neater to buy a high chair and booster seats than to let them eat at the coffee table in the family room, even though they seem to prefer that."

"Of course. That must seem like an adventure to them. They probably don't get to eat like that at home."

"They just like to roam as they eat. Strapping them in saves my walls and keeps the mess in one place."

"You definitely have thought of everything. I didn't have you pegged as a man who would flip out over a little dirt. After all, you are a rancher, and that can be pretty dirty from what I've seen."

"You're right. Which is why the boots stay at the door. No need to drag that mess all through the house. And if my clothes get too dirty, I drop them there too."

Alexandra immediately pictured a nearly nude Nathan standing before her, and her mouth began to water even as she broke out into a cold sweat. She grabbed her glass and took a long drink of iced tea.

"The stir-fry isn't too spicy, is it?"

She shook her head. "No. It's perfect. I like my food with a little kick to it."

"So do I." Nathan gave her a look before picking up his own fork.

Alexandra broke eye contact and glanced over at Chloe, who was happily chewing on her sandwich. Nathan had cut it into small slices, so it was just the right size for her little hands. Alexandra set a sippy cup of apple juice on the tray so Chloe could grab that whenever she wanted. She appeared content, so Alexandra turned her attention back to her food. But even as she ate, satisfying one hunger, she knew that the other hunger—the one that was suddenly a longing for physical contact with Nathan—would have to go unfulfilled.

Nathan seemed completely unaware of the lust that he was inspiring, eating his meal with gusto. The stir-fry was delicious. The chicken was tender and the vegetables were crunchy. Even so, Alexandra's ego took a hit as she realized the desire was one-sided. Oh, she knew that Nathan was attracted to her. The kisses they'd shared were proof of that. But she was realistic enough to know his passion might be the result of a sexual dry spell. He'd told her that he hadn't been in a relationship for a while. He might have kissed any woman that way.

The thing was, the desire she was experiencing wasn't a generic longing for physical touch. It was a specific desire for a particular man. She was lusting over Nathan. No other man would have the same effect on her.

"So, have you made up your mind about staying in Aspen Creek?"

Alexandra frowned. "I haven't given it much thought."

"Ahh," he said as if she'd said something profound.

"What does that mean?"

"It's simple, really. The fact that you haven't given it

any more thought appears to me that you have reached a decision."

"Really?" She held her fork suspended in midair, although she really wanted to put that water chestnut into her mouth. "And what decision would that be?"

"You're staying," he said confidently.

"How did you reach that conclusion?"

"The debate is over. That's why you aren't thinking about it. You feel comfortable in Aspen Creek and now it's home to you and Chloe. If it wasn't, you would still be trying to figure out your next move."

"You think?"

"Yes. You stopped looking for home because you've found it."

Had she? "Maybe. But my family is in Chicago. If Chloe and I move here, she won't see my parents, brother, and sister nearly as often as she would if we went back. Their relationships will suffer. And Chloe is the only grandchild."

He nodded. "That is a consideration. As someone who lives on the same piece of land as my parents and brothers, I understand how important family is. I can't imagine not seeing them as often as I do. Physical nearness is important."

"True. But it's not as if we're estranged. We can always visit each other. And I do feel at home here. As if I belong."

"I'm not surprised. Aspen Creek is just that kind of place. There is a sense of community. You and Chloe have made friends. You have a job you love, you have your aunt and a home. Why keep looking when you've found everything you want right here?"

"That's a good point."

"That's the only kind I make."

She laughed and resumed eating. "Oh, you are so full of yourself."

"That comes from being the oldest child. I always knew more than my little brothers."

"I bet you were a bossy big brother."

He gave a grin that made her heart lurch. "To hear them tell it, I still am."

"Really?"

"It comes from a place of love. Wanting to protect them. I can't stand by and watch them make mistakes without saying something."

"So you're trying to run their lives."

"Not at all. I give my opinion and then let them do what they are going to do. If it blows up in their faces, they can't say that I didn't warn them."

"And if it doesn't blow up in their faces? If it works out just the way they wanted it to? The way they expected it to?"

He shrugged his massive shoulders. "Then no harm no foul."

"Oh. Spoken just like a big brother. You guys are all so annoying."

"We come that way from the factory."

"You're blaming factory settings?"

"Only because it happens to be true. Big brothers know from the minute that our younger siblings are born that we have a responsibility to care for them. All good big brothers do just that."

She rolled her eyes. "You have got to be kidding me."

"Answer this. If it's not too personal."

She nodded. "Go ahead."

"How did your brother feel about Chloe's father?"

"Oh. That is a question."

"And if it is too nosy, please just ignore it. And forgive me."

She smiled. He sounded serious. And worried. "It's not

too nosy. And I don't mind answering. The truth is he didn't like Owen. He never came out and said the words. And he was always cordial. But he never treated Owen in the joking manner that he treated my sister's boyfriend. Or even some of my previous boyfriends. I guess I should have known there was a reason. But he never said. And I never asked."

He nodded. "It's hard to know what to do in those circumstances. You want to keep your siblings safe, but you know there's a line you can't cross and still have a good relationship with them. And no matter how it seems, we want to have good relationships with our younger siblings."

"I know. But when you're in the middle of it, you don't want to hear it."

"Which is why it's so hard to be a big brother."

"I'll give you that point."

He smiled. They had finished eating, so Nathan stood and picked up their plates. Chloe had eaten all of her grilled cheese sandwich and apple slices. She picked up her cup with both handles and then leaned back, noisily guzzling the last of her juice. When she finished, she dropped the cup onto the tray and let out a loud burp.

"Good one," Nathan said with a laugh.

"I've been trying to teach her table manners, but so far she hasn't caught on." Alexandra picked up Chloe. "If you'll excuse us for a moment. I need to wash up this little one."

"Take your time. I need to clean up the kitchen."

Alexandra held Chloe tight as she walked down the hall, being careful to keep her daughter from touching anything with her greasy hands. The last thing she wanted to do was create a dirty mess on his pristine walls. There were no pictures on the wall, which, given the beautiful artwork in the rest of the house, was a bit disappointing. Even so, the house had the same impact on her today as it had the first time she'd seen it. It was stylish without being showy. Comfortable. The overflowing toy box in the family room was evidence that he wanted everyone to feel welcome here. Even the ones with sticky hands.

She wiped Chloe's face and hands and then they went back to the kitchen. Chloe looked around, then began straining against Alexandra's chest, struggling to get down. Nathan was in the family room, digging through the toy box. There was a pile of toys at his feet, but he was pulling out even more. A couple of them were playing music and Chloe pressed more forcefully against Alexandra's chest.

Nathan glanced up. When he saw them, he smiled. His charming, boyish grin was almost sheepish. "I thought she might want to play for a while."

"You obviously know the way to Chloe's heart. She loves playing with musical toys." Alexandra stepped into the family room and then set her daughter onto the floor. Chloe immediately crawled across the room until she reached a musical ball. The minute she touched it, the ball rolled away from her. Not one to back away from a challenge, Chloe crawled after it. When she reached it, she slapped her hand on it, causing it to roll away. She let out a loud cry of frustration and began chasing it again.

"Looks like somebody needs help," Nathan said. He sat down on the floor, blocking the ball with his leg. Chloe crawled over and hit it again, but this time the ball couldn't escape. She laughed and then hit the ball over and over. With each touch, the song changed. Chloe plopped onto her diapered bottom and hit the ball over again.

Alexandra crossed the room and sat on the floor across from Nathan. Whenever the ball rolled away from Chloe, one of them would send the ball back into her direction, keeping her happy. After a few minutes, Chloe grew bored with the ball. Without missing a beat, Nathan picked up a stuffed giraffe and handed it to Chloe. She took the toy and smiled at Nathan. Then she crawled over to Alexandra and climbed on her lap, leaning her head against Alexandra's breasts.

"It looks like someone is getting sleepy," Nathan said.

It was naptime, so Alexandra wasn't surprised. Truthfully, she was glad to have a child who stuck to her schedule more often than not. Now though, Alexandra wasn't ready for the date to end and she wished that Chloe would stay awake a little while longer.

"Do you want to let her sleep on the couch for a bit? That way you can keep an eye on her and we can hang out longer. I don't have a crib since the grandparents are generally the ones who keep the kids overnight. Or would you rather I take you home so she can sleep in her own bed?"

NATHAN WATCHED AS Alexandra contemplated his question. A few long seconds had passed and she still hadn't responded. He was trying not to show how much her answer meant to him. He might be able to hide his feelings from Alexandra, but he couldn't hide them from himself. He wanted her to stay. That was troubling. The emotions she awoke within him were unexpected. Though he had no plans of becoming involved romantically with a woman now, his feelings weren't entirely unwanted. Alexandra was making him go against his plan.

Now he had trouble thinking clearly where she was concerned. It wasn't that he'd stopped believing in the perfect order of things. He still believed there was a time and place for everything. It was just that he was beginning to wonder if he might need to make adjustments to the order. Maybe

there were different times and places for the big events in
his life than he had once believed.

Nathan blinked. That thought was not something he'd
wanted to entertain for long, yet he couldn't totally rid
himself of it. Was he really thinking about reorganizing
his entire life simply because he was attracted to Alexandra? That didn't make a lick of sense. He barely knew
her. They'd only gone on two dates—three if you counted
today. Besides, he'd been attracted to a lot of women in
his life. Sometimes he'd acted on that attraction. Other
times he hadn't. But never once had he even considered
reordering his life.

"Well, to be honest," Alexandra said, pulling Nathan
out of his disturbing thoughts. "Chloe would be doing a
lot of her sleeping in her car seat. If you don't mind letting her lie on your couch, I am happy hanging out with
you for a while longer."

He breathed an internal sigh of relief. He knew he was
getting in over his head, but he didn't know how to dial
it back. Nor was he sure he wanted to. Truth be told, he
enjoyed having Alexandra around. He wanted to look at
her beautiful face for a while longer. He wanted to listen
to her sweet voice and inhale her intoxicating scent. He
could catalog the varied things he was finding pleasure
in, but honestly, he wanted to enjoy *all* of her.

"In that case, let me grab a sheet and blanket so our
little angel can sleep more comfortably."

"Thanks."

Nathan jogged upstairs to the linen closet. He grabbed
a sheet and a blanket, then returned to the family room.
Alexandra was standing beside the window, swaying back
and forth as she rocked Chloe the rest of the way to sleep.
Her back was to him and he took a moment to admire her
shapely figure. She was so sexy in her jeans and blouse. Al-

exandra must have sensed his presence because she turned around. When their eyes met, she gave him a soft smile. His heart squeezed, and for a moment, he was mesmerized by her and could only stare. He was struck not just by her beauty, but by her aura. There was a sweetness and calmness to her that touched him.

Chloe stirred and Alexandra brushed a kiss across her head. "She's just about fallen asleep."

That comment was a call to action, and Nathan strode into the family room. He covered one of the cushions with a sheet, then stepped aside so that Alexandra could lay Chloe down. She hovered a minute, watching as the baby stirred, moving around until she was comfortable. Chloe placed a thumb into her mouth and then was still. Smiling, Nathan covered her with a thin blanket. A tenderness swept through him, and he brushed a hand across her hair before stepping back.

"So…" he said, totally at a loss at what to say.

"So," Alexandra echoed.

Nathan shook his head in an attempt to get back on track. Alexandra hadn't agreed to stay here so he could gawk at her. Suddenly having Alexandra and Chloe around felt too natural. Too real. "Do you want something else to drink? Or maybe something to eat?"

"No, I'm fine."

Of course she wasn't hungry. They'd just eaten. He grabbed a couple of cushions from the large sectional and placed them on the floor in front of a sleeping Chloe. When Alexandra gave him a puzzled look he shrugged. "In case she rolls around, we'll be here to stop her fall."

"Good idea."

Sitting, he stretched his legs in front of him. Alexandra did the same. She was sitting close to him and the warmth from her body reached out, touching him and raising his temperature. Suddenly his mind was filled with images of the kisses they'd shared and a desire to kiss her again. His longing was a drumbeat inside him, growing stronger by the minute. His attraction to her and his desire for her was becoming an all-consuming force.

That was a problem.

How could he be around Alexandra and pretend to be in a relationship with her if the more time he spent with her, the more he wanted the relationship to become real? Just thinking about this puzzle gave him a headache.

"Why are you shaking your head?" Alexandra asked. There was a touch of humor in her voice.

He shook his head again and then laughed. He must look quite foolish to her. "You must think there is something wrong with me. First you see me talking to myself, and now I'm shaking my head."

She chuckled. "I was just wondering if it took you that long to answer yourself."

He grimaced. "I didn't know that you were so funny."

She dipped her head in a bow and then gestured her hand with a flourish. "I'm here all week."

And just like that, the lust that he had been trying to extinguish reignited. Their conversation faded away, and she seemed just as incapable of picking up the threads as he was. The truth was, he didn't want to talk. There was only one thing on his mind.

Their eyes met and he recognized the longing in hers. There was no use denying the serious attraction between them. And he was tired of fighting it. They were already sitting close enough to touch, but she leaned even closer to him. Her intent was clear, but still, he hesitated. Didn't move. He needed her to make the first move. She reached out and touched his face with trembling fingers. That soft contact was all it took to break through his self-control. He moved closer and brushed his lips across hers.

From the second their lips met, he knew the kiss was going to be hot. She opened her mouth to him and he swept inside. She tasted just as sweet as he remembered. But mingled with that sweetness was a fiery desire that matched his.

He slid an arm beneath her knees and his other behind her back, lifting her onto his lap. She wrapped her arms around his neck and they deepened the kiss. Time paused and then stood still. On and on the kiss went, until she broke away. He was panting too hard to do more than stare at her, his eyes asking the question that he was unable to voice. Why had she pulled back?

She pressed her palms against her chest, then answered his unspoken question. "I think that we're getting carried away here. This is supposed to be a pretend relationship. Making out like a couple of horny teenagers—as pleasurable as it is—is out of bounds."

Try as he might, he couldn't find an argument to dispute her. Perhaps because she was right. He nodded. She slid off his lap, and although his body was screaming for him not to let her go, he resisted the urge to pull her back into his arms.

"This is so much harder than I expected. You are so irresistible."

She giggled and looked directly at him. Longing still lingered in her eyes. "I know. Right? What is that?"

"I don't know. We're just incredibly attracted to each other." He knew that he could reignite the fire between them again with one kiss. But he respected her too much to try.

"Annoying, isn't it?"

He nodded. That was one thing that he appreciated

about Alexandra. One of many things. She understood the situation and didn't try to make it something that it wasn't. They were attracted to each other. Not in love.

"I suppose we should come up with a way to keep this under control," he said.

"That sounds like a good idea. Do you have a plan? Because I sure don't." Her expression was so open and honest. So irresistible.

"No. But if we are going to convince my family that we are a couple, I suppose our mutual attraction isn't a bad thing. We need to be comfortable with each other." It was a stretch, but he had to come up with a reason why it was a good thing he couldn't keep his hands off her. A reason that didn't involve his heart.

"And the best way to be comfortable is to practice," she said, taking his idea and running with it. Her eyes sparkled with mischief.

"And practice makes perfect. I am nothing if not a perfectionist."

"I don't like to do things halfway either."

He wondered if that meant she would go all the way, as the kids used to say in high school. He knew better than to ask because he didn't want to press his luck. Truthfully, he didn't know what answer was worse—*yes* or *no*. "So I guess that explains everything."

"Yep." She ran a hand over her hair, straightening it the best she could without a comb. His hands ached to experience the pleasure of running through her hair again, so he curled them into fists. He had been creeping up to the line, and he knew that the wise thing to do was back away before he crossed it.

They continued to speak quietly for a while, enjoying each other's company.

Chloe stirred and he and Alexandra turned as one to

look at her. As if feeling their gazes, the baby opened her eyes and gave them a sleepy stare before closing her eyes again.

"It won't be long before she wakes up," Alexandra said. "She'll be groggy for a few minutes, but then she'll be ready to play again."

"Will she be hungry?"

"Yes. I have a snack packed for her. And, of course, a diaper change." She paused briefly. "Unless you're ready for us to go home. We don't want to overstay our welcome."

"You aren't. That's why I invited you to stay while Chloe slept. It would be nice to spend a few more hours together if you don't have other plans."

"I don't have anything planned. Just dinner and playing with Chloe for a while. But you have toys here so that would be all that we need."

Chloe made a sound and they looked at her again. Her eyes were wide-open and she was smiling. She sat up and reached out to Alexandra.

Alexandra took her daughter into her embrace and kissed her chubby cheeks. "Look who's awake. I bet you want a new diaper."

Nathan reached into her diaper bag and pulled out a diaper as well as the vinyl mat. "I bet you could use this."

She took them from him. "Thanks."

He grabbed the sheet and blanket and then stood. "I'll give you some privacy."

"Thanks."

"Oh, and if you're free, would you like to have dinner at my parents' next Sunday? My brothers and their families will be there. I know you met them briefly at Miles and Jillian's wedding, but this will be a good opportunity for you to get to know everyone better."

She paused and then smiled. "I guess the plan is no good if we don't put it into practice."

"Is that a yes?"

She hesitated, and he held his breath, waiting until she answered. "Yes. We would love to have dinner with you and your family."

# CHAPTER FOURTEEN

THE FOLLOWING SUNDAY, Alexandra stood on Nathan's parents' front porch and looked around the sprawling ranch. There were acres of land with trees interspersed over the otherwise flat land. Naturally the mountains were visible in the distance. The view was spectacular, but she preferred the scenery around Nathan's house.

This house was more in keeping with what she thought a ranch house would look like. It was a large, sprawling, redbrick building with a wide front porch. Several chairs were grouped around a wicker and glass table on one side of the wide staircase. A swing and several rocking chairs were on the other. She could imagine sitting on the swing and looking out over the large lawn, sipping lemonade in the summer and hot chocolate in the fall.

She forced the cozy image away. She wasn't going to become a part of this family, so those peaceful evenings weren't going to be a part of her future. Once she and Nathan convinced his mother that they were involved, he wouldn't need her any longer. They could stage a breakup, then go back to their normal lives. Lives that didn't include each other.

When she'd agreed to pretend to be his girlfriend, she hadn't anticipated everything that would be involved. She'd imagined that they would have a few dates in popular spots where they would be seen. Word would get back to his mother that Nathan had a girlfriend, and that would be the end of it. Instead, she was about to sit down to a family dinner.

After their date last Saturday, Nathan had come to visit her twice during the week. She'd cooked dinner once, and he'd picked up carryout from a restaurant in town the other time. Nathan had insisted that the dates were important so that they could honestly say they were spending time together. Besides, he wanted to work on their cover story. Alexandra had to admit that she'd enjoyed her pretend dates a whole lot more than she had some real dates. They might be pretending, but Nathan was behaving like a real boyfriend. If she was interested in dating, he was exactly the type of man that she would want to be involved with.

He had also called her a few times during the week just to talk. They'd talked long into the night about Chloe's upcoming birthday party—Nathan had volunteered the ranch, but Alexandra decided to have the party at her aunt's house. They also discussed the big deal he was close to finalizing. Once again, he'd claimed that the phone calls were necessary in order to make their story realistic. Not that they needed to be all that creative. It was common knowledge that she and Nathan had met at the bachelor auction, so they didn't have to come up with a meet-cute.

Alexandra took a deep breath and then glanced up at Nathan. Suddenly she suffered a bout of nerves. She had never been much of an actress. The only time she'd been onstage had been third grade when she'd played an elf in the Christmas program. She'd forgotten her lines and had all but broken into tears. She knew that this wasn't entirely the same thing—she wasn't an eight-year-old explaining how toys were made—but she would be putting on an act.

Luckily, she wasn't alone. She had Nathan by her side. He could feed her lines to her if she got stuck. More than that, he wouldn't stand by silently and let his family grill her. Not that she expected a grilling. But she knew the drill. She'd met enough families of boyfriends to know that there would be some gentle questioning. If they got along well enough, there would be a bit of good-natured teasing.

She also had her secret weapon—Chloe. Her little girl was quite the charmer. Very few people could resist her. When she smiled, even the coldest heart melted. If Chloe became fussy, Alexandra would have the perfect excuse to take a break from the group.

"Ready?" Nathan asked.

"Yes." She smiled up at him. He looked so gorgeous in his blue shirt, black jeans, and his ever-present cowboy hat. Tingles raced down her spine. One thing was certain. She wouldn't have to fake her attraction. "I'm just trying to get a handle on my nerves."

"Why are you nervous?" He seemed genuinely confused.

"Because I want to make a good impression. I want your family to like me. Or at least not sit there wondering what in the world you see in me."

He brushed a gentle kiss on her cheek. She knew that he intended the kiss to be comforting. And it was. But it also stirred up longing inside her. A small part of her that refused to be silenced wished that this pretend relationship was actually a real one. The more time she spent with Nathan, the more she was coming to see that he was the real deal. Authentic. The kind of man that a woman could look for forever and not find. Yet here she was with him. And not with him.

Not that it mattered. She might be coming to care about him, but that didn't mean that he was also doing an about-face. The rational part of her believed that was a good thing. She already had enough balls in the air. She couldn't juggle another one.

"My family liked you when they met you at the reception. Once they know you better, they will love you. After all, what is there not to love?"

She felt herself blushing. "You had better dial back the charm."

He laughed and leaned in closer. "Why would I do something like that?"

She looked away. There was no way that she was going to tell him that she was starting to fall for him. Especially not when they were about to step into his parents' home. Neither of them needed that kind of pressure. The situation was fraught enough already.

Before she could think of a suitable reply, the front door swung open. Alexandra turned and looked into Nathan's brother's face. She recalled meeting Isaac at the reception. Even if she hadn't met him before, she would know they were brothers. The resemblance was strong.

"Hey. I saw your car out the window a few minutes ago. We're about to start taking bets on whether you plan to come inside or make a break for it."

"How was it looking?" Nathan asked.

"Not good. That's why I opened the door." He turned to Alexandra. "I don't know if you remember me from the reception. Come on in, I'm Isaac—"

"Of course. Nathan's brother. I remember you. And thank you," Alexandra said, stepping inside the house, Nathan right behind her. Chloe leaned back as she tried to see the two-story ceiling. Alexandra put her hand on Chloe's back to make sure that her little girl didn't tumble from her arms.

They stepped inside the living room where the family was gathered. For a moment, Alexandra was a bit nervous. She'd been honest when she'd said that she wanted Nathan's family to think well of her for his sake. But that had only been part of the truth. She also wanted them to like her for herself.

"Welcome," Nathan's mother said with a smile. "We didn't get to talk much at the reception. Hopefully we can remedy that."

The smile on the other woman's face was warm and welcoming, and Alexandra immediately felt at ease. "I look forward to that, Mrs. Montgomery."

"Please, call me Michelle."

"I will." Alexandra looked around. "I'm looking forward to getting to know all of you better. Nathan has told me a lot of good things about his family."

Isaac snorted and Alexandra wondered if she had gone too far. But when she saw the laughter in his eyes, she remembered that he was the jokester of the family.

Nathan quickly reintroduced the rest of his family. Alexandra smiled a greeting to each of them before she set Chloe on the sofa and retied her shoelace before picking her up again. The littles, as Nathan referred to his nieces and nephew, immediately rushed over to them.

"Baby," said a little girl who didn't look much older than Chloe.

"Yes, she is," Savannah said. She winked at Alexandra and then whispered, "Isn't it funny how little kids are so willing to call another kid a baby. But then, I guess to Mia she is."

"How old is your little girl?" Alexandra asked.

"A year and a half."

"She's a cutie."

"Thank you. She's also a handful."

"I like your baby," the other little girl said. Alexandra recognized her as the flower girl, Lilliana.

"Thank you."

"Bye," Lilliana said, abruptly. Then she and Benji

turned and ran away. Lilliana looked back. "Come on, Mia."

Mia tugged on Savannah's arm, held her face up, and pursed her lips. "Kiss, Mommy."

Savannah kissed the toddler and then watched as her little girl chased after the other kids.

Jillian walked over to them. "It's good to see you again. We didn't get to talk much at the reception."

"I understand how that goes. The bride is always the star of the show and in demand. Your wedding was beautiful, by the way."

"Thank you. I had a great time. But the reason we didn't get to talk had more to do with Nathan than anything else. He monopolized your time. It was as if he didn't want to share you with anyone else."

Alexandra felt her cheeks growing warm as she reflected back on the reception. She and Nathan had spent nearly every moment by each other's side. Time had seemed to fly with each pleasurable hour. She couldn't believe it when the band leader had announced the last dance. "Nathan is kind that way. He knew that I didn't know any other people and didn't want me to feel uncomfortable."

It also cut down on the risk that one of them would make a mistake that would blow the whole charade before they even started.

Savannah and Jillian exchanged glances and Alexandra realized that she hadn't fooled either one of them. But then, perhaps that was for the best. She and Nathan were supposed to be convincing his family that they were in a serious relationship.

"Is that what you really think?" Jillian asked.

Alexandra laughed. She had a feeling that she was going to like Savannah and Jillian quite a bit. "Not really. But given the way our relationship started, I wasn't going to get my hopes up."

"I understand completely," Savannah said. "It's hard to put your heart out there. There is always the fear that it will get broken."

Jillian nodded in agreement, and Alexandra wondered what kind of heartaches they had suffered. Given the fact that neither of them was a teenager, it was likely that they had suffered heartbreak of one type or another. That was just the way life went. Alexandra had endured her own pain from a broken romance. But unlike Jillian and Savannah, she hadn't found that one person who made taking the risk worth it. Given the fact that she was no longer interested in love, she wouldn't find that someone for quite a while. Being with Nathan gave her all the benefits of having a man in her life without taking the risk associated with a failed relationship.

"But when you find the right one, you discover that it was worth the risk," Jillian said. She was practically glowing and a newlywed, so clearly she'd found that man in Miles.

Chloe squirmed to get down, so Alexandra set her on the floor near her feet where she could keep an eye on her. But Chloe had other ideas and immediately crawled over to Nathan. When she reached Nathan, he immediately picked her up. She chortled happily and placed her head on his chest.

"Someone is going to be spoiled," Savannah said. "I can see it now."

"Chloe really adores Nathan. He's so good with her."

"Nathan was all business before, so it's good to see him have more in his life than the ranch."

"The ranch is important to him," Alexandra said, feeling oddly protective of him. "It takes a lot of work to keep it going. And Nathan is not the type to let others pull his weight."

"Hey, nobody is criticizing his choices," Jillian said, laughing. "I've known Nathan all of my life. He's been a good friend to me. Even when Miles and I weren't on speaking terms, Nathan and I kept in touch. I'm just glad that he's found someone that makes him happy. Someone who can help him see that he can find happiness outside of the ranch he loves so much."

"Oh." Alexandra felt sheepish. "I guess I jumped to conclusions. I'm sorry."

"Don't be," Savannah said. "We're both very protective of our Montgomery men."

"We'd wonder what was up if you didn't come to his defense," Jillian added.

Before Alexandra could reply, Nathan's parents announced that dinner was on the table.

"We helped," Lilliana said.

"We did a good job," Benji said, proudly.

Mia nodded and then clapped her hands.

"I can only imagine how much help they were," Jillian said.

"Should I have offered to help?" Alexandra said. She wanted to make a good impression after all, and sitting on her hands while others worked was definitely not the way to do it.

Savannah shook her head. "We helped a lot when we arrived so there was very little left to do. The kids' idea of helping is eating half an oatmeal cookie that we aren't supposed to know about."

"Really? Before dinner?"

"Grandparents' privilege," Jillian said. "Besides it's only about three bites. And it comes with the condition that they eat their vegetables, so it all comes out in the wash."

Alexandra thought of her own parents and recalled how they enjoyed spoiling Chloe. Of course, her daughter had been so young at the time and didn't have any memories of them, or of how special they had made her feel. That was one of the hardest parts of leaving home and moving to Aspen Creek. Breaking the bonds of a relationship that is so important to everyone.

Not that her family was out of their lives. She spoke with her parents several times a week and at least once a week with her brother and sister. And unless something unexpected happened, Alexandra's parents planned to come to town for Chloe's birthday party in two weeks. Even if they managed to come to town for a visit, Chloe wouldn't enjoy the regular spoiling that she would have gotten if she lived closer to her family.

Getting everyone around the table was a bit hectic, and there was good-natured teasing as Isaac sat beside Alexandra, pulling Savannah into the empty seat on his other side. Then Miles sat on Alexandra's other side, keeping Nathan from sitting beside her.

"Funny guys," Nathan said.

"We thought so," Miles said, getting to his feet.

"No matter how old we get, little brothers are a nuisance," Nathan said.

Everyone laughed at Nathan's put-out look, and Alexandra found herself joining in. After the blessing was said, everyone began serving themselves. Nathan explained that his mother usually had the children eat at the same table as the adults, but Benji and Lilliana had spent a lot of time with the other grandparents while Miles and Jillian had been on their honeymoon. Those grandparents let them use their own table for lunch and snacks. Somehow they had convinced Michelle to let them eat at their own table today. Chloe, however, still used a high chair and she was enjoying her bits of macaroni, chicken, and greens with the adults.

"Is the baby going to eat with us?" Lilliana asked.

"No. She needs a special chair," Alexandra said.

Lilliana shot Chloe a look that could only be described as pity before turning in her chair to eat the food Jillian had set in front of her.

"They like having their own table," Jillian said, taking her chair at the table.

"I remember sitting at the kid's table," Alexandra said. "But I recall wanting to eat at the big table for the longest time."

"Kids these days are made different," Isaac said. "They like having their own place."

"So Lilliana can talk Benji into doing something that will land them both in trouble," Jillian said with a grin.

"Like mother, like daughter," Nathan said, before turning to Alexandra to explain. "Miles and Jillian were friends as kids. She was always getting him into trouble. Lilliana is like the second coming of Jillian, and Benji is as laid-back as Miles was."

The conversation continued and Alexandra was instantly included. In only a few minutes time, she felt comfortable enough to join in the kidding and laughing. She glanced at Nathan and caught him staring at her, an intense expression on his face. The look made her heart pound and the blood in her veins began to pulse rapidly.

The surroundings faded away and Alexandra was only aware of Nathan. The deep, rich brown of his eyes, framed by dark, curly lashes. The way one eyebrow was raised just a smidge. The deep dimples in his cheeks. The warmth from his body reaching out to her. They were sitting so close that their shoulders brushed as they ate. It wasn't annoying. Quite the opposite. She liked it. His touch increased her attraction to him.

Chloe banged her cup on the table, and Alexandra immediately became aware of her surroundings. She looked away from Nathan and caught a glimpse of Isaac's expression. He was smirking as if he'd caught her and Nathan doing something wrong. Alexandra looked from him to her daughter. "What do you need, sweetie?"

Chloe babbled and then held out her cup.

"Looks like she wants more milk," Nathan said, coming to his feet. "I'll get her a refill."

"Thanks," Alexandra said.

"Who would have thought that Nathan would be so good with a baby?" Jillian asked.

"Certainly not me," Miles said. "Especially after the way he looked the first time we left Lilliana and Benji with him."

Everyone laughed.

"How did he look?" Alexandra asked.

"Like he had run ten miles," Jillian said.

"Nah. He looked like he'd been run over by a truck," Miles added.

There was more laughter as Nathan returned to the room. Chloe reached out for the cup, which he instantly placed into her hands. Then he placed a kiss on her head before sitting back down.

"What's so funny?" he asked.

"They were telling me about the first time that you babysat Lilliana and Benji."

He chuckled and shook his head. "Don't let those kids fool you. They may seem sweet and innocent, sitting there and eating like normal people, but let me tell you. They never stopped moving. Climbing all over the furniture.

Trying to find trouble to get into. I have never been so tired. Those were the longest two days of my life."

Laughing, Jillian corrected him. "It was maybe an hour or so."

"That's not better," Nathan said. "It just goes to show how exhausting they were."

"How are you going to handle it when Chloe starts running and climbing?" Miles asked.

Alexandra sucked in a breath as she waited for Nathan to respond. She knew this was only a fake relationship, but she couldn't stop her very real reaction.

"Chloe is a perfect angel, so I don't have to worry about her getting into any kind of mischief."

"Keep dreaming," Jillian said. Then she turned to Alexandra. "No offense."

"None taken." Alexandra replied.

"I'll tolerate no Chloe slander at this table," Nathan said.

Everyone laughed, and the conversation switched to other topics. Though Alexandra knew that Nathan was only pretending, her heart warmed at the affection he showed her daughter.

"DID YOU HAVE a good time?" Nathan asked Alexandra as they stepped inside her house a few hours later. Chloe had fallen asleep on the way home and Nathan was holding her in his arms as Alexandra closed the door behind them.

"I did. Your family is great."

"They felt the same about you."

She smiled and his heart skipped a beat. Though he'd been with Alexandra all day, he still hadn't become immune to her presence. Everything about her was enticing. From the way she nibbled her bottom lip when she was thinking to the way she tossed her hair over her shoulder when she laughed. There were so many things that he liked about her. So many more things that he wanted to learn. But that would take commitment, something neither of them wanted.

"I guess your plan worked. You don't have to worry about your mother setting you up on blind dates."

He didn't know why that comment bothered him. True, that was what this whole charade was supposed to be about. But several times during the day, he'd forgotten they were only pretending to care about each other. It had begun to feel very real. He'd been so proud of the way she'd fit in with everyone. His mother had been won over when Alexandra had insisted on helping to clear the table. His father had been impressed by her knowledge of sports. Jillian and Savannah had each told him how much they liked Alexandra. Isaac and Miles had also told him that he'd made a good choice. The littles had adored her and Chloe. Once Chloe could keep up with the others, he could picture the threesome turning into a foursome.

That is, if the relationship was real. Which it wasn't.

Alexandra's words were appropriate given the situation, so he nodded. "Even so, I don't think we should stop seeing each other. That would make them suspicious."

"I agree. What should we do next?"

"Everything. Dinner. Concerts."

"That sounds good, but one of the reasons I don't want to have a real relationship is Chloe. I don't have a lot of time, and I need to be with her."

"That goes without saying. She should definitely be a part of the plan. And I would like to teach her how to ride. We should spend more time on the ranch together."

"If you're sure."

"I am." He was surer of that than he was about anything else in his life. He wasn't ready to let Alexandra out of his life.

"I need to put Chloe to bed. Do you want to stick around, or do you have to get back to the ranch? One thing I've learned from being around you is that your day starts pretty early."

"I could say the same about yours."

"True. But that doesn't answer my question. Are you staying or leaving?"

"Staying. Definitely."

"Make yourself at home."

He nodded and sat on the couch. He didn't plan on staying long. Just long enough to get a few kisses. Despite how well dinner had gone, the date wouldn't feel like a success if they didn't make out for a few minutes. Alexandra was rolling back the clock and turning him into a horny teenager.

"I hope that didn't take too long," Alexandra said a few minutes later as she returned to the room and sat beside him.

"Not at all."

"Chloe had a good time today. Your family was so wonderful with her. You were wonderful with her."

"She's a sweet girl." Nathan realized that simple statement didn't come close to expressing what he felt for Chloe. That little girl had stolen his heart.

"I like her."

"And what do you feel about me?" he asked, moving closer to her.

"It would be easier to show you than to tell you."

"By all means, go ahead."

Alexandra gave him a flirtatious smile a mere second before she touched her lips to his. The kiss was soft, and he forced himself to let her take the lead. Gradually she increased pressure and then licked his lips. And that's when he lost control. He pulled her onto his lap and then deepened the kiss. The idea of taking this further crossed his mind, but the key in the door stopped him. Alexandra froze and then slid from his lap. They were straightening their clothes when Alexandra's aunt stepped into the room.

She looked at them and a wicked smile crossed her face. "Carry on. I didn't mean to interrupt your evening."

Nathan looked at Alexandra and then stood. "I was actually just saying good-night."

"Yes. We each have to get up early in the morning," Alexandra added, jumping to her feet.

"If you say so," Rose said. "I'm headed to bed myself. Good night."

With that, she turned and walked away. Nathan and Alexandra looked at each other and then burst out laughing. The sexual tension between them dissipated, but he knew with the least bit of encouragement, the fire could be restarted.

"I guess I should get going," he said reluctantly. Leaving Alexandra was becoming harder and harder.

"I know."

They walked to the door together. Nathan caressed Alexandra's cheek. "I'll talk to you soon."

"I'll look forward to that."

He jogged down the stairs and then got into his car. Before he drove away, he looked at the house, pleased to note that Alexandra was still standing in the doorway, watching as he drove away.

Even so, leaving her behind was still painful.

# CHAPTER FIFTEEN

"I HAVE SOME NEWS," Nathan said, excitedly.

"I can probably guess," Alexandra said, leaning against the pillow and adjusting the blanket. Chloe was asleep, Aunt Rose was in her room, and Alexandra was relaxed. She had been looking forward to their nightly conversation all day. There was something so intimate about talking with him in the quiet of night. "You have scheduled your meeting with James O'Brien, CEO of OB Marts. I know you've been after a deal with them for a while, to carry Montgomery beef. How many do they have again?"

He laughed. "Fifty. And you have a better memory for detail than I do. Heck, I should take you with me."

"When is it?"

"This Saturday. We're having dinner."

*Wait. What? He couldn't be serious.* "But this Saturday is Chloe's birthday party." She struggled to keep the panic from her voice.

"I know. But the party is at noon. My dinner isn't until seven. That gives me plenty of time to take pictures and push kids around on scooters. Or whatever happens at parties for one-year-olds before the cake and ice cream."

Alexandra blew out a sigh of relief. Though she and Nathan weren't officially dating, you couldn't tell it from their lives. They spent as much time together as she had with guys she'd actually been dating. They also shared the big and small events of their days with each other. Chloe loved Nathan and had gotten attached to him. He had become an important part of her life. She would notice if he wasn't at her birthday party. Even if she didn't notice, Alexandra would.

It was too late to go back and undo their fake dating scheme. They had grown too close. Their lives were now intermingled. Though she could tell herself that she had no right to expect Nathan to attend the party, she didn't believe that. They might not have talked about it, but their relationship had changed. It was no longer simply pretend. It was real.

"I'm glad."

Nathan's voice became deeper. Softer. "I won't disappoint Chloe. Or you. You both mean too much to me."

Her heart warmed at Nathan's words and the sincerity she heard there. "Thank you. Now tell me more about your meeting."

"We have worked out just about every detail. All we need to do now is sign the contracts."

"Congratulations. I know how hard you worked for this."

"It has been worth it. I am so happy to see the beginning of my five-year plan coming together."

"Your father must be so proud of you."

"He is."

Alexandra knew how much Nathan admired his father. It was clear from the sound of his voice how much making his father proud meant to him. "I'm proud of you too."

"Thank you. Only three days and the biggest deal of my life will be wrapped up."

They talked a few more minutes before they ended the call. Once they hung up, Alexandra set the phone on the bedside table. Now her day was complete and she could sleep easily. That thought had her bolting upright. She should be able to function without talking to Nathan. So why had she thought that? It didn't take long to come up with an answer.

She was in love with Nathan. The thought nearly stopped her heart. She pondered it for a moment and then realized that it was true. She didn't know how or when, but she had fallen in love with him. For a moment she didn't move. Barely breathed as she waited for the panic to hit her. It didn't come. Perhaps because Nathan was the type of man that she could trust with her heart.

He cared about friends and strangers alike. He loved and respected his family. Most of all, he loved Chloe and was wonderful with her. For the first time in a long while, she believed that it would be okay to love a man. More importantly, she believed it was okay for her daughter to love Nathan. There was no fear that he was unworthy of their love.

But uncertainty remained. Just because she had fallen in love didn't mean that Nathan had too. For all she knew, he was completely happy with the status quo. Although their relationship felt real to her, it didn't necessarily mean it felt real to him. It could all still be a charade to him.

Her heart ached at the thought. The truth was, she wouldn't know how Nathan felt unless she asked him. Since it was bound to be an emotional conversation—at least on her part—it would be best to have the conversation after Chloe's party and after he'd sealed his business deal.

That decided, she rolled over to go to sleep. The past couple of nights, she'd dreamed of Nathan. If she was lucky, he would make an appearance tonight.

The next day was busy at work, but she still managed to finalize arrangements for Chloe's party. Alexandra had invited the five children in her group at day care as well as Nathan's nieces and nephew. Everyone had responded to the invitation in the affirmative. Chloe's first birthday party was going to be a hit.

Alexandra's family would be arriving the Friday before the party. They had already sent a stack of presents ahead, but she had no doubt that they would be bringing even more with them. They hadn't seen Chloe in a while and Alexandra knew they were going to cram several months' worth of spoiling into a weekend.

Alexandra hadn't mentioned Nathan to her family. At the time she'd agreed to be his pretend girlfriend, she hadn't expected it to last this long or to feel this real. Now she was conflicted and unsure how she should introduce him to her family. It would have been simpler to introduce him as her friend if she hadn't invited his nieces and nephew to the party. But she had. Jillian and Savannah would be at the party. If Savannah described Nathan as her friend, that could raise suspicions. She didn't want to ruin things for Nathan simply to avoid a few questions from her family.

Nathan was bringing over dinner tonight, so hopefully they could come up with a solution that worked for both of them.

NATHAN STOOD IN front of the selection of toys, unsure which one to buy for Chloe. He'd narrowed his choices down to the final three. Each was different but had something that appealed to him.

"How long do you plan on standing here?" Isaac asked.

"As long as it takes."

"All of the toys you have are good," Miles said. "And take it from someone who knows. She'll probably play with the box and paper a lot longer than the toy anyway."

"Benji might have done that, but Chloe will know that the toy is the gift."

His brothers looked at each other and laughed.

Then Isaac smirked. "Of course she will."

"Why did I even ask you two to come with me?"

"I don't know. Why did you?" Isaac said. "Oh, I know. Because you had no idea what to buy. But if you're going to ignore our expert advice, we can just leave. After all, we have the gifts from our kids."

"You can't go wrong with any of them. So choose one," Miles said. "She'll love it and never know which toys you left behind."

Nathan knew that. "Give me a second."

"We'll go pay for ours," Miles said.

Nathan shooed them away and then turned his attention back to the toys. He picked up the music box. He knew that Chloe liked music. The exquisite, hand-carved music box wasn't exactly something she could play with. But it could be the beginning of a collection. He could give her one every year on her birthday. He liked the idea, so he placed the music box aside.

Next, he picked up the teddy bear family. The four bears were dressed in regular clothes, but there was the option to purchase fancy clothes for them. He'd selected snowsuits and raincoats for each of them. The bears were all huggable, and he could picture Chloe having fun with them for hours. He set them aside and then picked up the shopping cart toy. Chloe could practice walking while pushing it across the room. It also had shapes in varying colors that she could sort. She would have fun with this for hours.

He decided to get all of them. After all, a girl's first birthday was an important event that should be celebrated. Nathan scooped up all the toys and headed for the checkout. His brothers had made their purchases and were standing at the front door holding their bags. When they saw him, they came over.

Nathan glared up at them, daring them to say anything.

He must be losing his touch because Isaac grinned. "Decided to get them all."

"Yes. Do you have something to say about it?"

"Not to you." He turned to Miles and held out his hand. "Pay up."

"You bet on what I would get?"

"I thought for sure you would only get two," Miles said, digging out his wallet. He pulled out a twenty and gave it to Isaac.

"I knew you would get them all," Isaac said, slipping the money into his pocket.

"How?"

"I have a daughter. Miles is new to having a little girl. He'll soon discover how easy it is to spoil them."

Nathan should probably straighten out his brother and remind him that Chloe wasn't his little girl, but he didn't. He would have to explain about the whole charade with Alexandra, something that he wasn't inclined to do at this point. They had convinced his mother that their relationship was real, so there was no reason for it to continue. They could have the big fight and end things anytime without raising suspicions. He supposed he and Alexandra needed to arrange that for some time in the future. Just not now. Definitely not before Chloe's birthday. And really, there was no rush to break up. A few more months wouldn't hurt anything.

He set his gifts on the checkout counter, grabbed several different rolls of wrapping paper, a birthday card, paid for everything, and then he and his brothers returned to the ranch. After dropping his gifts onto the table in the entry, he headed to the stables. There was still a lot to do before he met Alexandra for dinner tonight. Nathan was grabbing his saddle when his phone rang. He looked at the screen and then hurriedly answered it.

"Mr. O'Brien. How nice to hear from you."

"I'll get right to the point. It's about our meeting Saturday."

Dread instantly filled Nathan. He couldn't believe the deal was falling apart. He inhaled and then calmed. "Yes? Is there a problem with the contract?"

"Nothing like that. We still want to partner with you. I'm certain we can work out the minor details. I'm just not able to meet with you on Saturday evening. Would it be possible to meet earlier in the day? Say, around noon? We could have lunch instead of dinner. That's the only time I'm available for the next few months."

That was during Chloe's birthday party. Hadn't he just thought of how important turning one would be for her? But on the other hand, he had worked on this deal for months. He couldn't walk away from it now. He could always stop in before the party started and give Chloe her gifts. Depending on how long lunch went, he could stop in after. He'd worked too hard to make this deal a reality to walk away now.

"That's fine. I'll see you Saturday at noon."

Nathan leaned back and stared at the ceiling. He knew he'd done the right thing. He just hoped that Alexandra saw it the same way. Since they were having dinner together, he would soon find out.

Although he tried to bury himself in work, a nagging sense of unease was never far from him. Alexandra knew how important this deal was to him. Surely she would understand why he had to miss the party.

He was telling himself that same thing hours later when he stood on her front porch waiting for her to answer the door. The aromas of the pizza, which Alexandra said she'd had the taste for, should have been making his mouth water, but instead his mouth was as dry as a desert. He was sure that once they'd talked, he would be able to relax.

The door swung open and Alexandra was standing there, looking as gorgeous as ever. She smiled brightly. "Come on in. That pizza smells so good."

He stepped inside. Chloe was sitting on the living room floor. When she saw him, she pushed to her feet and held out her arms. Nathan handed the pizza to Alexandra and then picked up Chloe and set her on his shoulders. She instantly pounded on his head, and he winced.

"One of these days you'll learn not to do that," Alexandra said.

"No. Eventually she'll learn not to slap me on my head. But until that day arrives, I'll get used to having a headache."

Alexandra laughed and Chloe echoed her.

They headed for the kitchen. Nathan set Chloe into her high chair and then grabbed plates from the cabinet. Alexandra poured juice for Chloe and then opened a bottle of wine.

"Where's your aunt?" Nathan asked.

"She has her regular card game tonight. I don't expect her until much later." Alexandra put a cut up slice of pizza on Chloe's plate. "She ate dinner earlier, so I don't know how much she'll eat."

Nathan and Alexandra placed a few slices of pizza onto their plates. Alexandra gave him a bowl filled with colorful salad and then started to eat.

When he only sat there looking at his food, she gave him a puzzled look. "Is everything okay, Nathan?"

He blew out a breath. Even though he wanted to have the discussion, he didn't want to ruin her dinner. Since it was obvious that something was on his mind, he might as well tell her. After all, the problem wasn't going to disappear. "Not exactly."

"Is there anything I can do to help?"

Of course that would be her first reaction. Alexandra was kind to a fault. "Not really. I got a call from James O'Brien this afternoon."

"Don't tell me that he wants to back out of the deal."

"Nothing like that. It's still a go."

"Then what?"

"He can't meet me for dinner on Saturday. He wants to meet at lunch."

"On Saturday?" Alexandra asked.

He nodded. "It's the only time that he will be able to meet for months."

"I see." Alexandra set her pizza back onto the plate. "And what did you say to him?"

"I told him that I would meet. What else could I do?"

"I don't know," she said sarcastically. "Maybe tell him that you have plans that you can't break. That's what I would do."

"I can come over before the party. Or maybe after. Chloe won't notice what time I come and leave."

She looked at him incredulously. "But *I* will, Nathan. And I won't have her be a second thought. If you don't want to keep your promises to her, then don't make them." She jumped to her feet so fast she knocked over her chair.

"You're overreacting here."

"I don't think so." Alexandra picked up the chair and scooted it under the table. "You know, this whole charade has been all about you. I played along and did everything that you asked for. I had a good time too, so I have no complaints about that. But when I need you to do one thing, *one thing* that you promised to do, you don't keep your word."

She was right and he knew it. The guilt souring his

stomach made him angry and he lashed out. "This isn't a real relationship. It was simply a pretend relationship to fool my mother. That's it."

The fact that it had started to feel real was immaterial and not something he wanted to even think about right now.

"Is she fooled yet?"

He nodded slowly. So fooled that when one of her friends asked about Nathan, she'd told her that Nathan had a serious girlfriend.

"Good. Then we've reached the part of the charade where we have a big blowup and end our relationship."

"Alexandra, don't be hasty." Panicked, he jumped to his feet and crossed the room, closing the distance between them. "We don't have to end everything simply because of a conflict between a party and a business meeting. Surely we can work this out."

She snatched her hands away from his and then hid them behind her back. She stepped away from him, putting the table between them. The emotional gulf between them was much bigger than the physical one. "Why? Nothing between us is real."

It certainly was beginning to feel real. But he wasn't going to say that now. Especially since his sharing his feelings wouldn't change a thing. He wasn't going to be able to attend Chloe's birthday party. Clearly that was a deal-breaker for Alexandra. He was searching for something—anything—to say that would get them back on track. Nothing came to mind.

Alexandra glared at him. "I think you should leave now. Feel free to frame our breakup in whichever way works best for you. I really don't care."

"Alexandra." He was pleading, but he didn't care. He didn't want her to walk out of his life.

"Just go. Please." Her voice broke on that last word, and he realized she wasn't just angry. She was hurt. She must think that he was rejecting Chloe in the same way that Chloe's father had. He wasn't. But nothing he said now would change her perception. Since Alexandra was struggling to hold herself together, he nodded.

"I'll go," he said softly as he walked away. Alexandra trailed behind him. When he reached the front door, he opened it, stepped outside, then turned to look at her. "I'll call you when I get home. Hopefully I can make you understand."

"Don't. There's nothing left to say."

"There is. This isn't the end."

Alexandra didn't reply. Instead she simply closed the door.

It wasn't the end, he told himself. It couldn't be.

ALEXANDRA LEANED AGAINST the front door and let the tears come. She didn't know why she hurt so badly. She'd known from the beginning that the relationship between her and Nathan was only temporary. A play they'd put on for his mother. Hadn't she just been thinking that the breakup scene was imminent? She hadn't expected this much pain. Reaching into her chest and literally pulling out her heart couldn't hurt more.

Of course, at the time she'd agreed to this farce, she hadn't been in love with him. Falling in love with him hadn't been even a remote possibility. Now she loved him with her entire heart. But if he couldn't love her and Chloe with all of his, there was no hope for them.

The idea of him not being a part of her life was excruciating. But she had survived worse. She would survive this too.

## CHAPTER SIXTEEN

"I NEED TO TALK," Nathan said the moment he had both of his brothers on the phone. After leaving Alexandra's, he'd driven aimlessly around Aspen Creek, trying to figure out how things had gone so wrong so quickly.

"About?" Isaac asked.

"Sure," Miles said. "Where are you?"

"I'm about ten minutes away from the ranch. Can you meet me at my house in fifteen minutes?"

"We'll be there," Miles said, speaking for Isaac as well.

"Thanks."

Nathan didn't know what he expected his brothers to say. Maybe nothing. But even if there was only a slight chance that one of them would have a bit of inspiration that could salvage things with Alexandra, it would be worth it. His head was spinning, and he couldn't think straight. Even so, he still believed there was a way to work things out. There had to be.

His brothers' cars were already parked in front of his house when he arrived, and they walked up the stairs together silently.

"What's wrong?" Miles asked the minute they were inside.

Nathan inhaled and then blurted out the painful words. "Alexandra and I broke up."

"What? Why?" Isaac asked.

"When?"

"Just now." He paced into the living room, and his brothers followed. Nathan stood in front of the windows and stared into the dark night. He blinked rapidly, not wanting to break down in front of his younger brothers.

"What happened?" Miles asked after a while.

Nathan turned around and faced them. Neither had taken a seat, so Nathan gestured toward the seating area. Isaac and Miles exchanged looks before they sat down.

"What happened?" Miles repeated.

"We had a fight." Nathan shook his head. He still couldn't believe how quickly things had gone sideways. Never in a million years would he have thought Alexandra would be so unreasonable. She hadn't even heard him out.

"About?" Isaac prompted.

Nathan shoved his hands into his jeans. "You know that I have that meeting with James O'Brien."

"We know. The first of your big deals. We already told you how great that is."

"Dad's pleased too. Anyway, we were supposed to meet for dinner Saturday night. He needed to meet earlier. At noon."

"That's the same time as Chloe's birthday party," Miles said.

"I know. When I told Alexandra I would have to stop by either before or after the party, she got angry." And hurt. The pain in her eyes had been unmistakable. It had hurt him too.

His brothers just stared at him. Neither of them spoke for a long moment. It was as if they were waiting for the other to say something. Miles blew out a breath. "And you blame her? You chose a business meeting over her daughter's birthday party."

It wasn't a question, but Nathan felt like he needed to answer it. "It's not as if I'm ignoring her. I'll see her before the party. Or after. Besides, all of her friends will be there. She'll be playing with them. Well, as much as a one-year-old plays with anyone."

"She might not know now that you chose to put business before her, but years from now when she looks at the pictures, it will be clear that you weren't there," Miles said.

"And Alexandra knows now. She's right to be angry," Isaac said. "You're putting her second. If you expect this relationship to last, you had better fix this."

Nathan looked at his brothers. There was no sense in lying to them. He knew they would keep his secret if he asked. Maybe if they knew the truth, they wouldn't be looking at him as if he were the biggest jerk in the world. He had lost Alexandra's respect. He didn't want to lose theirs too.

"We were supposed to have a fight, I just didn't know it was going to feel like this," he muttered.

"What are you talking about?" Isaac asked.

"You know how Mom started matchmaking. I didn't want to be bothered with it, so I convinced Alexandra to pretend to be my girlfriend. It wasn't supposed to last long. Just long enough to throw Mom off the scent. Then we were going to break up and go our separate ways."

"You expect us to believe that your whole relationship was pretend?" Miles asked. He shook his head. "We saw you together."

"Yes." At least at first. Somewhere along the line it began to feel real. He should have told Alexandra when his feelings had started to change. Looking back, he couldn't pinpoint the moment. It had happened so gradually, sneaking up on him. Now he admitted that fear had also held him back. Alexandra had been crystal clear that she didn't want a man in her life. She didn't have time for romance. If he'd told her how he felt, she might have bolted. He hadn't wanted to risk losing her.

So instead he'd hurt her.

"Then if it was all pretend, why am I here?" Isaac asked. "Why did you interrupt my time with Savannah and Mia? My relationship is real. If you and Alexandra planned on breaking up, why are you so upset?"

Nathan dropped into a chair and then rubbed his hand down his face. "I don't know."

"I do," Miles said. "It's because you're in love with her. And the idea of waking up tomorrow and knowing that she won't be a part of your life is tearing you apart."

"I wouldn't go that far." He couldn't have fallen in love with Alexandra. Yet he couldn't totally discount his brother's words. Not when he'd been coming to believe the same thing.

"Take it from someone who lost years with the love of his life. Don't be an idiot. Tell Alexandra that you love her and beg her to forgive you. And then call O'Brien and tell him that you can't meet at noon. Maybe you can split the difference and meet at four."

"And if he can't?"

"Then either cancel the meeting or get used to life without Alexandra and Chloe."

ALEXANDRA LOOKED AROUND the gaily decorated room and gave a determined smile. Her heart might be breaking, but she would keep up appearances if it killed her. Years from now when Chloe looked at the pictures from her first birthday party, she was not going to see a gloomy mother with eyes red from crying. She was going to see a smiling woman.

Alexandra's family had arrived yesterday, and as expected, they'd spoiled Chloe. Alexandra's father and brother hadn't noticed anything was wrong, but her mother and sister had taken one look at her and known. Alexandra had simply told them that she'd broken up with her boyfriend. They'd hugged her and let her know that it would be all right. Of course it would. After all, how long could a heart hurt when the relationship had been no more real than the flowering garden on the photographer's backdrop?

Nathan wasn't the first man to break her heart, but he would be the last. She and Chloe had been doing fine before they met him. They would do just as fine in the future. He'd called her twice, but she hadn't answered. To her, there was nothing that he could say that would change the situation. Either he was all in or he was all out. She couldn't teach her daughter to accept less than she deserved. Chloe was worthy of someone who would always put her first.

It wasn't as if Alexandra didn't understand how important this business deal was to him. Of course she did. But there would always be one more opportunity. One more customer. With her and Chloe out of his life, Nathan wouldn't have to choose. He could stick with his five-year plan. When Alexandra was strong enough emotionally that she could talk to him without breaking down and begging him to choose her and Chloe, she would tell him just that.

Judging from the message Nathan had left her, that conversation might not be necessary. The first time he'd called, he hung up without saying anything. Early yesterday he'd left a message that he had to go out of town for business. She didn't know why he'd bothered to tell her that. It wasn't as if they were continuing their charade. He no longer had to run his schedule by her.

The doorbell rang.

"Guests are arriving," her mother said, pulling her attention back to the present.

"Thanks, Mom." Alexandra checked her watch. It was only eleven forty-five. But then, perhaps someone was extra eager.

"It's time to get the show on the road," Victoria said.

Alexandra looked for Chloe so they could greet her first guest. Alexandra's father and brother were entertaining Chloe in the backyard while Alexandra, Clarice and Victoria put the finishing touches on the family room.

She opened the front door. And gasped. Nathan was standing there, a stack of presents in his arms. He looked more uncertain than she'd ever seen him.

"What are you doing here?" She'd meant to sound firm, but her voice was only a whisper.

"It's Chloe's birthday."

"Yes. But you have your all-important meeting. Remember?"

"I moved it."

"I thought he could only see you now."

"That was the only time he would be able to meet me here. His return flight was canceled, which was why he'd needed to meet sooner. So I flew out to Tennessee to meet with him yesterday. We signed the contract last night."

"How good for you. I'm happy for you," she said begrudgingly.

"I can tell," he said dryly.

"No really. I am. I know how much that deal meant to you." It had been more important to him than she and Chloe had been.

"It meant a lot. But not as much as I'd once believed. And certainly not more than you and Chloe."

She wanted to believe that, but she couldn't. "Since when?"

"Since I realized that I didn't want to pretend that we're dating."

Her heart sank. For one moment she'd actually thought… "Well, we aren't pretending any longer so… what are you doing here?"

He looked around and then set the gifts on a nearby table. Then he took her hands into his. "I want our relationship to be real. I want to date you for real."

"For real?"

He nodded. "I love you. I have for a while, but I just didn't know it. I know that probably sounds unbelievable, but it's true. Before we met, all that mattered was my five-year plan. I was happy with just having the ranch in my life. But ever since you and Chloe came into my life, my priorities have changed. The ranch still matters, but it is not everything. You and Chloe are."

"I wish I could believe that. But I can't. I know how much your plans for the ranch mean to you. I don't believe you can change your way of thinking just that easily. Even if you can, I don't want to get in the way of your plans. I may as well admit that I love you too. But sometimes love isn't enough."

"Sometimes it is."

"I need a man who puts me and Chloe first. I don't want to be selfish, and I know that sometimes business will come first. But not on special occasions."

"I know. It will never happen again." His voice was filled with undisguised desperation. Even so, she heard the sincerity there. "Please give me a second chance."

NATHAN HELD HIS breath as he waited for Alexandra's response. The past couple of days had been the worst of his life. He couldn't live without Alexandra and Chloe. Oh, his heart would still beat and his body would keep moving. He would go through the motions of living. But he would be dead on the inside.

Once he'd realized that Alexandra and Chloe meant everything to him, he'd known he'd do whatever it took to win Alexandra back. He'd called Mr. O'Brien and explained the situation. Then he'd offered to fly to Tennessee. He'd had to make a few adjustments to his schedule, but it had been worth it. He didn't know why it hadn't occurred to him sooner. If it had, he wouldn't have hurt Alexandra as he had.

"I'm scared," she said. "I want to trust you. If it was only me, I would. But I have Chloe."

"I know. If you don't believe anything else I say, please believe that I love her."

Alexandra nibbled on her bottom lip, a clear signal that she was thinking. Then she glanced at him. When he saw the expression on her face, his heart lifted. "I know Chloe loves you. It would be wrong to keep you apart simply because of my doubts."

"So you'll give me another chance?"

"Just one."

He breathed out a relieved sigh. "I won't need a third."

Nathan opened his arms and Alexandra went into them. He closed his arms around her and breathed her in.

He heard Chloe's excited chatter and turned. Her grandfather, Lemuel was holding her. When she spotted Nathan, she squealed and lunged toward him. Alexandra quickly introduced him to her family. He nodded and smiled. There would be time to get to know them better. But first his little angel was here, ready to celebrate her birthday.

"May I?" he asked, holding out his arms. Before Lemuel could answer, Chloe jumped into Nathan's outstretched arms. Nathan took her and held her against his chest. He'd missed his sweet baby. He brushed a kiss against her cheek and then wrapped an arm around Alexandra's shoulder, pulling her close. She leaned against him and smiled.

His life wasn't going according to his five-year plan. That was fine. Good even.

Life with Alexandra and Chloe was better than any plan he could have come up with.

* * * * *

# Second Chance Deputy

## Alexis Morgan

# MILLS & BOON

*USA TODAY* bestselling author **Alexis Morgan** has always loved reading and now spends her days creating worlds filled with strong heroes and gutsy heroines. She is the author of over fifty novels, novellas and short stories that span a wide variety of genres: American West historicals; paranormal and fantasy romances; cozy mysteries; and contemporary romances. More information about her books can be found on her website, alexismorgan.com.

Visit the Author Profile page
at millsandboon.com.au for more titles.

Dear Reader,

All of my books are special to me, but I am really excited about the release of the third book in my Heroes of Dunbar Mountain series. Every so often, a particular character comes along who is extra special and becomes incredibly real to me. They magically step out of the shadows of my imagination and demand to have their story told and very much on their terms.

Titus Kondrat, the hero in *Second Chance Deputy*, is definitely one of those. When I first started populating the town of Dunbar, my intent was to use Titus as one of the background characters. Boy, that sure didn't last long, because somehow he ended up playing pivotal roles in both of the earlier books in the series.

Even so, Titus remained a man with many secrets and a past that he still hadn't come to terms with. Enter Officer Moira Fraser, the only woman he's ever loved and the newest member of the Dunbar Police Department. Needless to say, things get interesting after that.

I hope you enjoy getting to know Titus and Moira as they deal with the problems of their shared past and the possibilities of a new future together.

Happy reading,

*Alexis*

# DEDICATION

This book is dedicated to my friend and
brainstorming partner, Janice Kay Johnson.
We've plotted an awful lot of books together
over the years, and it never gets any less fun.
I am grateful every day for her friendship
and amazing creativity.

# CHAPTER ONE

IT HAD BEEN an uneventful shift so far, especially for a Saturday night. Knowing that could change at any moment, Moira Fraser savored the quiet while it lasted. For now, she slowly steered her cruiser through the heart of town toward the church where Cade Peters, her boss and the chief of police, had just married Shelby Michaels. While Cade was relatively new to the area, Shelby and Moira had both grown up in the small town.

The difference was that Shelby had never left while Moira had only recently moved back after spending fourteen years living in Seattle. The city was only about one hundred and thirty miles from Dunbar, but it was a world away in size and intensity. She'd moved there to go to college, where her mother had expected her to get a teaching certificate and then hustle right back home. In a rare show of rebellion, Moira had majored in criminal justice, put on a police uniform and launched her career in law enforcement.

She'd loved her job in the big city and had been told she stood a good shot at moving up the ranks. While Moira had sometimes missed life in a small town, career opportunities in law enforcement in a place the size of Dunbar were extremely limited. Besides, the prior chief of police in town had been old-school, with no interest in hiring a female officer.

When she'd had to move back to town because her family needed her help, Moira had no idea what kind of job she'd be able to find. Fortunately, Cade Peters didn't share his predecessor's prejudices and immediately hired her, something she'd always be grateful for. To everyone's surprise—including hers—he'd also put her in charge of the small police force for the three weeks he would be away on his honeymoon. She'd heard rumblings that some members of the city council hadn't approved of his decision, but Cade had stood his ground.

One way or the other, she would justify his faith in her. She'd told him that one last time when she'd put in a brief appearance at the reception before resuming her patrol.

The church was now in sight, and she'd timed her arrival perfectly. The wedding guests stood clustered around the front steps as the bride and groom prepared to make their escape. Cade and Shelby held hands and laughed as they ran for the waiting limousine, passing by their friends and relatives, who stood on both sides waving colorful flags.

As the happy couple sped away to start their life together, Moira wondered if anyone had been able to find out where they would be spending their honeymoon. There had been a betting pool about the possible destinations. The suggestions ran the full gamut from the ridiculous to the sublime. Moira had five dollars riding on a Caribbean cruise, but she didn't care if she won. She just wanted her boss and his bride to have a solid three weeks of fun and relaxation without interference from anyone. It was still hard to believe that the city council had actually tried to order the newlyweds to go no farther away than nearby Seattle in case they needed Cade to come back early. She could only imagine how well that had gone over with him.

The crowd was rapidly dispersing, which meant it was time for her to get back to work. She resumed patrolling, taking her time as she circled the center of town again before gradually making her way to the outlying areas. Watching over her friends and neighbors was her favorite part of the job. She liked to think they slept better knowing someone was keeping an eye on things.

Still, she couldn't help but regret that she hadn't been able to spend more time at the reception. Since moving back to town two months ago, she had been working hard to reconnect with old friends, and Shelby had been one of the first to reach out to her. Unsurprisingly, Shelby had been too busy to spend a lot of time with any one guest at the reception. Even so, she and Cade made a valiant effort to personally greet everyone, especially those who'd come to town on such short notice. However, there were a few other people that Moira would've enjoyed hanging out with for longer than the half hour she'd been there.

Interestingly, there had been one person she'd expected to see but who had been missing in action—Titus Kondrat, the owner of the only café in Dunbar. Considering he'd been responsible for much of the excellent dessert buffet at the reception, it seemed odd that the man himself had been nowhere to be found. Not that she'd wanted to actually talk to him, but she made a habit of keeping a wary eye on him from a distance whenever she had the chance.

Oddly enough, from what she could tell, the police chief and Titus had become pretty good friends since Cade had moved to Dunbar. The two men seemed an odd match considering Cade was a by-the-book cop and Titus was... Well, that was an interesting question to ponder as she drove through the darkness. No one knew much about him since the man was amazingly closemouthed about his past.

Granted, people were entitled to their privacy, but for some reason that man set off Moira's Spidey-senses. They'd never actually spoken, but there was something familiar about him, most likely because he reminded her of a few criminals she'd helped put behind bars. The image of one guy in particular being led away in cuffs leaped to mind, but she refused to think about him right now.

After nearly ten years, the memory still hurt.

She couldn't picture Cade being best buddies with someone who might have flirted with the wrong side of the law, but there was just something about Titus that didn't add up quite right. That was a mystery to mull over another day, though. For now, she'd make another loop through town and then stop in at the office to check on a few things. Cade had told her to leave all the paperwork for him to deal with upon his return. Even so, she planned to make sure that she and the other officers kept on top of everything so the boss didn't return to a huge backlog of work. It would be easy to let things slide, but that wasn't happening on her watch.

As she turned back toward the police station, her phone rang. One look at the name on the screen and she couldn't help but sigh. No matter how many times Moira told her mother not to call when she was on duty unless it was an emergency, the message never got through. She could be calling because there was a real problem, but it was just as likely that she wanted Moira to pick up milk on her way home. She hoped that wasn't the case. There wasn't a store in Dunbar that stayed open past nine, and she didn't want to drive the twenty miles to the nearest gas station with a mini-mart.

She put the call on speakerphone so she could keep both hands on the wheel. "What's up, Mom?"

"I'm sorry, hon, but Gram slipped away again. I'm heading out to search for her, but I might need your help getting her back home."

"I'm on my way. I'll drive by her house first."

"Sorry. I know you don't like to be bothered at work."

"Don't worry about it, Mom. Besides, it's part of the job—I'd do the same for anyone. I'll text or call as soon as I have news."

"I appreciate it."

Her poor mother sounded exhausted, mainly because she probably was. Taking care of Moira's elderly grandmother 24/7 wasn't easy. It was the reason Moira had moved back home, but there was a limited amount of support she could offer her mom. Between her time on the job and the need to sleep occasionally, there weren't many hours left over to spend standing watch over her grandmother.

Two blocks later, she turned down the street where her grandmother had lived for most of her life. More and more Gram's mind got tangled up in the past. When that happened, she forgot that she now lived with her daughter and granddaughter, and would try to go back home. At least the old place was currently vacant, so she wouldn't be bothering anyone when she started knocking on the door trying to get in.

Moira could only hope that was where her grandmother had gone this time. Otherwise, they could be in for a long night of driving up and down every street in town looking for her. Thankfully, most folks in Dunbar knew Gram. If she was spotted, whoever found her would do their best to contain Gram until either Moira or her mother came to take her back home.

Ten minutes later, her phone rang again. She answered without looking at the number. "Mom? Did you find her?"

A rusty laugh was followed by "I'm pretty sure I'm the wrong gender to be your mom, Officer Fraser."

Next time she vowed to check the caller ID before answering. Besides, why on earth would Titus Kondrat be calling her? "Sorry about that, Mr. Kondrat. How may I help you?"

"I'm at the café. I believe I have your grandmother sitting in my kitchen drinking a cup of tea and eating a piece of cherry pie."

Could this get any worse? Of all people to find Gram, it had to be him. Not that she wasn't grateful. "I'll be right there."

"No rush. She's not a problem. Come around back, and I'll let you in."

The phone went dead before she could even thank him. Instead, she called her mom. "I've found her."

"Is she all right?"

"Yeah, she's fine. I'll tell you more when I find out how she ended up where she is."

"Thanks, hon. Again, I'm sorry you got dragged into this."

Moira was, too, but family had to come first. "Go on home, Mom, and relax. I'm not sure how long this will take, so enjoy the quiet while you can."

That her mother didn't argue was telling. "See you soon."

It took less than five minutes to reach the café. The dining area in front was mostly dark, with only a dim light shining through from the kitchen in the back. She'd heard that Titus often worked well past closing time prepping for the next day's meals. Come to think of it, that might explain why he'd left the reception early.

As instructed, she drove around the back of the café. The door opened and Titus stepped outside as soon as she parked the SUV behind a huge motorcycle. "She's doing fine, Officer Fraser. She and Ned have struck up quite the friendship and are enjoying each other's company."

Now that was a surprise. Gram rarely talked to anyone

she hadn't known for years. Moira didn't know everyone in town, but she couldn't remember anyone by that name. "Is this Ned new to town?"

Titus looked amused. "That's right. You probably haven't met him. He's a stray who decided to move in with me a few months back. Best guess is he's a German shepherd, golden retriever mix, but don't let Ned's size scare you. He's not the friendliest dog in town, but he has a soft spot for children and childlike souls."

That last category was a surprisingly accurate description of her grandmother these days. "If you don't mind me asking, where did you find Gram? She doesn't usually head in this direction."

"Actually, it was Ned who found her. He pitched a fit and all but dragged me a couple of blocks down toward Fourth Street. Between the two of us, we managed to coax her to come back here with us."

Moira would have loved to have seen that. Gram might be confused, but that didn't mean she couldn't be stubborn as a mule. "How did you know to call me?"

Titus shrugged. "Not many secrets in this town."

True enough. "Well, I'll get her out of your way. Thanks for calling me, Mr. Kondrat. My mom was pretty frantic when she realized Gram was missing."

"Actually, I don't think she's quite ready to leave. She had trouble deciding which flavor of pie she wanted. Right now, she's on her second mini pie and asked for a third." He glanced back inside and then opened the door. "Why don't you come in and have some with her? Maybe a cup of tea, too."

The notion was surprisingly tempting. "I shouldn't. I'm on patrol and could get a call any minute."

But as soon as she stepped inside the café, she knew she wasn't going to rush her grandmother out of there. Gram looked so happy sitting at a small table in the corner, eating pie with one hand while she gently stroked Ned's head with the other.

Without glancing at their host, Moira slowly approached the table and sat down. At least Gram had left home wearing a blouse and slacks instead of her nightgown, like the last time. She was also sporting what had to be one of their host's flannel shirts with the sleeves rolled up several times to accommodate her much shorter arms. Evidently, the dog wasn't the only one with a soft spot for those with childlike souls.

It took a couple of minutes before Gram acknowledged her presence. "I like this dog. Ned looks scary, but he's a marshmallow inside."

"I can see that."

Moira snapped a picture of her grandmother and texted it to her mother, adding a brief note that they'd be home after Gram finished her pie. She'd just hit Send when Titus set a pot of hot water, along with a cup and saucer, in front of her. A second later, he was back with a third mini pie for Gram and a piece of chocolate-cream pie for Moira. Eyeing all that chocolaty goodness, she knew it would take a lot more willpower that she could currently muster to resist the temptation to dig in.

Titus had put a tea bag, two packets of sugar and a lemon wedge on the saucer next to the tea. She picked up the tea bag and stared at the label in confusion. How had he known she liked her tea with two sugars and a squeeze of lemon, or that Earl Grey was her favorite flavor?

"I have other flavors of tea if you don't like Earl Grey."

His deep voice startled her. "No, this is great. It's actually my favorite."

Titus went back to chopping vegetables on a nearby counter. "It's the most popular flavor I carry."

So that explained it. She scooped up a forkful of her pie and closed her eyes in appreciation. "The pie is delicious."

He grunted an acknowledgment of the compliment and kept working. From that point, no one did any talking. Her grandmother happily finished off her last pie while she continued to pet Ned. Other than thanking Titus again for rescuing her grandmother, Moira couldn't think of a single thing to say to the man.

That didn't keep her from wishing she was on the other side of the table, where she could study him without being obvious about it. Gram had an unobstructed view of their host, but seemed totally oblivious to his presence. It was probably better that way. Something told Moira that Titus was the kind of man who was always hyperaware of his surroundings, and the last thing she wanted was for him to pick up on her interest in him. It was strictly professional, of course, but he wouldn't know that. Maybe it was the way he moved that seemed familiar, but she was almost sure they'd never met before she returned to the town.

He wasn't the kind of guy a woman would easily forget.

Moira had some personal experience with that sort of man. Ryan Donovan hadn't been easy to forget, either. They'd met nearly ten years ago, when she'd been fresh out of the academy. Over the course of two months, she'd fallen fast and hard for him. Looking back, she should have known that he was too good to be true. He'd been charming, handsome and sophisticated; she'd had a hard time believing a man like him would be interested in a small-town girl like her. It had taken her way too long to realize that he'd also been careful to avoid letting her snap any pictures of him. That alone should have raised suspicion.

Then came the horrific night Moira had been part of the local backup on a major drug bust, when she'd seen the DEA agents take Ryan into custody along with the rest of his associates. She'd heard a rumor that he'd worked a plea bargain for a reduced sentence. All she knew for sure was that she'd never seen him again nor had she wanted to. It had been ages since she'd thought about Ryan at all, and she was fine with that.

With no photos to refresh her memory, Ryan's image had faded over the ten years since she'd last seen him. The real question was why the man standing behind her had suddenly stirred up those memories. Ryan had been tall like Titus, but not nearly as muscular. His hair had been a much lighter color, and his eyes were blue, not brown. Still, there was an uncanny resemblance between the two men. Was it possible they were related somehow? Cousins, maybe, although Ryan had never mentioned his family that she could remember. Another warning sign she'd missed.

Clearly, the woman she'd been back then hadn't asked enough questions. As a result, the woman she was now would never trust any man so easily again, especially one as deliciously mysterious as Titus Kondrat. Before she could pursue that thought any further, her grandmother spoke up. "I'm tired, Moira."

"Then we'll go home, Gram. Mom will want to hear all about your adventure."

Her grandmother frowned as she looked around at the stainless-steel counters and the hodgepodge of pots and pans hanging from the ceiling on racks. "Why did you bring me here?"

Rather than point out that Gram had found her own way to the café, Moira settled for a white lie. "You had a hankering for some pie."

Gram studied the array of empty ramekins in front of her. "I ate all of those."

It wasn't a question, but Moira answered, anyway. "Mr. Kondrat said you couldn't make up your mind which flavor

you wanted, so he served you three of the little ones instead of a great big piece like he gave me. You also wanted
to pet Ned there."

Gram looked down at the patient dog and blinked several times as if actually seeing him for the first time. "He's
a handsome fellow, isn't he?"

Then she winked at Moira and added, "And so is his
dog."

Moira's cheeks flushed hot. "We should be going, Gram.
Mr. Kondrat has work to do, and Mom will be concerned."

Gram rolled her eyes. "Your mother is a worrywart, so
we shouldn't keep her waiting. The longer I'm gone, the
longer her lecture will be. Besides, it's quite a walk back
to the house."

Moira wasn't sure which house her grandmother was
thinking about, but she was right in both cases. "We don't
have to walk, Gram. I have my police cruiser parked right
outside."

"Why would you be driving a police car, Moira? Won't
they be upset that you borrowed it?"

It was far from the first time Moira had to remind her
grandmother about her job and the fact that she was all
grown up. "It's my job, Gram, and I'm on duty. I need to
get you back home to Mom so I can finish my shift."

To get them both moving in the right direction, she
stood up and reached for her wallet. "Mr. Kondrat, how
much do I owe you for...?"

One look at their host's face had her putting away her
wallet. "Sorry, I meant no insult."

He wiped his hands on a towel and tossed it aside. Then,
in a surprising show of gallantry, he offered his arm to her
grandmother. "Mrs. Healy, let me escort you to the car."

It was hard not to laugh a little about how her grandmother preened as she set her hand on Titus's outstretched

arm. Both dog and man carefully escorted Gram out to the cruiser, waiting patiently for Moira to unlock the doors. Rather than let her diminutive grandmother try to climb up by herself, Titus swept her up in his arms and gently settled her in the passenger seat.

Gram's mind must have cycled back to the present again. Sitting up straighter, she reached out to pat Titus on the cheek. "Thank you for the pie, young man. Please give Ned an extra treat for keeping me company. I didn't mean to be a bother."

"I will, Mrs. Healy, and you weren't any bother at all."

"I'll bring your shirt back." As she spoke, Moira couldn't help but noticed that Titus looked everywhere except directly at her. "And thanks again for everything."

He nodded and stepped back to close the door. Then he and the dog disappeared into the building without a single backward glance. And although she wasn't sure why, Moira found that disappointing.

# *CHAPTER TWO*

TITUS STOOD IN the shadows at the front of his café and watched as the police cruiser slowly turned back onto the main drag through town and disappeared into the night. As its lights faded in the distance, he finally spoke to his silent companion. "Well, dog, that was a close call. Still, it went better than I thought it might."

The unexpected encounter definitely hadn't answered the question he'd been pondering ever since he'd first heard that Moira Fraser had moved back to Dunbar—would she recognize him? The answer appeared to be no, but the odd looks she'd been giving him said that could change at any moment. It had been both a relief and a huge disappointment. "I probably shouldn't be surprised. It's been a lot of years since we last crossed paths."

Besides, he didn't look the same, starting with the fact that he'd packed on a lot of muscle since then. Heck, there were days he didn't recognize his own image in the mirror. His hair was back to its natural dark brown, he no longer wore contacts to alter the color of his eyes and his voice was now rough as sandpaper, thanks to the damage done to his vocal cords during a fight.

Then there were his tattoos. When he'd last seen Moira, he'd only had one or two. Now his forearms were almost entirely etched with ink, the designs all symbols chosen for reasons known only to him. Hidden among the swirls of color were the names of those he'd lost along the way—friends, coworkers, pets and the one woman who had meant far more to him than he'd ever admitted, not just to her but to himself as well.

Ned nudged the side of Titus's leg, a not-so-subtle reminder that he'd wallowed in the disaster of his past long enough. "Fine, fine. I'll get with the program."

By the time Titus reached the kitchen, Ned was already curled up and dozing in his bed. The dog had the right idea, but Titus still had work to do before they could head home for the night. They'd have to walk since he'd taken a long ride on his Harley after leaving Cade and Shelby's reception early and then driven directly to the café. Ned had shown up only seconds after Titus had parked the bike in the alley, even though he'd left the dog in the house when he'd left for work. He was beginning to regret installing a doggy door so Ned could go in and out as needed. It was only after the door was installed that Titus learned that a six-foot fence was no obstacle if Ned decided he wanted to hang out at the café.

Titus had meant to stay long enough to prep a few things for tomorrow's menu before calling it quits for the day. Instead, Ned had immediately planted himself in front of the back door to the café and herded Titus down the alley and out into the night. As much as Titus had wanted to refuse, the dog wouldn't budge on the issue. As it turned out, Ned had somehow sensed that Mrs. Healy needed rescuing. No matter how many times Titus tried to tell both the dog and himself he was nobody's hero—not anymore—there was no way he would have left the elderly lady out there on the street.

Yeah, he could have called 911 as soon as he'd found her and simply waited until whoever was on duty came to take her home. Instead, he'd loaned Mrs. Healy his shirt to keep her warm and coaxed the shivering woman into following him back to the café, where he could offer her hot tea and all the pie she could eat.

The relief in Moira's voice had been obvious when he'd told her Mrs. Healy was safe and sound in his café. So was the displeasure that he was the one who had found her grandmother. Not much he could do about that. At least now, maybe he didn't have to be so careful about avoiding Moira since she hadn't immediately called him by the name he'd used back in the day. He was no longer that man.

In truth, he never had been. Not really.

Things had gotten a little dicey when he'd screwed up by fixing Moira's tea just the way she liked it. He'd done so out of habit, not realizing his mistake until right after he'd set it down in front of her. She'd noticed, too. It was obvious from the way she stared at the packet of tea and the lemon wedge. What had he been thinking? At least she'd bought his explanation that Earl Grey was the most popular flavor that he carried, which was true. So was the fact that he carried it because it reminded him of her.

He picked up his knife and went back to work. Slicing and dicing always relaxed him. When he finish chopping the last of the vegetables, he made the pastry he would need for tomorrow's crop of pies and put it in the fridge to rest overnight. It took him another twenty minutes to clean up so the kitchen was ready for Gunner, the short-order cook who handled the early morning rush.

Finally out of anything useful to do, he dried his hands on a towel and tossed it in the hamper in the corner. Satisfied he'd done all he could to get ready for another busy day of feeding the people of Dunbar, he turned off the lights. Ned joined him at the door, ready to walk home.

Before starting out, he rolled the Harley into the shed behind the café and locked the door. His bike probably would have been safe enough out on the street, but there was no use in taking chances. It was a classic 1990 Harley-Davidson Fat Boy that he'd rebuilt himself. The long process had helped him get his head back on straight, and riding it still helped him find peace in moments of high stress.

Once it was secure, he looked around for Ned. The dog was busy sniffing his way up and down the alley, but he came running when Titus gave a sharp whistle. "Let's go home, boy. Tomorrow is another busy day, and I need to get some shut-eye."

Right before they turned down the narrow road that led toward their house, he caught a glimpse of one of the Dunbar police cruisers a few blocks away. There was no telling if it was Moira at the wheel or one of the other officers, not that he cared. He didn't realize that he'd stopped to stare until Ned lunged forward, yanking his leash out of Titus's hand. The dog gave him a disgusted look and then took off running for the house and his bed out on the front porch. No doubt he'd be sound asleep by the time Titus walked the last quarter mile.

"Dog, I don't know why I put up with you."

Which was a lie. Titus still wasn't sure which of them had actually made the decision to become roommates. All he knew was that his house no longer seemed quite so empty, even on the occasional night when Ned opted to sleep outside.

When he finally reached the porch, he stopped to top up Ned's water bowl with the hose. "I'll be turning in soon. If you want in, now's the time."

Ned slowly stood up and stretched. After testing the air one last time, he trotted inside and waited patiently to see where Titus was going to settle. When he headed for the bedroom, Ned jumped up on the couch and staked out the center two cushions, making it clear he wasn't in the mood to share his chosen bed.

Titus circled back to give him a good scratch. "I don't blame you, fella. This might just be one of those nights."

They both knew what he was talking about. Sometimes sleep only came in fits and starts as nightmares from the past kept Titus from getting any real rest. There was no use in both of them having to run on fumes tomorrow. After a quick shower, Titus crawled between cold sheets and stared up at the ceiling, reminding himself it was a good thing that Moira hadn't yet recognized him.

But even if that was true, it still hurt if she'd forgotten all about him when he'd never been able to get her out of his mind.

"YOU'RE DRESSED FOR work early. I thought your shift didn't start until this afternoon."

Moira finished folding the flannel shirt Titus had loaned her grandmother last night before answering her mother. "I don't have to be at the office until noon, but I have a few errands to run first."

"Is that the shirt Mr. Kondrat loaned Gram last night?"

"Yeah, I told him I would return it."

Her mom leaned against the washer and watched as Moira hung up the rest of the load. "I wish there was something I could do to thank him for helping Gram like he did. Normally I would bake one of my apple pies, but I'm guessing he has all the pie he could ever want."

Moira smiled. "Yeah, that's what I was thinking, too. I thought maybe I'd pick up a nice bottle of wine for him."

"Seriously? I shouldn't stereotype people, but don't you think he looks more like a beer kind of guy?"

Her mother wasn't wrong, but for some reason Moira thought he might also appreciate a bottle of Malbec. "Well, if he doesn't like drinking wine, he could always cook up something special with it."

Although it would be a criminal waste of such a nice red wine. It was time to change the subject. "How is Gram doing?"

"She's usually pretty connected in the morning. It's only later in the day when things go off the rails."

Moira hung up the last shirt and then gave her mother a hug. "I'm sorry you're having to deal with all of this. Any word from the facility we looked at last week?"

It had been hard for them to finally admit that something had to be done. Her mother had a job with the local school district, but she was running out of leave. Moira's hours changed almost daily depending on what shift she worked. More than that, if she was in the middle of a call, she couldn't simply clock out and rush home at a moment's notice.

It had been one thing to leave Gram alone once she started getting a little forgetful. But now, it wasn't safe to leave her by herself no matter what time of day it was. There was a lady in town who didn't mind staying with Gram for a few hours if necessary, but Mrs. Redd couldn't do it every day and didn't like to work evenings. That left them no option other than to look for more specialized care. They'd found a local group home close by that they'd liked and were waiting for a room to become available.

"Try to get some rest, Mom. If I can, I'll stop by before I report for duty."

Her mother's smile didn't quite reach her eyes. "I'll be fine, hon. Besides, you have enough on your plate while Chief Peters is gone. Don't spend all your time worrying about us."

Moira nodded as if accepting her marching orders, but

they both knew she would still worry about them. That didn't mean that she wouldn't take care of business at work.

"Do you need anything while I'm out and about?"

"Not that I can think of. Elsie Redd said she could stay with Gram while I do the grocery shopping this afternoon. You go ahead and run your errands. I'll put the clean clothes away."

Moira picked up Titus's shirt and kissed her mom on the cheek on her way out of the house. Outside, she stopped to draw in a deep breath of the cool morning air. It had become her ritual. It was a way of setting aside her problems at home before shouldering the ones that came with her job.

Sometimes it even worked.

MOIRA WAS RUNNING out of time if she wanted to deliver Titus's wine and shirt tonight. She could've stopped in the café before she started work or even on her dinner break. Instead, she'd chickened out each time, telling herself that Titus wouldn't want to be bothered while he was working. That was probably true, but it wasn't as if she wanted to show up on the doorstep of his house without warning. He might be busy there, too.

What if he had company? She hadn't heard any rumors that linked Titus's name with a particular woman in town, but that didn't mean he wasn't seeing somebody. Although Moira had a perfectly legitimate reason to show up with his shirt and the wine in hand, it didn't mean his lady friend would appreciate it.

The last time she'd driven past the café, the lights in front were still on, so chances were some members of Titus's staff were hanging around. Deciding to wait a while longer before trying again, she returned to the station to drop off some paperwork. Rather than drive the short distance to the café, she opted to do a quick foot patrol on the way through the small business district in town. She spent too much time in her cruiser as it was, and a little exercise would do her good.

Other than a couple of people out walking with their dogs, there wasn't much going on. That was a good thing, even if it meant she had no excuse to further delay her visit to the café. Sure enough, the lights in front were off this time around. Rather than bang on the front door, she'd go around back like she had on the previous night.

She walked around the side of the building toward the alley in back, but stopped when she heard voices coming from behind the café. She froze, unsure if she should turn back. Rather than make a rash decision, she crept a little farther forward, stopping at the corner of the building to listen. There were two men talking.

"Thanks for making the trip. They seemed in a hurry to get this latest batch."

That gravelly rasp was all too familiar, but who was Titus talking to? And, more importantly, what kind of batch was he talking about?

"Sorry I couldn't get here any earlier, man, but I'll make sure they get the shipment first thing tomorrow."

"Good. Let them know I've reached out to my contacts, and there's already more in the pipeline. When it arrives, I'll call you to set up the distribution."

"Sounds good. Now, I should hit the road."

Moira risked a quick peek around the corner. Unfortunately, the second guy was already closing the rear door of a white van that had definitely seen better days. Without backup close at hand, she couldn't risk getting caught. She retreated half a step to listen in case she could learn more about what they were up to. Luck wasn't with her. All she heard was the sound of a car door opening and closing, followed by the rough rumble of its engine starting.

Luckily, the van continued on down the alley in the other direction. She held her position for another couple of minutes, her mind chock-full of questions with no answers. Maybe she was overreacting, but all that talk about batches and pipelines and shipments had her flashing back to the drug busts she'd been part of in the past. Too bad she hadn't gotten the license plate on the van so she could run it when she got back to the station. The guy had been standing right in front of it when she peeked around the corner, and now it was too late. Even if she could still see the van, it would be too far away to make out the numbers and letters.

Maybe she needed to keep a closer eye on what went on behind the café at night. It seemed Titus had other reasons to hang around after closing time, ones that had nothing to do with chopping onions and carrots.

Taking a deep breath, and hoping she looked calmer than she felt, she started forward only to let out a shriek when she ran right into Titus as soon as she turned the corner. He reached out to steady her before stepping back. He crossed his arms over his chest and stared down at her with his mouth quirked up in a small smile as if he found the situation amusing.

"Tell me, Officer Fraser, did you hear anything interesting while sneaking around and listening in on a private conversation?"

He might think this was funny, but she didn't. "I heard enough to wonder what else you might be selling these days besides chocolate-cream pie."

He flinched just enough to signal she'd scored a direct hit. "Feel free to wonder all you want. Now, if you'll excuse me, I need to lock up and head home."

The smart thing would be to walk away, but instead of going into full retreat, she marched up to the door and let

herself in. Titus was expecting her, because he was leaning against the counter with his legs crossed at the ankle
and looking far more relaxed than he had been a few seconds before. Obviously trying to put her off balance, he
gave her a long look, starting at her head and wandering
southward, then back up again, his gaze snagging briefly
on the gift bag in her hand.

"Look, Moira, I don't know what you're doing here, and
I don't care. Right now, I'm tired and just want to go home.
Whatever you want will have to wait." He turned his back
to her and began wiping down the counter.

"I didn't come here to spy on you."

He sighed and tossed the rag he'd been using into the
sink. "Then why are you here? If it's for more of the chocolate pie, I'll send some home with you if that will get you
out from underfoot faster."

The pie sounded good, but she didn't want to be any
further in debt to him than she already was. "Actually, I
came to give you this."

When she held out the bag, he stared at it as if she was
trying to hand him a live snake. "What's that?"

Since he showed no inclination to take it from her, she
stepped close enough to set it on the counter. "Your shirt
and a thank-you gift for helping my grandmother."

"You shouldn't have."

Considering how uncomfortable Titus looked at the moment, he probably meant that. Too bad. "Ordinarily Mom
would've baked you a pie, but she figured you already had
enough of those. She thought you were probably more of a
beer guy, but I decided to buy you a bottle of wine instead."

When he remained frozen right where he stood, she
pulled the bottle out of the bag and forced him to take it
from her hand. He held the wine out at arm's length and
frowned at the label as if it would give him cooties.

"If you don't like what I picked out, feel free to regift it. I'm sure you know someone who would like a nice Malbec from Argentina."

He swallowed hard and then nodded. "It's a surprising choice for a small-town girl, but I won't be regifting this. It's one of my favorite wines. I might wait for a special occasion, but I will enjoy it."

Okay, then. The crisis had passed, although she couldn't imagine why this suddenly felt like a pivotal moment in their relationship. Not that they had one. When he gently set the bottle back in the bag after wrapping it in his clean shirt, she took that as a signal it was time to leave.

She made a show of checking her watch before opening the door. "Well, I should get back to the office. TJ is due to relieve me in half an hour."

Titus must have hustled locking up because he caught up with her before she reached the corner. He matched his stride to hers as they walked along the side of the building. "I didn't hear your cruiser when you arrived."

Moira pointed out the obvious. "That's because I walked."

"Well, that explains it."

She glanced up at him. "Explains what?"

"How you got so close without me noticing."

Rather than get tangled up in that whole situation again, she kept it light and gave him a superior look. "Sir, I'll have you know I am a highly trained police officer. How we do what we do is a trade secret."

That he laughed a little pleased her more than it should have. She had another question of her own. "But if you didn't hear me coming, why were you waiting for me when I came around the corner?"

Her imagination was probably working overtime, but for a second there was something oddly familiar about his expression before he finally answered her question. "Café owners have secrets, too."

Then he walked away into the darkness, leaving her staring at his back.

# CHAPTER THREE

IT TOOK TITUS longer than normal to get home, mainly because he'd stood watch until Moira made it back inside the station. She'd kick his backside if she found out he was looking out for her. He also knew that she was perfectly capable of defending herself, but he'd sleep better knowing that she'd made it to the end of her shift safely.

That didn't mean he wasn't still a little bit ticked off that she'd decided to spy on him and Ryder out in the alley. Instead of simply asking what they were up to, she'd immediately leaped to the conclusion that he was dealing drugs out of the back of his café. Yeah, she didn't know this iteration of him well enough to know any better. That didn't mean he appreciated her lack of faith in him. Logic didn't enter into the equation.

He could've settled the problem by admitting it had been a shipment of donated dog food and cat litter for a group of animal shelters in the area. Any one of the shelter managers would vouch for him if Moira wanted to verify he was telling her the truth. But, stubborn man that he was, he wanted her to simply trust him. Stupid, but he'd never been smart when it came to her.

Heaven knew he should've walked away from her the minute he realized she was going to be more than a passing interest for him. That mistake had caused them both a lot of pain. If…no, *when* she figured out that he and Ryan Donovan were one and the same, she'd likely gut him with a dull spoon. Or, worse yet, rat him out to the rest of the town by exposing the fact that their favorite chef had been arrested in a major drug bust a decade ago.

Ned was waiting for him on the front porch. "Sorry I'm late. Stuff happened."

The dog didn't want excuses. He only cared about the delay in getting his kibble delivered on time. As soon as Titus opened the front door, Ned shoved past him to stand over his food dish, his displeasure clear.

"Fine, fine. I'll feed you as soon as I set this bag down."

He unwrapped the bottle of wine and set both it and his clean shirt on the counter. After filling Ned's dish, he cut up a leftover hamburger and added a few pieces to the mix. He knew he was spoiling the dog, but a man had to take care of his friends. Ned gave the bowl a good sniff and acknowledged Titus's efforts with a slow wag of his tail.

With his roommate taken care of, Titus popped the top on one of the microbrews that Max Volkov had given him a week or so ago. After taking a long swig, he smiled. Moira's mother wasn't wrong. He drank far more beer than he did wine. A cold brew really hit the spot after a long day at work or while sitting out on Cade's porch sharing pizza.

Wine was more of a special-occasion beverage as far as he was concerned, especially a pricey bottle of imported Malbec. It was the kind of wine a man bought for the special woman in his life, which was why he'd only served that particular vintage once. Just staring at the label was stirring up all kinds of memories, ones he tried not to think about very often.

Knowing he'd missed his chance at having a real life with the one woman he'd ever loved hurt too much.

An argument could be made that he'd been a fool to settle in Dunbar. There were other small towns and other run-down cafés that he could've bought. But when he'd finally broken free from the chains of his past, he hadn't even considered any other option than the one he'd chosen. It was probably a sign that, despite his best efforts, he hadn't quite given up his love of adrenaline rushes and taking risks.

He'd chosen Dunbar for one reason and one reason only. It was Moira Fraser's hometown. She hadn't been living here when he'd signed the paperwork on the café, but he'd known there was always a good chance that she might move back. If nothing else, she had family in Dunbar and would come back periodically to visit them. Add in that his was the only eatery in town other than a take-out pizza joint and a tavern, their paths were bound to cross again at some point.

So far, it was obvious that Moira hadn't consciously recognized Titus. He could probably thank the damage done to his voice and face ten years ago for that. Regardless, her subconscious was clearly hard at work. Otherwise, of all the possible choices in fine wines, why had she bought him a bottle of the same kind they'd enjoyed with the only dinner he had ever cooked for her?

Rather than torture himself by adding the Malbec to the small wine rack sitting on the back corner of his kitchen counter, he tucked it away over the refrigerator in the small cabinet that he hardly ever opened. Out of sight and out of mind. Yeah, like that ever worked.

He finished off his beer and tossed the bottle in the recycling bin. "I'm going to bed, dog. Keep the racket down so I can get some sleep."

Rather than curling up on the sofa, Ned followed him into the bedroom and hopped up on the bed. Titus glared at him. "Fine, you can sleep in here if you want, but pick a side of the bed and stay there. No hogging the middle."

When Titus stepped back out of the bathroom, all he

could do was stop and stare. Ned had expressed his opinion on the subject by stretching out across both pillows at the top of the bed. Titus finally laughed. "Good one, Ned. Now move."

Satisfied that his effort to yank Titus's chain had been a success, Ned shifted to the far side of the bed and fell back to sleep within seconds. Still chuckling, Titus made himself comfortable and did the same.

WITH EVERYTHING THAT was going on, Moira felt a little guilty stealing time out of her day for purely selfish reasons. Her mom had taken Gram to a doctor appointment, so there wasn't anything she needed to be doing at home. Besides, she didn't have to report into the office until midafternoon. Finally, she reminded herself that even her boss had been known to sneak in a lunch date with his fiancée now and then. An hour to kick back and share a few laughs with a friend would do her some good.

The only drawback was where she and Carli were meeting for lunch—Titus's café. Short of driving to another town, there was no other choice. Besides, Carli would likely ask a lot of uncomfortable questions as to why Moira would want to do that. She didn't want to explain that it had been two days since she and Titus had last crossed paths, and she wasn't particularly excited about the possibility of doing so again.

How was she supposed to act around a man she'd pretty much accused of engaging in criminal activity in the alley behind his café? Looking back, she couldn't blame him for being a little ticked off about it, but she hadn't been wrong to wonder why they'd been tossing around words like *supplier*, *batch* and *pipeline*. It would be one thing if Titus had simply explained what they had been doing, but he hadn't. He'd even gone so far as to tell her that he had secrets.

No surprise there.

The door to the café opened, and Carli poked her head out. "Well, are you coming in or not?"

Was it too late to claim she'd been called into work early? It was tempting, but then she spotted the man himself standing not far behind Carli, smirking just enough to set Moira's teeth on edge. "I'm coming in."

As usual, the place was pretty much packed, but Titus led them to a table near the back that had just been cleared. He handed them menus, greeting Carli by name. His dark eyes briefly met Moira's gaze. "It's been a while, Officer Fraser."

As she stalked past him, she muttered, "Not long enough."

He kept pace with her, then leaned in close and whispered, "If I'd known you were coming, I would've made sure to have the chocolate pie on the menu."

The rough rumble of his voice sent a shiver straight through the heart of her, causing her to almost stumble. Luckily, she caught herself before anyone noticed. Well, anyone other than Titus himself. She was pretty sure he was laughing as he turned away to greet another customer.

Carli knew Moira liked to keep an eye on her surroundings and preferred to sit with her back to the wall, so she automatically took the other seat. There was no way Moira could ask her to switch places without raising yet another bunch of questions. Her friend knew her too well.

She and Carli had gone to school together and stayed in touch over the years. Whenever Moira had come home for a visit, they got together to catch up on each other's lives. At least once a year, Carli would come stay with Moira for a few days. Sometimes they took in a traveling Broadway show or else treated themselves to hours in the spa at one of the local casino hotels. They'd even gone camping a time or two.

The best part was if either of them was going through a rough patch, the other one came running with a bottle of wine and a shoulder to cry on. Carli had been there for Moira ten years ago when her love life had imploded, and Moira had reciprocated when her friend had gone through an unexpected and unwanted divorce.

The bottom line was that Moira was sitting across from the one person who could read her like a book. She'd have to watch every word she said and every move she made. The last thing she needed was for her friend to pick up on Moira's intense awareness of the man weaving his way through the café as he handed out menus to newcomers and glanced in her direction whenever he thought she might not notice.

"So how are things going with Chief Peters gone?"

Carli's question snapped Moira's attention back to her where it should be. "Quiet for the most part. The city council decided I need to give them daily reports to make sure I'm staying on top of things. Cade won't appreciate them poking their noses in department business, and it's a huge waste of time."

Her smile turned a bit wicked. "I make everything as dry as possible. Nothing like statistics and bar graphs to bore the socks off people."

Carli chuckled. "Serves them right."

Their server put in an appearance. She set a glass of water in front of Carli and a pot of tea in front of Moira—Earl Grey with lemon and two sugars. After she took their orders and left, Carli gave Moira a puzzled look. "Do you come in here so often that they already know how you like your tea?"

"No, actually I don't. It must have been a lucky guess."

Her friend studied her for several seconds. "That's pretty specific for a lucky guess."

The man was definitely messing with her. "Maybe that's how they serve it to everybody."

Still looking dubious, Carli glanced back over her shoulder toward the kitchen and then back at Moira. "I order tea sometimes. I always get a bowl with half a dozen different flavors of tea bags in it and no lemon unless I ask for it."

Then she pointed at the small container on the table that was stuffed full of sugar and sweetener packets. "Did Titus think there weren't enough of those on the table for one cup of tea?"

Before Moira could come up with any kind of explanation that wasn't completely ridiculous, Titus came back with their orders himself. After serving Carli, he set Moira's bacon-burger platter on the table. It was piled high with at least double the normal amount of sweet-potato fries and came with two bowls of dipping sauces. One was tartar sauce and the other was ranch dressing. Carli's eyes almost bugged out of her head, but at least she didn't say a word.

"Can I get anything else for you two ladies?"

Not trusting herself to be civil, Moira kept her eyes on her food and shook her head. Carli managed to be a little more polite. "We're good, Mr. Kondrat."

"Let me know if that changes."

As he walked away, Moira stuffed three fries into her mouth at once to avoid having to answer the litany of questions that Carli was bound to ask. The ruse failed miserably. As soon as she swallowed, her friend pounced. "Okay, what's up between you and Dunbar's mystery man? And don't tell me nothing is going on. I eat here at least once a week, and I've never seen him act like this."

"Like what?"

Her friend held up her fingers to count off the facts. "He

seated us himself. He usually just points and tells people where to sit. He sent tea to the table just the way you like it, and he delivered our food personally."

She stopped to point at Moira's plate. "That's enough sweet-potato fries for two people, so he knows you like them. You didn't ask for any special dipping sauces, but he brought your two favorites. Shall I continue?"

Even Moira had to admit Carli's evidence was pretty compelling. "Did anyone ever suggest you should've been a prosecuting attorney? After that list, any jury in the country would vote to convict."

Her friend leaned forward, elbows on the table. "Which raises the question of what you two might be guilty of. I won't be happy if you've been holding out on me."

Better to go with the safe part of the truth and hope that was enough to satisfy Carli's curiosity. "For starters, the only times I've eaten here, he's been working in back. However, Gram got out again the other night, and Mr. Kondrat found her. He brought her back here and served her pie and tea while he waited for me to come pick her up. When I arrived, she wasn't quite done with her treats, so he offered me tea and pie, too."

"And?"

"And what? Isn't that enough?"

Her friend's expression turned more sympathetic. "I'm so sorry about Gram, and it was nice of him to come to the rescue. Having said that, I get that might be why he knows how you like your tea, but it doesn't explain the fries, the dipping sauces or the way you avoided looking him in the eye when he was standing right there. I've never seen you act so skittish before."

Moira set her burger back on her plate. It was tempting to rail at her friend, but this wasn't Carli's problem. It was Moira's, plain and simple. She sighed as she dipped a fry in the ranch dressing. "I'm not afraid of Titus. There's just something about him that sets my teeth on edge. It's a cop thing, not a woman-versus-man thing. I've put a lot of men who look like him behind bars over the years."

That clearly shocked Carli. "But he's friends with Chief Peters."

"I know." She ate the fry and reached for another one. Talking about what it was like to be a cop with a civilian was never easy, even if the other person was a good friend. "You know me. I've never seen a puzzle I didn't want to solve, and that man is definitely a puzzle. No one knows where he came from or what he did before he moved to Dunbar. Heck, even Bea hasn't been able to figure it out, and you know all gossip flows through her bakery."

A shadow fell across the table, startling them both. She wasn't the only one relieved to see it was Rita, one of the two sisters who worked the day shift at the café. She had two pieces of pie in her hands, both of them chocolate-cream. She smiled at Moira. "It's your lucky day. It turns out we had exactly two pieces of your favorite pie left. Titus said it's on the house since he'd told you it wasn't on the menu today."

Moira unclenched her teeth long enough to be polite. "Thanks, Rita. Tell Mr. Kondrat we appreciate his generosity."

"Will do."

Carli waited until Rita disappeared back into the kitchen before speaking. "I don't remember the subject of pie coming up earlier when we gave her our orders."

"It didn't."

Knowing two words wouldn't satisfy Carli's curiosity, Moira surrendered to the inevitable. "Titus gave me chocolate-cream pie when I was here with Gram. It was delicious, and he must have noticed how much I liked it.

When he walked us to the table, he quietly mentioned that if he'd known I was coming in, he would've made sure there was chocolate-cream pie on the menu."

"Interesting." Her friend's eyes were alight with amusement when she added, "I assume you've noticed that he's an attractive man."

Seriously? "If you think he's all that, why don't you make him a casserole?"

Carli slapped her hand onto her forehead. "Gee, now why didn't I think of that? Especially when it worked so well last time."

Wow, there was a lot of sarcasm packed into that statement. Carli had been one of the women who had tried to catch Cade Peters's eye when he'd first moved to town by providing him with a whole lot of home-cooked meals. There had definitely been some sour grapes when he'd chosen Shelby Michaels instead, especially considering she hadn't baked a single casserole for him.

Moira smirked just a little. "I'm just saying."

"Okay, I'll tell you why. First, it obviously didn't work the last time. Second, Titus is a better cook than I could ever hope to be. Anything I baked for him would only be a big disappointment and would probably end up as a free meal for that huge dog that hangs around in the kitchen back there."

It was hard to argue with her logic. Besides, Moira wouldn't want to see her friend get hurt again. The meltdown of Carli's marriage had left wounds on her friend's heart that had only started to heal, and she needed a man who would treat her gently. Having seen the way Titus had been with her grandmother, she knew he was capable of toning down his intensity if the situation called for it. But that wasn't who Titus was at the core. She was convinced of that much.

Moira noticed two men, both members of the city council, headed for the door, and she stifled the urge to groan when they suddenly detoured in her direction. "Mr. Hayes, Mr. Crisp."

Julius Hayes checked his watch. "Officer Fraser, do you really have time to be socializing in the middle of the day when you're supposed to be in charge of the police department? I've heard that there have been reports of two incidents of theft over the past two days. Something about pet supplies missing from the feedstore and the market."

"I know about the thefts, Mr. Hayes. We wrote up reports and took statements from the two businesses. No one knows when the items were actually taken, only that their inventory of canned cat and dog food was off by several items. Neither business has security cameras, and no one saw anything. That doesn't leave us much to investigate, but we'll be checking back with the owners periodically to see if it happens again. Oscar is on duty and knows he can call me for assistance if need be. Since I'm on duty tonight, I'm not scheduled to report in for another hour."

Herb Crisp wasn't having it. "As the acting chief, you should be—"

Another unwelcome party joined the discussion, cutting off whatever the man was about to say with a simple look. He stared at them. "Gentlemen, since you've finished your two-hour lunch, I suggest you pay your bills and leave."

As entertaining as it was to see the two councillors bolt toward the cash register, Moira didn't appreciate Titus poking his nose in her business. "I was dealing with the situation. You didn't have to do that."

"Yeah, I did. I don't put up with anyone hassling my customers no matter who they are." He walked away without giving Moira a chance to respond.

Carli waited until Titus reached the two councillors to

ring up their checks before speaking. "Wow, that was intense. I bet those two will never do that again."

"Maybe not, but I don't want or need Titus butting his nose in my business. If he does it again, we'll be having words." Because she didn't need him making her look as if she needed a big, strong man to run interference for her, especially in front of the two councillors who had questioned Cade's decision to leave her in charge.

"We'd better get the pie boxed up to go while we finish off our burgers. I really should report in."

Carli finished cutting her burger in half to make it easier to manage and then pointed her knife in Moira's direction. "Fine, but just know I can't remember the last time I've seen you this worked up about a man. You might not realize it, but you can't seem to tear your eyes off Titus even when you're mad at him."

Moira realized it, all right. Try as she could to convince herself it was all because of what had gone on in the alley the other night, that story didn't hold water. No, there was just something about the way that man moved that drew her gaze every time he wandered through the diner. There was such power in those broad shoulders and lean muscles. And silly as it was, she'd always had a thing for men with their sleeves rolled up to reveal powerful forearms. She would have never thought she'd find that many tattoos attractive, but she'd really like to study his artwork up close.

Carli snickered. "There you go doing it again."

Having a fair complexion made it impossible to hide the fact that she was blushing. "Enough, Carli. Please."

"Okay, I'll lay off for now. Just know we'll be revisiting this conversation at another time."

Surrendering to the inevitable, Moira shrugged. "That's what I figured."

Hopefully she'd have better answers for her friend about this odd compulsion when the time came. Sadly, she wouldn't bet on that happening.

## CHAPTER FOUR

TEN MINUTES AFTER Moira went on duty, her day took a definite turn for the weird. Oscar had ducked his head in the door long enough to say that two people had shown up at the front desk wanting to report a major crime. He'd been about to relieve TJ out on patrol, so Moira told him to escort the pair to the conference room and tell them she'd join them shortly.

She closed out the file she'd been updating and picked up her clipboard that held blank report forms. Oscar hadn't mentioned any names, but she recognized both people. A widow in her early seventies, Mrs. Zimmer shared a duplex with her cousin about two blocks away from where Moira lived. Edward Sandis had a small house in the same neighborhood. He'd retired from the forestry department a few weeks back.

Considering they had both reported their pets missing within the last few days, it wasn't surprising when they each pulled out a flyer that featured Mrs. Zimmer's calico cat and Mr. Sandis's long-haired dachshund. Assuming they were there for a status update on the department's efforts to locate the missing animals, Moira set her clipboard on the table. "I'm sorry, but there hasn't been progress. We've all been keeping an eye out for Bitsy and Clyde. I've also checked in with a couple of the closest animal shelters to see if they've picked up any strays that fit their descriptions."

Mr. Sandis waved off her apology. "We know you've done your best, Officer Fraser. That's not why we're here. We wanted to update you on what's happened since we first reported the problem. I learned that her cat was missing when our paths crossed when I was posting my flyers. In fact, they disappeared within an hour of each other. Needless to say, we've both been doing everything we can to find both of our pets."

He smiled at the older woman. "We've each cruised different parts of town looking for Bitsy and Clyde with no luck. Until yesterday, that is."

Then he pointed at two plastic bags sitting in front of him on the table. From where Moira was sitting, it looked as if they each held what looked like a typewritten note and a legal-size envelope. After sliding them across the table toward Moira, Mr. Sandis said, "We've had a break in the case. The two of us found these letters in our mailboxes yesterday afternoon. We put them in the bags like they do on television to protect the forensic evidence. Thought you might want to dust them for fingerprints or something."

Moira didn't want to rain on their parade, but that wasn't going to happen. Small police departments like theirs didn't have their own labs. Instead, they depended on the county sheriff's department for any forensic investigations. It was doubtful—if not laughable—that the sheriff would waste limited resources on a missing pets.

That didn't mean Moira wouldn't give it her best effort to figure out what was going on. Picking up the bags, she quickly scanned the notes. The messages were identical:

If you want your pet back, put $20.00 in the enclosed sandwich bag and leave it in the old phone booth behind the abandoned gas station.

"Seriously? You think someone is actually holding your pets ransom? For twenty dollars?"

It was hard not to groan when both people immediately nodded. By that point, Mrs. Zimmer was smiling big-time. "Yes, that's exactly what happened."

Moira tried to get her head around the idea. "It seems more likely to me that someone saw your flyers and decided to see if you'd pay up on the off chance it would get your pets back."

"But that's just it. We did put the money in the old phone booth. When I woke up this morning, Bitsy was back home."

It had to be a coincidence. "Did she look like she'd been living on the street for a few days? Was she starving?"

Mr. Sandis picked up the conversation. "No, actually, I'd have to say that wherever Clyde has been, he was well treated. His nails were clipped, he'd had a bath and his coat had been brushed. He hasn't looked that good since the last time my wife took him to that fancy dog groomer in Seattle."

"The same with my cat. I don't know what brand of pet shampoo the kidnapper used, but Bitsy's fur was so soft and smooth. Smelled good, too."

Moira was happy for them, but she wasn't sure what they wanted her to do now. "I'm glad it's all turned out for the best. However, I'm pretty sure the sheriff's office won't have time to process the evidence, especially since the pets have come home."

Mrs. Zimmer looked disappointed by Moira's assessment of the situation, but Mr. Sandis didn't look surprised. "I thought that might be the case. But all things considered, I thought it was worth a shot."

"What things?"

He brought up a picture on his cell phone and passed it

over. "When I went to take down the flyers on Clyde and Bitsy, I saw these."

The picture was a close-up of three more flyers about missing pets—two small dogs and another cat. All of them were from the same general area where Mr. Sandis and Mrs. Zimmer lived.

"I hadn't heard about these. I'll have to check with Oscar and TJ to see if either of them have taken reports about more missing animals. Is it okay if I forward these pictures to myself? I'd like to reach out to the owners to see what I can learn."

"Sure thing. Do you want to keep the ransom notes, too?"

She reached for her clipboard and began to fill out the form. "Yes, I need to log them in as evidence."

That had both of her guests sitting up straighter in their chairs. This was probably the closest either of them had ever come to being part of an official police investigation. If she was a betting woman, either or both of them would head straight for the bakeshop down the street to announce the news. It was tempting to ask them to keep the information to themselves for the time being, but she decided that it probably wasn't possible to keep a lid on the situation for long, anyway. Besides, there was no telling how many people they'd already talked to before deciding to bring the ransom notes to the police department.

It didn't take long to finish the report. She wrote the case number on the back of her business card for each of them and then stood. "Thanks for bringing this to our attention. I'll reach out to the other pet owners to make sure they know to contact our office if they get a note like this or if their pet comes home."

"That's great." Mr. Sandis held out his hand. "Thanks for taking this seriously, Officer Fraser. I know compared to the cases you probably handled in Seattle, a lost cat or dog may not seem all that important. But if you'd heard my wife crying when we thought we'd lost Clyde forever, you'd know how much it meant to us."

"I understand, Mr. Sandis. Please tell your wife that I'm so pleased that Clyde is back home where he belongs."

She walked with them to the front door of the station. He was right, of course. It was highly unlikely that her former department would have paid much attention to this kind of case. It was a prime example of how police work in a small town was understandably different from working in a major city. She might have some regrets about walking away from her job in Seattle, but that didn't mean she wasn't going to do her best to serve the people of Dunbar.

As she returned to her desk, she pondered the case. What kind of person kidnapped a cat and then asked for such a paltry ransom amount? Especially when it sounded like they'd spent a fair amount of money on grooming products and pet food, returning the animal well-fed and shampooed. Well, unless the kidnappings tied in with the stolen pet supplies.

It was a puzzle all right. Shaking her head, she went back to reading the report she'd been working on when Oscar had interrupted her. Once that was finished, she'd start making some phone calls.

THE FIRST HOUR Moira was on patrol was blissfully quiet. Unfortunately, a call from Dispatch changed that. "Tell Shay Barnaby I should be there in less than five minutes."

Moira hung up the call and picked up speed. A few blocks later, she spotted the commotion that had been reported to Dispatch. Evidently, some truckers had gotten rowdy enough at Barnaby's tavern that Shay himself had escorted them out of his fine establishment. Considering his reputation, he'd probably used his boot to hurry them on out the door. She wasn't taking the situation lightly, but she would've liked to have seen that for herself. In his midthirties, Barnaby was a former Recon Marine, and no one with a lick of sense would take him on when he got riled up.

He understood the nature of his clientele and on the whole was pretty tolerant of their behavior. If he couldn't handle the kind of crew that routinely hung out in the tavern, he had definitely picked the wrong line of work. From what Moira had heard, only one thing would result in him tossing out paying customers: someone had said or done something to offend one of his employees. Moira actually respected the man for being so highly protective of his staff. This time a trucker had gotten a bit handsy with one of the servers, a definite no-no. When the guy's two drunken buddies had laughed, Barnaby had ordered all three of them to vacate the premises pronto.

The trio had made the mistake of thinking they stood a chance against Shay Barnaby. He had them out the door and back on the street before they knew what hit them. In the process, he'd also confiscated their keys to make sure none of them got behind the wheel until they sobered up. That was smart of him, even if it left the three wandering around on the street with nowhere to go and no way to get there even if they did.

Hence the call to Moira. Left to their own devices, there was no telling what kind of trouble they would get into. She parked her cruiser and got out, but not until she put in a call to the county sheriff's department to let them know she would likely need an assist.

She walked toward where the trucker and his friends were wandering around, peering in shop windows as if on the hunt for another watering hole. As soon as one of them spotted her headed their way, they stood shoulder-to-shoulder and watched her approach. When they stepped off the sidewalk into the glow of a nearby streetlight, she recognized the guy on the left. Jimmy Hudson had been a year ahead of her in school, and his mother still lived about a block from her mom's house.

"Jimmy, looks like you might need to call someone to come get you. If you don't have your phone handy, I can make the calls for you."

He squinted in her direction. "Do I know you?"

"I'm Moira Fraser. We went to school together." She tapped the badge on her uniform shirt. "Actually, it's Officer Fraser now. Do you still live with your mom?"

He snorted with laughter and jerked his thumb toward the guys standing next to him. "No, I live with them."

Then he gave her what he probably thought was a sexy leer and waggled his eyebrows. "As you can see, I'm all grown up. Maybe you should come home with us."

Praying for patience, Moira tried a different tack. "Do you live within walking distance or do I need to call someone to come pick you up?"

Jimmy puffed out his chest and widened his stance. "Doesn't matter. I parked my truck out back. I can drive myself home as soon as you arrest that Barnaby guy for stealing my keys."

He waved his hand in the general direction of his two companions. "Theirs, too. He had no right to do that. We didn't do anything wrong."

"That's not what I heard. According to Mr. Barnaby, he asked you to leave because you disrespected at least one member of his staff. You know he doesn't put up with that kind of stuff. He also doesn't let people drive who've had too much to drink."

"I apologized to her." Jimmy frowned and added, "At

least I meant to. He tossed us out before I had a chance. When you go inside to get our keys, you tell him that it's all his fault."

Like that was going to happen. "First things first. We need to get the three of you home. Then I'll talk to Barnaby about your keys. You can pick them up at the station tomorrow, provided you cooperate and go home quietly."

When Jimmy turned his back to her to confer with his buddies, she knew they weren't going be smart about this. It was time to check on those reinforcements from the county. The trouble was that the county deputies were likely out on their own calls.

While the three men were distracted, she checked back to find out how much longer it would be until help arrived. Hearing the best-case scenario was an ETA of fifteen to twenty minutes, she quickly dialed TJ's number. He answered on the second ring, sounding blissfully alert despite the late hour. He was out his front door and running for his car before she finished explaining. She only needed to keep a lid on things long enough for him to get there.

Jimmy abruptly turned back around, an ugly smile on his face. "We don't want to go home. We want to go back inside. Barnaby can't refuse to serve us because of a little misunderstanding with that waitress. He never asked for our side of the story."

That was probably because Barnaby had seen it play out in real time, but pointing that out wasn't going to help the situation. Moira offered the best deal she could. "Jimmy, for the last time, the three of you need to go home and sleep it off. Otherwise you're going to end up behind bars, and it won't be here in Dunbar. You'll be the guests of the county, and none of us want that to happen."

He made a show of looking up and down the street.

"Funny, I don't see any county deputies anywhere around here. It's just us and one lady cop all by her lonesome."

When he took several steps in her direction, Moira stood her ground. "You don't want to do this, Jimmy. What will your mama say?"

"Don't know. Don't care."

He kept coming. "Like I said, you've got no backup. Chief Peters is out of town on his honeymoon. That old cop, Oscar something, he wouldn't be much help even if he was here."

Jimmy wasn't wrong, but Moira wasn't going to admit that in front of a civilian. "Who can I call for you?"

One of the others finally chimed in. "Like he said. We don't need no calls made. Make Barnaby give our keys back or things are gonna get rough."

Moira wasn't the only one who jumped when Titus prowled out of the shadows from across the street with that huge dog at his side. He was on Moira's left, a few steps behind her, as if making it clear that he was there as backup, not trying to take charge of the situation. That didn't keep him from injecting himself into the conversation.

"What was that you said, Toby? Because it sure sounded like you were threatening Officer Fraser."

The cold fury threaded through his words had all three men taking a step back, even as it had Moira's temper flashing hot. She had the situation under control with additional support on the way. But now wasn't the time for that discussion; that would come later, when the current problem had been dealt with. The guy Titus had called Toby swallowed hard and held up his hands as if hoping to placate the furious man standing beside her.

"Sorry, Titus. I didn't mean nothing. We were just messing with her. We didn't know she was yours."

Moira cringed. *Great.* The last thing she needed was

for rumors linking her name to Titus's to start circulating in town, especially if the city council caught wind of him backing her up on a call. They already doubted her ability to do her job. Before she could set Toby straight, Titus did it for her.

"Officer Fraser is her own woman, knucklehead. But from what I heard from Shay Barnaby, Officer Fraser is not the first woman you nitwits insulted tonight. I won't stand for it and neither will Barnaby. You're all banned from my café and his tavern until further notice."

Well, wasn't that just dandy. Nothing like throwing gas on the fire. He had to know that kind of threat wasn't going to help the situation. She glared at him and then at Toby. "Like he said, I speak for myself. Here's how this is going to play out. Settle down now and I'll make sure you get home. We'll return your keys in the morning. The other option is spending the night behind bars. It's your choice."

Toby had sobered up enough to realize how much trouble they were in, but Jimmy was still going full steam ahead. "I ain't afraid of either of you. Besides, it's still three against two."

Titus's dog barked and flashed his teeth, maybe to point out that the odds were actually even. She didn't know about Jimmy, but she wouldn't want to face off against Ned…or his owner, for that matter.

"Not three, Jimmy. I'm out of this." Toby stumbled back a few steps, holding up his hands. His bloodshot eyes pleaded with Moira to believe he no longer wanted to be part of this disaster. If he actually meant it, it would help even up the odds.

She pointed toward the sidewalk behind him. "Toby, go sit down on the curb. Officer Shaw will be along any second. He'll drive you home when we're done here."

Toby immediately backpedaled over to the curb and

sat down. The as-yet-unnamed third member of the group looked at Jimmy, her and then Titus. "Is that offer good for me, too?"

When she nodded, he joined Toby on the curb, putting several feet between them. Both men were smart enough to keep their hands in plain sight and didn't move an inch. Rather than follow their lead, Jimmy made a break for it, making a quick turn to charge back toward the tavern.

He might have been a football star in high school, but his glory days were long gone. Moira caught up with him before he'd gone ten feet. Using his own momentum against him, she had him on the ground and cuffed before he knew what hit him. He tried to roll over, but she held him in position. That didn't mean she wasn't relieved to see TJ finally arrive. He parked his car and came running.

"What can I do?"

"Let's get him into the back of my cruiser. The county deputy is on his way. He can take him to the county lockup."

She nodded in the direction of the other two. "They made smarter decisions. I told them you'd see they got home. I'll pick up their keys from Shay Barnaby after we're done here. They can get them back in the morning."

They dragged Jimmy up to his feet. "This one will get his back when and if the judge says he can."

When they'd tucked Jimmy into the back seat of her vehicle, TJ frowned. "Sorry you had to do this all by yourself."

She hadn't, not really. But when she looked around for Titus, he had disappeared as quickly as he had appeared. She fully intended to rip into him but good for showing up unwanted and uninvited, but that discussion would be private. His intentions had been good—it just wasn't his job.

It was hers.

TITUS STARED UP at the stars overhead as he replayed the confrontation in front of Barnaby's in his head. Looking back, it was obvious that Moira had already called for backup before he had charged into the situation. There wasn't a doubt in his mind that the woman would come looking for him sometime soon.

"Darn it, dog, I screwed up big-time."

Ned didn't care. He was too busy sniffing around the bushes along the front edge of their yard. He took it personally if another dog or any other critter decided to make a pit stop in his territory. He stopped at one bush long enough to grumble a bit before lifting his leg. His job done, he trotted to the porch and waited for Titus to catch up.

As he unlocked the door, he couldn't help but admire the way Moira had faced off against the three fools without backing down an inch. She'd given them every possible chance to make a smart decision. It had even worked two times out of three. Chalk that up as a win for the good guys. Too bad Jimmy hadn't made the same decision.

None of them would be happy about being banned from the café and Shay's place for any length of time, but it served them right.

He flipped on the lights and headed into the kitchen. Ned followed along in case Titus had somehow forgotten that he'd already fed him earlier. "I'm not falling for that again, dog."

But then he tossed Ned a couple of his favorite treats. "Thanks for backing Moira up tonight. She might not appreciate our efforts, but I couldn't simply hang back and watch."

Because if Toby and that other guy hadn't come to their senses, she would have had her hands full on her own. He grabbed a couple of protein bars out of the pantry and a beer from the fridge, then headed for the sofa. Ned joined him, taking up far more room than one dog should. Titus turned on the news and settled back to unwind a little before heading to bed.

Stroking Ned's head helped with that. "I give it until tomorrow evening before Officer Fraser shows up to read me the riot act for getting involved. She has no idea how close I came to clocking Toby for shooting his mouth off about things getting rough for her."

He couldn't help but grin a little. "If that had happened, I have no doubt Jimmy wouldn't have been the only one sitting behind bars tonight. Think how much madder she'd be if she were to find out that Shay and I had planned ahead of time that he'd call me if he had to toss anyone out while Cade is gone."

Ned heaved a big sigh and rolled over. "Yeah, I know. It's not your problem."

When the phone rang, Titus considered ignoring it. Right now, he just wanted to kick back and relax for a while before turning in for the night. Sadly, he wouldn't be able to do that if he didn't check to see who was calling. Seeing Rita's name on the screen, he knew he had to answer. She wouldn't be calling for no reason, especially at this hour.

"Hey, Rita, what's up?"

A few seconds later, he had to ask her to back up and repeat about half of what she'd said. This time, she spoke at a more reasonable pace, but that didn't make the news any better. Realizing how stressed she sounded over having to abandon her post, he decided to lie. "No, I get it. Don't you worry about the café. I have names of a couple of people in town who said they might be willing to be on call in an emergency. Both of you go and help your sister. Once things settle, text me when you'll be heading back."

After asking her a few more questions, he said, "Let me know if it's a boy or a girl."

He should've foreseen the possibility of something like this happening when he hired the two sisters as his primary servers. The only person he knew in town who didn't have a regular job was Max Volkov. He had no idea if Max had ever worked in a restaurant, but Titus was willing to give him a crash course in the basics if he could come in for even a couple of hours until Titus could make other arrangements. Eyeing his companion, he asked, "Well, Ned, how do you feel about waiting tables?"

The dog opened his eyes briefly and then went right back to sleep.

"Yeah, that's what I thought."

## CHAPTER FIVE

THE LAST THING Moira wanted to do first thing on her day off was to confront Titus Kondrat about the stunt he'd pulled the night before. No matter how good his intentions, she couldn't let something like that stand. She knew he was working, but what she wanted to tell him wouldn't take long, ten seconds tops. A simple "Don't ever do that again" would get the message across. Then maybe she could quit stewing about it and get on with her day.

When she reached the café, the line was out the door and halfway down the block. The place always did a brisk business during peak hours, but she couldn't remember seeing a backup like this. When she spotted a familiar face, she made her way through the crowd, promising those waiting that she wasn't cutting the line and would leave as soon as she asked someone a quick question. Mrs. Redd was actually her mother's friend, the one who sometimes stayed with Gram when both Moira and her mother had to be away from home.

When she tapped Mrs. Redd on the shoulder, the woman jumped. She'd been busy brushing something off her sleeve, frowning as she did so. "Moira, I didn't see you. I was just at a friend's house, and her cat shed all over me. I hope you're not hoping to cut in line. Well, unless you have to be on duty soon."

"No, I was just wondering why the line is so long this morning."

The older woman sighed. "Neither of the waitresses showed up for work today, so Mr. Kondrat is by himself. It's taken me thirty minutes to get this close to the door. To tell the truth, I'd go back home, but the special is his French toast. He makes it with challah bread, you know. It's delicious."

"I bet it is. Thanks for the information."

Moira retreated to a safer distance to consider what she could do to help the situation. It wasn't her problem, of course, but the café was the only place in town to get a meal. A fair number of the locals ate breakfast there before starting their workday. If they gave up and left, they'd either have to do without, go back home to eat, or else drive another twenty miles to the nearest diner.

Only one plan of action made sense. Titus might not like her poking her nose into his business any more than she'd appreciated his help last night, but too bad. She jogged down to the corner and headed for the back entrance of the café. One glance in the window only strengthened her resolve. It was total chaos.

When she let herself inside, the guy manning the grill didn't even glance in her direction. She approached him carefully, not wanting to startle him. "Gunner, where are the aprons?"

He pointed toward a drawer across the room. "You gonna work today?"

She nodded. "Yeah, I might be a bit rusty, but I'm pretty sure it will all come back to me. Does Titus use one of those fancy computer things to take orders or does he go old-school?"

Gunner laughed as he flipped fried eggs onto a plate. "Right now, the man wouldn't care if you carved the orders on stone tablets if it would get people served faster."

"Are the tables still numbered in the same order? One by the door and on around from there?"

"Yep."

First up, she made quick work of loading the dishwasher and setting it to run. That done, she picked up a pad of order slips, grabbed a couple of pens and then stuffed everything in her apron pocket. Spotting a rubber band, she slicked her hair back into a ponytail before washing her hands and heading out into the fray.

Before approaching any new customers, she decided delivering the backlog of orders sitting on the pass-through window should get priority. She loaded up a tray with the plates and added the packets of butter, bottles of syrup and other necessities.

"What do you think you're doing, Officer Fraser?"

"I'm helping out."

Titus nudged her aside with his hip to pick up the tray and grumbled, "Thanks, but I don't need any help."

So it was all right for him to poke his nose in her business last night, but not for her to offer to help him? "Yeah, you do, like it or not. And just so you know, I've put in way more hours working at this café than you have. I started busing tables here when I was fourteen and worked as a waitress during the summers all the way through high school and college."

She pointed toward the front window at the line of people still waiting to get in. "Those people need to get fed and soon."

With a look of pure frustration, he jerked his head in a nod. "Fine. Yell if you have questions."

As he stalked away, she set out another tray and repeated the same process. Titus came back for it within a couple of minutes. He didn't seem any happier about her being there, but he didn't say a word. When the backlog of orders was under control, she grabbed the cart that the servers used to clear tables after people had finished their meals. Despite the passage of years since she'd last worked at the café, evidently some skills didn't need to be relearned.

As she wiped down the last table, she noticed several people waiting near the door. On her way toward them, she gathered up several stacks of menus that were scattered around the room and returned them to the bin where they belonged.

Pasting on a smile, she asked the people at the front of the line, "How many?"

"Four, Moira."

"This way."

Titus glared at her from across the room, but she ignored him and returned for the next group. Once she had all the tables filled again, she started a fresh pot of coffee before taking the previous one with her as she circled the room topping off drinks for customers between taking orders from those who were waiting.

"Officer Fraser, a moment of your time, please."

Moira came to an abrupt stop next to where Otto Klaus was sitting. "Mr. Mayor, what can I do for you?"

"You're supposed to be in charge of the police department. Shouldn't you be doing that job instead of busing tables? That's not what we're paying you for."

She forced a smile. "Actually, it's my day off, although I still check in on a regular basis. The other officers know to call if they need backup. When I saw the line outside, I figured Mr. Kondrat might need a little help."

Otto didn't look any happier. "I hope Titus is grateful. I hear tell Rita Leoni and her sister Beth left to help their older sister. Seems she went into labor early."

So that's what had happened.

"Is there anything else I can get you? More coffee?"

Otto waved her off. "I'd like my check."

"I'll let Titus know."

She caught up with the man in question a second later. "The mayor would like his bill."

He studied her for a second. "Did he say something to upset you?"

"Seems he thought I was blowing off my real job to work here." Seeing the flare of anger in his expression, she stepped in front of him. "It's not your problem, and I already set him straight."

When his expression relaxed, she asked, "So should I take orders, bus tables or wash dishes?"

He glanced around the room. "If you'll take orders, I'll deliver the food and run the register."

"Sounds good."

Before she could walk away, he grabbed her arm just long enough to stop her. "Thanks for doing this, Moira."

She pointed a finger at him. "I'm still mad about last night, but you're welcome."

His mouth quirked up in a small smile. "Fair enough."

IT WASN'T UNTIL ten thirty that Titus finally had a chance to catch his breath. to make sure Moira and Gunner also got a break, he locked the front door and posted a handwritten note that the café would reopen sometime between eleven and eleven thirty. He'd barely sat down at his usual table in the back corner when Moira walked out of the kitchen and headed in his direction.

She plunked down two plates containing sandwiches and cups of soup and then walked away. A few seconds later, she was back with glasses of water and two slices of pie. Without asking permission, she sat down across from him. When Titus didn't dive right in, she pushed the plate closer to him. "Eat while you can. Things will pick up speed again all too soon."

A wise man knew when to argue and when to accept his marching orders. "Yes, ma'am."

Apparently satisfied that he was taken care of, Moira picked up her own sandwich and took a big bite. It was hard not to stare as she took pleasure in the simple act of eating. The truth was there was so much he admired about Moira even if the mad rush they'd dealt with had left its mark. Her ponytail was a bit bedraggled. There was also a grease stain on her apron and a smudge of what was probably flour on her cheek. She'd never looked more beautiful to him, not that he was about to tell her that.

The woman was already mad at him. No use in making matters worse.

They ate in companionable silence. She wasn't wrong. He needed to refuel before people started arriving for lunch. The breakfast rush lasted way longer than normal because he hadn't been able to find anyone to fill in for Rita and her sister. If Moira hadn't shown up out of the blue, it would have been a total disaster.

Never in his wildest dreams would he have ever expected Moira to be the one who would ride to the rescue. He owed her big-time, which reminded him… "I'll need you to fill out some paperwork."

She frowned at him. "What kind of paperwork?"

"So I can pay you for today."

"Nope, no paperwork. For one thing, you haven't even asked if I have an up-to-date food handler's card."

The thought hadn't even occurred to him. That could be problematic if the health inspector found out. "I don't suppose you do."

Feeling a bit smug, she pulled out her wallet. "And you

would be wrong. I used to volunteer at a local soup kitchen in Seattle, so my card is current."

That simplified things, although he wasn't above bending a few rules if it meant his customers got fed. Meanwhile, she pointed at him with her fork. "Besides, as the mayor so graciously pointed out, I already have a job. I was just helping out my friends and neighbors."

Now, that was an interesting thought. "So now we're friends?"

It was hard not to laugh at the shocked expression on Moira's face. Before she could sputter out an answer, he stopped her. "Never mind. I know you didn't do it for me. You took an oath to serve and protect. I just didn't realize the *serve* part referred to French toast and coffee."

"Not funny, Titus."

For some reason, sparring with her gave him a new boost of energy. He might just make it through the day after all. "Yeah, it is, but I'm still grateful. If you won't let me pay you for your time, at least let me reward your efforts with the pie of your choice. I won't have time to bake it today, but I promise I'm good for it."

She was already shaking her head. "You've already fed me lunch. That's enough."

"Okay, chocolate-cream it is. I'll even throw in a couple of those cherry mini pies for your mom and grandmother so you don't have to share."

It was fun watching the by-the-book cop warring with temptation. "Fine. I'll take a pie and the mini ones for Gram and my mom."

With that settled, he finished off his meal, taking his time because he knew the second they finished eating she would rip into him about last night. As it turned out, he was wrong about that. She didn't wait that long.

"Titus, last night cannot happen again. Civilians getting involved in police business, no matter how well intentioned, is a recipe for trouble. If you had gone vigilante on those guys, the repercussions would have been serious for both of us. And what if Ned bit one of them? You could have ended up being ordered to have him put down for being a vicious animal."

He swallowed hard at the thought of that prospect. She was right. That didn't bear thinking about. He'd jeopardized Ned without meaning to.

Meanwhile, Moira met his gaze head-on, something few people were comfortable doing. "If you doubt my abilities as a cop, especially in public, other people will as well. Cade trusted me to do the job. Take your lead from him."

He leaned back in his chair, feeling pretty darn defensive by that point. "I never once said you couldn't handle your job."

Moira's pretty face was now set in hard lines. "Then why were you there last night?"

"I was out walking Ned."

She snorted, giving his weak excuse all the respect it deserved. "Fine, you were walking your dog and just happened to end up in a stare-down contest with those three drunken truckers. Regardless, no more, Mr. Kondrat. Do you understand?"

Rather than answer her question, he asked one of his own. "Any reason you've reverted to calling me by my last name? I'd think after everything we've been through in the past few days, we'd be on a first-name basis."

Moira was getting more exasperated with him by the second. She shoved her empty plate to the side and leaned forward, forearms on the table. "Fine. Titus, don't follow me around when I'm on duty. I'd hate to have to toss you in a cell for interfering in police business, but don't think I won't."

He mirrored her position, narrowing the distance between them. "Does that mean it's okay if I follow you around when you aren't on duty?"

Her eyes flared wide and then narrowed. "Are you making fun of me?"

It was hard not to laugh at her outrage. "Absolutely not. Just asking for clarification."

"Let's keep it simple. Don't follow me around—period."

Then she stood and gathered up their dirty dishes. Jerking her head in the direction of the door, she said, "Looks like people heard about the backup this morning and decided to get in line early. Do you want me to start seating people and get their drinks while you take orders?"

"Sounds like a plan, but are you sure you want to spend your whole day here with me?"

After setting their dishes on the cart, she gathered up a stack of menus and headed for the door. "You'd be surprised what I'd be willing to do to get my very own chocolate-cream pie."

Okay, that put a whole lot of thoughts in Titus's head that he had no business thinking about her. Definitely time to change the subject. "Just so you know, Max Volkov should be here any minute now. He said he could bus tables and wash dishes."

"That's nice of him."

Titus wasn't so sure. "That depends on how many dishes he breaks. Seems that's why he got fired after only a week at his last restaurant job."

He started to walk away but then turned back. "By the way, don't mention the pie to him. I'm guessing you remember when Max first showed up in Dunbar and claimed the Trillium Nugget belonged to his family instead of the historical museum down the street. The whole town was up in arms over his attempt to make off with that big chunk of gold, Dunbar's most prized possession."

She looked a bit puzzled about where he was headed with this. "Yeah, it was quite the deal."

Titus grinned at her. "Well, I told Max he owed me free labor for letting him hang out here at the café back when everyone else in town hated him."

She was still laughing as she opened the door and let the waiting horde rush in.

THE REST OF the day passed in a blur. Moira had forgotten how exhausting standing on her feet all day could be. At least she'd had on her running shoes when she'd thrown herself into the fray to help feed what felt like the entire population of Dunbar. When Titus finally locked the front door and turned off the lights in the dining room, her poor feet were screaming in protest.

Max was still finishing up the last of the dishes when she took a seat at the same table where she and her grandmother had enjoyed their pie the other night. There wasn't anything left for her to do around the café, but she didn't have the energy to walk back home. She'd asked Max for a lift, but he'd walked to the café, too. Upon hearing that, Titus had offered to drive her home once he took care of a few more things. She didn't want to ask her mother to come get her since that would mean leaving Gram on her own. Neither of them liked to do that even for a short time. Since Carli was working tonight, that wasn't an option, either.

In the end, she'd reluctantly accepted Titus's offer. She sipped a cup of tea while the man started prepping things for the next day. At least he'd managed to hire some temporary help to cover until Rita and her sister returned. Max put up the last of the clean dishes and then took a seat across from Moira.

"Whew, I don't know if I could ever get used to working at this pace full-time."

She smiled at him. "You get used to it after a while, but it's why I always leave a big tip when I eat out."

He looked around. "With my new appreciation for how hard everyone works here, I'm going to up the ante when I tip from now on."

"My staff will appreciate it." Titus picked up two plates and headed their way. "I figured both of you could use a little something to eat about now."

After setting down the plates, he immediately snatched them back up and switched them around. "Sorry about that. The salad without the nuts is Moira's. She's allergic to them. The last thing she needs is another trip to the emergency room for a shot to counter the effects."

Max picked up his fork and dug right in. "Good catch."

Moira started to do the same, but then it hit her that she'd never ordered anything that had contained nuts here at the café, or even mentioned her allergies to the staff. The problem wasn't particularly life-threatening, but she preferred not to take any chances. The real question was how Titus knew that she needed to avoid nuts, much less that she'd ended up in the emergency room not long after she became a police officer.

Rather than ask questions in front of Max, she ate her salad and quietly watched Titus as he went back to chopping veggies. A few more pieces of the puzzle he represented started falling into place even if others didn't seem to fit at all. Once they were alone, though, she would demand some answers.

At that moment, he glanced back over his shoulder and winced before quickly turning away when he saw her watching him. Oh, yeah, that man was hiding something, and she had just realized what it was.

The night she'd gone to the ER, she hadn't driven herself there. No, someone else had rushed her to a nearby hospital—Ryan Donovan, her erstwhile boyfriend at the time. Not even her mother knew about that evening because she worried enough about Moira being on her own in the big city. Instead, Moira had told her mother a different part of the truth—that her doctor had recommended that she get some allergy testing done and discovered that she had a mild problem with nuts.

Max finished off his salad and put his plate and silverware in the dishwasher. "I'm heading out, Titus, but let me know if you need me again."

Turning back to Moira, he smiled at her. "When I called my wife to tell her that I'd be later than expected, she said to remind you that the book club will be meeting at our house the week after Shelby and Cade get back."

"Tell Rikki I'll be there unless I have to work."

"I will. 'Night, you two."

Moira waited until Max was gone before getting up to lock the door. This next conversation needed to be private. When she turned back around, Titus was once again leaning against the counter with his arms crossed over his chest, doing his best to look relaxed. However, she'd learned a lot about reading body language over the course of her career. To a casual observer, Titus might look cool, calm and collected, but there was a lot of tension in his shoulders and panic in the depths of those deep brown eyes.

Positioning herself a few feet in front of him, she met his gaze head-on. "Ordinarily I would now ask how you happen to know about my allergies. But all things considered, I don't have to, seeing as you're not Titus Kondrat at all."

She prowled a few steps closer, a mix of anger and betrayal feeding her fury. "So tell me, Ryan Donovan, how long have you been out of prison?"

# CHAPTER SIX

TITUS KNEW MOIRA had finally connected all the dots, but having that name flung in his face still came as a shock. It sure had taken her long enough to see through the surface changes in his appearance to recognize the man she used to know, maybe even loved. Heaven knew he'd been dreading this moment, but somehow it also came with a huge dose of relief. He doubted she felt the same.

"So, Moira, it's been a while. I guess I owe you an apology. I never meant—"

The sudden chill in the room had nothing to do with the setting on the thermostat and everything to do with the hard-eyed, furious woman glaring at him. She cut him off with a slash of her hand. "Don't play nice now. I bet you've been having a big laugh behind my back, so I don't want an apology. Not from you, especially not now. An explanation might be nice, though."

Her face was flushed, but he didn't know if it was temper or embarrassment that accounted for those rosy cheeks. He'd never meant to hurt her, and the last thing he'd ever do was laugh at her. Ned had been dozing in his bed, but now he was up and moving. The dog positioned himself between Moira and Titus, as if unsure which one of them needed his protection right now.

Titus stroked the dog's head, desperately needing that small connection to help keep himself grounded in the moment. "I've never laughed at you, Moira. And if I could have told you the truth back then, I would have."

"What? They don't let prisoners write letters these days? Or make phone calls or send emails?"

Stubborn woman. "I couldn't contact you at the time without putting people at risk, myself included."

She stared at him for the longest time. "Why? Did you rat out your low-life associates?"

"In a manner of speaking."

"Don't play word games with me. Not now."

"You're right." Knowing this moment had been bound to come sooner or later, he'd prepared for it. "Give me a minute. I'll be right back."

Without waiting for her response, Titus headed for the staircase that led up to his office on the second floor. He should have known she wouldn't do as he said. She walked into the room before he'd even had time to unlock the file cabinet. He pulled out the manila envelope he kept tucked all the way in the back.

Turning to face her, he reluctantly held it out to her. "Your answer is in there."

She dumped the contents out of the envelope onto his desk. After staring at the worn leather wallet for a second or two, she slowly picked it up and then looked at the badge and picture inside. She held it up to the light to study the ID photo and then ran her finger over the badge as if to verify it wasn't plastic. Such a distrustful woman, but then she had good reason to be.

Her expression was incredulous when she finally asked, "You're DEA?"

"Make that past tense. I haven't been for a long while now, especially since my cover was blown."

She abruptly shoved the contents back into the envelope, then tossed it on his desk. "Is that why you look so different?"

Moira waved her hand toward his head and down to his feet. "Your hair is dark, not almost blond, and your blue eyes have magically turned brown. You're a lot more muscular, and you've picked up all those tats along the way. You don't even sound the same."

She didn't know the half of it. "When you saw me get taken away in cuffs, the goal was to preserve my cover as Ryan Donovan. It didn't work, however. Although the task force rounded up most members of the drug ring that night, a few had slipped through the cracks. They caught up with me a short time later and expressed their displeasure."

Her face turned pale. "How badly were you hurt?"

"Collapsed lung, shattered kneecap, broken ribs, internal bleeding." He rubbed his hand over his nose and cheeks. "Multiple facial fractures. The doctors worked from pictures to piece everything back together. They came pretty close to getting it right."

He tried not to think about that period of his life much. It had taken time, but his injuries had eventually healed. Mostly, anyway. When she didn't immediately speak, he filled the silence himself. "I walked away from the DEA and went to culinary school. The rest is history."

She flinched, as if his words had cut her to the quick. "Like me?"

He sighed. "No, never you, Moira. Like I already said, I would've clued you in back then if it wouldn't have put you and others in danger."

"And in the ten years since?"

"All things considered, I thought it best to let you get on with your life."

Her temper flashed hot. "It wasn't solely your decision to make. I should've had a say. Maybe not when the drug bust went down. I get that, but what about later, once the dust settled? Well, unless everything you claimed to feel about me, about us…was a lie."

She clenched her hands into white-knuckled fists. "Tell me, Agent Kondrat, was I only another piece of your cover story?"

Now he was getting angry. She hadn't been the only one left hurting ten years ago. Walking away from her had cost both of them a lot of pain. "I never lied to you, not about anything that mattered."

Her answering snort said it all. "Do you expect me to believe that when you lied about virtually everything I knew about you? Heck, I don't even know your real name."

She drew a ragged breath, still fighting for control. "I thought it was bad enough dealing with the knowledge that I was a cop who fell hard for a charming criminal. It's so much worse finding out that the man I cared about wasn't even real."

By that point, her blue eyes were bright with tears. Knowing he'd made this strong woman cry was a real gut punch. "I use my real name these days. Ryan Donovan was a persona the DEA created for me to use when we were working to bring down that drug ring. When you and I met, I'd already been undercover for more than a year working my way up the food chain."

She poked an accusing finger into his chest. "I told you I was a cop that night at that dance club. You had to know that would complicate things for both of us. Why didn't you walk away then?"

Titus caught her hand before she could poke him a second time. "Honestly, if I'd had a lick of sense, I would have."

He wanted to brush away the tears trickling down her

cheeks, but dropped his hand down when she jerked back out of his reach. "Trouble was, I didn't want to."

She wasn't buying it, but it was nothing less than the truth. Back then, there was something about her that had drawn him like no other woman had ever been able to do. He'd been foolish enough to think they could share a few laughs and then he would walk away, no harm, no foul. Instead, he'd hurt the only woman who'd ever mattered to him and all but destroyed himself in the process.

"How did you end up in Dunbar, of all places?"

Okay, that one was tricky. She was already mad at him. He'd thrown the dice and bet everything on rebuilding his life in her hometown just so he might someday have this very conversation with her. Clearly, telling her that wasn't going to go over well at all. It was proof positive he wasn't firing on all cylinders when it came to anything to do with Moira.

"After I left the DEA, I went to culinary school. After gaining some experience, I wanted to buy a café. This one was on the market and fit my requirements."

That earned him a huge eye roll. "Which were?"

He ticked the reasons off on his fingers—at least those he could safely share. "Small town, updated kitchen, steady clientele and close to Seattle."

"And you're asking me to believe the fact that it was my hometown didn't enter into your decision."

Okay, that wasn't something he particularly wanted to admit to, but leave it to Moira to jump to the right conclusion. "Yes, Moira, I picked Dunbar because it was your hometown. I figured we'd run into each other eventually."

"Well, now we have. I hope you're happy. I'm not."

After one more glare hot enough to melt the polar ice caps, she did an abrupt about-face, then marched back downstairs and out the door, slamming it hard enough to rattle the windows. He shoved the envelope back in the file cabinet and locked it. Ned was waiting for him at the bottom of the steps, his head cocked to the side as if asking what Titus had done to upset his new friend.

Now wasn't the time for long explanations. "Come on, dog. We need to make sure she gets home in one piece."

As soon as they were out the door, they took off at a dead run. It might have been faster to drive, but he doubted she'd get in the truck with him. Instead, he and Ned kept a fast pace, heading in the general direction of her mother's house. He finally stopped when he realized Moira was nowhere in sight. There were several routes she could've taken, and the woman could really move when she wanted to. Luckily, he had Ned as his secret weapon. "Find her for me, boy."

The dog immediately put his nose to the ground and ranged back and forth until he finally caught her scent. He woofed softly and turned off the main road onto a side street. Sure enough, Titus spotted her two blocks ahead. He kicked it into high gear, determined to reach her before she could take shelter inside her house.

They needed to talk, and neither of them needed an audience.

Moira glanced back in their direction and then picked up the pace as well. That didn't keep him from gaining on her. She was a fast runner, but his longer legs trumped her speed. When he caught up with her, he blocked her way. She tried to step around him, but he wasn't ready to give up.

"You have to be tired, Moira. At least let me walk you home."

"I'm perfectly capable of getting there on my own."

"Never said you couldn't."

Under normal circumstances, the woman was more than

capable of taking care of herself. But right now, thanks to him, she was both tired and upset. He doubted she was more than marginally aware of their surroundings. Shortening his stride to match hers, he stepped aside and let Moira set the pace for now.

A few steps later, without so much as glancing at him, she asked, "Does Cade know about your past? About us?"

"Absolutely not. What happened between you and me is nobody's business but ours. As to the rest, Cade probably has his suspicions about my former employment, and I've been thinking about telling him the truth. The man knows how to keep a secret, and I don't want my past becoming public knowledge."

She shot him a quick look. "Why?"

"Because there are still a few people out there who have long memories and a taste for revenge."

Before he could stop himself, he rubbed his throat. As soon as he realized what he was doing, he dropped his hand back down to his side, but not before she noticed. "The same ones who are responsible for why your voice sounds so rough these days?"

"Yeah."

Not that he wanted to talk about it. During the fight, his voice box had been permanently damaged. The doctors hadn't been sure if that last part was from actual physical trauma or from him screaming so much. It was just another in a long list of bad experiences he'd just as soon forget about. To his surprise, Moira reached out to squeeze his hand. "I'm sorry."

"Not your fault. I got careless."

They were now in sight of her family home. He slowed down, pretty sure she wouldn't want her mother or neighbors seeing him escorting her to the front door. "Thank you again for helping out today."

"I didn't do it for you."

No, she'd done it for her friends and neighbors. The woman had a generous heart.

Unfortunately, he seriously doubted that generosity would be extended to him in the near future, if ever. That was probably for the best. It would make it easier for him to maintain some distance from her. When he'd moved to Dunbar, he'd hoped they could eventually be friends, but now he wasn't sure that mere friendship would ever be enough. "I'll let you know when I have your pies ready."

Moira shook her head. "Forget it. I don't want them."

She wasn't the only one with a stubborn streak. "You'll get them, anyway. I bet your mom won't turn them down. She'd probably think that would be rude. Your grandmother wouldn't for sure. She likes my pies."

He risked a small grin. "In fact, I think she likes me, period. She's also quite fond of Ned."

Apparently, Moira didn't find his assessment of his standing with her family amusing. "That's because they don't know the truth about you. Mom might not know all of the details, but she does know that I went through a bad breakup back in the day. If she found out that it was you, she'd come after you with her rolling pin."

"So that's where you get your fire." He fought the urge to brush back a lock of hair that had escaped her ponytail. "All things considered, I'd probably let her give it her best shot."

Moira didn't respond, but she patted Ned on the head, giving him a quick scratch. "Thanks for seeing me home, Ned. You might have questionable taste in owners, but you're a good dog."

Turning her attention back to him, she said, "As for you, keep your distance. Not just now, but for the foreseeable future. Whatever we once shared wasn't real, because the man I thought you were never existed. I was in love with a ghost."

Okay, enough was enough. He might have had secrets that he couldn't share at the time, but how he'd felt about her hadn't been a lie. If their relationship, however fleeting, hadn't been so incredibly special, they wouldn't both be hurting so much right now. Maybe it was time to remind them both of that fact. Moving in too quickly for Moira to escape, he caught her in his arms and pulled her in close to his chest. He was several inches over six feet, while she was about five-ten. That made her short enough to tuck under his chin when they slow-danced, but tall enough to kiss without having to bend down too far. He'd always loved how well they fit together. "What we shared was real all right, Moira. Otherwise, losing it wouldn't have hurt so much."

Defiant to the end, she met his gaze without flinching. "You were pretending to be a man you weren't, so you were only playing a part in a play. Nothing was real."

"Yeah, it was. So is this."

Keeping his hold on her gentle, he moved slowly. If she'd wanted to break free, she could have. Instead, she watched him as he closed the last bit of distance between them. When he kissed her, it was as if the past ten years had never happened. At first, she didn't give in to the moment, but gradually Moira softened in his arms as he gently coaxed rather than demanded her cooperation. He'd always wondered if he'd only imagined the way she could bring him to his knees with a simple kiss. Now he knew the truth. This woman had laid claim to his heart and never given it back.

Not that there was anything simple about this kiss, which tasted of lost love and so many regrets.

Then without warning, she jerked free of his embrace

and immediately wiped the back of her hand across her mouth. Did she actually think that would erase the reality of what had just happened? The defiant gesture would have infuriated him if he hadn't seen the slight tremor in her hand before she could hide it.

"Like I said, Kondrat, stay away from me. I have enough on my plate right now without you playing mind games with me."

Then she walked away, her head held high, and never once looked back in his direction. He waited until she let herself into the house before heading back toward the café. He was bone-tired and ached from head to toe after the emotional wringer he'd just been through. Regardless, right now sleep would be beyond him. Too many memories and too many regrets running rampant in his head. Better to take out his frustration on innocent vegetables rather than lie in bed, staring up at the ceiling.

When Ned tried to turn toward home, Titus didn't stop him. "Go ahead, boy. I'll be along eventually."

Then he walked off alone, as usual.

# CHAPTER SEVEN

MOIRA CHECKED HER appearance in the mirror over her dresser. Her hair was swept up in a high ponytail, her makeup mostly hid the dark circles under her eyes and her uniform was neat and tidy. Although she couldn't quite put a finger on the reason why, she still felt as if she was a cartoon cop made from pieces of construction paper pasted together by a small child with a whimsical sense of humor.

Last evening, she'd burned through what little energy she'd had left trying to maintain some semblance of normalcy in front of her family. Even though she'd done her best to pretend that everything was fine, her all-too-perceptive mom had realized that something was wrong. Moira had waved off her concern, claiming that she was simply tired after being on her feet all day. After all, it had been years since she'd put in a full day working in the café. At least the news that Titus intended to pay her with pie had proved to be enough of a distraction to avoid any more unwanted questions.

Even going to bed early hadn't done much to replenish her depleted energy level. That probably had more to do with the emotional toll of learning the truth about what had happened to Ryan…or Titus—whoever he was. How could she have so totally misread the situation? Granted, she'd barely been out of the police academy at the time, but there had to have been some clues that she'd missed that all wasn't as it had seemed.

For one thing, she hadn't heard anything about him standing trial, not that she'd expected to have to testify. After all, she and her fellow officers had been at the big drug bust solely to do traffic control. It had only been by happenstance that she'd been in the perfect position to watch Ryan being dragged out in cuffs along with his low-life buddies. Even now, so many years later, she could remember the bitter heartbreak and disgust she'd felt as it all played out like a bad movie.

As the man she loved had passed right by her, he kept his eyes pinned firmly on the ground, never once glancing in her direction. At least he'd given her that much. None of her coworkers knew anything about the man she'd been dating, only that he'd left town suddenly with no explanation. Carli was the only one who knew the truth. Well, most of it, anyway. Moira only had vague memories of the night she'd poured out her troubles to her friend as she and Carli overindulged in pizza, washed down with copious amounts of wine. Her hangover the next day had been one for the record books.

As tempting as it was to see if her friend was available for another girls' night of whining and wine, Moira couldn't risk it right now. Her emotions were too raw, and Carli already suspected there was something simmering between Moira and Titus. She'd be sure to read far too much into the fact that Moira had let him kiss her brains out last night. Besides, one drink too many would increase the chances of the truth of Titus's past slipping out. She might be furious with him and all the deception, but she was a cop to the core. There was no way she would put a former officer's life at risk because of hurt feelings.

She picked up her service belt and strapped it on before retrieving her weapon from the small gun safe in her bedside table. As ready as she'd ever be, she headed into the kitchen to grab a couple of protein bars to eat on the way to the office. It wouldn't be much of a breakfast, but the last thing she wanted this morning was to sit down at the table with her mother. The woman had an uncanny knack for accurately reading Moira's mood. If she thought someone had upset her daughter, the woman was likely to go on the warpath.

She'd almost made it to the door when her grandmother walked into the kitchen. "Morning, Moira. Off to work already?"

"Yes, I have some paperwork to take care of before I go out on patrol." She noticed Gram looked more like her old self. She'd taken the time to neatly style her hair and even put on a little makeup. "How are you feeling this morning?"

Her grandmother rolled her eyes. "More clearheaded than usual if that's what you're asking."

She stopped talking, then poured herself a cup of coffee and continued, "Clearheaded enough that I could tell you were pretty upset when you got home last night, even though you tried hard to hide it from your mom."

Pointing out the window, she changed subjects without waiting to see if Moira would offer up an explanation. "By the way, I happened to be looking outside when you walked up to the house. It was hard not to notice that you had an escort out there waiting and watching to make sure you made it inside without a problem."

It was surprising Gram hadn't mentioned that last night. Regardless, Moira didn't want to have this conversation. It was a huge relief when her grandmother finally looked in her direction. "I'm pretty sure that was Ned out there standing guard. Does his owner know you borrowed his dog?"

At least Gram hadn't seen Titus, which was a huge relief. "I didn't ask him to follow me home from the café. He decided to do that all on his own. Besides, I'm not sure that dog thinks he's actually owned by anyone."

Her grandmother huffed a small laugh. "You're probably right about that. Did I hear you tell your mother that Titus is paying you with pies for helping him out at the café yesterday?"

"Yeah, he insisted he owed me something when I refused to let him offer me any money. I didn't do it to earn extra cash."

Gram moved on to making herself some toast. "A man like him has a sense of pride. He probably doesn't want to be beholden to anyone."

That was very likely true.

She kissed her grandmother on the cheek. "Have a good day, Gram. I've got to hit the road."

Gram set her cup on the table and followed Moira to the door, grabbing her hand to keep her from leaving just yet. "I know you love your job, honey, but you need more in your life than being a cop. I've always suspected something happened back when you first joined the force that left you a little gun-shy in the romance department. Since you stayed in law enforcement, I have to think that it didn't happen on the job. But whatever it was, it changed you."

She gave Moira's hand a quick squeeze before releasing it. "Life can get pretty lonely when you don't have someone special waiting for you at the end of the day. I miss your grandpa every day, and your mother feels the same about your dad. Just ask her."

Her smile turned a little wicked and her faded blue eyes sparked with mischief. "You could do a lot worse than a man who knows how to cook and loves his dog. I shouldn't have to point out that Mr. Kondrat isn't hard on the eyes, either. There's something about those broad shoulders and tattoos."

Then she giggled like a schoolgirl. "I'm just saying."

Before Moira could do much more than sputter at her outrageous behavior, Gram walked out of the room. Sadly, she sincerely wished she could say her grandmother was wrong, but it never paid to lie to herself. The Ryan Donovan iteration of the man she'd known ten years ago had been sophisticated and handsome enough to grace the cover of any fashion magazine. Whenever the two of them had gone out, he'd drawn the attention of women as they passed by.

The Titus Kondrat version, though, was far rougher around the edges. It was more than the gravel in his voice or the tattoos, although they were part of it. Life had left its mark on him in other ways. There was an edginess to him that ran bone-deep, especially when he tore through town on that big Harley he liked to ride. At the same time, the man could be surprisingly gentle when the occasion called for it, just like when he'd gallantly escorted her grandmother from the café and helped her into Moira's vehicle.

That stood out in stark contrast to the night outside the bar when Titus took exception to the three truckers threatening Moira. On that occasion, he'd worn a veneer of barely leashed violence like a second skin. She might not have appreciated him interfering in police business, but she couldn't deny that she was drawn to his alpha-male nature on some level.

Not that she'd ever admit that to anyone, especially the man himself. The situation was too complicated—he was too complicated. His ability to switch personas was a good reminder that he wasn't to be trusted. There was no way to know what was real and what wasn't. She couldn't bet her heart on a man she couldn't trust.

After glancing at the time on the kitchen clock, she hustled out the door. While she wasn't going to be late for her shift, she wanted to get there early enough to clear out some paperwork before she was due on patrol again.

When Moira walked into the office, Oscar was working at the front desk. He smiled and pointed to a paper bag sitting on the counter. Her name had been scribbled across the front in felt-tip pen. There was a matching one sitting next to it with Oscar's name on it.

"That Kondrat fella dropped those by a little while ago. Since we're all putting in extra hours with Cade gone, he thought we might appreciate a treat. I put the others in the fridge, but I knew you were on your way in."

If the gift had come from anyone else, she would've been pleased by the gesture. But she was pretty sure this wasn't Titus being thoughtful. No, this was him messing with her. It was tempting to toss the bag in the trash, but that would only have Oscar asking questions she didn't want to answer, especially because the older officer was known to share juicy tidbits of gossip with Bea at the bakeshop down the street. From there, the information would make the rounds from one end of town to the other with lightning speed. After that, the phone calls would start, and no one needed that kind of grief.

It was time to get down to business. "Anything I need to know about?"

"Nothing much going on other than the usual speeding tickets and such." Then Oscar frowned. "We have gotten a couple more reports involving missing pets. No evidence of foul play, so they could have wandered off. Maybe coyotes got them. That happens once in a while. I told the people to reach out to local shelters and to post flyers around town."

"That's pretty much all anyone can do." She finally

picked up the paper bag. "I'll be in Cade's office if you need me. Then I'll be heading out on patrol in an hour."

"I made a pot of fresh coffee if you want some."

Moira grimaced as she walked away. She could use some caffeine about now, but the truth was that Oscar's coffee was a little too high-octane for her taste. Still, it was better than nothing. She stopped in the break room to pour herself a cup, adding extra sugar and cream to mellow out the acid brew.

When she was safely ensconced in Cade's office with the door closed, she finally opened the bag Titus had dropped off. When she saw that it was a sandwich, a bag of chips and a couple of sugar cookies, she breathed a sigh of relief. So maybe she'd been wrong about him messing with her. Regardless of his intent, she knew the food in the bag would be one heck of a lot better than the protein bars she still hadn't eaten.

Rather than save the meal for later, she decided to dive right in. After setting aside the cookies to snack on while on patrol, she opened the bag of salt-and-vinegar potato chips. It was most irritating that Titus had remembered that was her favorite flavor, just like he still knew how she liked her tea. That didn't mean she wasn't going to eat them; it would be a shame to let them go to waste. She munched on the chips between returning a few phone calls.

Once she caught up on those, she unwrapped the paper on the sandwich far enough to see what kind it was. It turned out to be turkey and Swiss cheese on a brioche bun, no tomato, no onion and light on the mayo. Now the jerk was just showing off, not that it would stop her from eating every bite. It wasn't until she finished removing the wrapper completely that she realized Titus had written her a note on the inside of it.

Rather than read it immediately, she folded the paper

back up and stuck it in her pocket to deal with later. It wasn't as if she even cared what the man had to say. She had no intention of getting involved with Titus again and had made that very clear to him last night. She'd even almost convinced herself that it was the wisest course of action. Her time would be far better spent concentrating on her job. With that in mind, she made quick work of the sandwich because she had files to update, people to serve, a job to do.

About halfway through the first file she tried to read, she gave up and set it aside. There was no way she could focus on the work at hand with that stupid wrapper burning a hole in her pocket. Grumbling under her breath, she pulled the note back out and gingerly unfolded it on top of the desk.

After skimming over it, she growled under her breath as she started over at the top and read it more slowly. Her emotions bounced all over the place, running both hot and cold, as she absorbed the brief message.

I know you don't want to hear it and maybe don't believe it, but I am sorry about what happened between us. Who knows, maybe someday you might even forgive me. For now, enjoy your meal. If you're reading this, at least you didn't throw it away. I figured that was a distinct possibility, but you always were a sucker for salt-and-vinegar chips. Be safe.
Titus

Sorry now that she'd given her curiosity free rein, she wadded up the wrapper and tossed it in the trash. An hour later, she finished the last report and logged off the computer. It was time to start her patrol. Before heading out to the parking lot, she filled her thermos with coffee and tucked the cookies she'd saved from earlier into her pocket to eat later.

She made it halfway to the parking lot before doing an abrupt about-face and marching back into Cade's office to retrieve the note from the trash. Despite her best efforts, she couldn't convince herself that she only did so to prevent anyone else from finding it. If that was true, she could've simply shredded the darn thing. Instead, she read it over one last time before folding it neatly and stashing it in her jacket pocket.

Maybe Titus was truly sorry for hurting her; it wasn't as if she knew what went on in that man's head these days. Regardless, it didn't change anything. Not really. They'd both moved on, started new jobs, built new lives. All that was left of their shared past was a mix of memories, both good and bad. Nothing that was worth losing sleep over. Eventually they'd figure out how to live life in a small town without getting in each other's way. It shouldn't be that hard. All it would take was a little effort on both their parts. Easy-peasy, no sweat.

And maybe if she kept repeating that, she might eventually believe it. On that happy note, she headed out to stand guard over the citizens of Dunbar.

Two nights later, she was back out on the road and bored out of her mind. Mostly, she was happy to have an uneventful shift. Other times, though, it felt as if she was driving in circles and accomplishing nothing. For one thing, it was hard to vary her route very much in a town with only six hundred people. There were also a few places that she made a point of checking on more frequently than others. Shay Barnaby's bar was definitely at the top of that list, but there hadn't been any notable trouble there since the night Shay had given Jimmy and his buddies the boot.

Maybe it was because Jimmy's antics had ended with him spending a few nights behind bars. Somehow, Moira thought it was more likely because he and his two drunken companions had also been banned from both the bar and Titus's café for the foreseeable future. Nobody wanted to have their name on that list.

As she did a quick turn through the neighborhood where her family lived, Moira spotted her mother's friend walking along the sidewalk. It seemed odd for Mrs. Redd to be walking that late at night, so Moira slowed to a stop and rolled down the passenger-side window.

"Hey, Mrs. Redd, is everything okay? Do you need a lift home?"

The older woman had been facing away from Moira. When she turned around, she was holding a cat. "Oh, hi, Moira. Everything is fine. I was too restless to sleep and thought a little fresh air would help."

Moira pointed toward the calico kitty. "Who's your friend?"

Mrs. Redd stroked the cat's head several times before setting it back down on the ground. The animal took off like a shot, disappearing into the bushes next to the closest house. "I don't know her name, but she must live close by. I see her fairly often when I walk by here."

She smiled at Moira. "I guess I should head home myself."

"The offer of a ride is still open."

Mrs. Redd shook her head and started walking. "It's not far and the exercise will do me good. Tell your mother and grandmother I said hi."

"Will do."

Moira slowly pulled away, still keeping an eye on Mrs. Redd in the rearview mirror. She lived on the next street and should be all right for that short distance. Regardless,

Moira decided she'd circle the block to make sure Mrs. Redd arrived home safely.

Ten minutes later, Moira headed for the two-lane highway that led into town to watch for late-evening speeders. When she reached the spot where she liked to set up shop, she backed into position. She'd barely gotten situated when a huge pickup truck went roaring past. She clocked the nitwit at thirty over the limit. Flipping on her lights and siren, she hit the gas to pull back out onto the highway.

That's when things went horribly wrong.

Her left front tire hit a deep pothole she missed seeing when she pulled in. The resulting jolt shot straight up her spine as it flung her forward and back. When the vehicle finally quit rocking, she was surprised the airbag hadn't deployed. She put the vehicle in Park and turned off the flashers and siren before sitting back long enough for her pulse to return to normal. Finally, she put it back in Drive and slowly pressed on the gas pedal.

The cruiser lurched forward and then rocked back again, making it clear that she had bigger problems than letting that speed demon escape. After turning on her emergency blinkers, she got out and used her flashlight to take a close look at the driver's-side wheel. The news was anything but good. Not only was the tire flat, but she was also willing to bet that there was structural damage to the suspension on that corner. Great.

She got back in the vehicle and notified Dispatch that she was out of commission. Next on her list, she called Oscar to see if he could take over patrol an hour earlier than expected. Once she had the rest of her shift covered, she called for a tow. Manny Lopez, owner of the garage in town, answered on the third ring. That was the good news. The bad was that he was finishing up another call, so it could be half an hour before he arrived.

She gave him the location of her vehicle. "I'm parked safely off the highway, so just get here when you can."

With that much settled, she made herself comfortable and considered her options. Manny might be able to give her a ride, but his shop was on the opposite end of town from where she needed to be. If he got another call in the interim, he might not have time to chauffer her around. Should that happen, she supposed she could wake her mother and ask her to come get her. She probably wouldn't mind, but it would mean leaving Gram alone, never the best idea. Unfortunately, her present location was at least two miles from the city center, making it a long walk back to the office. Before she could decide which was the best of two poor options, another vehicle came whizzing by—an all-too-familiar motorcycle.

A few seconds later, it circled around and headed back toward her. The big bike sent up a spray of gravel as its rider pulled off the pavement to stop beside her. She slowly lowered the window and stared at the one man she didn't want to talk to right now. Or ever.

Without saying a word, Titus climbed off his bike and immediately squatted down by the front wheel, using his cell phone's flashlight app to examine the damage. After straightening back up, he rested his hands against the truck and smiled at her.

"Well, Officer Fraser, it looks like you've got a bit of a problem. It's a good thing I happened along right now."

Yeah, it was, not that she would admit it.

"I've already called Manny to come."

"And how soon is he going to get here?"

There was no use in lying about it. She checked her watch. "I'm next in line, so about another fifteen minutes or so."

"Okay, that's one problem taken care of." Titus stepped

back. "That leaves the question of how you're going to get back to the police department."

She knew where this was headed, and she didn't like it one bit, even if it beat both of her other two choices. "I could call my mom."

"I'm betting she's already in bed asleep. It would be a shame to wake her."

"That's what I was thinking. I was going to walk."

He turned away to study the road. "Not the smartest thing to do this hour of the night. There aren't many street-lights out this far, making it hard for a passing driver to see you. There's also not much of a shoulder, leaving you walking too close to the road for safety."

His mouth quirked up in a small grin. "And who knows what kind of riffraff would be out at this late hour?"

Even she had to laugh at that. "True enough."

"Tell you what, Officer Fraser. I don't make a habit of picking up hitchhikers, but I'm willing to make an exception in your case. Meanwhile, get whatever you need out of the vehicle before Manny gets here. Once you hand over the keys to him, I'll give you a lift back to town. You can take care of whatever you need to at the station, and then I'll take you home."

"I don't have a helmet to wear. It's the law, you know."

He leaned in close and whispered, "I won't tell if you don't. You can wear mine, and I promise to go slow and drive safely for a change."

When she still hesitated, he opened the door and held out his hand. "Come on, Moira, trust me just this once. You can go back to hating me once I get you back to town."

The only trouble with his offer was the uncomfortable truth that, despite her best efforts, she didn't actually hate him at all.

## CHAPTER EIGHT

TITUS FIGURED MOIRA'S stubborn determination to keep him at arm's length was currently at war with her common sense. There was always the possibility that Manny could take her wherever she needed to go. If that happened, there wasn't much Titus could do about it, but evidently he'd made a good argument against her calling her mother. Moira was already busy gathering up everything she needed from the vehicle. Once she had it all together, she reluctantly turned it over to him to stash in his saddlebags just as Manny pulled up.

Titus watched as Moira walked away to talk with Manny. He suspected she was still hoping he would offer to give her a ride. It was a relief when the man shook his head and held out his hand to take her keys. Moira's shoulders slumped just a little in disappointment, but the moment of weakness didn't last long. By the time she headed back in Titus's direction, she was back to being all business.

"Okay, let's go."

Victory was his, but Titus wasn't about to rub it in. Instead, he pulled off his leather jacket and handed it to her. "Put this on."

It was no surprise when she tried to refuse it. "I have a jacket."

"Yours doesn't match my black helmet. I have an image to maintain." He walked behind her and held it up for her to slip on. "Besides, the leather will protect you, not just from the wind but also from a bad case of road rash should something go wrong."

She slid her arms into the sleeves. "And you think that flannel shirt you're sporting would be adequate protection for you?"

He didn't dignify that question with a response. Her safety came first. Rather than argue, he focused on adjusting his helmet to fit her. When he was satisfied, he led her over to the motorcycle. "Have you ever ridden one of these?"

She lifted her chin to give him a superior look. "Yes, I rented a scooter to ride on the beaches over on the coast in Ocean Shores. I didn't crash once."

Now she was just jerking his chain. There was no comparison. He suspected he was sneering a bit when he said, "My Harley would eat those scooters for breakfast."

He liked that she laughed and patted the handlebars on his bike. "Sorry, Harley, no offense intended."

Then she shot him an amused look. "I forgot how sensitive guys are about the size of their motorcycles."

Okay, that was funny. "Tell me, Officer Fraser. When did you get to be such a smart aleck?"

Without waiting for her to answer, he launched into a brief safety speech before climbing on the bike. Then he held out his hand to help her get situated behind him. When she tried to scoot back far enough to avoid touching him, he grabbed both of her hands and tugged them around his waist. "Come on, Moira. I don't have cooties. Hang on tight. It will make it easier for me to balance the bike with an inexperienced rider on the back."

After a second, she leaned in close to his back and tightened her arms around him. He started the engine and carefully guided the bike onto the highway. He maintained a slower than normal speed until she finally relaxed into him. Then he gradually picked up the pace, taking the curves just fast enough to make things a little exciting for both of them.

She tightened her grip a bit, but at least she wasn't screaming for him to slow down. He'd always suspected she was a bit of an adrenaline junkie. Too bad he'd promised to take her directly to the station. Otherwise, he'd be tempted to circle back around to the highway and let her see just how the Harley could eat up the miles.

He wasn't going to do that, though. She didn't need another reason not to trust him. But maybe someday he'd coax her into going on a long-distance ride with him. For now, he'd play the gallant knight and take her to the station. From there, he'd drive her home if she'd let him.

One good deed wouldn't make up for the mistakes of the past, but maybe it was a start.

AN HOUR LATER, he pulled into the driveway at her mother's house. As soon as he did, a light came on up on the second floor. Seconds later, the curtain on that window twitched to the side, and her mother peered out at them. Moira immediately scrambled to get off the bike. As soon as she did, he dismounted as well.

Her eyes widened with what looked surprisingly like panic. "Where do you think you're going?"

"Nowhere, but unless you're going to keep my helmet and jacket, I'd like them back."

She'd already removed the helmet and tossed it to him as the front door opened and her mother stepped out on the porch. Moira all but shoved the jacket at him, too. "Take this and go."

He glanced at Mrs. Fraser and back to Moira. "What's the problem?"

"One of the few rules Mom always insisted on was that I not ride on a motorcycle."

*Seriously?* "Last I looked, Officer Fraser, you're an adult. Can't you make that decision for yourself?"

"Yes, but I try not to upset my mother any more than I have to. She worries enough because I'm a police officer. She lost a brother in a motorcycle accident when she was a teenager."

Now he felt bad about laughing. Rather than respond to Moira, he pushed past her to go speak to her mother himself. "Mrs. Fraser, sorry if my motorcycle woke you up. Moira's cruiser broke down out on the highway, and I stopped to see if I could be of help. I swear I drove carefully."

To his surprise, the woman smiled at him. "Thanks for bringing her home, Mr. Kondrat."

His mission accomplished, he winked as he passed Moira on his way back to his bike. "I'm sure I'll see you around, Officer Fraser. Sleep well."

By the time he drove away, Mrs. Fraser had already disappeared back into the house, but Moira paused long enough to watch him drive off. He wanted to think that she was reluctant to see him leave, but it was far more likely that she was wishing he'd disappear from her life just as easily as he disappeared into the night.

It was tempting to head back out to the highway and try to outride his regrets. With some effort, he resisted the urge, knowing that wouldn't be fair to Ned, who was waiting at home for Titus to feed him.

At least when he finally made his way to bed, he could dream about those few minutes when Moira held on tightly and trusted him to get her home safely.

THANKFULLY, IT HADN'T taken Manny long to replace the damaged suspension, so things were back to normal by

Monday afternoon. Moira was relieved to have her cruiser back, and she could be back out on patrol.

All things considered, the town had a pretty low crime rate, but there had been another report of a missing cat. Not that anyone had seen anything. From what she could tell, all of the missing animals had simply disappeared. She felt bad for the owners, but there wasn't much the police could do. Heck, even if she spotted an animal out wandering the street, how was she supposed to distinguish it between a pet and a stray unless they were wearing a collar with a tag on it?

Even so, to keep everyone happy, she'd assured the distraught owners that she and the other officers would keep an eye out for anything suspicious as they patrolled their neighborhoods. Who knew how much good it would do, but at least they could say they'd tried. She'd also stopped in to talk to the managers at the feedstore and the market. The good news was that no more pet food had disappeared, something she was happy to put in her report to the council.

She also made a point of driving by Titus's café once or twice a shift, especially at night. She definitely owed the man for giving her a ride home the other night. However that didn't mean she'd give him a free pass on whatever he and that other guy had been up to in the alley when she'd dropped by to give Titus the bottle of wine she'd bought for him.

Doing so made her conscience twinge a bit. He'd been kind to her grandmother and had gone out of his way to reassure her mother after he'd brought Moira home on his motorcycle. He was also friends with her boss, a man she thought was an excellent judge of character. It could be that she was completely off-base in thinking Titus was up to something. Maybe she should do this one last drive-by and call it good.

With that in mind, she turned down the side street that crossed the alley behind the café. Slowing to a crawl, she killed her headlights as she eased up to the intersection. Most nights the only vehicles in the alley were either Titus's Harley or his old pickup truck. Tonight, she was disappointed to see the van was back. There was no sign of the other guy, but Titus was in the process of locking the doors on the back of the van. She continued to watch as he climbed into the driver's seat and started the engine.

As soon as he drove off, she followed, while maintaining what she hoped was a safe distance. Unfortunately, there weren't many cars on the street this late in the evening, making it almost impossible to hide the fact that she was tailing the man. There were two cars between them, one of them driving at a steady five miles an hour under the posted speed limit. Normally, Moira would have no problem with that, but right now it meant that she was falling farther and farther behind her target. She could have passed the slowpokes, but that would only draw Titus's attention in her direction.

It was a huge relief when both cars turned off at the same cross street. She resisted the urge to gun the engine to close the distance between her and Titus. By this point, it was obvious that he was heading out of town. The stop sign at the end of the block marked the last intersection within the city limits. From there, the road became a two-lane road that led to the state highway that connected two east-west interstates. It would be interesting to learn if Titus was going toward Seattle, Tacoma, or even Spokane on the east side of the state.

How long should she follow him? In another quarter mile, they would cross into the county sheriff's jurisdiction. There was also the fact the Dunbar Police Department was shorthanded right now. If she had actual knowledge that a crime was being committed, it would be one thing. Curiosity wasn't a good enough reason for her to stray so far from her normal territory.

The decision was made for her a few seconds later when she got a call about some minors drinking alcohol and being a nuisance. She listened to what the dispatcher had to say. "Got it. I'll be there in less than five minutes."

She did a U-turn and headed back toward town. She checked her rearview mirror one last time before picking up speed. Unless she was mistaken, Titus had just stuck his hand out of the driver's window long enough to wave goodbye. Torn between laughing and wanting to punch something—or someone—she hit the gas and went back to work.

TITUS STARED AT the bag sitting on his desk. He still owed the goodies it contained to Moira for the day she'd spent working at the café. Considering his mood, he should probably drop them off at her mother's house rather than delivering them to Moira at the police station. He hadn't actually appreciated her tailing him last evening. He glanced down at Ned, who was curled up in his bed in the far corner. "So what do you think, dog? Shall we walk down to the police station and pay an unscheduled visit to Officer Fraser?"

Ned tipped his head to the side as if actually pondering the wisdom of that idea. He rose to his feet and gave himself a good shake before heading out of the office and down the steps to the kitchen below. "I guess I got my answer."

At the bottom of the steps, Titus waited until Gunner finished plating up an order to catch his attention. "I'm going to deliver this order of pies. I shouldn't be gone long. Call if you need me."

"Will do." The other man eyed the bag and smiled just a little. "Tell Moira hi for me, even though I'd suggest you leave that at the front desk for her. You tend to get all riled up whenever the two of you cross paths. Gotta admit that it makes for an unpleasant work atmosphere."

The man wasn't wrong. Being around Moira did tend to twist Titus up in knots. That didn't mean it was okay to take his bad moods out on his employees. "Like I said, I won't be gone long."

He grabbed Ned's leash on the way out. The dog didn't much like being tethered to Titus as they walked through town, but Ned's size and attitude tended to make people nervous. Or maybe it was Titus himself who was the reason some folks gave him and the dog a wide berth as they walked by. He evidently had that effect on some people. Go figure.

The police department was not far from his café as a crow flies, but he took a more circuitous route than necessary. He did it partly to give Ned a chance to stretch his legs a bit, but mostly he preferred to avoid walking by Bea's bakeshop whenever he could. Her place served as gossip central for the town. He didn't much care what rumors Bea spread about him; it wasn't as if she actually knew much about him or his past. No one in Dunbar did. But that didn't mean he wanted to offer up fodder for the gossip mill if it might link his name to Moira's. She deserved better, especially when she was currently in charge of the police department.

He crossed the street and continued to the next intersection before turning in the direction of the police department. It amused him that Moira had failed miserably to disguise the fact that she was trailing him last night.

Thanks to some finely honed survival skills, he almost had a sixth sense that warned him when someone was a little too interested in his business. Besides, that huge black SUV decked out with lights on the roof that she drove everywhere was hardly inconspicuous.

It had been tempting to lead her on a merry chase, but he hadn't wanted to keep the people he was supposed to meet waiting any longer than necessary. They'd already made special arrangements to accommodate his schedule. Still, knowing them, he was pretty sure they would have found it hilarious if he'd pulled up with a suspicious cop hot on his tail. He doubted Moira would've thought it was funny. A smarter man would clear the air and simply tell her what she wanted to know, but it made him mad that she assumed the worst about him.

A soft nudge against his legs accompanied by a low growl broke through Titus's spiraling temper and made him realize that he'd coasted to a stop. He glared down at Ned, who glared right back. "What do you want, dog?"

Ned had about as much patience as Titus did. He expressed his displeasure with a soft growl as he circled Titus's legs, tangling him up in the leash. Before he could get free, Ned lunged forward, nearly tripping Titus in the process. With some fancy stepping, Titus managed to free himself without falling down or dropping the pies. He gave the leash a sharp tug to bring the unruly dog to a quick halt. When Ned begrudgingly sat down, Titus patted him on the head. "Okay, let's try this again."

Ned started forward again, this time carefully matching his pace to Titus's. "Should we see if we can get in the back door of the station or go in the front?"

Like the dog cared about that. Titus headed for the front of the police department. It was a huge disappointment that it was Oscar Lovell standing at the front counter. While he didn't have any problems with Oscar, the man was related to Bea at the bakeshop. The pair appeared to have an on-going competition over which one learned the juiciest bits of gossip first. Such was life in a small town, something Titus was still getting used to.

Oscar eyed Titus with interest. "Morning, Titus. What can I do for you?"

He tilted the bag so Oscar could see its contents. "I have a delivery for Officer Fraser. Is she in?"

Seeing the disappointment on Oscar's face, Titus bit back a sigh. "I should've thought to bring extras for Dun-bar's finest. Dessert is on me the next time you stop at the café."

"That's right decent of you." Oscar jerked his head in the direction of Cade's office. "Moira is working in back. If the door is closed, knock first."

"Thanks, Oscar."

"Before you go, here's a couple of treats for your friend."

He handed the dog biscuits to Titus rather than offer-ing them to Ned himself. Titus didn't blame him for being cautious, even though Ned always behaved himself around people who might feed him. A dog who had spent much of his life living on the street knew better than to ever turn down a free meal.

After tossing the treats to Ned, Titus led him down the hallway to Cade's office. The door was open, but he knocked on the door frame, anyway. When Moira looked up from her computer screen, her expression instantly morphed from welcoming to suspicious.

"Titus."

"Moira."

She rolled her eyes. "Is there something you need? I have work to do."

He held up the bag. "I brought your pies. Sorry it took

longer than expected. Things have been a bit busy lately. You know, late-night errands to run. Stuff like that."

She gave him a dark look at that last comment. Clearly, the woman's sense of humor was on hiatus today. "You could've left me a message to pick them up at the café and saved yourself a trip."

"Ned and I were out and about, anyway."

At the mention of his name, Ned circled around to stand next to Moira. To her credit, she positively cooed as she pet him. "You're such a handsome boy, Ned. Are you sure you wouldn't be happier living with someone else? Maybe somebody reputable?"

Titus smirked. "Ned knows when he's got a good thing going. As long as he has a warm place to sleep and a steady supply of food, he's got no room to complain."

He held up the sack again. "So do you want these or not?"

Leaning back in her chair, she pointed at the corner of the desk. "You can set them there."

After putting them down as instructed, Titus tugged on Ned's leash. "Come on, boy. Officer Fraser has work to do, and so do I."

He started out the door, but stopped long enough to add a reminder. "I wouldn't leave the cream pie sitting out for long, but it will be okay for a short time."

She glanced at her computer and back to him. "Thanks, Titus. Gram and my mother will be thrilled. They love your desserts."

"And you?"

"I would think you'd be above fishing for compliments, Titus. But I do, too."

"Good to know. See you later, Moira."

Then he grinned at her. "Or maybe not. I'll be staying

in town tonight, so no need for you to cruise by the café this evening to see what I'm up to."

Happy to have had the last word, he whistled as he walked away.

## CHAPTER NINE

As it turned out, Titus hadn't lied about his plans for the previous evening. He had indeed stuck close to home, not that Moira had taken his word for it. She'd still driven by the café three times while she'd been out on patrol. On her last pass, Titus had just locked the café's front door. He had Ned with him, and the pair set off in the direction of their house. She'd slowed to the speed he was walking and rolled down the passenger window.

"You look kind of tired. Do you want a lift home?"

He waved her off. "Thanks, but I need the exercise."

"I wasn't talking to you. I was asking Ned."

That startled a laugh out of the dog's owner. "Funny. I'm sure Ned would love to shed all over your official vehicle, but he needs to burn off some energy. Otherwise, he'll keep me up to all hours."

Moira moved on to another subject. "By the way, both Mom and Gram asked me to thank you again for the pies. Theirs didn't last long. I'm crossing my fingers that they didn't find the last piece of the chocolate that I stashed in the vegetable drawer."

That seemed to please him. "Let me know the next time you want to dust off your waitress uniform and earn a couple more. I make a mean banana-cream, too."

She bet he did. "I'll keep that in mind. Good night, Ned."

Looking back, that conversation had been the high point

of last night's shift. A few minutes later, she'd gotten a call about an accident on the edge of town that resulted in two people having to be airlifted to the trauma hospital in Seattle. She'd helped control traffic while the county completed its investigation of the incident and got the two damaged vehicles cleared. By the time she'd gotten home, she'd been too wound up to relax right away. At least her piece of pie had been right where she'd left it. Coupled with a cup of chamomile tea, it had soothed her nerves enough to let her sleep.

Tonight was going better. At least, so far. She decided to take advantage in the lull to return Titus's pie plate and the mini-pie ramekins. She regretted the decision as soon as she turned down the alley behind the café. There was Titus picking up a pair of pet carriers and setting them into the back of the same van he'd been driving two nights before.

When her headlights hit him, he slammed the doors shut and turned around to face her. She continued forward, parking a short distance away but leaving her headlights on to illuminate the scene ahead of her. After putting her vehicle in Park, she got out and started toward Titus.

"Mr. Kondrat, did you just load some cats into that vehicle?"

"And if I did?"

After speaking to several stressed-out pet owners earlier, she was in no mood to play games. "Can you prove that they are yours?"

He patted his pockets and shook his head. "I must have left the paperwork in my other pants."

"Not funny. Several pets have gone missing recently. Two owners received ransom notes and had to pay up to get their animals back."

Now he was looking at her as if she was crazy. "Come on, Moira, what exactly are you accusing me of now? The last time you jumped to the conclusion I was dealing drugs. Now it sounds like you think I'm heading up a cat-rustling gang or something."

Okay, putting it that way did make her feel a bit foolish. She backed off a bit on the attitude and tried again, "Sorry, I didn't mean it to come out that way."

He arched an eyebrow, conveying his disbelief about that. There wasn't much she could say because he wasn't wrong. "Okay, maybe I did, but let me start over. Are those cats strays? We've had reports of pets gone missing, several of them cats. I was hoping maybe those might be two of them."

He opened the back of the van. "I'm sorry to hear that, but these two are a couple of feral kittens."

She peered around him to study them. "What are you going to do with them?"

Titus offered her a teasing smile. "Normally I'd tell you that I'm trying out a new recipe for the café, but I suspect you're not in the mood for tasteless jokes. They're actually the last of a litter that I've been trying to round up for the past month. They're young enough that they might still be able to make a good pet for someone."

She couldn't quite hide her own smile when he poked his fingertip through the door of the closest cage to gently stroke the small calico cat inside. "So I repeat, what are you going to do with them?"

"I'm taking them to a no-kill cat shelter about twenty miles from here. They'll spay or neuter them, give them their shots and then farm them out to someone who fosters kittens. Once they figure out if these fur balls can adjust to living with people, they'll try to place them in a permanent home."

As he spoke, she noticed the stack of bags piled up behind the two cages. She leaned in closer to read the labels.

Then, feeling a little slow on the uptake, she finally connected the dots. "You're taking them and that stack of pet food and cat litter to the same shelter."

When he nodded, she sighed. "Just like you and that other guy were doing the last time I saw you loading up this van."

"Yup."

She smacked him on the arm. "Why didn't you just tell me that at the time?"

"Because it made me mad that you immediately jumped to the wrong conclusion. You should have known better."

She felt compelled to state the obvious. "At that point, I didn't know who you were."

"Sure you did, at least on some level."

Moira had no idea what he was talking about. "How do you figure that?"

"Remember the wine you bought me?"

The man was making no sense. "Yeah, what about it?"

"It's the same wine I served when I cooked dinner for you the night before everything went wrong."

Darn it, he was right about that. "But wait, even if that's so, I hadn't given it to you yet. There was no way you knew at that point if I was starting to see through all the changes you've made in your appearance."

He didn't deny it. "That's true, but maybe I wanted to think you'd remember me no matter what happened back then."

Was that regret she heard in his rough voice? "Why would you care?"

He shoved his hands in his hip pockets and leaned against the back of the van. "Because I never forgot you."

"It's been almost ten years, Titus. I won't believe that you haven't dated other women in that time."

At least he didn't deny it. "They don't matter. They never did."

Her brain didn't buy that for one second; her heart desperately wanted it to be true. "I've dated other men."

"I know."

"What's that supposed to mean?" Before he could answer, she retreated a step. "Have you been spying on me?"

Because that would be seriously creepy.

"No, but there's no way a woman as beautiful as you are wouldn't have had your fair share of admirers. The real question is how you've stayed single so long. There had to have been someone along the way who meant more to you than a casual date."

It must have been the night for some honesty. "Yeah, there was one who came close, but he eventually realized he couldn't handle the fact that I was a cop. Seems he wanted someone who worked regular hours and didn't strap on a weapon when she went to work. Between you and him, it shouldn't be surprising that I'm a little gunshy when it comes to men."

There was more than a hint of anger in Titus's dark eyes as he narrowed the distance between them. "I'm sorry if he hurt you, but I'm not sorry it didn't work out. Partly because it was better to find that out before you married him."

Then he caressed her cheek with his fingertip. "But mostly, for selfish reasons. From the first night we met, I thought you and I were a perfect fit. Nothing has happened to change my mind about that, even if you do have an unfortunate habit of accusing me of all kinds of bad things."

"What do you expect? You let me spend ten years believing you were a convicted felon. It's going to take a while to get used to thinking any differently."

His dark eyes met her gaze head-on. "I'd appreciate if you'd put more effort into doing that."

"Why?"

"Because I'm convinced you might still feel something for me even if you're fighting it." His mouth quirked up in a small smile. "I'm not a patient man by nature, Moira, but you're worth waiting for."

His words were a balm to her badly bruised ego, but that didn't mean she was eager to take a chance on a man who had already broken her heart once. She pointed at Titus and then back at herself. "The two of us might have fit once. But as I've said before, the man I thought I loved was an illusion. As it turned out, *you* weren't real, not in any meaningful way."

"Oh, I'm real all right, Moira, and so is this."

Then Titus gently wrapped her in his arms and once again kissed her. It was even more potent than the first time as the man gave it his all, doing his best to convince her that she wasn't making the biggest mistake of her life. When he finally released her, he looked a bit stunned. No doubt she did, too. Worse yet, she wanted a lot more of the same. That wasn't going to happen. Not now. Maybe ever.

It was definitely time to retreat before she did something she might regret—like surrender to the same attraction that had cost her so much pain ten years ago. "I'm sorry, but we can't do this again, Titus. You let the lies between us stand for ten years. I won't risk that kind of hurt again."

It took every bit of strength she could muster to walk away.

But she did it, anyway.

# CHAPTER TEN

"I RECOGNIZE THAT LOOK."

Titus plunked down Max Volkov's lunch on the table, along with his own. He took his seat and glared at the other man. "What look is that?"

"The same one you and Cade were giving me grief about not so long ago."

As he spoke, Max moved his plate a little closer to his side of the table as if afraid that he might have offended Titus to the point that he'd revoke Max's right to eat in his café. Any other time, Titus would have found that amusing, but he wasn't in the mood at the moment. Evidently sensing his irritation, Max held up his hands. "Sorry, man, I didn't mean to poke the bear. I'll shut up now."

Titus leaned back in his own chair and did his best to chill out. "You can relax, Max. I was thinking about someone else, not you."

"Good to know." Max lowered his hands and grinned. "So back to the subject at hand. What's Moira done to upset you?"

Titus tightened the grip on the glass of water he'd just picked up, momentarily imagining it was Max's neck. After drawing a slow breath, he gently set the glass down on the table and met his friend's amused gaze. "What makes you think my mood has anything to do with Officer Fraser?"

When Max didn't immediately answer, Titus tried

again, this time with a little less growl in his voice. "Seriously, what have you heard?"

"Actually nothing, not even at Bea's bakery. I hung out there yesterday afternoon while I did some online research. Her voice carries, so I heard pretty much everything she said while I was there. Your name didn't come up at all. The only mention of Moira had something to do with missing cats."

Okay, that was good. Titus tried again, "So again, why did you think she's done something to upset me?"

Max's smile was sympathetic. "Because I saw what happened at Cade's wedding reception when she walked in. As soon as you spotted her, you went into full retreat and never came back. If it's any comfort, I'm pretty sure no one else noticed."

Titus wasn't in the habit of pouring out his woes to anyone other than Ned. The dog was a good listener, but not all that great at offering advice. However, this wasn't the best place to spill his guts. He looked around the crowded café to make sure no one was paying undue attention to their conversation while he considered how much to tell Max.

Finally, he said, "This goes no farther than this table. You can't even share it with Rikki. That's more for Moira's sake than mine. They're becoming friends, and it should be Moira's decision how much she shares."

Max frowned. "I don't like keeping secrets from Rikki, but I will this once."

Titus decided to throw the dice and believe Max would keep his promise. "The problem is that the lady and I have a bit of history in the distant past. Let's just say that it had to do with her job in Seattle and leave it at that."

It was hard not to laugh as he watched Max try to process that little bombshell. He started to say something and then shut his mouth before a single word came out. Considering he was both a reporter and a writer, the man no doubt had at least a double dose of both imagination and curiosity. There was no telling what kind of scenario was playing out in his head right now, but Titus bet it was a dandy.

After a bit, Max shot him a wicked grin and waggled his eyebrows. "I'm not going to push for details. However, you should know that I'm pretty sure whatever happened involved handcuffs."

This time Titus gave in to the urge to laugh. "No comment."

"I knew it!"

Then Max mimed zipping his lips as his expression turned serious. "If you need to talk, I'm available. I'll even bring the pizza and beer."

That was decent of him, but Max had other people in his life now whose needs should come first. "You're a newlywed. Doesn't your wife prefer that you stick close to home?"

"Normally, yeah." Max rolled his eyes in exasperation and then pointed his fork at Titus. "But you stepped up to help me protect my family. I'll never forget that."

Titus had been a loner most of his life and sometimes forgot what it was like to have people who actually cared about him. Maybe it was time to share some of his secrets with a friend. "I appreciate the offer, but I'm fine."

It was obvious Max wasn't buying what Titus was selling. Trying to head off any more offers of a shoulder to cry on, Titus pointed toward Max's plate. "Eat. I didn't spend all morning cooking for you to let it go cold."

Max laughed and offered Titus a salute. "Yes, sir. And if I clean my plate, do I get pie?"

"For here or to go?"

Max rubbed his hands together with greedy glee. "Why can't I have it both ways?"

Titus gave Max a considering look. "What would Rikki say about you pigging out on pie twice in one day? Not to mention you didn't even ask for extras to share with her and Carter."

"You know you can be a real jerk sometimes, Titus." He took a big bite of his lasagna and swallowed. "I'll take three of your mini pies to go. I wouldn't want to deny my new wife and son the pleasure of one of your desserts."

It was hard not to be jealous of the man's unabashed happiness about his life these days, not that he didn't deserve it. "You're a good man, Max Volkov, and for that reason they'll be full-size pieces."

MOIRA DEARLY WANTED to rub her temples in case that would ease her headache. Instead, she maintained perfect posture and did her best to keep her temper under lock and key. How did Cade deal with this kind of stuff day in and day out without exploding? It might've been cowardly on her part, but she would have cheerfully slipped out the back of the station if she'd known Otto Klaus was on his way to see her. In her experience, the mayor rarely had an actual opinion of his own. Instead, he chose his course of action based on which way he thought the political winds were blowing.

Right now he was staring at her with what he probably thought was an intimidating glare. Moira wasn't impressed. She'd faced down far too many hard-core criminals to cower in front of a sulky small-town mayor. "Officer Fraser, I remain convinced that you overreacted."

She worked hard to keep her expression neutral. "You've already said that, Mr. Mayor. Twice, in fact. That said, those four teenagers were minors in possession of alcohol, which is illegal. I can print out a copy of the exact law if that would help you better understand the situation. I've already provided copies to both the teenagers involved and their parents."

Otto flushed bright red. "I don't need a copy of the law, Officer Fraser. What I need is for you to realize that you mishandled the situation. It was only a few beers."

"Yes, I'm aware of that. But that doesn't change the fact that the kids were underage, in public and had every intention of driving under the influence. I could have arrested the lot of them or even called the county sheriff to take them into custody. I offered them a fair alternative."

The man simply wouldn't give up. "None of them have any history of prior problems. You should've let them off with a warning. I'm sure they've learned their lesson."

Okay, that did it. She leaned forward, elbows on the desk, and met Otto's gaze directly. "No, they haven't, Mr. Mayor. In fact, they think they're above the law. Two of the boys went so far as to tell me that their football coach wouldn't allow me to force them into taking the alcohol-and-drug counseling program that the high school offers. Something about it interfering with football practice."

"But—"

She cut him off, "That's when I brought them into the station instead of letting them call their parents for a ride."

Otto looked horrified. "You put teenagers in a cell?"

"I told them to wait in there, but I didn't close the door. It's the same thing Chief Peters did the last time something like this happened. When all of the parents arrived, I took them into the conference room to explain the policy that Cade established for first-time offenders. They have to complete the counseling at the high school. Once they do that, their record is cleared. Failure to so means the charges stand. That wouldn't result in jail time, but it will affect their insurance rates."

It would have been nicer if Otto had simply accepted

Moira's judgment on the best way to handle the situation, but at least telling him she was following Cade's precedent had calmed him down. "We will revisit this situation with Chief Peters when he gets back, Officer Fraser."

She could only hope that Otto hadn't already tried to call Cade—she wouldn't put it past him. He and several of the council members clearly didn't understand the concept of the police chief being entitled to vacation time.

"Believe me, Mr. Mayor, it's important to impress on kids the dangers of messing with alcohol. I've been a police officer for more than ten years now and have lost count of the number of horrendous accidents I've responded to that were caused by someone driving under the influence. I'd rather those parents be a little mad at me for playing hard-ball now than to have to knock on their door one night to tell them their son or daughter won't be coming home ever again. No one should have to live with that kind of pain."

Otto swallowed hard and finally nodded. "You're right, of course. I will talk to the counselor at the school to see if they can work their sessions around the football practice schedule."

"That seems fair."

She finally relaxed and sat back. Unfortunately, the mayor wasn't done yet. "One more thing. Have you had any progress in locating the missing pets? My office has gotten multiple calls, and several of the council members are concerned that you might not be putting enough effort into solving the problem."

She could guess which two members he was talking about. "All of us are watching for any suspicious activity while we're out on patrol, Mr. Mayor. We've been in touch with the local shelters and the county animal control people. We've advised the owners to post signs in public areas in case someone has spotted the animals. I've also talked

to the county sheriff's office to see if the problem is occur-
ring in other areas besides Dunbar. To date, they haven't
received any similar reports. Is there anything else?"

"No, that was all."

He trudged out the door. If she wasn't so mad at him,
she would have laughed. She couldn't imagine anyone less
suited for public office than Otto Klaus. At least she'd finally convinced him that she'd handled the problem with
the teenagers according to department policy. Still, that
wouldn't keep him from coming trotting back to whine
some more as soon as the parents involved found out that
siccing the mayor on her hadn't changed anything.

That was a problem for another day. While she pondered
what to do next, she closed her eyes and finally massaged
her temples. It might have even helped if she didn't suspect yet another concerned citizen was headed her way.
She checked to make sure her ponytail was still high and
tight, picked up a pen and tried to look busy as she waited
to see who was about to darken her door.

When she finally looked up, she wasn't sure how to
react. On the upside, it wasn't the mayor or any of the irate
parents. On the downside, it was her grandmother standing
there looking a bit confused. Moira was up and moving
before she even realized she'd made the decision. "Gram,
what are you doing here? Where's Mom?"

Because it was a bad thing if Gram had managed to
wander this far from home without her daughter noticing she was gone. Moira needed to call her mom, but not
until she got her grandmother settled into a chair. Before
she could do that, a second person appeared, this one even
more surprising.

Titus stepped across the threshold and gave her grandmother an exasperated look. Ned followed right behind

and immediately parked himself next to Gram, who smiled and stroked his head. "Hi, Ned."

Titus looked a bit chagrined when he finally spoke. "Boy, she's quick. Ned found her again, and we were closer to here than the café. TJ stopped us at the front counter because you were meeting with the mayor. When Gram asked to use the restroom, I led her down the hall to the ladies' room. The mayor was just leaving your office, so I ducked back out of sight, figuring you wouldn't want your grandmother's adventures broadcast all over town."

He shot Gram a hard look. "Honestly, I was only out of sight for thirty seconds, but she still managed to get past me. At least she headed here and not out the back door."

Moira appreciated his concern for Gram; she truly did. But knowing Gram had turned into a real escape artist upped the ante on Moira's headache. It was pounding out a harsh rhythm and making her feel queasy. Keeping a hand on the desk to maintain her balance, she made her way back to her chair, reached for her phone and called her mother's number.

While she waited for her to pick up, Moira motioned Titus toward the chair next to Gram's. Her mom answered on the second ring. "Hi, what's up?"

Her mother sounded pretty cheery considering the circumstances. "Mom, do you know where Gram is right now?"

Nothing but silence for several seconds before her mother spoke. "I left her at home with Elsie Redd while I did the grocery shopping. I'm on my way home now. Why?"

"She's sitting in my office. Titus and Ned found her again and brought her here."

Her mother's sigh was heartbreaking. "Elsie's trying to call me. I'd better take it. Then I'll come pick her up."

"No need, Mom. You go on home and deal with the groceries. I have less than an hour until I get off shift today. Gram can keep me company until then while you take a breather."

"Are you sure?"

"She's fine. She's petting her buddy Ned right now."

"I'm sorry, Moira."

"Don't worry about it, Mom."

After she disconnected the call, Moira leaned back in her chair and closed her eyes. It was probably rude to ignore her guests, but she needed a chance to gather her scattered thoughts. A second later, Titus broke the silence. "Have you taken anything for that headache?"

She pried her eyes open to see nothing but concern reflected in his gaze and winced when she made the mistake of shaking her head. "I was about to when Mayor Klaus decided to pay me a visit. If I hadn't had a headache before he showed up, I would have had one by the time he left. I have some acetaminophen in my locker."

"Go take some now. I'll keep an eye on your grandmother."

She didn't even try to argue. "I'll be right back."

"Take your time, Officer Fraser. I'm in no rush to get back to the café, and Ned is happy to keep your grandmother company."

"Thanks, Ned." Moira pushed herself up out of the chair and moved toward the door. "And you, too, Titus. Looks like I owe you another bottle of wine."

He waved off that suggestion. "No, you don't. Besides, I still have the first one. I plan to serve it if you ever let me cook dinner for you."

Even though she suspected she already knew the answer, she had to ask… "You're talking about at the café, right?"

He caught her hand as she passed by. "We both know

you're smarter than that, Moira, but we can write your confusion off to the headache. It would be at my place, and I promise to be on my best behavior."

She tugged her hand free and kept walking without responding. It was hard to stay mad at a man who had once again stepped up to make sure her grandmother was safe. That made it all the more important to take her pills and get back to her office. Then she would shoo Titus and Ned back out the door before she did something foolish, like accept his invitation. She had enough to contend with between Gram wandering off, the mayor second-guessing her every decision and the mystery of the missing pets. She couldn't handle another complication in her life, especially one as tempting as Titus Kondrat.

After a quick stop at her locker, she washed down the pills with a glass of water in the break room, hoping like crazy that they'd kick in fast. Before returning to the office, she grabbed a bottle of water for Gram, a few of the cookies Oscar's wife had baked and a handful of doggy treats for Ned. She also poured two cups of coffee, adding cream and sugar to hers but leaving the one for Titus black, like he preferred. He wasn't the only one who remembered little details like that from their all-too-brief time together in the past.

She distributed the makeshift refreshments and sat back down at her desk. Titus seemed content to sip his coffee in silence. It wasn't long before Gram spoke. She kept her hand resting on Ned as she looked around the office in confusion. "Moira, why am I here?"

No matter how many times it happened, it was excruciating to hear the hint of fear in her grandmother's voice. As usual, Moira tried to reassure Gram with a version of the truth that wouldn't cause her distress. "You went for a walk and ended up close to where I work here at the police department. Ned and Mr. Kondrat thought the three of you would surprise me with a visit."

For a second, she thought her grandmother had accepted the explanation, but then Gram shook her head. "In other words, I got lost again."

She immediately turned to Titus, looking distraught. "I'm so sorry I've caused you so much inconvenience."

When Titus responded to Gram's apology, he did it with such amazing gentleness. "It's no inconvenience to spend time with a beautiful woman, Mrs. Healy."

He winked at Moira as he wrapped Gram's fingers in his and pressed a soft kiss to the back of her hand. "It's even better when I'm enjoying the company of two at the same time."

Gram's cheeks flushed as she giggled like a schoolgirl. "You'd better watch out for this one, Moira. He's a charmer."

That he was, but he was also the most aggravating man Moira had ever met. She offered Ned the last treat she'd brought for him. "Thanks again, Titus. I can take it from here. I'm sure you've got stuff you need to be doing at the café."

At least he took the hint. He finished off his coffee and set the empty mug on the corner of the desk. "Yeah, those pies don't bake themselves."

Before leaving, he smiled at her grandmother one last time. "Take care, Mrs. Healy. Have Moira bring you and your daughter for dinner at the café sometime soon. Ned would be glad to see you, and I'll spring for dessert."

Gram leaned down to give the ever-patient Ned a big hug. "We'll do that."

"Come on, dog. Let's hit the road."

Ned slipped past his owner into the hall. Before following his buddy, Titus pinned Moira with a hard look.

"About that dinner I mentioned earlier—you used to love my crème brûlée. To be honest, I understand why you're not interested in picking up where we left off. That doesn't mean we can't be friends."

She listened as the sound of his footsteps faded down the hall toward the front of the station. At least the acetaminophen was taking effect, already reducing the syncopated rhythm that had been playing on repeat in her head. That was the good news. The bad news was that she wasn't the only one who hadn't forgotten a single detail about that dinner ten years ago. The only question was what would happen if she allowed Titus to talk her into a do-over.

Would it be just as special? Even if it was, where would that leave them? They'd been very different people back then, and they'd each gone through a lot of changes in the ensuing years. What was Titus hoping to accomplish? More important, was it worth the risk of having her heart broken again just to see if the spark of attraction they'd enjoyed back then could be rekindled?

Rather than sit there and let her thoughts continue to spin in circles, she decided it wouldn't hurt to knock off a few minutes early. TJ had the front desk covered, and she wasn't on patrol tonight. She logged off the computer and stood up. "Gram, can you please wait here while I check in with my coworker out front? It won't take long, and then I'll drive you home. Mom is expecting us."

Gram slowly nodded. "She's going to be upset, isn't she? I don't mean to cause everyone so much trouble."

There wasn't much Moira could say to that. "Maybe we should pick up a pizza for dinner. Mom is always happier when she doesn't have to cook. We'll order her favorite even though I'm not all that fond of olives. Don't you think that will help her mood?"

Looking more like her old self, Gram grinned. "It couldn't hurt."

## CHAPTER ELEVEN

FEELING RESTLESS, Titus paced the length of the living room and back again for the fourth time in the past ten minutes. "Maybe I should've taken Max up on his offer. Some company would be nice about now."

Ned's lip curled up in a canine sneer to express his disdain over his roommate's comment. At least that's how Titus interpreted it. "Sorry, boy. I didn't mean you weren't good company. It's just that Cade, Max and I started hanging out together whenever one of them was having woman troubles. Sad to say, now it's my turn."

The dog stood up long enough to turn around three times before curling up again, this time facing away from Titus. His message was pretty clear. Ned had heard enough whining for the time being. "Dog, normally I would remind you who pays for that expensive kibble you like so much, not to mention all those treats you think you deserve."

Titus kneeled down by Ned's bed and stroked his fur. "However, I think it's time to stop feeling sorry for myself. I'm the one who screwed up everything ten years ago, and I can't blame Moira for not wanting to pick up where we left off."

Ned gave Titus's hand a quick lick, which was as close to sympathy as Titus was probably going to get from anybody tonight. He gave the dog another pat on the head just as the doorbell chimed. "Who could that be?"

As soon as he asked the question, he figured he could

guess. Just because he told Max not to bother coming, that didn't mean the man would actually listen. Sure enough, Max was standing on the front porch with a huge pizza box in one hand and a six-pack of a local microbrew in the other. "Surprise!"

It was tempting to grumble a bit, but Titus was actually glad to see him. "Come on in."

Ned indulged in a long stretch before slowly dragging himself out of his bed to join them by the door. Max smiled down at the dog. "Let me set this stuff down, boy, and then I'll give you a proper greeting."

Turning his attention to Titus, he nodded toward the pizza box. "Coffee table or kitchen table?"

Oh, right. Titus should probably make some effort to play host. He pointed toward the couch. "Might as well be comfortable. I'll grab plates and napkins from the kitchen and be right back. Would you like a salad to go with the pizza?"

Max set the pizza on the coffee table and surrendered the six-pack to Titus after removing two for immediate consumption. "Actually, that sounds good if it's not too much trouble."

"It won't take but a minute. Make yourself at home."

On his way out of the room, he called back, "Keep an eye on Ned while I'm gone. After living on the street and dumpster diving for dinner, he's an expert on opening pizza boxes."

In the kitchen, he gathered the ingredients to make a Caesar salad. While he worked, he pondered why Max had landed on his doorstep after they'd agreed that Rikki would prefer her husband of less than three weeks to stay home.

It could simply be Max's reporter's curiosity, but Titus rejected that idea. No, he was pretty sure that Max's presence was motivated by something else. He'd already made it clear that he felt he owed Titus for helping to capture the woman who had terrorized Rikki a few weeks back. But after giving the matter further thought, he rejected that idea, too. Guys might not spend a lot of time spilling their guts to each other, but that didn't mean that kindred spirits didn't recognize one another. Max had come bearing pizza and beer because evidently that's what the male half of the population did when a friend was operating in crisis mode. Not that Titus had ever experienced the phenomenon firsthand before moving to Dunbar.

Before exchanging his badge for an apron, Titus had specialized in undercover work for the DEA. That meant he'd spent more of his time hanging out with lowlifes and criminals than he did his fellow agents. After leaving the agency, he'd bounced around a lot as he worked to polish up his culinary skills. The bottom line was that it had been a long time since he'd stuck around one place long enough to actually make friends.

He only knew the broad strokes of Max's past, but he suspected that something other than needing to do research had driven Max to remain out on the road for weeks at a time. It wasn't until Max had met Rikki Bruce that he found someone who made it worthwhile to give up his wandering ways. The only question was if Titus and Max both having problematic pasts would provide a solid basis for friendship.

Figuring there was only one way to find out, he picked up the salad bowl and plates and headed for the living room. His guest was ensconced at one end of the sofa with Ned stretched out beside him with his head in Max's lap. The pair looked pretty content with the arrangement. Titus set the bowl and plates on the coffee table, then took his own seat on the opposite end of the couch.

Max eyed the salad with interest. "This looks great. A lot fancier than I was expecting."

As usual, Titus didn't know how to respond when someone acted as if the meals he prepared were anything out of the ordinary. "It's just a salad."

It was a relief when Max just laughed and dug right in.

Although Titus had the necessary skills to prepare the kind of expensive meals that were featured in five-star restaurants, it hadn't taken him long to figure out that wasn't the type of cooking he wanted to do for the long-term. Instead, he prided himself on preparing hearty and delicious food for ordinary people, the kind of stuff his grandmother always said would stick to a man's ribs. He liked to think that she would have approved of his career choice.

Nana Kondrat had taken in Titus not long after his mother had remarried, which was less than a year after his father had been killed in combat. His stepfather hadn't much liked Titus from the get-go, mostly because Titus had resented Will's concerted efforts to erase all reminders of his predecessor as soon as he moved in with Titus and his mother. Almost overnight, the pictures of Titus's father had disappeared. Also gone were his medals, as well as the flag that had been presented to his widow and son at the funeral. Starting almost from day one, Titus and Will had faced off on too many occasions to count. Unfortunately for Will, Titus had already been nearly as tall as he was now even though he'd been in his early teens. His stepfather had found it difficult to discipline someone who towered over him.

After one particularly bad confrontation, his mother had once again sided with Will and ordered Titus either to toe the line or leave. To her surprise, he'd gone for curtain number two and walked out. It had taken him three days to hitchhike to where his grandmother lived. He'd be eternally grateful that she hadn't hesitated to open her heart and her home to him.

He credited Nana with saving him.

A movement off to his right dragged Titus out of the past and back to the present. Max had finished off his salad and leaned forward to open the pizza box. "I got the pizza with everything on it. I hope that's okay."

Titus finished up his salad, too. "That's fine. I pretty much eat any kind of pizza."

Max narrowed his eyes. "Even the ones with pineapple on them? Because that might be a deal-breaker on any chance of friendship we might have had."

Titus waggled his hand in the air, indicating he could take it or leave it. "Let's just say I can live without it."

"Fair enough."

Max slid two huge slices of pizza onto each of their plates. "Can Ned have some?"

The dog's ears perked up at the mention of his name. Titus had rules about such things and figured he'd better explain them now if they were going to make a habit of hanging out together. "I'll cut him a few small bites after we're done eating. Otherwise, he'll gulp them right down and then mooch for more."

Max patted his canine companion on the head. "Sorry, boy. I guess we'd better do as the man says."

The dog snorted, his opinion on that concept clear. Then he avidly watched every bite that Max took in a clear attempt to guilt him into bending the rules this one time. Titus hoped Max managed to resist the temptation. Ned already thought he ruled the roost. He wasn't exactly wrong.

It didn't take long to finish off most of the pizza. Titus carried everything back into the kitchen and made good on his promise to give Ned a few bites. After grabbing two more of the beers from the fridge, he rejoined his guest on the sofa.

"Thanks for coming tonight."

"No problem. And just so you know, I'm not neglecting my family by being here. They both had other plans. Some repeat customers checked in to the B and B today who have kids about the same age as Carter. He was having a great time hanging out with them when I left. Rikki was determined to spend the evening getting caught up on paperwork. Between our trips to Portland to pack up my stuff and buying all the things we need to set up my office here, we've let a few things slide."

"Have you decided to sell your place in Portland?"

"Not right away. I've listed it for rent with a property-management company for now." Max stopped talking long enough to shift positions to face Titus more directly. "That's enough about me. Let's get back to the conversation we started at the café today. I believe you mentioned something about you and Moira having a bit of a past when she was a cop in Seattle. I remember asking if it might have involved handcuffs, but in a good way. I've been on pins and needles all day wondering if I was right about that."

Titus didn't know whether to laugh or punch Max on the arm. Finding it hard to dive right into a long explanation, he stood back up. "Give me a minute."

He headed for the chest of drawers in his bedroom. While he hadn't brought his badge from the café, he did have a couple of other bits and pieces from his past he could share with Max.

When he returned, Ned was back on the couch, too. But this time he was sitting on the center cushion as if waiting to cuddle up by Titus this time. At least Titus hoped that was the dog's intention. He might need that small connection to maintain some semblance of control while he stirred up a whole bunch of bad memories.

With that in mind, he took a big gulp of his beer and set it aside. "I'm betting you've heard a lot of theories and wild guesses about where I came from and what I was doing before I moved here and bought the café."

"A few." Max chuckled a little. "Honestly, I've written down some of the more interesting ones in case I want to try my hand at writing a thriller when I finish the book I'm doing about my great-grandfather. Do you know how many people believe you learned how to cook while behind bars? Seriously, since when does prison cuisine include things like chicken and dumplings and Dutch apple pie?"

Titus was well aware of the whispers that had dogged his footsteps since he'd taken over the café from its previous owner. He found that theory pretty amusing. "For the record, I learned how to make chicken and dumplings from my grandmother. Nana was one heck of a cook."

Another sip of his beer did little to soothe Titus's parched throat, but he wasn't going to stop talking now that he'd finally gotten started on the story. "You already know that Moira was a police officer in Seattle. She and I met at a dance club just by happenstance and really hit it off."

He stared down at the envelope in his lap. "I should've walked away that night. It would have been better for both of us if I had. Instead, I used every excuse I could come up with to see her as often as possible."

He finally dumped the contents out of the envelope and handed the picture on top of the pile to Max. "To be completely accurate, though, the man she met that night was this guy—Ryan Donovan."

Max studied the picture for several seconds and then held it closer to the lamp on the end table to get a better look. "He looks enough like you to be your cousin or maybe even your brother. His nose looks a bit different, and his hair looks lighter. He also has a more slender build."

"Believe it or not, that *is* me. At least it was ten years ago."

He'd expected Max to immediately pounce on the fact that Titus was now living under a different identity. Instead, he pointed at the picture again. "Who is this other guy? He looks familiar."

Someone Titus wished he'd never met. "You might have seen his face on the news. His name is Cian Henshaw. At the time that was taken, he was the second-in-command of a large drug-trafficking ring that operated up and down the West Coast."

Max swallowed hard and looked up in confusion. "I can't help but notice that the two of you look pretty darn chummy in the picture."

"We were. You would've liked him, too. Cian was charming, funny and generous with his friends." Titus leaned over to point at the watch he'd been wearing when the photo was taken. "He gave me that for my birthday. I looked it up later to see what it cost. Even on sale, the price tag would've topped ten thousand dollars. I don't like thinking about how much product he would've had to move just to pay for it."

The silence stretched out almost to the breaking point before Max finally spoke. "So which one of the alphabet-soup agencies were you working for?"

Titus blinked, both surprised and relieved that Max had immediately jumped to the right conclusion. "I was a DEA agent working undercover."

"And Moira didn't know?"

"No, and I couldn't risk telling her. It nearly killed me to lie to her every minute of every day we spent together. However, I'd been undercover for a year already and couldn't simply walk away because I happened to fall hard and fast for a beautiful woman."

"Did this Henshaw fellow know you were dating a cop?"

"No, so at least I did that much right. I kept those two parts of my life completely separate. Moira and I had been dating for about two months when the whole thing blew up. The DEA received intel that forced them into moving on Henshaw and his organization hard and fast. I happened to be with him at the time, so I got swept up in the same net as everyone else they could corner. Rather than out me at the scene, the agency tried to protect my cover."

He handed Max another newspaper clipping. "They used some of the local police force to help with the raid that night."

Max's eyes were huge as he studied the picture in the paper. He pointed at one person in particular. "That's you being led away in cuffs."

When Titus nodded, Max moved his fingertip to tap on one of the cops in the background. "And that's Moira."

"Yep. That was the last time I saw her before she moved back here to Dunbar and went to work for Cade."

Max handed back the newspaper and the picture. "Let me see if I've got this straight. You never told Moira you were DEA, and she was there the night you were arrested, along with Henshaw and his associates. You knew she had to be kicking herself for not realizing that she had fallen in love with a criminal, and yet you made no effort to tell her any different."

"Pretty much."

"And somewhere along the way, you decided that the best way to rectify that situation was to buy a café in her hometown and then sit back and wait to see if she would figure out you and Ryan Donovan were one and the same."

By that point, Titus had some serious regrets about consuming so much pizza and beer. "I have to admit that it wasn't my smartest idea. In my defense, my original plan was to let the dust settle after the raid and then tell her the truth. I owed her that much even if she couldn't find it possible to forgive me. Unfortunately, life interfered."

"I take it she knows now."

Titus kept his focus on petting Ned. "She does."

Max gave a long, low whistle. "Am I right in thinking she wasn't happy when you finally told her the truth?"

Titus couldn't help but chuckle. "That's putting it mildly."

Once again, Max surprised him. Instead of laughing, too, he sympathized. "We both know you wouldn't have walked away from her unless you had no choice."

Without waiting for Titus to offer up some excuse, he picked up the picture of Titus standing by Cian again and frowned. "There's got to be more to the story than you've told me so far. What happened to turn the guy in this picture into the man you are now? And I'm not just talking about the surface changes."

Good question. He leaned his head against the back of the couch and closed his eyes. "I said the agency tried to protect my cover—I didn't say they succeeded. The raid that night was only partially effective. They rounded up the majority of the intended targets, but a few managed to avoid capture. Somehow, Cian's younger cousin learned I was a cop. Two weeks after the raid, he and a few of his buddies managed to corner me on the street."

He realized he was rubbing his right knee, once again trying to soothe the still sharp memory of what it felt like to have his kneecap shattered with a tire iron. That had been only one of multiple broken bones he'd suffered that night, but it was the one that continued to play a starring role in his nightmares and flashbacks. He'd still been conscious when it happened. The broken bones in his face had been inflicted after he'd finally passed out.

"I was in the hospital for a month recovering from the multiple surgeries needed to patch me back together. After that, I was transferred to a rehab facility for a long stint while I learned to walk again."

He forced himself to meet Max's gaze. "The gravel in my voice was a by-product of that night in the alley, probably from screaming so much."

At this point, Max was ashen. "I don't know what to say, Titus, other than I'm sorry. Both that it happened and for prying."

"Don't sweat it, Max. It was a long time ago."

Besides, he'd come this far and might as well finish it. "When I was discharged, the agency transferred me to a desk job in an office on the other side of the country. The idea was to see if I would recover to the point where I could return to working out in the field. Looking back, I think I knew I was done wearing a badge before I even got out of rehab, but I gave it a shot and then walked away."

He stroked Ned's fur. "I did a two-year culinary program at the community college and then worked at a long list of restaurants and tried out a variety of styles of cooking. It didn't take long for me to realize that I wouldn't be happy working for anyone else long-term, so I also enrolled in some business classes."

"You were still living on the East Coast?"

"Yep."

Max was looking slightly better and even managed a small smile. "And when you were ready to open your own place, you looked around and decided the only place where you could put your new skills to use was in Dunbar, Washington, population six hundred."

"Pretty much. I figured the people here would appreciate hearty meals and good desserts."

"I don't doubt that's true, but I'm guessing the real reason was you were hoping the one person who mattered to you would move back to her hometown at some point."

"I know that sounds ridiculous, but yeah."

How could Titus explain that it had never seemed like a crazy idea to him? He'd been a man on a mission to set things right, to find some way to turn back the clock to the minute he'd first met Moira and felt something inside him click into place. No one and nothing had ever felt so right since.

But instead of shaking his head in disbelief, Max shook his head with a look of wonder on his face. "All I can say is that was one genius plan. It ranks right up there with me moving to the one town where virtually everyone hated my guts on the off chance I could coax Rikki into giving me the time of day."

Now that was funny. "An interesting parallel I hadn't considered. At least one of us has had his nefarious plan work out."

"Fingers crossed that yours meets with success, too. So what comes next?"

"Good question. Do you want another beer in case a little more alcohol helps inspire an even more genius plan?"

Max held out his empty. "What the heck, it couldn't hurt."

# CHAPTER TWELVE

MOIRA'S AFTERNOON HAD started off badly and then gotten worse. For the past fifteen minutes, she'd been on the phone talking to yet another citizen complaining about the failure of the Dunbar police force to locate his missing pampered pet. She wasn't quite clear on what breed Sir Nigel was, but Mr. Humby made it quite clear that the dog had his own bedroom, which was filled with a record number of first-place and best-in-show trophies.

To prove it, the guy had insisted on texting her a series of photos before insinuating that she was cowering in Cade's office when she should be out on the street organizing a manhunt. Or dog hunt. Whatever. He was right about one thing. She needed to hit the road again as soon as she managed to end the call.

Responding to his next threat, she said, "Mr. Humby, there's no need to call city hall." Mainly because the last thing she needed was for the mayor and his buddies on the council hassling her more than they already were. "I'm sorry, but I've been out on patrol and had only just returned to the office right before you called again. You were already at the top of my list of people to contact."

"I'm not sure I believe you, Officer Fraser," he huffed in disgust. "I had already left several messages, and you hadn't bothered to respond to any of those."

That was because he'd called three times in less than an hour. At the time she'd been responding to a pretty bad fender bender on the other side of town. The man's fourth call came in before she'd even had a chance to sit down.

"I'm sorry about the delay, Mr. Humby, but I was responding to an emergency. Until the ambulance and tow truck arrived, I wasn't in a position to return phone calls. You may choose not to believe me, but the truth is I had just returned to the office five minutes before you called this time."

There was a heavy silence on the other end of the line, followed by a deep sigh that now sounded more resigned than angry. "I apologize, Officer Fraser. I wasn't aware, and I shouldn't have implied that you were shirking your duty."

He'd more than implied it, but she let it go. If she got upset every time someone had questioned a cop's job performance, she would have spent most of the past ten years angry. That would be a waste of both her time and energy. "And as I was about to say, I will be going back out on patrol as soon as I finish returning calls. If I learn anything about Sir Nigel, I will get in touch immediately."

"I would greatly appreciate that. He means everything to me and my wife."

She hesitated before hanging up. "There is one thing you should know. Several other pets have gone missing recently. A couple returned on their own, and I hope Sir Nigel does the same. The thing is, two others came home only after their owners paid a ransom demand. The good news is that both animals had been well-cared for during their absence. There's no way of knowing if this is what happened to your dog. But if you do get demand for payment, please let me know."

There was a quaver in Mr. Humby's voice when he spoke. "We live on a fixed income, Officer Fraser. I will make some calls to see how much cash I can raise on short notice, but what happens to Sir Nigel if I can't raise the money?"

At least she could reassure him on that score. "That's the odd thing. Each time the ransom demand was less than thirty dollars."

"Seriously? That's almost an insult to a dog like my Nigel. What kind of criminal mastermind are we dealing with here?"

"I have no idea, Mr. Humby. I would ask that you not broadcast what I just told you. I wouldn't want to spook the kidnapper."

"My lips are sealed. I appreciate the warning."

After a brief hesitation, he added, "Stay safe while you're out on patrol, Officer Fraser."

She accepted the peace offering. "Thank you, Mr. Humby. I'll do my best."

The last question after she made her remaining phone calls was if she had time to pick up a meal to go. She'd been about to make her lunch before leaving home when Oscar had called for an assist. She'd been going nonstop since and worked straight through lunch and well into the dinner hour. To make it all the way to the end of her shift, she definitely needed to refuel. Fast food wasn't her favorite cuisine, but drive-up windows were sure convenient in a pinch. Unfortunately, the closest one was nearly thirty miles away, too far to go when duty required she stick closer to home.

That left only one recourse—calling in an order to the café. She'd love to actually sit down at a table and take the time to enjoy her meal, but she'd have to settle for getting one of Titus's roast-beef sandwiches and a couple of sides to eat as time and duties allowed. She'd do a circuit through town before picking up her meal and parking somewhere while she ate. That way, she could still respond quickly if something came up that required her attention.

It would be nice if one of the staff at the café answered the phone, but with the way her day had gone so far, she had little doubt whom she'd end up talking to. Sure enough, it was Titus's deep rumble that greeted her. "Officer Fraser, I've been thinking about you."

She wasn't about to ask why. "I need to place an order to go."

Maybe Titus picked up on the stress in her voice, because he simply asked, "What would you like?"

She kept it short and sweet. "A roast-beef sandwich with the usual fixings and a side salad. Iced tea to drink. I'll be there in about thirty minutes to pick it up."

"Drive around back and honk. I'll bring it out to you. See you soon."

"Wait, you didn't get my credit-card number."

"Did I ask for it?"

She pinched the bridge of her nose, trying to hold on to her temper. "No, that's why I asked you to wait. We aren't done."

"You're right. In fact, we're far from it."

He managed to thread a whole lot of extra meaning into those few words. When she couldn't do more than sputter in response, he had the nerve to laugh. "Like I said, honk when you get here."

When the line went dead, she slammed her hand down on the table. "Someday that man will go too far."

And if her real fear was that the two of them would never go far enough, well, that was her secret to keep.

TITUS CHECKED THE clock for the umpteenth time. Moira had said she'd be there in thirty minutes, but an hour and a half had passed and still no sign of her. Maybe she'd gotten a call. That would be the most logical reason for the delay, but his gut feeling was that something more was going on. He could only hope that he was wrong, but there was just one way to find out. He called the police station directly. Instead of either Oscar or TJ picking up, it kicked over to Dispatch.

"Nine-one-one, what is your emergency, Titus?"

At least it was someone he knew. "I'm sorry, Jackie, there's no emergency. I was trying to reach one of the officers at the Dunbar Police Department. I didn't realize that the call would get patched through to you if they couldn't answer. My apologies."

"Who were you trying to reach? I can pass along a message if the officer checks in."

"Ask Officer Fraser to give me a call. She has the number."

"Will do."

He hung up and resumed staring out the back window of the café, watching for any sign of her cruiser in the alley. Finally, he grabbed his jacket and whistled for Ned. The last of his staff had left for home already, so there was nothing keeping him there except Moira's order. He grabbed it off the counter in case he found her to save them both a trip back to the café.

"Let's take a look around, Ned."

Hoping to cover more territory in less time, he opened the driver's door on his pickup and stood back to let Ned jump in ahead of him. Once out on the road, he started by circling the center of town and gradually moved outward from there. When he got as far as Shay Barnaby's place with no sign of trouble, his tension eased up, but only a little. Instead of returning to the café, he decided to do another sweep before giving up. It wasn't until he reached the park on the opposite side of town from the tavern that he finally spotted Moira's cruiser.

It was parked at a weird angle, partly on the road and partly on the grass. The lights were flashing on the roof, but there was no one in the vehicle and no sign of Moira in the immediate vicinity. Titus's pulse picked up speed as he considered his options. "Moira would remind me that I'm no longer a cop and that I should call for assistance."

Ned growled, expressing his opinion of that idea. Clearly, he understood the possible urgency of the situation. "I agree, boy. I'll make the call in case she's in trouble, but that's not going to stop me from taking a look around before backup arrives."

He pulled his flashlight out of the glove box before getting out, then held the door open for Ned to join him on the ground. They made their way over to the abandoned cruiser and took a quick look at the interior. No obvious sign of trouble, so he stepped back and studied the surrounding woods. Where could she be?

That's when he noticed Ned had gone on point, sniffing the air like crazy with his ears pricked forward. "Show me, boy."

The dog trotted forward, stopping every so often to get his bearings. They'd gone about a hundred feet into the trees when Titus finally heard Moira's voice. She was too far away for him to make out the words, but her tone was calm and professional. That made him feel marginally better, but he still didn't like the fact that she was alone in the woods with a person or persons unknown.

He dialed TJ's home number, hoping to catch the young officer at his house. "Officer Shaw speaking, Mr. Kondrat. What's wrong?"

"I was out for a drive when I spotted Officer Fraser's cruiser parked near the entrance on the south side of the park. The lights are flashing, but there's no sign of her. My dog took off running into the woods. When I caught up with him, I could hear her talking to somebody. Rather than go charging in, I thought it best to call you first. Stay on the phone while I move closer to see what's going on."

"You should wait for me to arrive. I'm only about a mile from there."

"Sorry, but a lot can happen in the time it would take you to get here. If Moira gets mad, I'll make sure she knows you tried to get me to do the smart thing."

"I'm on my way." There was the sound of a car door opening and closing again. "And for what it's worth, I wouldn't wait, either."

The kid had a good head on his shoulders. No wonder Cade was so high on his newest hire. "When you see the cruiser, head straight into the trees about a hundred feet or so. I could hear her talking at that point. I'm going silent now to see how close I can get without putting her in danger. I don't want to draw unwanted attention in my direction if she's in the middle of something."

"Got it."

Ned stuck close to Titus without having to be told. He kept his nose to the ground, still stopping occasionally to listen before moving on. There wasn't enough moonlight filtering down through the trees to make maneuvering through the woods easy for man or dog. More than once, Titus came close to taking a header when he tripped over a rock or root jutting out of the ground. At least the trees were starting to thin out a bit, as if they were approaching a clearing of some sort.

That made navigating easier, and he could hear Moira speaking more clearly. There was definitely an angry edge in her voice now. That was worrisome enough, but it was the other person involved in the conversation who set Titus's teeth on edge. Ned started to growl deep in his chest, so Titus wasn't the only one reacting badly to whatever was going down just ahead. Unless he was mistaken, Moira was facing off against the same guy she'd tangled with outside Shay Barnaby's place last week. Jimmy something, not that his name was important at the moment. What had that jerk done now?

It was time to give TJ an update before moving closer to the confrontation. Titus moved back farther into the trees before speaking. "Sounds like Moira is dealing with that Jimmy guy who spent a couple of nights as a guest of the county jail. I'm almost within sight of them. Near as I can tell, they're talking for now. I'll let you know if that changes."

"Hang back if you can. I can see Moira's vehicle, so I should catch up with you shortly."

"I'm going silent again."

Without waiting for a response, Titus moved back, closer to where Moira and Jimmy were still facing off. This time he positioned himself where he was slightly behind Jimmy's position. If it all went sideways, he'd have a better shot of reaching Jimmy before the man would even see Titus coming. Easing forward and a few more steps to the right, he had an unobstructed view of the situation. Nothing about it made him happy.

Moira was sporting her best cop face as she stared down her opponent. Jimmy was perched on top of a picnic table as he glared right back at Moira. It might have been more impressive if he wasn't swaying back and forth and having trouble staying upright. The scattering of empty beer cans on the table and the surrounding ground made it even more obvious the man had been doing some serious drinking.

For the moment, the conversation between the two had apparently ground to a complete halt. Moira relaxed her stance as if she had all day—well, actually, all night—to deal with the situation. Her calm silence wasn't having the desired effect on Jimmy, though. Titus braced himself for action as the man became more agitated as the seconds ticked by. When Jimmy finished off the beer in his hand, he tossed the can aside and reached for another.

"You have no right to kick me out of the park, Officer. I'm a citizen, and I pay taxes."

He paused to belch loudly before continuing his tirade. "At least I did pay taxes when I still had a job."

He pointed a shaky finger in Moira's direction. "And it's your stupid fault that I don't have one anymore. My boss didn't much appreciate me not showing up for work the next morning without calling in. Funny how the county jail doesn't care about such things. They eventually let me call my mother to hire an attorney to get me out of there, but I couldn't call anyone else."

"I'm sorry to hear about your job, Jimmy, but I don't see how that was my fault. Maybe if you can lay off the beer, he'll reconsider. If you want to get into a program, I can put you in touch with some people."

He popped the top on his beer and downed at least half the can without even pausing to draw a breath. After setting it aside, he went back to pointing. "For your information, Officer, what I drink on my own time is not his business. Yours, either. If you'd gotten my keys back from Shay Barnaby like I told you to, none of this would've happened. I wasn't drunk and disorderly—I was hanging out with my friends. We didn't cause no trouble, leastwise not until you showed up and started throwing your weight around. You even got my friends to turn on me. Toby hung up on me when I tried to call him."

His head wobbled as he looked around the clearing, as if he expected to see his former buddy standing around.

"The big coward let your cop friend drive him home like he was some kid too young to have a drivers' license. Now that I think about it, I'm madder at him than I am at you."

Moira finally spoke again. "I'm sorry you're upset, Jimmy, but I still have to ask you to leave the park. It closes at sundown, which was a while ago. If you come along peacefully, I won't write you a ticket this time."

As long as Jimmy remained seated, Titus would continue to hold his current position. TJ should be arriving any second now and could step in if Moira needed support. With luck, Titus and Ned could then melt back into the trees without getting involved. Not that he wasn't fighting a strong urge to go charging to the rescue, anyway, even though Moira had the matter well in hand. Unless that changed, he'd stay right where he was.

To help keep himself grounded, he stroked Ned's fur, taking comfort from the dog's warm presence at his feet. A few seconds later, a twig snapped, ratcheting up Titus's already high stress level. The noise came from somewhere behind his current position. Ned stood up, on full alert.

"It's me, Mr. Kondrat. Can you ask your dog to stand down?"

"Sit, Ned. Officer Shaw is Moira's friend."

After giving the air a good sniff, Ned turned his attention back to the clearing and sat down, leaning into Titus's right leg. TJ sidled up to stand next to Titus on the other side. "Sitrep?"

"The man's drunk and upset. She's trying to talk him down. I've only heard part of the conversation, but he blames her that he lost his job while he was locked up. Something about the county jail not letting him call in sick to work or something. Moira just reminded him that the park closes at sundown and that he needs to leave. She even offered not to write him a ticket if he cooperates."

TJ shook his head. "Fat chance of that happening. I've dealt with Jimmy a time or two myself. Once he digs in his heels, he never backs down."

The second Moira shifted slightly, Titus knew she'd run out of patience. "Mr. Hudson, we've been out here long enough. I have to get back on patrol, and I can't do that until I know you've made it home safely."

The man jerked as if her words had hit a raw nerve. "And where would that be? Toby kicked me out after I punched him for letting me go to jail by myself. My mother paid the attorney to get me sprung, but she said until I got sober I wasn't welcome at her house. With no paycheck coming in, I can't afford a motel."

He shifted forward, sliding down onto the seat of the picnic table and planting his feet on the ground. "I'm not going anywhere because I ain't got nowhere else to go."

Then he sneered as he looked at her. "And I'm betting you can't make me this time. I still haven't figured out who helped you take me down that night outside of the bar. Ain't no woman alive who could do that without help. Was it that other cop or did that Kondrat guy and his dog ambush me? Everybody knows that guy did hard time. I should sue him for attacking me for no reason. His dog, too. Then I'd have money."

Under other circumstances, that last bit would have been funny. Right now, though, TJ was giving Titus a dark look. "You and the dog were there that night? I didn't see you."

"Ned and I were out for a walk. Ned didn't like the way those guys were talking to Moira and growled. He was on his leash the whole time and didn't go anywhere near them. From what I could see, she had things handled and backup was on the way. You must have arrived right after we left."

Actually, he knew exactly when TJ pulled up because he was watching from the shadows between two nearby buildings. Moira had been mad enough that Titus had been there at all. If her coworker had known he had almost waded in and knocked heads to protect her, she would have tossed him in the slammer right next to Jimmy.

All of which meant it was probably time for him to make a strategic retreat again. Once he was back at the road, he'd text Moira and tell her that he'd put her dinner in her SUV. "Now that you're here, Ned and I will head home."

But before he'd taken a single step, Jimmy went into launch mode. Titus let go of Ned's leash, ready to do battle.

## CHAPTER THIRTEEN

MOIRA KNEW BETTER than to take her eyes off the target, but that didn't mean she wasn't aware that she and Jimmy were no longer alone. A few seconds ago, a movement off to her right had caught her attention. A man was now standing in the deep shadows under the trees, watching her and Jimmy, and he wasn't alone. The ambient light might have been too dim to make out his features, but she knew exactly who was standing watch—Titus and Ned.

A slow burn of frustration flowed through Moira's veins, but she made every effort to hide it. Darn the man, she'd warned him once already not to follow her around, even if this time she was almost glad he was there. With luck, she wouldn't need his help, but there was no telling how this was going to play out. She pulled out her cell phone to call TJ and ask him to come running. Before she could, he stepped into sight. Since she hadn't called him, it only made sense that Titus had done the honors. At least he'd thought that far ahead.

That didn't mean she was going to stand here all night waiting for Jimmy to either pass out or go on the attack. At the rate he was downing beers, it could go either way. He finished off the one he'd just opened and tossed the empty down with the others. He reached into the cardboard carton sitting next to him on the table only to realize it was empty. Frowning, he looked around, as if wondering who had stolen his last beer.

"Jimmy, let me give you a ride…"

She immediately regretted making the offer again, because where could she take him? If his roommate had kicked him out and his mother wouldn't let him come home, where else was there? The only possibility she could think of was sure to light his already short fuse, but something had to change. They couldn't stay out here in the woods all night. "Jimmy, if you need a place to sleep, I can let you use the cot in the cell at the police department."

He came up off the picnic table in a blur of motion, his fists clenched as he bellowed, "I'm not going back to jail. That's why I'm in this mess in the first place."

TJ darted out of the shadows with Titus right on his heels. Moira veered in his direction, determined to prevent him from making a huge mistake. "Stop, Titus! TJ and I will handle Jimmy."

Somehow.

She moved closer to Jimmy, aiming for calm but not sure how successful she was being as she tried again, "I didn't say you were under arrest, Jimmy. I'm simply offering you a warm place to stay tonight. The cot might not be all that comfortable, but it has to beat sleeping on a picnic table. If you can think of someplace better, I'm open to suggestions."

His face flushed red as he sneered, "I have all kinds of suggestions for you, lady, and none of them involve me spending another night in jail."

He staggered two steps forward and almost tripped. When he caught his balance, he spun around as if trying to figure out if someone had pushed him. The quick move only succeeded in sending him stumbling back toward the picnic table. Moira held her ground, waiting to see what he'd do next. At least Titus and the dog had retreated to the edge of the trees, leaving her and TJ to deal with the real problem.

One way or the other, it was time to bring this little party to a close before Jimmy did something that set Titus off again. Like she'd told him last time, she wouldn't put up with vigilante justice. By that point, Jimmy had now regained his balance, if not his composure. He glared at TJ. "Where'd you come from?"

Without giving him a chance to respond, Jimmy focused on Titus. "What are you doing here? I told you and that dog the last time to stay out of my business."

He shook his fist in Titus's direction. "It's bad enough I don't have a job or a roof over my head. But thanks to you and your buddy Barnaby, I can't even get a hot meal in town. I've been living on gas-station food and cheap beer."

Continuing his tirade, he spun back toward Moira. "I was out here minding my own business when that lady cop showed up to hassle me. That ain't right. I wasn't bothering nobody. Not this time."

At least Titus kept his mouth shut this time while TJ peeled off to head in Moira's direction. He positioned himself near enough for her to hear him whisper, "How do you want to play this?"

"Best case, I want to get Jimmy out of here without the situation getting any worse."

She glanced toward Titus, who was leaning against a handy tree with Ned by his side. He'd been talking to the dog but turned in her direction as if he'd sensed her watching him. Something occurred to her. Every time there was a problem of some kind, Titus's immediate response was to bring food. He'd done it back when her boss had tossed his now wife in jail overnight for obstructing a police investigation. He'd also offered her grandmother pie and tea when he'd found her out on the street. More recently, he'd brought sandwiches and treats to the police station. Maybe she could take advantage of his generosity one more time.

She took a step closer to Jimmy to keep his focus on her. "Jimmy, I'm going to make you a onetime offer. If you agree to come along to the station peacefully, I'm going to ask Titus to bring you one of those hot meals you mentioned. You'll feel better once you've eaten, and you can get a good night's sleep on the cot. Come tomorrow, we'll figure out what can be done about your other problems. How does that sound?"

It was a relief that Jimmy didn't reject the idea out of hand. He squinted at Titus as if trying to decide if the offer was on the up-and-up. "You got any of the meat loaf special left? It's my favorite."

Titus didn't hesitate. "I believe I do. I can heat up a couple of slices along with all the fixings."

He moved back into the clearing while making sure he didn't get between her and Jimmy. "Come to think of it, I also have that bread pudding you had the last time you came in. While Officer Fraser gets you settled in at the station, I'll go back to the café to fix your dinner."

Moira suspected she wasn't the only one holding her breath as they waited to see what Jimmy decided. Finally, he nodded. "I'll go with her."

Then he looked down at the cans scattered on the ground. "First, I should pack up all of those. Shouldn't leave a mess in the park. Bad example for the kids."

He nearly toppled over when he bent down to pick up the closest can. In a quick move, TJ caught him before he hit the ground. "Easy there, Jimmy. Why don't you sit for a spell?"

Moira positioned herself on his other side, careful not to crowd the man now that he was making some effort to cooperate.

Titus bent down to pick up the closest can from the ground. "Jimmy, would you hold Ned's leash for me while I pick up the cans for you? It won't take but a minute."

Jimmy finally sat down and latched on to Ned's leash. Titus made quick work of dumping all of the empties back into the carton. When he finished, he took back Ned's leash. "I'll head to the café. It won't take me long."

Meanwhile, TJ gave Jimmy a helping hand off the bench. "Come on, Jimmy. Let's head back out to where Officer Fraser parked her vehicle. It's not far."

Moira waited until the two men disappeared into the woods before she confronted Titus. She also needed the time to figure out what she actually wanted to say to him. Maybe she'd start with the basics and go from there. "I warned you about following me."

"You did."

"And yet here you are."

Instead of being properly cowed by her disapproval, he gave her an aw-shucks grin. "You didn't pick up your dinner, and I hate to have good food go to waste. When it was time to lock up and go home, I figured I'd take your meal with me in case I happened to see you while I was out and about."

Oh, brother. "Right, and you just happened to be driving by the park, which is in the complete opposite direction from your house."

He shrugged. "What can I say? I have a poor sense of direction sometimes."

She was fighting a losing battle and knew it. "You called TJ."

"I did. I was only going to hang around until he arrived. If Jimmy hadn't started getting all worked up, you would've never known I was even here." His teeth gleamed in the moonlight when he smiled again. "Former undercover cops have some serious skills when it comes to skulking around in the shadows, you know."

Fighting the urge to grin right back at him, she shook her head sadly. "Sorry, big guy, but I've got news for you. Those skills you're so proud of are seriously rusty. I saw you approach the first time and then retreat. I'm guessing that's when you called TJ, and then you came back again."

"Well, that is disappointing. At least give me credit for not charging to the rescue...not that you needed rescuing. I learned from my mistakes."

Maybe he had.

He stared down at her, his dark gaze intense. "I wish the mayor and the council had been here to see you in action. You were amazing."

His assessment meant a lot, but she was glad it was dark out so he couldn't see her blush. Meanwhile, it was time for her to also give credit where credit was due. "I know I didn't give you much choice, Titus, but I appreciate what you're doing for Jimmy. It likely made the difference in getting him to come along peacefully. He still would've ended up sleeping in the cell, but with the door locked. Not only would charging him involve a lot of paperwork for me, but it wouldn't help his current situation at all."

"It's just some leftover meat loaf." As usual, Titus looked uncomfortable with her gratitude and immediately changed the subject. "Speaking of that. I still have your sandwich and salad, but they're pretty old by now. We'd better catch up with TJ so the two of you can get Jimmy settled at the station. I'll fix enough food for all three of you."

Not only was the man a natural-born protector, but he also had such a generous heart. She wasn't wrong in believing that the guy she'd fallen in love with ten years ago hadn't been real, but her heart badly wanted to believe the man standing in front of her was. After taking a quick peek to make sure that TJ and his companion were out of sight, she caught Titus's head with her hands and tilted his head to the perfect angle for a quick kiss. It was unprofessional, not the right time and absolutely perfect.

He frowned down at her. "Not that I'm complaining, but what was that for?"

"You're a smart man. Figure it out for yourself."

They started walking, and he snapped his fingers as if the answer had just come to him. Leaning in close, he whispered, "I've got it. You're hoping I have enough bread pudding to go around."

She couldn't help but laugh, which felt pretty good. It had been a long day and a tough one at that. An hour ago, all she'd wanted was for it to end, so she could crawl into bed and pull the covers over her head. But right now, walking through the woods in the darkness with Titus Kondrat, well, there was nowhere else she wanted to be.

"You look like heck."

Titus dropped into the seat across from Max. "Thanks. Good morning to you, too. If you're going to be a jerk, maybe you should take your breakfast and go straight to… someplace else. The door's back that way."

Rather than being offended by Titus's ill temper, Max now looked concerned. "Seriously, is everything okay?"

Needing the energy boost that caffeine would give him, he waited to answer Max's question until he'd gulped down almost half a cup of the miracle cure that was dark roast. Setting his mug back down on the table, he sighed. "Yeah, despite appearances, I'm fine. Mostly, anyway. It's been a while since I pulled an all-nighter."

Max's eyes flared wide in surprise. "Tell me you were doing something fun that involved our favorite lady cop."

Not a question that Titus wanted to answer in public, but at least Max had the good sense to keep his voice down. "It did involve Officer Fraser, but unfortunately Officer Shaw was there as well. We...well, actually *they* were dealing with a situation. My contribution was limited to meat loaf."

That was as much as he wanted to say on that subject, so he gave Max's plate a pointed look. His friend took the hint. "Fine, I'll eat."

Rita swung by to top off his coffee. To Titus's surprise, she also set a plate in front of him that was piled high with ham and cheddar scrambled eggs with a side of hash browns. "What's this for?"

"It's for you to eat. Gunner pointed out that you're running on empty, which we all know makes you a bit...well, let's just say, temperamental. We've got everything covered right now, so take your time and relax."

He arched an eyebrow. "Remind me, who's the boss around here?"

Rather than cower at the growled question, she laughed at him. "You are, sir. That means it's the job of us minions to see to your every need."

She pointed at the plate. "And right now, you need to fuel up."

Turning her smile in Max's direction, she asked, "Mr. Volkov, can I get you anything else?"

"Nope, I'm good. I'll make sure he cleans his plate."

Great, everyone was a comedian today. "*He's* sitting right here and can decide for himself how much he wants to eat or even if he wants to eat at all."

Titus glared first at Max and then at Rita. Judging by how she kept laughing as she walked away, he needed to work on his intimidation skills. It didn't help that Max wasn't making any effort to hide his amusement as he stuffed his face with the spinach-and-mushroom omelet he'd ordered.

What made matters worse was knowing that Gunner and Rita were right. Drinking all that strong coffee on an empty stomach hadn't been the smartest thing to do. Neither was shoving the food in his mouth as fast as he could. With some effort, he forced himself to slow down and actually enjoy his meal. When he'd finished off the eggs and most of the hash browns, he set down his fork and pushed his plate over to the side of the table.

Max had finished his meal as well, which left him free to start pestering Titus with more questions. "So Moira was acting in her official capacity during your late-night encounter with her."

Titus set down his cup without taking a drink. "You're not going to be happy until you wheedle every detail out of me."

Looking a bit insulted, Max said, "I'll have you know that I do not wheedle. I'm a highly trained reporter. I investigate."

"Right now, you're a highly trained pain in my backside."

Max fell silent for several seconds. "Fine. I'll back off for now, but I'm available if you need to talk about anything."

Once again, Titus wasn't sure how to deal with having so many people who seemingly cared about his personal well-being. It wasn't that he didn't believe them. What he didn't understand was why they would care so much. Max already knew more about Titus's past than anyone else did…including Moira. That wasn't right, and he'd have to change that if he ever hoped to get past the defenses she rebuilt every time he thought they'd made some progress.

It wasn't fair to treat Max like a guinea pig, but Titus had to start somewhere.

"She called and ordered a dinner to go last evening. She was supposed to pick it up thirty minutes later, but she never showed. She warned me once not to interfere with her job, but I got worried. After I locked up the café, I went looking for her. I eventually found her out in the park dealing with a situation."

"So despite her telling you not to follow her around while Cade is gone, you did it, anyway."

"Pretty much. I can't remember if I told you about the night that her vehicle broke down, and I gave her a ride back to the office and then home. I was worried something like that had happened again, especially when I spotted her cruiser at a weird angle by the park with the lights flashing."

Come to think of it, she never explained why she'd left it that way. Not that it mattered right now. "Anyway, I took it to mean that she'd spotted something—or someone— and took off running. Ned and I went through the woods to see what was going on, and I called Officer Shaw in case she might need his help."

"Was she mad about you showing up?"

"Put it this way, she wasn't exactly thrilled, but it ended on a good note." He was thinking about the way she'd kissed him afterward, not that he was going to share that private moment with Max. "Anyway, I ended up coming back here to fix a meal for her, TJ and someone else, who shall remain nameless. By the time I finally got home, I couldn't unwind enough to go to sleep."

"How much rest did you actually get?"

"Not enough."

Or any at all, actually. He'd ended up going out walking until it was time to show up for work. It wouldn't be the first time that he'd had to go without sleep and still function. That's why he'd been guzzling extra strong coffee since he'd arrived at the café to fix the breakfasts he'd promised to Jimmy and whoever had ended up babysitting him last night. Luckily, Oscar Lovell happened to stop in to buy a breakfast sandwich to go. Since he was about to go on duty, Titus had asked him to deliver the meals instead of taking them over himself.

Meanwhile, Max was talking. "Anything I can do to help? Rikki isn't expecting me back at the B and B until this afternoon. I can wash dishes, seat customers—whatever you think I can handle."

"I appreciate the offer, but we're good."

"Just let me know if that changes." Then Max looked past him toward the door. "Wow, Officer Fraser looks like she's not doing much better than you are this morning."

Titus risked a quick glance in her direction. Had Moira been the one who had ended up watching over Jimmy? She and TJ had still been arguing over who should get stuck spending the night at the police station when Titus had left. Or maybe something else had happened that had required her attention. There was always the possibility that Mrs. Leary had wandered off again. He hoped not, for her sake, as well as for Moira's and her mother's.

To his surprise, Moira didn't wait for Rita to direct her to a table. Instead, she looked around the room and then made a beeline in his direction. Max immediately started to stand up. "I should be going."

He probably thought Titus would prefer to be alone with Moira. Any other time, that might've been true, but right now he would rather have the other man there to provide a buffer between him and Moira. "Stay where you are. I'm not sure what's happened now, but I might need you to referee."

Max settled back into his seat. "If you're sure…"

For the first time all morning, Titus felt like smiling. "When it comes to that particular woman, I'm never sure about anything."

# CHAPTER FOURTEEN

MOIRA HAD TO be out of her mind, but right now she didn't care. There was a perfectly good empty table on the near side of the café. She could sit there, order a cup of coffee with some kind of pastry and enjoy a few minutes of relative peace before moving on to the next stop on her lengthy list of errands. She could've also done the same thing at Bea O'Malley's bakery a few doors down and not run the risk of running into Titus Kondrat.

Instead, here she found herself bypassing the empty table and heading straight for the man himself. The department owed him for the meals he'd so generously donated to the cause last night. As the person temporarily in charge, it was her duty to officially thank him. She'd already tried to pay for the food, but he'd refused to take a dime from her even when she'd assured him that she could put it on her expense account.

That much was true even though there was no guarantee that she'd actually get reimbursed. She wasn't sure if Cade could okay providing meals for someone who wasn't exactly a prisoner since no actual charges had been filed. She'd let Jimmy off with a warning, making him more of a guest than an actual prisoner.

She forced herself to maintain a steady pace across the short distance to where Titus was sitting with Max Volkov. It would be better if she didn't discuss police business in front of a civilian other than Titus, but right now she couldn't muster enough energy to care. By the time she reached the table, Titus was up and pulling out a chair for her. As much as she normally appreciated such courtesy, it would've been better if his actions hadn't drawn so much attention in their direction.

Rather than comment on it, she did her best to act as if having the most mysterious man in town demonstrating some good old-fashioned manners was something that happened every day. When she was settled, Titus walked away after saying he'd be right back. That left her sitting with Max, someone she still didn't know all that well.

He must have picked up on her unease. After a brief hesitation, he quietly spoke. "Titus was just telling me that it was a late night for him and that it probably was for you as well. He didn't share much in the way of details other than he did some cooking to help you out last night. From the way he's been swilling down coffee, it's obvious he's dragging a bit this morning."

So she hadn't been imagining the exhaustion she thought she'd seen in Titus's eyes. She hadn't gotten much sleep herself, but that was because she spent the night sitting at Cade's desk and wading through paperwork until all hours. Ordinarily, she would've caught some shut-eye on the cot in the break room, but Jimmy hadn't actually been locked up. Knowing that he could go wandering whenever the mood struck, she hadn't been willing to take that risk.

At least she was scheduled to be off after TJ came in at ten. Her original plan had been to go home and crash for a few hours, but then an unexpected phone call had put that idea to rest. As soon as Titus settled in one spot long enough for her to thank him, she would focus her sleep-deprived brain on dealing with the new problem that had been dumped in her lap.

He reappeared carrying a tray containing a pot of tea

and a stack of small plates. The top one held three huge cinnamon rolls. He set the tea and a mug in front of Moira and then slid one of the rolls onto each of the two extra plates, keeping the third one for himself. Finally, he handed out the three forks he'd stuck in his shirt pocket.

He got rid of the tray while she eyed the gooey goodness. When he returned, she pointed out the obvious. "You've already fed me once this morning."

He picked up his fork and dug right in. "Consider it dessert."

Okay, that was funny. "I wasn't aware that people were in the habit of eating dessert with breakfast."

Not that it was going to stop her. She took a bite and nearly moaned as the flavor of yeast laced with cinnamon and maybe a bit of cloves hit her tongue. "Did you make these or did Gunner?"

Titus gave her a suspicious look. "Does it matter?"

"Of course, it matters." She scooped up a bit of the icing and licked it off her finger. "I wouldn't want to kidnap the wrong guy and force him to become my pastry slave for life." Max almost choked on the bite he'd just taken as Titus gave her a considering look. When he didn't immediately answer, she asked again, "Seems like an easy question. Was it you or Gunner?"

His voice was a deep rumble when he finally responded. "Considering your nefarious plans, I'm tempted to lie. However, since I told you enough lies in the past, I'm not going to now. Gunner produced this batch, but I taught him how to make them and let him use my recipe."

"Well, that does pose a problem, doesn't it?" She smiled just a little. "Which one of you makes the pies? Oh, and the chicken and dumplings?"

He nudged her with his shoulder. "That's all me."

She nudged him back. "Okay, then it's settled. I won't be kidnapping Gunner."

He swiped his hand across his forehead and grinned at Max. "Whew, that was a close one. I almost lost the best cook I've ever worked with."

Max pointed his fork at Titus. "That's great for you two—you get to keep your cook while she gets pastries and dumplings for life. What about the rest of us? Are we supposed to go without your pies while you spend all your time baking for her?"

Before either of them could answer, he aimed the tines in her direction. "And you, Officer Fraser, you're sworn to protect and serve. How can you call it *serving* if you keep all the pie for yourself? Sounds like some serious dereliction of duty to me."

Boy, she'd needed this bit of silliness. Playing along, she raised her hands in surrender. "You're right, Mr. Volkov. It would be unbelievably selfish of me to keep Chef Kondrat's skills all to myself."

"Don't I have a say in this?"

As he spoke, Titus gave her one of those looks that made her wish they were someplace a lot more private, although it was probably better that they weren't. "Nope. It's your civic duty as owner of the only full-service eatery in the entire town."

Then she leaned in closer and whispered, "But if you want to bake me a chocolate-cream pie now and then, I won't tell anyone."

"It's a deal."

She liked that she'd made him smile and that he wasn't looking quite so tired now. The interaction felt comfortable and a little bit familiar. More like the easy relationship they'd had when they'd first met than the sometimes awkward, sometimes infuriating encounters they'd had since she'd learned the truth about who he was. Titus had definitely changed in the ten years since they'd been together in ways that went far deeper than the tattoos that were so much a part of his persona now. However, more and more often she caught a glimpse of the man she'd known and liked so much back then. He'd been more...lighthearted, she supposed was the best description. She suspected that was true for her as well.

Unfortunately, it was time to get down to business and finish her cinnamon roll. "I can't stay long. I wanted to thank you again for helping out last night and feeding everybody this morning. We all appreciated it."

He acknowledged her gratitude with a bare hint of a nod. "How was the unnamed party doing this morning?"

Again, she probably shouldn't respond in front of Max, but it wasn't as if anything ever remained secret for long in Dunbar. "Having two square meals and a decent night's sleep seems to have made a big difference. We discussed some options, and I'm hopeful he might start making better decisions."

Titus looked pleased by that. "Good to hear."

"Yeah, I took a chance and talked to his employer myself. Turns out our guy is only suspended. If he gets some help, his job will be waiting for him. His mom also said he can return home until he can get things arranged."

"Boy, you have been busy this morning. I hope you-know-who appreciates it."

"Me, too." She checked the time. "Oops, I'd better be going."

When she started to stand, he stopped her. "Shouldn't you be off duty by now?"

"Yeah, but something's come up." She relaxed back in her chair again. "I promised to help find someone who can umpire a couple of little-kid baseball games later today.

It's the local fall ball league. Evidently, Cade had volunteered to be a substitute ump when the regular guy can't make it. Since Cade's still on his honeymoon, that leaves them shorthanded. Thomas Kline, the guy in charge, has called everyone he could think of with no luck. I would do it myself, but I don't know the finer points of baseball. I played volleyball and soccer when I was in school."

Titus went perfectly still, then blurted, "If they're that desperate, I could do it. I played center field from junior high school all the way through college. The rules can't have changed all that much."

She didn't know which one of the three people at the table were the most shocked by Titus's offer. Max looked dumbfounded, but only slightly more so than Titus himself. After a second, he frowned and pointed at the swirling tats on his arms. "Look, I know what people suspect about my background. That's my fault for not telling them the truth. If you think having me there wouldn't go over well with the parents, just say so. It won't hurt my feelings."

Something in his voice made her suspect that might not be true. She hastened to reassure him without being too heavy-handed about it. "It's not like you're a stranger to the people in town, and they know you and Cade are friends. That should ease any doubts they might have. From what Thomas told me, they run into more problems when one of the parents gets dragooned into umping and either makes a bunch of mistakes or doesn't seem to be impartial."

Max chimed in with, "So what you're saying is that you need someone neutral so both sides can be mad at him without feeling guilty."

He meant it as a joke, but it was probably true. "Yeah, I'd say so."

Max rubbed his hands together. "I can tag along in case Titus needs backup. I was a pretty good shortstop back in the day. I'll bring Rikki and Carter, too. I think the kid would get a kick out of watching the games. We're hoping to sign him up for T-ball in the spring."

Problem solved. "I'll call Thomas back and ask him to drop off a copy of the rule book for each of you. We should arrive at the park around four thirty. The first game is scheduled to start at five."

Titus looked surprised. "We? Are you coming, too?"

Would he rather she didn't? "I figure somebody ought to be there cheering for the umpire and his assistant."

Titus looked slightly less freaked out by what he'd just volunteered to do. "And to protect us from irate parents?"

She laughed and patted him on the arm. "That, too."

THE BASEBALL DIAMOND was located on the back side of the same park where she'd found Jimmy the previous night. Right now, the people starting to pour into the park were there to watch their kids play baseball. It had been years since Moira had attended one of her cousin's games, but she remembered having a great time hooting and hollering when one of the kids got a hit or made a great catch. She was looking forward to doing that again, but she was also concerned about Titus's role in the games. He would do his best to be both impartial and accurate with his calls. The only question was if the parents would give him a fair chance.

Since she wasn't on duty, she hoped to get lost in the crowd rather than look as if she was there in her professional capacity. With that in mind, she'd stopped off at home long enough to take a quick shower and change into civilian clothes. That was also why she'd borrowed her mother's car instead of driving her official vehicle. Unfortunately, her hope of blending in died when someone called her name as soon as she stepped out of the vehicle.

It took her a second to spot her friend Carli waving at her from across the parking lot. Moira waved back and cut through the line of cars to reach her. "I didn't expect to see you here."

Carli fell into step with her as they started down the path that led through the trees to the baseball field. "Some of the kids in the Sunday-school class that I'm teaching this year are playing today. I promised them I would come. How about you? Do you know someone in the game?"

Great. This could get awkward. She'd already been debating whether she could safely reveal to Carli that Ryan Donovan and Titus Kondrat were one and the same man. She trusted her friend's discretion, but Titus hadn't chosen to share his past with the locals for good reason.

Carli was still waiting for an answer, so Moira went with an almost accurate version of the facts. "I was in the café this morning talking to a friend. Titus Kondrat overheard me saying that I'd been asked to find someone who would be willing to umpire the games this afternoon. To my surprise, he volunteered. Since I got him into this situation, I thought I should be here to show my support."

It was too much to hope that Carli would take the explanation at face value without peppering Moira with a bunch of questions she didn't want to answer. Instead, she tugged Moira off the path, where they could talk without blocking the people coming up behind them. As soon as they were out of the way, Carli said, "Run that by me again."

"Titus is working behind the plate, and Max Volkov will be umpiring out in the field."

"So Titus was eavesdropping while you were talking to Max Volkov?"

That sounded bad for some reason. Knowing she was about to lose complete control of the conversation, Moira swallowed hard and tried again, "Actually, the three of us were sitting at the same table eating cinnamon rolls when the subject came up."

Carli did a little victory dance, a huge grin on her face. "I knew I was right. There is something going on between you and the mystery man. I want all the details."

Feeling a little panicky, Moira glanced around to see if anyone might be listening to their conversation. Most people walked by with barely a glance in their direction, but this still wasn't the time or place for this conversation. "Look, it's complicated, and I can't explain everything here. I promise I'll share what I can the next time we get together."

"Well, that's disappointing." Carli put her hands on her hips in an attempt to look intimidating. "My social calendar is wide open, so pick a night. I'm guessing you would rather not share all the details in front your mom and grandmother, so we'll meet at my place. You can even stay over if it's the kind of conversation that will require multiple bottles of wine."

"It just might."

Her voice cracked just a bit, which had Carli frowning big-time. "Do I need to borrow some kid's bat to make sure Titus knows to toe the line when it comes to how he treats you? I won't stand for another jerk hurting you like that guy did back in the day."

It was hard not to laugh at the irony. "We'd better get moving. I don't want to miss anything."

When Carli made no move to start down the path, Moira tried again, "I told Titus and Max that we needed to be there by four thirty. I don't want them to think I bailed on them."

"We're not going anywhere until you answer my question. Do I need that bat or not? Will he treat you right?"

While Moira appreciated her friend's determination

to protect her, it still wasn't a conversation she wanted to have. She and Titus weren't in a relationship, not the kind Carli was talking about. The truth was Moira didn't know what they had. Yes, they'd exchanged a couple of kisses, but those had been done on impulse. He hadn't said a word about officially getting involved again, and she wasn't sure that's what she wanted, anyway. What if they tried and it all went wrong again? Wouldn't it be better to settle for being friends? Safer, at least. That might actually be the best scenario considering they lived in such a small town.

But it would also be pretty disappointing.

# *CHAPTER FIFTEEN*

TITUS LOOKED AROUND the baseball field and fought the urge to take off running. What had he gotten himself into? He'd spent most of the afternoon reading and rereading the rule book Thomas Kline had given him. Considering the kids in the first game were seven and eight years old, it was doubtful he'd need to know much about the more obscure rules and regulations. That didn't mean he wasn't nervous.

At least Max had called to say that he and Rikki were definitely bringing Carter to watch Max and Titus umpire the game. That was good. For sure, Thomas Kline had been relieved to learn that Moira had been able to round up two volunteers to help out. Titus figured that "two suckers" was a better description, but he'd faced tougher situations and survived. Now, if only the person who'd gotten him into this mess would show up. He could use some moral support.

He'd been on the receiving end of curious looks from some of the parents as they arrived, but no one had actually approached him. A few of the kids had stopped and stared at him in confusion, as if wondering why he was out of his normal environment at the café. It was kind of like back when he was six and ran into his first-grade teacher at the grocery story. Who knew that teachers didn't actually live at school?

"You're looking a bit freaked-out there."

He slowly turned around, trying to look far calmer than he actually felt. "It's about time you got here."

Moira jerked her head toward the bleachers. "I ran into Carli out in the parking lot. She had questions. You know, about how you happened to overhear me mentioning I needed to find an umpire for the game."

"You make it sound like I was sneaking around to listen on your conversation. As I recall, you were sitting right next to me at the time."

"Yes, I know. That information was clarified upon cross-examination. Carli has an uncanny knack for sensing when I'm not being totally honest with her."

A glance in the same direction verified her friend was watching the two of them with great interest. "And was she satisfied with your answers?"

"Not exactly. Ever since that day she and I ate lunch together at the café, she has suspected that there's something going on between the two of us. I tried denying it then, but wasn't all that successful. Probably because I don't like lying to my friends. Having said that, you haven't chosen to share your past with many people here in Dunbar. I figure that's your right, so I've danced around the subject."

She sidled up closer and whispered, "But you better be careful around Carli. She's already asked if she needed to borrow a bat. Something about using it to convince you to treat me better than that jerk Ryan Donovan did back in the day."

Great. "So she knows about him...me...us and what happened."

"She doesn't know that you're him, if that's what you're asking." Moira stared up at him, her blue eyes so solemn. "But she's the one who helped me pick up the pieces."

There was something he should be saying that would soothe the pain in that single sentence. For the life of him, he couldn't think what it might be, especially standing at the edge of a baseball diamond in front a small crowd. He kept it simple. "I promise she won't need the bat."

"Mr. Kondrat, here's your gear. I have some for the other guy, too."

Neither of them had noticed Mr. Kline's approach. At least he seemed too distracted to have been listening to their conversation. "You can leave Max's stuff with me. I'll see that he gets it."

"I've told the coaches from both games how you stepped up to help out tonight. They're pretty levelheaded as far as coaches go, so you shouldn't have any problems. If you do, I'll want to hear about it. We have rules about such things and do our best to enforce them. Sometimes people get caught up in the moment and forget baseball is a game and supposed to be fun, especially at the age these kids are."

Then he gave Titus a considering look. "Somehow I don't think you'll run into any problems you can't handle."

Thomas winked as he looked past him to Moira. "And you have some serious backup, too."

"I'm a civilian tonight, Mr. Kline. I'm here to support Titus and Max since I got them into this, but I plan to cheer for both teams."

"Smart woman." He pointed off to the left. "Looks like your friend has arrived. I'll be around long enough to make sure the first game starts off okay. After that, I'm umpiring a game at the middle school. If you wouldn't mind taking the gear with you, I'll pick it up at your café tomorrow."

Titus nodded. "No problem, and lunch will be on me."

"That's mighty nice of you, Mr. Kondrat. I'll see you then."

By that point, Max had gotten Rikki and Carter settled in the bleachers. It looked like they'd hit the refreshment stand on the way in. Both were chowing down on hot dogs and there was a small bucket of popcorn sitting between them. Nothing like junk food to make a sporting event more fun.

After getting his wife and new son settled, Max crossed the field to join him and Moira. Titus gave him his share of the gear designed to protect the umpires from fast-moving baseballs. As he began strapping on a shin guard, Max looked around before whispering, "I hope I don't make a complete fool of myself doing this."

Moira handed him the other shin guard. "Relax, Max. This isn't the big leagues, and you're both a lot bigger than the players are even if they are armed with bats. Besides, I'm betting you can outrun the little rascals."

"Thanks for making me feel better…not. We all know the parents and grandparents are the scary ones."

"True enough. And on that positive note, I should head over to the stands before Carli thinks I've forgotten about her. Good luck to both of you. Afterward, I'll buy the first round at Barnaby's. Maybe even the second."

Max finished fastening the straps on his chest protector. "Thanks for the offer, but I'll have to take a rain check. It'll be Carter's bedtime by the time we get done here. I don't like to miss story time."

It was disappointing, even if understandable, why Max would prefer to spend time with his new family. Titus hoped it didn't mean that Moira would retract the offer. He'd love a chance to spend some time with her when she wasn't on duty and they weren't surrounded by his employees and customers.

But he'd rather know now than spend the next couple of hours wondering. "Will Carli be coming, too?"

To his relief, Moira hesitated only a second before nodding. "I'll invite her, but I don't know if she has other plans."

As she walked away, Titus wondered if it was bad on his part to be hoping Carli had somewhere else she needed to be. Regardless, he was relieved that Moira seemed okay with the idea of hanging out with him at the tavern for a drink or maybe even two. Things were looking up.

IT HAD BEEN obvious that both Max and Titus were jittery before the first game started. After all, neither of them had any umpiring experience. That didn't account for why she was on the edge of her seat and as tense as any parent in the stands. It wasn't as if Moira had a child in the game to worry about. No, instead she had the umpire, a man who was perfectly able to take care of himself. If Titus could handle going undercover in a drug cartel, he could handle this situation.

She'd heard a few murmurs from people sitting around her who obviously didn't know who he was. No matter how protective she was feeling, it wasn't her job to leap to his defense. Luckily, someone else spoke up. In the process, she learned a few things about Titus that she hadn't known about, starting with how he routinely donated money to local programs for kids. As near as she could tell, the man was a soft touch whenever there was a fundraiser going on in town.

It was a sure bet he would've never told her about his efforts to support the community like that. The man liked keeping his cards close to his chest. She also couldn't help but notice that an awful lot of the players themselves knew him. It probably wasn't normal practice for the umpire to offer high fives as the kids came charging across home plate, but they seemed to expect Titus to celebrate with them. Since he did the same thing for both teams, no one could claim he played favorites. Funny how he seemed more at ease with children than he did with most adults.

Considering kids usually were pretty good judges of character, she liked what that said about him.

Max was also doing a good job dealing with the kids. She wondered if either man realized that they'd probably be getting calls the next time a substitute umpire was needed. Somehow, she doubted either of them would mind.

"You're looking pretty starry-eyed there, lady."

Moira shot a quelling look in her friend's direction. "I am not."

When Carli rolled her eyes in disbelief, Moira tried again, "I'm the one who got Max and Titus involved in this. I'm simply happy that things have gone smoothly so far. That's all."

"You keep telling yourself that. I get why you might want to convince me that's all it is, but you're not usually in the habit of lying to yourself. Seriously, I haven't seen you this interested in a man in a long time. Maybe you should ask Titus out and see how it goes."

Right then one of the players hit a home run, and the crowd went wild. Moira was excited for the kid, but she was also grateful that all the resulting hooting and hollering as he ran the bases made any further conversation impossible until the noise died down. After everyone returned to their seats, she drew a slow breath and braced herself for Carli's reaction to what she had to say next. "I already invited Titus and Max to Barnaby's for a drink after the game."

"And did they say yes? Because I'd be surprised if Max would go unless Rikki could get a babysitter at the last minute."

"He took a rain check, so it would be you, me and Titus."

Carli looked horrified by that prospect. "Oh, no. You're not roping me into chaperoning the two of you."

"It's just a drink, Carli. My way of thanking him for stepping up to help out. It's not like it's a date."

"But it could be if you'd just admit you're interested in the man." Carli kept her eyes trained on the game. When she finally spoke again, there was a heavy dose of sympathy in her voice. "Believe me, I get it, Moira. We both know it's hard to put yourself out there again, but not every guy is like Ryan or my ex."

Carli finally turned to face Moira. "I have to believe that if I ever want to be happy again. It's not that I want to dive right into something serious. It would be safer to dip my toes in the dating pool a few times to test the waters. But eventually I want someone to call my own. Someone I can trust to build a future with me, maybe even start a family."

Moira not only heard the longing in Carli's voice, but she also understood it. She told her the same thing she'd told her before. Maybe eventually Carli would believe her. "You deserve a nice guy who is smart enough to recognize how special you are."

"Ditto to you, too."

Crossing her fingers, Moira asked, "So will you come to Barnaby's with me?"

"I've never been there, but I'm pretty sure it's not my kind of place. Have you ever been there?"

Moira was fairly certain her answer wouldn't reassure her friend at all. She leaned in closer to keep this part of their conversation private. "Only professionally, and then only outside in the parking lot."

Obviously, that possibility hadn't occurred to Carli. Wide-eyed, she whispered back, "So if you've raided the place, how will the owner feel about you showing up? Won't he be unhappy about having a member of the local police hanging out there?"

"I'll be there as a private citizen. Besides, the owner

has been known to call us himself when he has problems with a customer. From what Cade has said, Shay Barnaby wants his customers to enjoy themselves, but he doesn't put up with bad behavior. We usually get called to deal with the ones he's already tossed out."

"I wonder what constitutes bad behavior in a tavern that caters to a pretty rough crowd."

"Actually, I'm not sure, but I guess we'll find out. So you'll come, right?"

Carli sighed dramatically. "Fine, I'll come."

The bleachers began emptying out, signaling the second game had ended. Moira stood and stretched a few stiff muscles. She'd forgotten how uncomfortable it was to sit on wooden bleacher seats for so long. Once the exodus slowed down, she and Carli made their way to the field, where Titus and Max were stripping off their gear and stuffing it back into the duffels Mr. Kline had provided. Rikki and her son stood nearby, the little boy talking a mile a minute to Titus. From the sound of it, this had been the first real ball game he'd ever seen.

"And I had two hot dogs and popcorn and a purple snow cone!"

Titus took suitably impressed as he kneeled down to better hear Carter in the midst of the crowd. "Sounds like you liked the food even more than the game."

The little guy frowned as he gave the matter some thought. "I liked watching Dad a lot. You, too, Mr. Titus. Mom and me think you both did a good job."

Titus ruffled Carter's hair. "I'm glad you think so. It was our first time umpiring, so it was a bit scary."

For some reason, the little boy thought that was hilarious. "You shouldn't have been scared of a bunch of kids."

Titus's gravelly voice was laced with amusement. "It wasn't the kids I was scared of. It was the parents. Sometimes they don't think the umpires are being fair to their kids and yell at them."

"Then they're being mean. You'd never be unfair."

Then the little guy held out his arms to offer Titus a hug. She wasn't sure how he would respond, but he swept Carter up and hugged him back. Whatever he whispered to him restored the boy's happy smile. When he set him back down on the ground, Max and Rikki each took one of Carter's hands. Rikki smiled at Titus. "You'll have to come for dinner soon, Titus. Carter and Max built another model together. This one is a wooden clipper ship."

"Let me know when."

"We will." Max looked down at Carter. "Come on, kiddo. It's almost story time, and I've been waiting all day to find out what happens in the next chapter."

After the trio headed off for the parking lot, Moira waited until Titus picked up the two duffels and slung the straps over his shoulder before speaking. "Are you still up for having a drink with the two of us?"

He nodded. "Sounds good to me. Can I hitch a ride with you? I walked over from the café."

"Sure thing." She turned to Carli. "Do you want to ride with us or would you prefer to drive yourself?"

"I'd better take my car. I don't want to leave it here in the parking lot after the park closes."

"Good thinking."

Even if that meant Moira would have to be alone with Titus for the time it took to get to Barnaby's. "If we get there first, we'll wait for you outside."

"Okay. Also, I have church in the morning, so I won't be able to stay long."

"You're not the only one. I'm back on the day shift."

Titus entered the conversation. "Look, I know you think you owe me for helping out with the game. If you'd rather not do this, just say so. I know all about how hard it is to work all day after a late night."

Gosh, how could she have forgotten that he'd been up late helping her out last night and still had to be ready bright and early to open the café on time? "I'm sorry, Titus. I forgot that you've got to be running on fumes by now. We can reschedule. Your choice."

He stared at her for what felt like a long time before he finally answered, "Actually, I could use a cold one. And what do you say we add in some of Shay's hot wings? I've been trying to get him to share his recipe, but the selfish jerk won't even give me a hint."

Feeling like she was about to do a high dive without knowing how deep the water was, Moira found herself grinning. "I say yes."

## CHAPTER SIXTEEN

TITUS SETTLED INTO the front seat of the car and tried to get comfortable. There wasn't quite enough legroom for a man of his height, but they didn't have all that far to go. A few minutes into the ride, he noticed Moira's white-knuckled grip on the steering wheel. He had no doubt she likely had second thoughts about this outing. She also kept checking the rearview mirror to make sure her friend hadn't changed her mind about joining them. If that happened, he figured there was better than a fifty-fifty chance that Moira would suddenly think of something at work that required her immediate attention.

That would be disappointing but not surprising. He'd known he was playing with fire by accepting Moira's impulsive invitation to join her and Carli for a drink and some hot wings at Barnaby's. Considering how antsy both of the ladies were acting, he had to wonder if either of them had ever been in Barnaby's before tonight. That would certainly explain Carli's nervousness about the situation. Maybe Moira's, too, but he suspected that had more to do with the push-pull nature of her relationship with him.

Moira could handle anything that happened at the bar, but he had concerns about Carli. Still, Shay never let things get too far out of hand. Early on, he'd posted a short list of rules that he expected to be followed or else. It hadn't taken long for Shay's customers to learn that the former Recon Marine was a man of his word.

"We're here."

Titus sat up taller and looked around. He'd been so lost in his thoughts that he hadn't realized they'd arrived. "Is Carli still with us?"

"Yeah, she parked two spots down from where we are." Moira looked a little uneasy. "I'm guessing she won't stay long, but don't take it personally. She went through an ugly divorce a while back. Her ex already had his next wife waiting in the wings before he even told Carli he wanted out of their marriage. From what I heard, he married the woman the day after the divorce was finalized, and his new wife gave birth to their first child three weeks later. All of that has left Carli a bit skittish when it comes to dating or meeting new men."

That explained a few things. "I kind of got that impression. It's taken some time, but she's finally quit jumping whenever I approach her in the café. I was hoping I wasn't actually that scary. That would be bad for business."

Moira smiled at that last part as he hoped she would. He barely knew Carli, but even the brief description of what she'd gone through had him wanting to punch something. He flexed his hands several times to work off some of the tension. "She has to know she's so much better off without that guy. That doesn't mean I wouldn't like to give him a hands-on lecture on how a man should treat his woman."

Not that he had much room to talk considering how he deceived Moira ten years ago.

She started to open her door but stopped to look back at him. "I'm sworn to uphold the law, so I probably shouldn't admit to what I'm about to say. When I found out what happened, I asked friends of mine to keep an eye on Carli's ex. You'd be surprised by how many times he got nailed for speeding the first couple of months after he left her."

When they both got out of the car, he stopped to grin at her over the roof of the car. "Good for you. Does she know?"

"Nope. I'm not even sure she would have approved. She's not normally a vindictive person."

He snorted at her assessment of her friend. "Sorry, but isn't she the one who offered to borrow a bat in case I needed a reminder to treat you right?"

She offered him a wide-eyed, innocent look. "Yep, come to think of it, she did. Well, what can I say? Women are complicated."

At that point, Carli joined them. She looked at Moira and then at Titus. "What's so funny?"

Titus immediately clamped his mouth shut and left it up to Moira to explain. "Um, we were just laughing about something someone said at the ball game."

Moira was complicated all right; she was also sneaky. Technically, she wasn't even lying to her friend since Carli had made the comment about borrowing the bat at the park. Meanwhile, Moira looped her arm through Carli's. "Come on, let's head inside. I've been craving those hot wings ever since Titus mentioned them."

Carli glanced at Titus, looking a bit concerned. "Are they really that hot? I don't like things that are too spicy."

Titus hastened to reassure her. "That's not a problem. Shay offers them with different levels of heat, which are rated from one through five. We can order the mildest version."

Moira wasn't having it. "Nope, not for me. I like them hot."

They'd reached the door. As he hustled ahead to open it for them, Titus tried one more time to warn Moira that she might be biting off more than she could chew…literally. "You probably won't believe me, but I've seen grown men cry after biting into the hottest ones. You might want to start with the threes and work your way up from there."

The stubborn woman scoffed as she headed inside. "You two can play it safe if you want to, but I'm more of a go-big-or-go-home kind of girl."

"Don't say I didn't warn you."

He followed her toward an empty table near the front of the bar. The music was blasting loud enough to make conversation difficult while they were on the move. When they were seated, he studied the list of all of the available microbrews. Good, it looked like Shay had added a couple of new ones to the menu since the last time Titus had stopped in.

Moira plucked the list from his hand and studied it before passing it over to her friend. He wasn't surprised when Carli checked out the pitifully short list of wines that Shay bothered to keep on hand. The bar's usual clientele tended to go for beer or the hard stuff. People who preferred wine normally headed to somewhere fancier in one of the bigger towns in the area. After a bit, Carli wrinkled her nose and set the list back down on the table.

It was a bit of a surprise when Shay himself appeared to take their order. "It's been a while, Titus."

"I've been busy."

The truth was the bar was often too loud and too crowded for his personal tastes. Meanwhile, he performed the necessary introductions. Shay smiled at Carli first. "Welcome to Barnaby's, Ms. Walsh."

When she nodded, he turned his attention to Moira. "And, Officer Fraser, it's nice to finally meet you in person."

She smiled at him. "Please call me Moira."

Since Titus usually came in alone, he was surprised when Shay didn't ask how he'd been lucky enough to show up with two attractive women this time. It would've been funny to see his reaction to finding out that Moira wanted to buy Titus a drink for umpiring a kids' ball game. Instead, Shay was still playing the role of good host to new guests to his establishment. "So what can I get y'all?"

Titus didn't know where Shay was from originally, but he suspected it was someplace well south of the Mason-Dixon Line. He'd heard more than one woman exclaim over his soft drawl and good manners. It hadn't even occurred to Titus that he would be introducing Moira to one of the few eligible men in Dunbar. It might not be the smartest thing he'd ever done considering the unpredictable nature of his relationship with her. It was definitely time to place their order, so Shay could move on to his other customers. "I'll have that new pale ale on the menu. Moira, what would you like?"

"I'll have the same."

Shay jumped in to ask Carli himself, no doubt noting she was back to studying his limited wine list. "And what can I get for you, Ms. Walsh? I stock a decent red, but I also have a new Riesling I'm trying out that's not on the list yet. It's not too dry, but not too sweet, either."

Carli set aside the menu and offered Shay a shy smile. "I'll have a glass of that. Thank you."

He smiled back. "Let me know what you think."

"I will."

Titus noticed one of the bartenders was desperately trying to get Shay's attention and pointed back toward the bar. "Looks like you're being paged, Shay."

He shot his employee an exasperated look and bellowed, "Hold your horses, Jody! I'll be there in a minute." Then, bringing his attention back to Moira and Carli, he turned down the volume on his voice. "Sorry about that. Can I get anything else for you folks?"

Titus figured he'd give Moira one last chance to show some common sense. "Carli and I will split an order of the mildest hot wings."

Then he pointed toward Moira. "This one insists she wants the hottest ones."

Shay blinked in surprise. "Are you sure? Usually the only people who order those are the ones who've lost a bet of some kind."

At least his explanation gave her pause for thought. "They're that hot?"

"Yes, ma'am, they are." Shay grinned at her. "I'll tell you what—if you'll go with an order of the threes, I'll throw in one of the fives for comparison."

This time Moira didn't hesitate. "It's a deal."

Titus waited until Shay walked away, then muttered, "Smart move, but how come you believed him and not me?"

He'd love to know the answer to that question, but Carli derailed that conversation by pointing to a neon sign on the wall. "I've never heard of a bar that has a written standard of conduct."

Then she glanced around as if checking to make sure that Shay wasn't close by. "I assume Mr. Barnaby is the one who posted it, but was he serious?"

Moira answered before Titus could. "Yeah, Cade said the number of times that we have to deal with problems here has gone way down since people realized what happens when someone doesn't follow Shay's rules."

Carli looked around the bar with great interest. "Remember back on my twenty-first birthday when you, me and some other friends were going to go out for drinks to celebrate? My folks made me promise that we'd go anywhere other than this place."

Moira grinned at her. "Growing up here, we all heard

tales about the shenanigans that happened here." Then she gave Titus a considering look. "I think an argument could be made that it hasn't changed all that much."

Feeling obligated to defend himself, Titus leaned back in his chair and crossed his arms over his chest. "Shay has never had cause to toss me out of this place. Isn't that right?"

He directed that question to the man himself, who had just walked up to the table. "That's true. Titus is always on his best behavior whenever he comes in. A model citizen and inspiration to us all. In fact, if I ever get around to posting a customer honor roll, he'll be right up there near the top."

Even Titus had to laugh at that, although he was pretty sure Shay hadn't necessarily meant it as a compliment. Meanwhile, Shay unloaded the tray one of his servers was holding. "Here are your drinks, your wings and my dinner."

He carefully handed Carli her wine and then set beers in front of Titus, Moira and himself. What the heck was Shay doing? No one had issued him an invitation to join them. Moira looked a little surprised, but she didn't say anything. Neither did Carli, but then maybe they thought this was normal behavior for Shay.

Once he was settled in, Shay met Titus's gaze, a glint of amusement in his expression. "Sorry if I'm intruding, but I decided it was unfair for Titus to keep the two prettiest ladies in here all to himself."

Carli immediately blushed while Moira rolled her eyes, which made Shay laugh. "I also wanted to be close at hand if you ran into problems with that hot wing I promised you. It's not too late to change your mind."

MOIRA LOOKED FIRST at Shay and then at Titus. The bar owner looked amused, but Titus not so much. Meanwhile, the server was back, this time with a tall glass of milk. Shay took it and leaned across the table to set it next to Moira's personal basket of wings. "The one in the separate wrapper is the hot one. Normally we ring the bell to announce someone is about to do something entertaining. However, I'll save you that particular embarrassment, Moira."

"Thanks a lot, Shay."

He laughed at the distinct lack of sincerity in her words. "You're welcome. I will, however, wish you good luck."

There was no dignified way to get out of the corner she'd backed herself into. Bracing herself as she prepared to release an inferno in her mouth, she picked up the wing and took a respectable bite out of it. Then she waited for the burn to begin. Seconds passed with only a mild tingle teasing her tongue and lips.

It wasn't until she finally looked up at Shay that she knew she'd been had. "Cute, Mr. Barnaby. How many people fall for that trick on any given night?"

He cracked up, his deep laughter ringing out across the room, drawing far more attention to their table than she was comfortable with. "Actually, none. Normally, I give people what they ask for. But you looked like you might be having second thoughts and I opted to let you rethink your decision. That one was a two, but the rest are level threes. If those aren't hot enough, next time we'll know to serve you the fours."

Then he jerked his head in Titus's direction. "Besides, your guy was looking a little bit worried."

She started to protest that Titus wasn't her anything, but she doubted it would convince Shay that his assessment of the situation was wrong. Heck, she couldn't even convince herself of that. At least he'd turned his attention to the man in question.

Shay flexed his shoulders, giving his already impressive muscles a little more definition. "While I don't mind a good dustup now and then, even I would have second thoughts about taking Titus on."

He was joking. She hoped so, anyway. While Moira was used to dealing with some pretty tough characters, it dawned on her to wonder how this particular exchange was affecting the fourth member of their party. She got her answer when Carli abruptly stood. "Hey, are you okay?"

Her friend's smile looked a little brittle. "Yes, but it's time I headed home. Like I said before, I have to be up early in the morning."

Carli turned her attention to Shay. "You were right about the wine. I liked it quite a lot. It was nice meeting you."

Wow, her friend sounded as if she meant that. Moira wanted to ask if that was true, but now wasn't the time or place. "I'll walk you out to your car."

Her friend waved her off. "No, you don't have to do that. Stay and enjoy yourself. I'll be fine."

Before she'd gone two steps, Shay was up and moving. "I'll see you out. I prefer that our lady customers never have to walk out by themselves."

Carli pointed toward the list of Shay's rules. "I don't see that rule listed on the board."

He gave her a flirtatious grin. "It will be when I eventually get version two-point-oh posted."

The couple continued toward the door still bickering about the subject until they disappeared from sight. Moira didn't know what to make of the interaction. "What just happened?"

Titus shrugged. "I'm not sure, but you can trust Shay. He'll see that she reaches her car safely."

Moira was inclined to believe that. She suspected Shay had a big dose of the same protective nature as Titus did. It was one of the many reasons she was finding it nearly impossible to maintain a friends-only relationship with him. She gave in to the temptation to scoot her chair closer to his and play with fire by giving his bicep a quick squeeze. He looked a little surprised by her bold move, but then he grinned and flexed the muscles in his arm.

She let her hand slide down to his forearm and asked him one more question. "So was Shay right? Should he be worried if the two of you ever came to blows?"

Titus stared at her hand as she slowly traced one of his tattoos with a fingertip. "It's best we never find out."

She withdrew her hand and feigned a stern look. "Speaking as a member of local law enforcement, I heartily agree. Now, let's finish our wings. Tomorrow is a workday for both of us."

# CHAPTER SEVENTEEN

Titus opened one of the packets that came with the hot wings and used the wipe to clean the sticky sauce off his fingers. Moira finished the last of her wings and did the same. "I can see why you'd like to steal Shay's recipe. Those are some of the best wings I've ever had."

She pushed the basket toward the center of the table and looked past him at the door. "Shay's back already, so it must have been quiet out in the parking lot tonight."

Titus shrugged. "No one would dare mess with Carli with Shay offering her his personal protection."

Once again, Shay didn't wait for an invitation and parked himself across from Moira. "I watched until your friend drove out of sight to make sure she got away safely."

Moira offered him a bright smile. "Thanks for doing that. I'm sure she appreciated it."

That actually had Shay laughing. "You would've thought so. Instead, she spent most of the time telling me she was a grown woman and perfectly capable of finding her car in a parking lot all on her own. When I tried to open her car door for her, she actually told me to back off."

Titus couldn't help but smirk a little. "She must be immune to all that Southern charm of yours I've heard so much about."

"At least some folks think I have some charm." Shay gave him a superior look. "That's more than I can say about you. Frankly, I'm amazed your café does as well as it does considering your reputation for growling at people."

Sadly, that was a fairly accurate assessment of Titus's personality, but as far as he could tell, Moira didn't mind his less-than-sunny disposition. Meanwhile, Shay caught the attention of one of the servers and then stacked up the basket that held his half-eaten dinner and the two that had held the hot wings. When she reached the table, he handed them to her and then pointed at the empty bottles. "The next round is on me."

Moira shook her head. "Sorry, but I probably shouldn't have another drink since I'm driving."

Shay didn't argue and instead switched gears. "Bring coffee instead along with a fresh burger and fries for me. Get them another basket of mild wings, too."

Titus was never good at small talk, but Shay seemed all too willing to take on that role. "So, Moira, how do you like policing a small town after working in the big city? I bet things seem a bit dull after everything you must have dealt with in Seattle."

She scrunched her nose a little. "I wouldn't call it dull, just different. I also like being close to my family. They're a big part of the reason I moved back to Dunbar."

"I get that. When I decided to leave the military behind, I wasn't sure what I wanted to do next. Inheriting this place made the decision for me. That I have an aunt and a few other relatives scattered around the area was a bonus."

Shay turned his attention to Titus. "I don't think I've ever heard how you ended up in Dunbar."

Moira bit her lower lip, maybe trying to hold back a laugh. She knew full well why he had moved to Dunbar, but also that story wasn't something Titus was in the habit of sharing with just anyone. He settled for a partial version of the truth. "I wasn't happy working in fancy restaurants and wanted to find a small café where I could get to know my customers. I also liked the Pacific Northwest and living near the mountains, so Dunbar fit the bill. I guess I'm a small-town guy at heart."

Shay looked a bit doubtful, but he didn't say anything. Luckily, their food arrived, putting a hold on the need for any further conversation. Titus wasn't hungry for more wings, so he concentrated on drinking his coffee. Moira made more of an effort to enjoy the wings while Shay devoured his dinner. No doubt he was used to having to make quick work of a meal while he had the chance.

When he finished off the last of his fries, he studied the small dance floor, where several couples were giving it their all to some fast-paced country song. Then he gave Moira a considering look. "Any chance you'd like to dance?"

Titus wished he'd thought of asking her first, but he didn't say anything. He didn't own Moira and knew she wouldn't take it well if he let his inner caveman loose in the bar. He sipped his coffee as Moira glanced toward the other couples and then back to their host. "Why not?"

Shay escorted her to the dance floor just as another song started. Titus's fingers ached from the tight grip he had on his cup. At least it wasn't a slow dance. He watched Moira and Shay as they quickly found their rhythm together. A smile lit up her face, making her even more beautiful, even if it wasn't directed at him. That thought had him up and moving toward the jukebox. After scanning the choices, he stuffed several quarters in the slot and impatiently waited for the current song to end.

Before the last note died away, he was across the dance floor holding his hand out to Moira. He let out a slow breath when she didn't hesitate to take it. When Shay didn't immediately retreat, Titus tugged Moira in close to his side, but didn't say a single word. Instead of taking offense, Shay laughed. "I'm surprised you waited this long."

"Don't be a jerk."

"Sorry, but I have to go with my strengths."

Then Shay aimed a large dose of his Southern charm in Moira's direction. "Thank you for the dance and the info. Enjoy your dance with this guy."

As Titus swung her into his arms, she gave him a puzzled look. "Do you two not get along?"

"We do most of the time." He stared past her to where Shay was leaning against the bar and watching their every move. When he realized Titus had noticed, he laughed and turned his back to focus his attention on whatever the bartender was telling him. "Tonight he's just having fun poking the bear. I think he's jealous that I'm here with the prettiest woman in the place."

He twirled her out and back in again. "So what info was he talking about?"

Moira looked around, probably wanting to make sure Shay wasn't close enough to hear their discussion. "He asked a few questions about Carli."

So Shay was interested Carli. That was a relief, even if Moira didn't seem all that happy about it. "What did you tell him?"

"The truth about her situation."

"Which is?"

"That Carli is still getting over a bad breakup and taking things slow. You know, basically being pretty selective about the kinds of guys she wants to date."

He bet that went over well with Shay. The man also wasn't the kind to give up easily if he was interested in Carli. For some odd reason, Titus felt obligated to defend him. "You know Shay's not a bad guy, and he's very protective of the women who work here."

"I told him that I'd heard that about him. I just didn't want him to take it personally if she's not interested in going out with him."

Of course, Shay would take it personally. Who wouldn't? Not that Titus was going to argue with her. For the moment, he didn't care about Shay or even Carli. He wanted to enjoy this dance with this woman. His woman, whether she knew it or not.

Apparently, Moira wasn't done with the discussion. "Carli is an adult and can make her own choices, but I still worry about her. Her ex did a real number on her self-esteem, and I think she needs someone who will take things slow and treat her well. The proverbial nice guy next door."

Considering how Carli had argued with Shay all the way out to her car, Titus had to wonder if Moira's assessment was on target, but it wasn't like he claimed to be an expert when it came to women. The one thing he knew for a fact, though, was that having Moira back in his arms felt perfect.

The song finally came to an end. When Moira started to step back, he held on to her hand. "One more dance, and then we should probably head out."

When the music started up again, a slow ballad this time, she studied him for a few seconds before closing the distance between them to rest her head against his shoulder. They fell into an easy rhythm as if they'd danced together forever. It had been the same way the night they first met, and he'd missed it every day since. Her soft sigh made him hope that she had, too.

They swayed slowly as the singer told a story of heartbreak and dreaming of second chances. Maybe it had been a bit heavy-handed on his part to pick that song, but he hadn't been able to resist. "This is nice."

She didn't say anything for the longest time, but neither did she try to put any distance between them. Finally, as the last notes of the song faded away, she murmured, "Yeah, it is."

Maybe it was time to push for something more. "We should do this again sometime soon. Maybe head into Seattle and make an evening of it."

Before she could respond, Shay was back and holding out her phone. "You left this on the table. Someone is trying to reach you."

She checked the call log. "It's Oscar. I've got to call him back."

Shay pointed toward the hallway that led toward the restrooms. "If you need someplace more private, you can use my office. It's across from the ladies room."

"Thanks, Shay."

Moira was off and running. So much for spending any more time together. He and Shay wandered back to the table to wait for Moira to return. There was always a chance that Oscar only needed to ask her a question or something.

"So you and her…"

Shay didn't finish the sentence, but he didn't have to. Titus kept his answer simple. "Working on it."

"I can see why. I like her."

"So do I."

Shay leaned back in his seat, arms crossed over his chest. "A cop seems like an odd choice for you, what with your reputation and all."

"You mean the one where people think I got my ink in prison and also learned how to cook there?"

The other man laughed. "Yeah, that one."

"Next time you stop in the café, remind me to show you my diploma from the culinary school where I got my degree."

"I might just do that. But for the record, I never believed the prison theory. It never rang true to me."

Interesting. Most people bought in to the rumors without hesitation. "Why not?"

"I haven't known Cade Peters for long, but the man is definitely a straight arrow. I can't see him being best buddies with an ex-con."

Titus huffed a small laugh. "It could just be that he loves my chicken and dumplings too much to risk offending me."

"Couldn't blame him for that. I also don't think Moira would've enjoyed a slow dance with a man who has a shady character." Shay focused on something back over Titus's shoulder and then met his gaze head-on again. "I'm not asking for details about your past. We all have secrets. I'm just saying that of all the people in Dunbar, you've ended up with two cops as friends. Makes me wonder what you might have in common with them."

Then he stood up. "But that's a conversation for another day. Your lady is headed back this way."

When Titus reached for his wallet, Shay waved him off. "Forget it. You can treat me to some of those chicken and dumplings I've heard so much about."

Titus tossed some cash on the table to tip their server. "That's the Thursday special, so make sure you come in early enough to get some or call and let me know to put some back for you."

"Will do. Thanks for coming in tonight. Bring the ladies back anytime."

He walked away before Moira reached the table. "We should go. Oscar is tied up on a call that will take another hour or so to handle. I need to cover until the next shift starts. I'll drop you off at home."

"No need. I can walk if you can drop the duffels off at the café in the morning for Mr. Kline to pick up."

Still, she hesitated. "If you're sure. It's pretty late to be out and about."

"My house is only a fifteen-minute walk from here. I'll be fine."

Outside, he followed Moira over to where she'd left her car. "Are you going to snap at me like Carli did at Shay when he wanted to open her door for her?"

"I guess we'll have to see."

She pushed the button on her key to unlock the car. But instead of leaving immediately, she leaned back against the car and stared up at the sky. After a few seconds, she let out a slow breath. "Tonight was fun."

He inched closer to her. "It was. Well, except for watching you dancing with Shay. I could have done without that."

She gave him a curious look. "Would you have asked me to dance if he hadn't?"

Feeling he was about to step on a land mine, he gave her the honest answer. "I would have if I'd known you would actually say yes."

He expected her to laugh or maybe roll her eyes, but her expression turned serious. "I'm pretty sure I wouldn't have been able to resist."

Well, that was encouraging. He traced the line of her cheek with a fingertip. "And if I asked you to kiss me now, would you?"

Her mouth quirked up in a small smile. "Oh, I don't know. I should get back out on patrol."

That wasn't a definite no, but he couldn't delay her much longer. "Then we better get down to business."

He kept the kiss gentle and on the innocent end of the scale. Now wasn't the time to push for more. She tasted so sweet, and it felt so right when she wrapped her arms around his neck. Like coming home. Like there might be a future for them. Like maybe she was starting to forgive him for all of the mistakes he'd made in the past.

He savored the moment for a little longer before stepping back. "I haven't forgotten that you never answered me when I mentioned the two of us going out on a real date."

She pretended to think about it as she opened her car door. "No, I guess I didn't."

"Well?"

Her answering smile was all tease. "I'll think about it. I'll see you in the morning."

Just knowing that was true made him surprisingly happy. "Stay safe out there, Officer Fraser."

"I'll do my best."

He closed her door for her and watched as she drove off into the night. When her car disappeared from sight, he started for home. Ned wasn't going to be happy with him for staying gone so long, but Titus could buy his forgiveness with a couple of treats. As he walked, he couldn't help but wonder if he could sway Moira's decision about the whole date thing with another chocolate pie.

It was worth a shot.

## CHAPTER EIGHTEEN

MOIRA WAS DEAD tired and ready for the night to be over. Oscar had finally finished the call that had kept him tied up for several hours, but then he got an emergency call on the other side of town. At this point, there wasn't much use in her going home, considering she was due back at the office in just a couple of hours.

She turned at the next corner, planning on doing another circle through town before returning to the station. But when she spotted a familiar figure walking down the sidewalk, she sped up until she drew even with him. Rolling down the passenger window, she called out, "Titus, why are you still out walking? Is everything okay?"

He walked another couple of steps before finally stopping. "I can't find Ned. He wasn't at home when I got back. He was in the house when I left for the park, but he has a doggy door so he can hang out in the backyard. Maybe he jumped the fence again. But even if he did, he never stays gone this long."

Titus ran his hands through his hair in frustration. "I thought I'd better go looking for him."

"Get in. We can cover more territory driving than you can walking."

She wasn't sure he would do as she suggested, but he finally opened the passenger door and climbed in. "I'm worried something might have happened to him."

There was no mistaking the fear in his voice. "We'll find him."

She probably shouldn't make that promise, but right now she'd do anything to ease Titus's pain. "Let me know if you see anything you want to check out. We can also use the spotlight if that will help."

"I'm probably overreacting, but he's never stayed gone this long." He pounded his fist on his thigh in frustration. "I should've gone straight home from work. If I'd done that instead of umpiring the games, he'd be home safe and sound."

Moira winced. Was she supposed to apologize or something? It wasn't as if she twisted his arm into helping out. He was the one who volunteered. Besides, he'd had a good time cheering on the kids. If he'd been that concerned about leaving Ned alone, he could have also gone straight home after the games ended. Rather than point any or all of that out, she kept her mouth shut and kept driving. It was better to cut the man some slack, especially considering both of them were operating on minimal sleep.

Right now, finding Ned was all that mattered.

They rode in silence, going slowly so she could safely check out her side of the road as he scanned the right side. As they approached the intersection ahead, she asked, "Which way now?"

He closed his eyes and drew a slow breath. "I have no idea. I've been up and down this whole area multiple times already."

The ambient light in the car cast his face in harsh shadows. Hating how worried he looked, she considered their options. "Let's drive by the café in case he's waiting for you there. He's done that before, hasn't he?"

"Yeah, he has, although most of the time he either rides to work with me or we walk together."

"It's worth checking. After that, I'll drive you home to see if he's already found his way back. No matter what, you should try to catch some sleep."

"I'll probably shower and change clothes. I have to be back at work in a couple of hours. Once things are up and running, I'll go back out looking again."

"I'll let the officers on duty know to keep an eye out for Ned. You've probably already thought of this, but don't forget to call the shelters, too. Someone may have picked him up."

"I'll put up some notices in town if he doesn't show up soon."

A few minutes later, they circled the block around the café, but there was no sign of Ned anywhere. She had an awful feeling that their luck wouldn't be any better at Titus's house, but she kept her fingers crossed that she was wrong about that.

Titus was out of her car and charging toward his front porch before they even came to a complete stop. She turned off the engine and followed after him. He cupped his mouth and yelled, "Ned, you get yourself home right now!"

When there was no response, he tried one more time. "No treats for a week for worrying Moira like this, you worthless dog!"

They both stood in silence, hoping for some sign that the dog would respond. After a few seconds, Titus's shoulders slumped in defeat. "Like I said, thanks for trying to help, but you'd better go. You have better things to do than haul me around."

"I'll be back on duty soon. Let me know if Ned shows up."

"I will."

She started to walk away. She'd gone a few steps when Titus caught up with her. "Look, what I said earlier in the car was just me blowing off steam. I don't regret helping out at the games, and I enjoyed hanging out with you and Carli at Shay's place."

"Call if you need me."

"I will."

He started back toward the house but stopped again. "I'm not used to having anyone to care about, and I'm obviously not very good at it. I screwed up big-time ten years ago, and I'm doing it again with Ned. It might not have seemed like it at the time, but you got off lucky when things didn't work out for us."

His words hit her hard. "That's not true, Titus."

She stepped close enough to place her hand on his back. She hoped her touch would offer some comfort, but he shrugged it off. "You'd better get going. You've wasted enough time on me for one night. Maybe even for a life-time."

His words sent a shaft of pain right through the heart of her. "Don't talk like that, Titus."

"Why not? It's the truth."

When he walked away again, she had no choice but to let him go.

TITUS MADE QUICK work of his shower and changing clothes. After that, he settled on the couch and tried to come up with a plan of action, to do something—anything—to help bring Ned home. With his nerves stretched to the breaking point, he did his best to relax in the hope that even a short nap would get his brain back to firing on all cylinders, which didn't work at all. He'd been right when he'd told Moira that he wouldn't be able to sleep. Not when every sound, every creak of the house, had him up checking the front porch to see if it was Ned out there wanting in.

Finally, he gave up and did the only productive thing he could think of. After uploading a recent picture of Ned, he designed one of those depressing lost-pet notices to post around town. He offered a reward for any information at all. Good news would be preferable, but even the alternative would be better than not knowing. After printing off a few copies, he headed out the door to post a few on his way to the café. If Max stopped by for his usual coffee and breakfast sandwich, he'd ask him to post a few as well.

It wasn't much of a plan, but it was all he had. Darn that dog, anyway. How dare he worm his way into Titus's life only to disappear again? He couldn't wait to give the fur ball a piece of his mind as soon as he came strolling back home.

If he came home at all.

Outside, the sun was just starting to crest the horizon, but the darkness suited Titus's mood better. He'd have to warn Gunner and the rest of the staff that it would be better if he didn't have to deal with the public any more than absolutely necessary today. That would make more work for the others, but it would be easier for them in the long run.

He managed to hang about ten of his notices before he gave up and hustled the rest of the way to the café, arriving about fifteen minutes later than normal. Gunner was already hard at work in the kitchen. Keeping his back toward Titus, he grumbled, "Must be nice to sleep in on a workday. I guess that's one of the privileges of being the boss man."

When Titus didn't respond, Gunner finally turned around. He immediately wiped his hands on a towel and started toward him. "What's happened?"

"Ned is gone. I spent most of the night looking for him. There's no sign of him anywhere."

Gunner pulled out one of the chairs at the small table in the corner and all but shoved Titus down on it. "Stay put while I fix you something to eat."

"I'm not hungry."

"Tough. You haven't slept, you've got a full day of work ahead of you and then you'll be back out on the street hunting for Ned."

Instead of walking away, Gunner fidgeted in place for a few seconds. "I might complain about Ned being underfoot all the time, but I don't mean it. He's a good dog, and when I finish my shift I'll hit the street and do some looking myself. Between all of us, we'll find him."

Before Titus could manage to string together any kind of rational reply, Gunner stalked off and started slamming pans around. In a matter of few minutes, he was back with a plate full of scrambled eggs, fresh fruit and buttered toast. On his second trip, he brought a large cup of black coffee and a glass of orange juice.

"That should hold you for a while. Let me know if you need anything else."

Titus stared at the plate for a few seconds before he finally picked up his fork and dug in. Gunner wouldn't expect him to gush over his meal, but the least he could do was make a serious effort to clean his plate.

As it turned out, Gunner was right. The food replenished Titus's energy, at least enough so that he could get started on his usual routine at the café. He started by brewing fresh coffee and making sure they had enough sets of silverware rolled up in napkins to get them through the early morning rush. As he made a few more, he heard Gunner talking to Rita and Beth. The resulting cries of dismay made it clear what he'd told the two sisters. Two seconds later, they were headed his way.

He didn't know what he expected them to say or do, but having both of them hug him at the same time was definitely a big surprise. While he got along with all of his employees, he wasn't much of a touchy-feely kind of guy. Still, it felt good to hang on to them for a few seconds. Finally, he released them and stepped back.

Rita's eyes were suspiciously shiny. "I'm so sorry, Titus. You must be worried sick about Ned. This isn't like him."

"He was a stray when he moved in with me. Maybe he decided it was time for him to find a better gig somewhere else."

Rather than agree with him, Rita shook her finger at him. "I can't believe you said that, Titus Kondrat. Everybody knows that dog loves you. We'll organize a search and find him. Just you wait and see! Your friend Max will help. Moira, too. Make some posters, and we'll plaster the town with them."

It was hard to talk around the lump in his throat. "I already started on that this morning."

"Good. Now, go open up before those folks start pounding on the door to get in."

She gave him a gentle shove to get him moving. "I know it's easy to tell someone not to worry, but you'll get through the day with our help. If Ned shows up on his own, we'll all take turns yelling at him and then stuff him full of treats. If he still hasn't come back by the time we get off work, then we'll kick the search into high gear. You're not alone in this. We all love Ned."

He jerked his head in a small nod and headed toward the door as ordered. To his surprise, Rita called after him, "And in case you don't already know it, we love you, too."

That surprise announcement had him stumbling over his own two feet. At the last second, he caught his balance.

That saved him the indignity of falling flat on his face in front of not only his staff, but also the line of customers staring at him through the front windows. Maybe things were taking a turn for the better.

THANK GOODNESS THE morning all but flew by. He wasn't sure how many more words of sympathy or pats on the back he could handle without exploding. Yeah, everyone meant well, but he wasn't used to such an outpouring of support and didn't know how to deal with it. At some point, Rita had run off more copies of Ned's poster and handed them out to any customer who was willing to post a few in their neighborhood. Again, the number of people who stepped up to bat for Titus and his missing pet was a bit staggering.

He did his best to accept the sympathy in the spirit of how it was offered. That didn't mean he was comfortable with all the attention. It was a huge relief when his phone rang, and he saw it was Moira calling. He smiled—sort of, anyway—at the two elderly ladies who were fussing over him at that moment. "I'm sorry, ladies, but I have to take this call."

"We'll be praying for you and Ned, Mr. Kondrat."

"Thank you."

He held the door open for them as he answered the call. "Moira, what's up?"

"I know this probably isn't a good time, but I need you to come look at something. Can I pick you up in two minutes? It shouldn't take long."

His heart about stopped. There was only one reason he could think of that would have her asking him to leave the café just as the lunch rush was about to start.

"Yeah, I can. But why? What's happened? Have you found him?"

"No, I haven't. Cross your fingers, but there may have been a break in the case."

"What kind of break?"

"I'm not completely sure, but keep your hopes up. I'm on my way."

## CHAPTER NINETEEN

MOIRA COULD HAVE told Titus more on the phone, but she was less than two blocks away. By the time she turned down the alley behind the café, he was already outside pacing back and forth across the narrow expanse. He stopped as soon as he spotted her headed his way. Just as he had the night before, he yanked open the passenger door before she had even brought the big vehicle to a complete stop.

As she waited for him to get settled in and his seat belt fastened, someone rapped on her window, startling her. She breathed a sigh of relief when she recognized Gunner. He started talking as soon as she rolled down the window.

"We'd all appreciate it if you let us know when you have some news about Ned. Also, do what you can to make that guy get some rest. He's held up better than any of us expected, but he needs to shut it down soon before he collapses. We can handle the rest of the day, the prep for tomorrow and lock up afterward. No one wants to see him come back anytime soon."

Titus grumbled, "I'm sitting right here, Gunner."

The other man scoffed. "Heck, I'm not telling her anything I haven't already said to your face at least three times today, so don't bother snarling at me. I quit being scared of you ten minutes after I started working for you and don't see any reason to start up again."

Moira did her best not to laugh, but that was funny. She wasn't the only one who saw Titus for who he really was.

Even when he'd claimed she'd already wasted too much time on him, he was trying to protect her from what he saw as his own failures. They'd talk about that later. For now, they had more pressing matters. "If we get any news about Ned, we'll let you know. I'll also keep an eye on Titus for you. I'm not scared of him, either."

Gunner laughed and stepped away from the SUV. "Do that."

He did an about-face and headed back into the café, where Rita was waiting for him. As Moira eased the vehicle down the alley back toward the main road, she said, "It's nice of your staff to pick up the slack for you, but I can't say that I'm surprised. You've done the same for them."

"Yeah, yeah, I'm a real charmer." He crossed his arms over his chest and glared at her. "Now tell me what's going on. Where are you taking me?"

"We're heading for your house. TJ noticed something odd when he was out on patrol and asked me to come take a look. I did a drive-by and then called you. I want you to see it with fresh eyes, and then we'll talk."

Titus looked like he might explode at any second. The combination of no sleep and worry had taken its toll on him. She hadn't gotten much more sleep that he had, but at least her best friend hadn't gone missing. In short order, she turned into his driveway and parked. "Tell me if anything has changed since you left for work this morning."

Titus made no immediate effort to get out of the SUV. Instead, he leaned forward toward the windshield, as if those few inches made all the difference in how well he could see his house. After a second, Titus frowned. "What's that stuck on the front door? An ad of some kind?"

She had her suspicions as to what it was, but she wasn't

ready to jump to any conclusions. "So whatever it is wasn't there the last time you were here?"

"No, at least I'm pretty sure it wasn't." He leaned back in the seat again and frowned. "Although to be honest, I can't swear to that. I left in a hurry to start putting up notices about Ned."

No surprise there. "So here's the thing, Titus. I asked TJ to drive by a few times on his shift in case Ned came back and was sleeping on the front porch. TJ said he was pretty sure someone stuck that up there between the last two times he passed by your place. Our best guess is that it's been there no more than an hour and a half. Let's go check it out."

Moira half expected Titus to take off running, but he waited so they could approach the porch together. When they reached the steps, she stopped to snap a few pictures with her cell phone. After that, she pulled two pairs of gloves out of her pocket and offered a set to Titus. "It's not likely we'll get any forensic help from the county lab, but I'd still prefer to avoid contaminating any evidence."

She pointed toward the plastic bag taped to his front door. "You already know about the recent uptick in missing pets. A couple eventually came back of their own accord, but there have been several instances of a ransom demand for return of the animals. I probably should've thought about that being a possibility when you first said Ned had gone missing, but he doesn't exactly fit the profile of the other victims. They've all been cats or else small dogs. I couldn't imagine any stranger would try to dognap an animal the size of Ned. I'm sorry I didn't tell you sooner."

"No problem. I can see why you felt that way. Most people are a bit reluctant to approach Ned when they first meet him. There are a few adults he took to immediately, but he doesn't always go out of his way to make friends. Well, except when it comes to kids or people like your grandmother."

Those same things could be said of the dog's owner, too. The man and the dog were definitely kindred spirits. Meanwhile, Moira watched as Titus pulled on the gloves before reaching for the zip-top plastic bag. Using care, he peeled off the tape and then gently opened the bag, pausing several times to let her take more pictures. Finally, he removed the single sheet of paper from inside and set the plastic bag on the porch railing. Drawing a deep breath, he slowly unfolded the note and held the paper so they could both read it at the same time. The note was written in a shaky hand, but the message was clear. Titus needed to pony up some cash to get Ned back. Just like with the other incidents, he was supposed to stuff it in an unlabeled envelope and leave it in the phone booth next to the vacant gas station outside town.

He glared at the paper as if he couldn't believe his eyes. After folding it up again, he stuffed the note back in the plastic bag and handed it to her. "Seriously, whoever took him is asking for just sixty dollars to give him back? I'm insulted on Ned's behalf."

This wasn't a laughing matter, but Moira couldn't help herself. "Sorry, but you're not the first person to have that reaction. One of the earlier victims was a purebred champion with a ton of trophies and blue ribbons. His owner was furious that anyone would ask so little for the return of his pride and joy."

Titus looked incredulous, but Moira simply nodded. "It looks as if whoever is doing this operates on a sliding scale, maybe based on the size of the hostage. The demands I know about have been between twenty and thirty dollars, but Ned is two or three times bigger than any of the other animals, at least the ones that were brought to my attention."

His dark eyes looked haunted. "But they were returned unharmed?"

At least she could reassure him on that account. "Not only that, they appeared to have been well-fed. They'd also been bathed, and their coats brushed."

That information must have been the tipping point for Titus's ability to deal with the situation, because he grabbed for the porch rail and held on while he dropped down to sit on the porch steps. He braced his elbows on his knees and rested his face in his hands. "So you think I'll get Ned back."

Moira sat next to him and gently rested her arm across his back. "No guarantees, but based on the previous cases, I'd say it looks promising. After the first two people paid the ransoms, their pets reappeared early the next morning. No one saw anything. They just woke up to find their pets back home. They were even tethered to the front porch to make sure they didn't wander off."

Titus didn't say anything for the longest time. When he finally lifted his head to look around, his coloring had improved even if his hands were still shaky. "I've been scared sick that he'd either been hit by a car or else someone grabbed him to use in a dog-fighting ring."

He slowly rose to his feet, once again holding on to the porch rail for balance. "I'll get an envelope from inside and then hit the ATM for some cash. I could take it out of the till at the café, but I don't want anyone to know what's going on."

"Good thinking. Come on, I'll give you a ride."

He shook his head. "I appreciate the offer, but it's probably better that I'm not seen with you anywhere close to the drop-off location. If the kidnapper is watching, it could set off alarms if he or she thinks I've involved the police."

She rested her hand on his sleeve. "Are you sure you should be driving?"

He jerked his arm away from her. "I can handle it. Don't fuss over me."

Okay, that was enough. She growled right back at him. "Don't get all defensive, Titus. It's my job to worry about the safety of all of the citizens in Dunbar. It's my professional opinion that you should not be out driving right now. If something bad happened, you'd never forgive yourself."

To soften the moment, she added one more bit of truth. "And I can't stand the thought of you getting hurt. Let me call Max for you."

After a second, he sat back down. "Tell him to hurry."

"I will."

She stepped away to call both the office and then Max to explain the situation. It was a huge relief that he was home and available. "I'll tell him you're on the way. Thanks for doing this for him."

After hanging up, she returned to the porch and sat down again. It was time for her to head back to the station, but she didn't want to leave Titus alone. Max had promised to be on his way in matter of minutes. While they waited for him, she shared her own frustration. "I need to put an end to this situation before Cade gets back. He went to bat for me before he left, and I'd hate to disappoint him. He shouldn't have to come back to a bunch of angry citizens complaining because I couldn't figure out who was stealing their cats and dogs, especially for what's essentially chump change. Seriously, how weird is that?"

Titus shook his head. "It is a weird way to pick up some extra cash. In dribbles and drabs instead of one big money grab."

He was right. "I'd been wondering if the low ransoms were because it was kids doing this. Depending on their age, it might have seemed like a lot of money to them. Certainly their parents wouldn't be as likely to question them having a small amount of extra cash."

But the more she thought about it, that didn't make sense. Where would kids stash their captives without getting caught? There was another possibility. "But maybe this could be someone who desperately needs a small influx of cash."

"That makes more sense than anything I can think of right now." He nudged her shoulder with his. "Although I'm not at my sharpest right now. The question is what are we going to do about it? I don't want anyone else to go through the same scare about their pet as I have."

Moira mulled it over for a few seconds. "I hate to admit it, but I agree it's better not to have any kind of police presence near the drop-off. There's no telling what would happen if we were spotted and panicked the culprit when they come for the ransom. Too bad the drop isn't someplace with security cameras. If we had more time, maybe we could borrow some equipment from the county sheriff's office, or maybe find one of those motion-activated cameras that hunters use to track animals."

Titus sat up straighter. "I'll ask Max to give me a ride up to Leavenworth. We should be able to buy one of those there."

"Save the receipt in case I can put it on my expense account."

"No, Ned's my responsibility."

It was tempting to argue the point, but she knew stubborn when she saw it. With neither of them operating at peak capacity, it was simpler to let Titus have his way for now. She could always bring up the subject when Cade returned to see what he thought.

"I'm guessing you and Max can handle the installation."

"Can't be all that hard. He may even know something about how they work. I'm betting he's done a few freelance articles on wildlife photography at some point."

There wasn't much more to say on the matter. She could only hope for Titus's sake that Ned showed up on his doorstep soon. The man wouldn't find any peace until that happened. "Promise me after you install the camera and drop off the money, you'll try to get some sleep. I have another hour on my shift, and I'm counting the minutes until I can go home and pull the covers up over my head."

For an instant it seemed like he wouldn't respond, but he finally did. "I can't promise I'll sleep, but I will stay home and zone out in front of the television. Since Gunner is doing the prep, I don't need to go into work until tomorrow."

She'd take what she could get. To pass the time, she took advantage of the moment to do something she'd been wanting to do for a while now. Leaning in closer, she studied the swirl of tattoos on his closest arm. After a bit, she frowned. What had originally looked like a geometric pattern now appeared to be highly stylized letters. Cocking her head to the side, she tried to make sense of them. After a bit, she poked the first letter. "Okay, I give up. What does that say?"

He twisted his arm to give her a better look. "That's my grandmother's name. She's the one who took me in after I ran away from my mother and stepfather. I lived with her until I left for college. There's no telling where I would have ended up without her in my life. I had it done not long after she passed away."

There was a lot to unpack in those few words, leaving

her with so many questions about his past. Now wasn't the time. "Do you have other names hidden in among all that artwork?"

He pointed out another spot. "That's the emblem for my father's unit with his name and rank written below it. Dad was killed while serving in the army when I was in my early teens."

Well, rats. What she'd hoped would be an innocent distraction to pass the time while they waited for Max was turning out to be a disaster. "I'm so sorry."

"Me, too. He was a great guy, and I miss him every day. I always wonder what he would think of some of my life choices. For one thing, I'm the first in four generations not to serve in the military."

She knew the answer to that one. "If he was anything like you, he'd be proud that you were a good cop and sacrificed a lot trying to bring down a drug ring. He'd also be glad you found a career that makes you genuinely happy and that you have so many friends who care about you. Just so you know, I also got an earful about you at the game while you were umpiring. Seems you do a lot for the people here in town. When help is needed, they all said you step up without asking for anything in return."

She glanced up at him to see how he was reacting to her assessment of his life. "Why, Titus Kondrat, I do believe you're blushing."

The look of disgust he gave her had her holding up her hands. "Your secret is safe with me. If anyone asks, I'll deny to my dying breath that you're a nice guy underneath all those tats and bad attitude."

To hide her grin, she turned her attention back to his tattoos. A ripple of shock rolled through her when she recognized one final name written on a small heart tucked in between the stems of two beautiful roses. She said the letters aloud as she traced them with her finger. *"M-o-i-r-a."*

She dragged her gaze up to meet his. "You have my name on your arm."

The corner of his mouth quirked up in a small smile. "I do."

"Why would you do that, Titus? More importantly, when did you do that?"

He caught her hand in his and held it. "When I got out of the hospital, I had a lot of time on my hands while I went through all the physical therapy and other rehab I needed. I somehow found myself getting inked. Once I started, I decided I didn't just want a bunch of meaningless artwork, so I had the artist add in the names of people, places and things that meant something to me. The first three names were the obvious ones—my grandmother's, my father's and yours. Ned's will be next."

A second later, he used the knuckle on his forefinger to lift her chin and close her mouth. There was a twinkle in his eyes that had been missing since his furry companion had disappeared. "What's the matter, Officer Fraser? You're looking a bit frazzled there. Must be the lack of sleep."

Before she could frame a coherent question, a car pulled into the driveway. Titus jumped to his feet. "Well, that'll be my ride. I'll keep you posted about what happens."

Then he was gone, leaving her staring at his back.

## CHAPTER TWENTY

TWELVE HOURS LATER, Titus shifted on his bed, trying without success to get more comfortable. He pointed the remote at the television and clicked through the channels, trying to find something that could hold his attention. He would've been happier sitting on the couch, but he didn't want to hang out in the living room for fear the kidnapper might be scared off by any sign of life inside the house.

It was half-past four in the morning, so his miserable night would finally end. The only question was what would happen between now and when the sun finally crested the horizon.

It had taken all the willpower Titus could muster to stay home instead of staking out the gas station to see if Ned's captor claimed the ransom. He kept reminding himself that he'd promised Moira he would stay home and get some rest. He'd given her his word, and he needed her to learn she could trust him if they were ever going to have any kind of future together. It also wasn't worth the risk of spooking the kidnapper. Who knew what would happen to Ned if Titus was spotted lurking in the shadows at the gas station.

He finally gave up in disgust and shut off the television. The silence settled around him, making him feel more alone than ever. His solitary life didn't used to bother him, but that had changed the day Ned moved in to stay. He still had no idea why the dog had chosen Titus to be his new owner out of all the other people in town, but he done his best to make sure Ned never had cause for regret. At the time, Titus hadn't been looking to adopt a pet of his own despite his volunteer work for the local shelters, but then he wasn't actually the one who made the final decision. He'd left that up to Ned.

Regardless, even Titus had to admit that it had done him a world of good to have someone who actually needed him. Yeah, the people he employed at the café depended on Titus for their income, but there were other jobs to be had. He liked them and considered their welfare with each decision he made regarding the café. That wasn't the same as having someone waiting at home every night who was happy to see him walk back through the door.

Titus might have started making connections with people right after he moved to Dunbar, but the process had definitely sped up once he opened his home to Ned. It had been the first real move toward letting himself get close to others, to push past the barriers he'd built to hide behind.

The thought of going back to being that alone again... No, he wouldn't even think about that possibility. Besides, he had other friends now: Cade, Max, Gunner, Rita and Beth. And, God willing, he'd have Ned. And then there was Moira. Although he'd tried to warn her off, she kept coming back to help him. Maybe he hadn't screwed up as badly as he thought he had when it came to her. A man could only hope.

In the distance, he heard the chime that signaled he had a new text message. He rolled up to his feet to retrieve his phone, which was charging on the kitchen counter. He must have dozed off at some point, because he'd missed messages from both Max and Moira before this most recent one. He sent a quick response to Max, telling him he was hanging in there, but there was still no sign of Ned.

He also thanked him again for helping to get the camera set up. After promising that he'd let him know if there was news, he moved on to Moira's two messages.

The first one had come in over an hour ago and was short and to the point. *You doing okay?*

The second was longer. *Hey, checking in again. I hope you were able to catch some shut-eye, but figure that's not happening. Call if you want to talk. I'm up.*

Should he? Why not? Moira wouldn't have made the offer if she hadn't meant it. He grabbed a can of pop out of the fridge and settled in at the table before making the call. It was a relief when she answered on the first ring.

"Any news?"

"Not so far. I'm scared to look out front for fear of… well, I'm not sure what, exactly." He stopped to take a calming breath before continuing. "I figure Ned will let me know when he gets home."

*If he gets home.*

He shoved that thought back down into the darkest depths of his mind. Time to change topics. "What are you doing up at this hour?"

Moira sighed. "Gram had a rough night. Sometimes she can't sleep and gets agitated. When that happens, one of us stays up to make sure she doesn't try to slip out of the house."

He could hear the near exhaustion in her voice. "I'm sorry. Is she doing better now?"

"I fixed her a cup of herbal tea and put one of her favorite old movies on to play. She dozed off in her recliner about an hour ago. It didn't seem like a good idea to wake her up just to send her to bed, so I covered her with a blanket and turned off the lights. I'm sitting in the kitchen killing time until Mom takes over so I can get ready for work."

"That's gotta be tough on all of you."

"Yeah, it is. But speaking of sleeping, were you able to get any rest?"

"No, but not for lack of trying. I've been hiding out in my bedroom to avoid being seen from the front of the house."

She chuckled. "Sounds like we're each doing a lot of skulking around in the dark tonight."

"It would be more fun if we were skulking around together. We should try it sometime."

"Maybe I'll give you a call the next time I have to do a stakeout."

Curiosity got the better of him, so he asked, "Does that happen a lot here in Dunbar? Because I'll bring the snacks."

"Sadly, not very often. But if you're going to bring some of your mini pies, I might just fake one."

His mind filled with the image of the two of them sitting alone in the dark and quietly talking for hours about anything and everything. Oh, yeah, he would be totally down with that. "Just name the time and the place."

"Oops, I'd better go. I think Mom is headed this way. Keep me posted on...well, you know."

Titus didn't want to hang up, but Moira's family needed her right now. With everything she had going on with her job and her grandmother, it was a wonder that she had enough energy left over for anyone else. Especially him, but he wasn't going to suggest that she stop.

"You'll be the first one I call. If...no, make that *when* Ned shows up, we'll have to retrieve the camera. I think it would be best if you or one of the other officers went with me to do that since it might have the evidence you need to put a stop to this. I'll sleep a lot better when the culprit is behind bars."

"We all will. What time do you have to leave for work?

If Ned isn't back by then, I'll make sure to swing by your place periodically to check on things."

He didn't want to set foot out of the house until he got his roommate back, but he was needed at the café. "I'll have to leave by five thirty to help Gunner open up."

"Okay, we'll start doing drive-bys after that."

"Thanks, Moira. That's above and beyond, but I appreciate it."

Once they hung up, he checked the time. He needed to head for work in less than an hour. Before leaving the kitchen, he stopped long enough to fill Ned's bowl with fresh water and to put out some treats, just in case. Having done everything he could to prepare for his roommate's imminent return, he headed down the hall to shower and get dressed.

TITUS WAS IN no shape to be around anyone right now, but he had no choice. He'd barely found the strength to open his front door when it came time to leave for the café. His gut told him that if Ned had been returned, the dog would have made his presence known. Even knowing that, he'd been so hopeful that he would step out on the porch to find him sleeping in the bed Titus kept out there for him.

Seeing the bed empty had left Titus feeling physically ill. Instead of ducking back inside and slamming the door, he forced himself to head off to work like he would on any other day. It was tempting to ride the Harley, but he opted for the pickup, the safer option all things considered. Besides, he'd need it to retrieve the camera later since Max had made him promise to take him along for the ride.

The trip to the café was both too short and too long. He needed more time to prepare himself for the barrage of questions that would come flying his way about Ned's continued absence. But he also needed to get to the café, where he could lose himself in the routine of feeding people. It was unusual for him to beat Gunner to work, but the other man's rattletrap car was not in its usual spot across the street. At least that would give Titus a chance to get inside and settle himself a bit.

But as he turned down the alley to park the truck, he slammed on the brakes and rubbed his eyes to make sure he wasn't seeing things. Realizing his eyes were working just fine, he jumped out of the truck and ran for the small porch at the back door of the café.

"Ned!"

The dog was tied to the railing of the steps. He'd been lying down, but he lurched to his feet, barking and wagging his tail like crazy. Titus sat down on the steps and gathered his friend in close, burying his face in the dog's silky fur. It took a few seconds to be able to believe that Ned was back, safe and sound.

Titus unfastened the rope that had been used to tie Ned to the railing. "Come on, boy, let's go inside."

As soon as the door opened, Ned shoved past Titus to sniff his way around the kitchen, maybe wanting to make sure that nothing had changed in the short time he'd been away. When he reached his bed, he sat down on the cushion with an expectant look on his face. Titus wasn't about to deny the dog anything he might want. "I'll get you some treats, boy."

After grabbing a handful out of the jar, Titus leaned against the wall and slid down to sit next to the basket. Still waiting for his pulse to return to some approximation of normal, he fed Ned a treat and then texted Max to tell him the good news. He followed that up with a quick message to Moira. He'd just sent it when Gunner arrived. As soon as he spotted Ned, he grinned and headed straight for him. "I see you came back, you worthless mooch. Don't think I'm going to be slipping you bits of bacon after the scare you put us through. Not to mention what a pain in the backside your owner has been about the whole affair. What kind of friend are you to go wandering off like that?"

Titus reached over to give his buddy a thorough scratching. "It wasn't his fault. Ned was kidnapped. I paid the ransom last night."

Gunner stepped back in shock. "Seriously? Who would do something like that?"

As Titus explained the situation, the door opened and closed again as Moira joined the welcome-home party. He left it up to her to respond to Gunner's question. "We don't know yet, but I'm going to do everything I can to make sure they don't do it again."

She kneeled by Titus's side. "How is he?"

"Fine, near as I can tell." Titus leaned in close to take another sniff of Ned's fur. "For one thing, he's had a bath."

Clearly puzzled, Gunner asked, "How can you tell that?"

"It's a different scent than the shampoo I use on him. He's also had his nails trimmed."

By that point, Gunner was frowning in disbelief. "So you want me to believe Ned was kidnapped and held prisoner at a doggy spa?"

Moira stood. "Actually, the same thing happened to some other animals who've gone missing lately."

"Well, that's just plain weird, even for Dunbar."

"You'll get no argument from me on that point." Titus pushed himself back up to his feet. "I hope it's okay, but Max wants to go with us to retrieve the camera. He should be here any second now. I need to get back to help with the early morning rush. Do you have time to go with us now?"

"Yeah, I told Oscar what was going on. He'll cover for me."

"Then we should go now."

Ned beat them both to the door. Titus didn't even try to convince him to stay with Gunner. After clipping on Ned's leash, he let the dog lead the charge back outside. Just as promised, Max came jogging around the corner. Ned barked a greeting and allowed yet another one of his human friends to praise him for returning home. Afterward, the four of them piled into Moira's SUV and headed for the drop site.

The parking lot was empty with no one else in sight when they arrived. It was no surprise that the envelope that had contained the ransom was long gone. Once again, Moira took pictures of everything, including the camera they'd mounted on a nearby tree. When she was satisfied that she had everything documented, she passed out gloves. After putting them on, Max carefully removed the camera and handed it over to Moira.

Titus explained the setup on the camera. "We had it set to take a quick series of photos and then a short video whenever it was activated."

The three of them stood close together as they checked out the pictures. The first set caught a coyote on the hunt. Moira skipped through those pictures and video to get to the next one. It showed a trio of deer making their way from the trees on the other side of the road to the open field behind the station. Interesting, but not helpful.

"There's one more to go."

Titus tamped down his growing anger as he waited for her to push the button. If they failed to learn the identity of the kidnapper, someone else in town would likely go through the same pain and fear that he had.

Max grinned as he pointed to the screen. "We got a human this time."

Yeah, they had, but it was impossible to tell if it was a

man or a woman in the first photo. Whoever it was had come dressed in dark pants and a sweatshirt with the hood cinched down tight to hide his or her face and hair.

The second picture wasn't much better, but the third time was the charm. After studying the last photo for several seconds, Moira held the camera so that all three of them could watch the video. After watching it once, she played it again as if having a hard time believing what her eyes were telling her.

When it was finished, Max pointed to the figure on the screen. "I'm guessing you both recognize that person, but I don't. Who is it?"

Titus gave him an honest answer. "No one I would have expected to see."

Moira nodded, looking grim. "But we're definitely going to go see her now."

## CHAPTER TWENTY-ONE

MOIRA WASN'T SURE she should have allowed Titus to come with her, but it would've been a major fight to get him to wait at the café to find out what she learned. Titus wasn't the only one who had insisted on coming along for the ride. When they'd tried to leave Ned at the café, the dog had dug in his paws and refused to leave Titus's side. In the end, he'd ridden in her back seat with his nose stuck out the window, happily sniffing the wind.

While Moira could play hardball with the best of them, she couldn't bring herself to separate the pair right now. She was pretty sure it would be a long while before Titus let Ned out of his sight for any length of time. Besides, she was a firm believer that a victim had some rights. Both Titus and Ned deserved their chance to confront the woman who had put them through the wringer over the past two days. The dollar amounts in the kidnappings didn't add up to a huge amount, but the pet owners had paid a high price in worry and fear.

Once they reached their destination, Moira parked her cruiser on the street and led the parade up the driveway. Before stepping onto the porch, she laid out some ground rules for her companion. "I'll do all the talking, Titus. It's my job."

"I know."

She pressed the doorbell and then stepped back as she

called out, "We're here on official police business. Please open the door."

The curtain on the front window twitched as if someone had peeked out, but then it fell back into place. When there was no further response, Moira raised her hand and knocked on the door, putting considerable oomph into her effort to show she meant business.

Finally, there was the click of the lock being turned, and the door opened just a crack. "I'm sorry, Moira, but I'm not entertaining visitors right now. Perhaps if you could come back later this afternoon."

When the door started to close again, Moira blocked it. "I'm sorry, Mrs. Redd, but that's not going to happen. I'm here investigating a series of crimes, and I have reason to believe that you are involved."

The older woman gasped. "Moira Fraser, your mother and grandmother will both be horrified to learn how rude you're being to me."

Titus had been standing off to the side, but he'd obviously heard enough. When he took a step closer, Moira maneuvered so she remained between him and Mrs. Redd. "I wouldn't be here if I didn't have hard evidence that you kidnapped Mr. Kondrat's dog. In fact, it's a slam dunk that you're behind the recent crime spree of missing pets."

Calling it a crime spree was a bit of a stretch, But at least she'd managed to get through to the woman. Mrs. Redd opened the door wide and stared at Moira and her two companions. Ned whined and wagged his tail, as if happy to see the older woman, another indication that she'd treated her captives well.

After a second, Mrs. Redd seemed to shrink in on herself. "You'd better come inside."

Moira followed her mother's friend down the hall and into the living room. Titus followed close behind with Ned by his side. Their unwilling hostess motioned toward the sofa and chair. "Have a seat. Can I offer you any refreshments?"

Titus took one end of the sofa while Moira took the other. Ned jumped up on the middle cushion and lay down. Stroking the dog's head, Titus grumbled, "We're here for explanations, not to be entertained."

He was right about that and had every right to be angry. Regardless, they'd get more from the woman if they kept the conversation civil. Moira gave him a reproachful look and then turned her attention to Mrs. Redd. "What we need is an explanation about what's going on in your life to make you do something like this. You're not the kind of person who would turn to a life of crime for no reason."

The older woman sank down on the chair, her face pale. Her hands trembled as she looked everywhere but at her guests. When she spoke, her voice was a mere whisper. "I live on a limited income. As long as nothing unexpected happens, I do okay."

Ned sat back up and stared at her. Before Titus could stop him, he hopped down off the sofa, sat next to her feet and leaned against her legs. Mrs. Redd stroked his fur with a soft smile on her face. "You're such a good boy, Ned."

Turning her attention to Titus, she bit her lower lip before speaking. "I'm sorry, Mr. Kondrat. You're such a polite young man, and you're always so generous with your customers. I often get an extra dinner and sometimes even another lunch out of those delicious meals I order at the café. Regardless, I should never have taken Ned home with me. You must have been worried sick about him. Neither of you deserved that."

Moira wouldn't have been surprised if Titus snarled at the woman again, but she should have known better. Like his dog, the man had a soft spot for people who were in pain. He leaned back and released a long, slow breath. "Just tell us what's going on."

Mrs. Redd sounded so tired when she finally came clean. "If it had been only one unexpected expense, I would have been all right. But this house is getting old, and I had several big repair bills all at once. I've been keeping up on the payments, but I admit that it's been a struggle. Then my doctor put me on a medicine that's very expensive. I don't have to take it forever, but it's still more than I can afford on top of everything else."

She kept stroking Ned's head. "I honestly don't know why I thought holding pets hostage was a good idea. I was bound to get caught eventually, but I kept telling myself I'd stop after one more. That somehow I'd find another way to get the money."

Mrs. Redd stopped to stare at the small diamond ring on her hand. "The alternative would've been to sell my wedding ring, but that would've been like losing my husband all over again."

The woman's story made Moira's heart hurt. Now what was she supposed to do? If she actually arrested Mrs. Redd, that would only add to her financial woes. "Do you have any other pets visiting with you right now?"

"Oh, no. Ned was the last one." She sat with her shoulders hunched, making her look older and more fragile than she actually was. "I'd already made up my mind to stop."

Moira believed her. "That's a step in the right direction."

"I know it doesn't change anything, but I took good care of the animals while they were with me."

"I could tell." Titus looked down at Ned. "I don't know what you used on his coat, but it feels softer and looks shinier than what I've been using."

His comment triggered an interesting idea. Moira mentally poked and prodded it for a few seconds as she considered all the possible ramifications. She wasn't sure what the mayor and city council would think, but she decided to give it a shot.

"Mrs. Redd, we both know there will have to be consequences for what you've done. So here's my thought. Have you ever considered earning some extra money grooming animals for your friends and neighbors? You obviously have a talent for it. Or maybe boarding a dog or cat if their owners need to be out of town occasionally?"

The older woman sat up a little straighter. "I hadn't, but I actually enjoyed taking care of my…guests. They were good company."

"I can't make any promises because I don't have the authority to make this decision. However, I'm willing to make the suggestion if you're interested. Of course, you might have to do it for free for the owners of your guests. It would be like doing community service to make up for what you've done."

Explaining all of this to her boss might prove interesting, but she suspected that Cade would likely be grateful for a solution to the problem. No one would want to see Mrs. Redd behind bars.

By that point, Titus was looking marginally happier. "Officer Fraser, I can write a letter to Mayor Klaus and the city council in support of the plan if that would help."

Moira smiled first at him and then at Mrs. Redd. "I'll make some calls and let you know."

THE NEXT EVENING, Moira picked up the pizza for the girls' movie night that she had promised to spend with Carli. They'd immediately settled on opposite ends of the couch to watch the rom-com Carli had chosen. Sadly, less than half an hour in, Moira had already lost track of the plot and all interest in the pizza.

"Where are you tonight?"

Moira dragged her eyes away from the television to see what Carli was talking about. After all, the answer was pretty obvious. "I'm here with you. Remember you invited me over for pizza and a movie."

"I know I did, but it doesn't feel as if you're here at all. I'm not complaining. I'm worried. Something is bothering you. Does it have to do with Mrs. Redd and what she did? I thought you'd worked something out with the mayor and the city council."

"I did. In fact, they were thrilled with the solution I came up with. Otto was even making noise about writing up an official commendation for my record. We need to wait until Cade gets back to make it all official."

"That's great, but something definitely has you all tied up in knots."

Feeling a bit defensive, Moira frowned at her friend. "What makes you think that?"

Carli shifted to face Moira directly as she started counting off her reasons for concern. "First, you've barely spoken a word all evening. Second, since when do you only eat a single slice of pizza? Seriously, it's not like you to let all that delicious pepperoni go to waste."

Then she pointed toward the glass of wine on the coffee table. "And you've barely touched your drink. I bought that bottle specifically because it's one of your favorites. Add all that up, and it's pretty clear that at least your head is somewhere else."

Her friend wasn't wrong, but Moira still tried to deny it. "I don't know what you're talking about."

"Yes, you do." Carli narrowed her eyes as she pointed at Moira. "If I were a gambler, I'd bet all of my money that whatever has you all tied up in knots has to do with Titus Kondrat."

Moira winced at her friend's accurate summation of the situation. "I'm sorry. I'll do better."

Carli turned off the television. "I don't want you to pretend you're enjoying yourself. I want to know what's wrong. Do I actually need to borrow a bat and go have a talk with that man? Because I will."

Okay, that image never got less funny. "No, that won't be necessary. I'm not upset with Titus. It's more that I don't know what to do about him."

"Why not?"

"He's not who I thought he was." She reached for her wineglass and took a big swig. "No, that's not right. It's more that he's not who he used to be."

Her friend sipped her own wine, shaking her head. "Honey, if you think that was any clearer, you're sadly mistaken. Try again."

"I'm saying it's who Titus used to be that is the problem." Maybe it was time to lay it all out there for Carli. "Promise me that what I'm about to tell you won't go any further. There are reasons why Titus is closemouthed about his past. Good ones. But if I don't tell you some of it, none of this will make sense."

Looking solemn and not a little confused, Carli held up her hand. "Consider me sworn to silence."

"Okay then. Here's the thing. Titus is Ryan. Well, he never really was Ryan at all, but I didn't know that back then. I do now."

Carli sat up taller, her eyes wide with disbelief. "I never met Ryan, but you told me a lot about him. That he was charming, a fancy dresser and a fast talker. What is it about Titus that could possibly remind you of that jerk?"

"That's just it. Titus doesn't just remind me of Ryan. He is…no, he actually *was* Ryan Donovan ten years ago, when I knew him. It was the name Titus used when he was an undercover cop. That's all I can tell you about that time in his life. The truth is that Titus was never arrested or sent to prison, but a bunch of things happened afterward that were out of his control. For his safety and mine, he had to stay away."

"So you're saying when you were dating Ryan, you were actually dating Titus even though you didn't know it."

When Moira nodded, Carli frowned. "And somehow ten years later he magically ended up living in your hometown. How come you didn't recognize him as soon as you saw him?"

"I might have figured it out sooner, but I think he used to avoid letting me get anywhere close to him. For sure, he did look vaguely familiar, but part of what I can't tell you altered his appearance permanently. Also, when he was Ryan, Titus's hair was almost blond, he wore blue contact lenses and he was built along leaner lines. More like a swimmer. His wardrobe was also much more upscale."

Carli held up her hand as if she needed a second to absorb that much information. Finally, she said, "And now he has dark hair, brown eyes, is totally ripped and has a huge collection of flannel shirts."

"Yep, and the tats are a new addition, too." Moira leaned forward and whispered, "He has my name inked on his left arm. It's on a small heart between two roses."

"Wow, that's a lot to take in." Carli blinked several times and then said, "I'm guessing it's no accident that he opened a café here in Dunbar."

"Nope. He figured if he moved here, we would cross paths eventually."

"What was he hoping would happen? I mean, if all he wanted was forgiveness, he could've reached out years ago. More importantly, now that you know the truth, what do you hope will happen? Because that's the real question."

"Yeah, it is. Even though what Ryan and I had seemed so special, it wasn't built on anything real." Moira set her glass back on the coffee table. "Since I moved back to Dunbar, I've gotten to know Titus better than I ever really knew Ryan. He's a good man, and he has no problem with me being a cop. That's more than the last guy I seriously dated could claim."

She swiped a stray tear from her cheek. "My heart wants to give us another chance, but he recently told me I shouldn't waste more of my time on him. He was upset about Ned disappearing when he said it, but what if he really meant it?"

Her friend's expression turned sympathetic. "But what if he didn't, Moira? You said yourself he was hurting at the time."

"We're not the same people we were ten years ago."

"No, you're not, but maybe that's not a bad thing. How do you feel about this version of Titus? And how does he feel about you?"

Moira closed her eyes and let images of Titus flood into her mind. Him high-fiving kids at the ball game. The gentle kindness he'd shown both her grandmother and Mrs. Redd. The way he showed up with food whenever there was trouble. And how right it felt when he kissed her.

"I like him, more than I ever thought possible." As soon as she admitted that much, she knew *like* wasn't a strong enough word for how she felt about him. But if she was going to find the courage to admit that she actually loved Titus, he deserved to be the first to know. "I think he feels the same, too."

At least she hoped so.

Carli stood and offered Moira a hand up off the couch. "As much as I normally enjoy your company, you're not going to find answers sitting here with me. You're a smart woman and know what you've got to do."

Yeah, she did. "You're the best friend ever."

"I know. Now, pack up the rest of the pizza, go find the man and see what happens."

Moira did as ordered. Before heading for the door, she gave Carli a quick hug. "This is crazy."

"Just know that I'm rooting for you. If you two can find something special despite everything you've been through, then maybe there's hope for me, too."


NED WOOFED AND stared out the front window. Titus was already up and moving before the doorbell rang. He'd been half expecting Max to show up wanting to learn the full story behind Ned's capture, but it definitely wasn't him standing on the porch looking shy and not at all sure of her welcome.

Titus stood back out of the way. "Moira, this is a nice surprise. Come on in."

She held out the pizza box in her hand. "I thought this might go with that bottle of Malbec I gave you."

He lifted the lid, noting there were two pieces missing. "Did you get a discount because someone else ate part of it?"

She blushed. "Actually, I'm supposed to be over at Carli's watching a movie and sharing a bottle of pinot grigio."

"And yet here you are with me."

"I am."

She remained close to the door as if she had doubts about whether she wanted to stay at all. He had to do something to get her to hang around long enough to find out why she had deserted her best friend and headed for his place. Rather than peppering her with questions, he fell back on his default setting.

"While I could reheat the pizza, I actually have something better that's ready to serve. Besides, I told you I'd save the Malbec for when you'd let me cook dinner for you. This might be more spontaneous than I expected, but you'll love my saltimbocca."

"Sounds fancy."

Laughing, he headed for the kitchen and hoped she'd follow. "It's just chicken cutlets with mushrooms, prosciutto and cheese in a wine sauce."

To give her something to focus on, he pointed at a cabinet and then at a drawer. "Why don't you set the table while I put the finishing touches on dinner?"

She made quick work of her assigned duty. When she'd arranged everything to her satisfaction, she stood next to him at the stove. "That smells delicious. I'm glad you made extra."

"Me, too."

He tasted the sauce and added a touch more salt. "It needs to simmer another minute or two to thicken. Keep an eye on it for me while I open the wine."

When he served their meal, she hesitated before picking up her fork, looking a little panicky. "Moira, eat. We can talk about whatever brought you here afterward."

She rolled her shoulders as if trying to shed some of her tension. It must have worked because they were able to carry on a casual conversation for the duration of the meal. When he cleared away their empty plates, he said, "I'm sorry, but I don't have any dessert to offer you."

Staring at him in mock horror, her hand on her chest, she gasped, "You mean you don't keep chocolate-cream pie on hand on the off chance that I'll show up at the door with a half-eaten pizza?"

He topped off their wineglasses. "I will from now on if it means you'll do this again soon."

And just that quickly, all of her tension came roaring back. "About that—I thought we should talk."

"Okay, but let's take this discussion to the couch."

"Shouldn't we do the dishes first?"

"No, they can wait. I'm not sure whatever you need to talk about can."

He tugged her up from her chair. "Come on, and bring the wine. I suspect we might need it."

Ned was zoned out on the couch, taking up more than his fair share of space. "Move it, dog."

Most of the time, Ned would have either ignored the order or else taken his own sweet time moving out of Titus's way. Maybe he sensed something serious was afoot, because he immediately vacated his spot and headed for his fallback position on the chair. Titus sat down in his own usual spot and then tumbled Moira down next to him. He held her there with his arm around her shoulders before she could put any distance between them.

If she'd fought to get away, he would've let her go. When she settled in closer after only a few seconds, he gave her a nudge. "So tell me what's going on. Why did you abandon Carli to show up on my doorstep?"

"I had questions, ones she couldn't answer, not even when I told her you were Ryan." Moira swallowed hard and met his gaze with worried eyes. "I swore her to secrecy."

He didn't know where this conversation was headed, but at least he could reassure her on that much. "It's fine, Moira. My past is bound to come out eventually. I already told Max some of it, and I plan to tell Cade when he gets back. Since neither man likes keeping secrets from their wives, that probably means Shelby and Rikki are both going to find out soon as well."

She looked relieved. "Anyway, Carli already knew about me and Ryan...you, that is. She saw how hard it was for me to get over you. Looking back, I should have recognized the signs that something wasn't right. I'm not sure if I was incredibly naive or willfully blind."

Interesting. "What kind of signs?"

"We were together for two months, and I didn't have a single picture of you. The fact that I never met any of your friends. You never talked about your family." She waved her hand in the air. "None of that matters now. The point is that I trusted you, and we both know how that turned out."

Titus struggled to draw a full breath, all the pain from that time in his life bearing down hard on him. "I hate that I hurt you. I never meant for that to happen."

Moira twisted to look up at him. "If I mattered back then, why didn't you find a way to tell me the truth?"

"Because I was a coward."

She immediately scoffed at that idea. "How do you figure? Cowards don't live a year undercover knowing every minute that something could go fatally wrong. That takes nerves of steel."

He huffed a bitter laugh. "Risking my own life wasn't scary, but knowing I could be putting you at risk if Cian Henshaw or his people found out about you was terrifying. There was also the fact that you were in love with the very flashy Ryan Donovan. What if you didn't feel the same way about plain old Titus Kondrat?"

He liked that she didn't immediately dismiss what he was telling her. Finally, she threaded her fingers through his, holding his hand in her lap. "So what changed, Titus? It's been a long time since all of that blew up in our faces. You could've tracked me down long before now. Instead, after all this time, you moved here and waited to see if I'd ever show up. How long did you plan to stay in Dunbar, especially if I never moved back?"

The woman had a talent for asking the hard questions.

"Honestly, I didn't think that far ahead. Early on, I focused on getting the café up and running. I was lucky that Gunner wanted his old job back and that Rita and Beth were looking for work. Once we opened, I made sure I stayed too busy to have time to think much past the next week's menu."

Ned raised his head to give Titus a long look. He got down from the chair, stretched and then circled around the coffee table to lay his head on Titus's knee. The familiar connection made it easier to keep talking. "Things started to change when this fur ball first showed up. I hadn't had anyone in my life who belonged to me since my grandmother passed. Once Ned claimed me as his owner, somehow Dunbar became my home, not just a place to hang out until the real part of my life would finally begin."

It was time to throw the dice and see what happened. He muscled Moira up from where she was sitting to settle her on his lap. It meant a lot that she didn't resist, and even more when she cuddled against his chest. "That last part happened the day you moved back to town."

"Why didn't you say something when I first got here?"

"Didn't you hear me when I said I was a coward? Besides that, you deserved time to settle in. You were dealing with a new job and your grandmother's issues. The last thing you needed was me showing up on your doorstep."

She pondered that for a few seconds before finally nodding. "When I first came back, I secretly thought it would only be a temporary move. You know, we'd get Gram situated somewhere safe, and then I could go back to Seattle and get my old life back."

"And now?"

Because if that's what she wanted, he'd have to let her go even if it would almost destroy him. She leaned in closer to tuck her head under his chin. "You're not the only one who has realized how special Dunbar is. I like being so close to my family and friends. I'm also happier working for a small police force. Helping and protecting people I actually know is surprisingly satisfying. I would miss all of those things if I moved back to Seattle."

Then she cupped his cheek with her hand. "Most of all I would miss you. You're not the man I knew back then, but I'm not the same woman, either. Carli is a smart lady. She asked how I felt about the man you are now."

"And what did you tell her?"

"I said that I liked you, but that was an understatement." She offered him an uncertain smile. "What I feel for you is way more than that. I'm pretty sure that I've fallen in love with the real you, and I thought you should be the first one to hear me say those words."

It was everything he'd hoped for and way too terrifying to believe. He covered her hand with his. "Considering all the bad things you suspected me of, when did this surprising change of heart happen?"

Her cheeks flushed pink. "First, I should apologize for some of the things I said, but I think I was running scared. I haven't been this attracted to a man in a long, long time."

He waved that off. "You have solid instincts, Moira. That's what makes you such a great cop. They were screaming that something about me didn't add up right. Don't forget that I could have saved both of us trouble if I had told you sooner that Ryder and I were helping out the local animal shelters."

"True, but I still shouldn't have jumped to the worst conclusion possible."

He smiled down at her. "Let's call it a draw as to which of us was in the wrong."

"It's a deal. And so, back to your question—I think it was when I realized how often you take care of people.

It's the way you show up with food whenever something is going on, and how you're always so gentle with my grandmother. You offered Max a safe harbor in the café back when half the people in town hated him and stepped up to help him and Cade end the threat to Rikki and her son. And most of all, you trust me to be able to handle whatever my job throws at me even though it goes against your protective nature. That last one is huge."

Moira paused to kiss his cheek. "The list goes on, but all of those things define who you are—the man I love."

His heart felt lighter than it had in years. Maybe ever. "That's good, because I love you, too. Always have, always will."

Then he kissed her, taking his time to make sure this woman knew just how amazing she was. Learning that she loved him felt as if all the broken pieces of his life had suddenly snapped back together. The two of them sat in silence, maybe needing a little time to come to terms with the abrupt change in their relationship. When she finally stirred, he tightened his hold on her.

"Before I let go, I have two questions for you."

She settled back in. "Okay. Ask away."

Feeling as if he was about to step off the high dive without knowing how deep the water was below, he asked, "I might be moving too fast, but I have to know—are you going marry me? Because I want it all—you, me, Ned, maybe even a couple of kids."

There was a quick intake of breath, and then she nodded without speaking. "Sorry, Moira, but I need to hear you say the words."

She pushed away from his chest to look him straight in the eyes. "Yes, Titus Kondrat, I'm going to marry you."

The determination in her words meant everything. The second question had more to do with logistics. "Now that we have that much settled, I have to know one more thing. Can we elope like Max and Rikki did, or are you going to make me jump through the kind of hoops that Shelby put Cade through?"

That had her laughing. "I don't want or need all those fancy bells and whistles. We'll keep things simple. You know, a few friends, my mom and Gram. I'm thinking Carli and Shelby should be my bridesmaids. Max and Cade can be their escorts."

Then she reached down to pet Ned. "And your buddy here will be our ring bearer."

He could deal with that. "Perfect."

She sighed contentedly. "It will be."

So this was what real happiness felt like. Before he could share that thought with Moira, she asked a couple of questions of her own. "Can I have chocolate-cream pie instead of a wedding cake? And if so, do I have to share it with anyone?"

He laughed and kissed her again. "Lady, you can have anything you want."

\* \* \* \* \*